Stepping Stones

The Journey of an Imperfect Daughter

~A Novel~

Janet Robinson

"Everyone is worth knowing."
O Henry

Stepping Stones: The Journey of an Imperfect Daughter is a work of fiction. Names, characters, and situations are the product of the author's imagination. Any resemblance to persons living or dead is coincidental.

ISBN-13: 978-1481891516
ISBN-10: 1481891510

Cover design by Imagine Graphics

CONTACT JANET ROBINSON

www.janet-robinson.com
www.facebook.com/janet.robinson.author
www.twitter.com/JanetRobinson21
1020.writers.block@gmail.com

Dedication

For my children, Hunter and Haylee, who are beautiful
both inside and out.
I have truly been blessed beyond measure.

For Whitney Summerlin and my niece, Casey Cothran,
who are both most amazing young women.
I can only wish I had been as beautiful
and as intelligent and independent
when I was your age.

And for my mom and dad,
who both believed in my creative talent
and always encouraged it.
I miss them every day. Every single day.

Acknowledgements

I've always loved to write, but I didn't know I was a good writer until my ninth grade English teacher announced it to the class one day while she was reading every one of my essay questions aloud. I still remember the moment so clearly, and I remember her looking at me and saying, "Writing is your niche. It's your thing. It's what you're good at." Mrs. Rebecca Gregory caused something to spark within me that day, and I have never forgotten it. It has stayed with me all these years.

My senior year of high school, another English teacher, Dr. Cliff Browning, would push me to be the best writer I could be. He was a true inspiration, and I constantly worked to impress him.

Teachers should never underestimate the influence they have. Their words are powerful, and those words can stay with students all their lives. Teachers play a vital role in shaping the character of those they teach. I am a writer today because of the words spoken to me long ago, encouraging me to write.

I am also very blessed to have friends and family members who believe in me and support me. A special thank you to all of those who read this story and offered advice and encouragement: Janice Robinson, Leigh Pene, Casey Cothran, Sallie Johnson, Gayla Reaves, Kathy Slay, Michelle Green, and Travis and Cheri Norwood. I appreciate all of you more than you will ever know.

Stepping Stones

The Journey of an Imperfect Daughter

All things are possible
for those who believe.
Mark 9:23

Janet Robinson

The most beautiful people we have known
are those who have known defeat,
known suffering, known struggle, known loss,
and have found their way out of the depths.
These persons have an appreciation, a sensitivity,
and an understanding of life
that fills them with compassion, gentleness,
and a deep loving concern.
Beautiful people do not just happen.

Elisabeth Kubler-Ross

Prologue

"I'm not worth anything. Literally."

That statement was the only thing written one day in my diary when I was thirteen years old. I don't remember the context of it or what had occurred, but I do remember the feeling. It was a palpable feeling that permeated my entire youth. I have fought my whole life to prove myself wrong. Sometimes I have it mastered and believe the battle is won. Other times, I'm still that same thirteen-year-old girl desperately needing affirmation.

My dad once told me to channel my hurt into something positive. *Don't be self destructive because the people who cause the hurt will win. Prove them wrong and do something useful. Something meaningful.* I think that's where my ambitious spirit began. Before he uttered those words, I was unmotivated and believed every hurtful thing that was said to me. Afterwards, and to this day, those words still ring in my ears, echoing as I have trudged my way through any situation that seemed impossible. I see his wisdom in giving me something hopeful to cling to, to remind me every day of my life that I am far better than what they see. A child with such low self-esteem would need such a motto to live by. But enduring the pain, even while trying to remember such advice, sometimes proved very difficult.

I look back now at every step of my life and how it brought me to this point. Adversity builds character, or so they say—and they would be right. Everyone who struggles has the potential to come out better on the other side. Not everyone is so lucky though. Some drown in the pain, their lives ruined for the most part. But then there are those who use such pain as a springboard to a better, more fulfilling life. That's what my dad's words were meant to do. And ever the daddy's girl, I clung to them. I would like to say I did the instant he uttered them, but that would not be true. It took me a few years to understand such wisdom, but eventually I caught on.

I have reached a point in my adult life where I can look back and reflect on what has transpired. What challenges were met and overcome; and which ones were lost, crashing and burning into oblivion only to be soothed by mint chocolate chip ice cream that I would sneak out of the freezer at two o'clock in the morning. What is in our psyche that craves attention? That desperately desires affirmation. That needs someone to say, "You are an amazing person." Those who receive it readily do not notice its absence. They are oblivious to the anemic soul that is shunned. They are quite content in all their accomplishments and the lavish praise that follows. They never struggle; they never sadden; they never want—or so I believe. Therefore, one is left to wonder what kind of life they end up living when everything always goes their way. How do they ever survive the inevitable challenges that occur in adulthood? As for me, I was fully prepared for the world's disappointments. I wasn't surprised by any of them, and I even laughed at a few.

So here is the story of my journey. Every thought, every memory, and every story my dad told me. I listened carefully and paid attention. I remember it all very well. Such memories, good and bad, stay with us forever. They never leave us because they form the very fabric of our character, stitched together to create the tapestry of who we are. Every single moment in our lives is important. Nothing is insignificant. No one is insignificant. My struggle has been to think that about myself, that I am significant. Maybe one day I'll believe it.

Roda Allen-Emerson
December 2025

Chapter 1

~October 1975~

My parents met fall of freshman year when Rutgers played North Carolina. My mother, Paige Martin, being a seasoned gymnast, opted for a spot on the cheerleading squad. She craved the excitement of the games, knowing that would be the true experience of college life rather than being confined to competing in a gymnasium on uneven bars and balance beams. My dad, Paul Allen, was on a baseball scholarship. He didn't play football but would sometimes watch the games from the sidelines rather than the student section. A few of his friends played football, so he would get a pass to hang out on ground level.

My dad thought he had noticed my mother first, but he found out later that she had been watching him. She waited, however, for him to approach her. He was handsome with wavy brown hair, green eyes, and the cutest crooked smile. He was tan from spring and summer ball, and from the occasional trips to the coast. She had the most striking blue eyes and long blonde hair. They had been glancing at each other during the game; and as soon as it ended in a close defeat for the Scarlet Knights, my dad approached her in the helpful manner of picking up her pom poms. It was the only time she was glad her team lost; otherwise, she would have been on the field celebrating with the rest of the squad, and the good looking new guy would be lost forever among the crowd.

She found him to be witty and charming, and he found her to be warm and friendly. They talked for a while and made a date for that night. He picked her up at her dorm and took her to a

3

popular hangout for dinner and then a movie afterwards. It was the perfect start to a college romance. They were inseparable, sharing the same likes and dislikes. They were compatible in every way.

~*December 1976*~

My dad waited until they had dated more than a year before he considered taking her home to meet his parents. He wanted to be sure that she was the one. His family was from Troy, New York; just outside of Albany. Her family was from Alexandria, Virginia. Over three hundred miles apart with the university in between. He had planned for her to meet his family over Christmas break their sophomore year. They thought it might be possible, but my mother's parents had planned a surprise trip to Europe. She would be gone the majority of the time but was scheduled to be back before New Year's Eve. So they made a date to be together then. There wouldn't be enough time to visit his parents, but my dad had a wonderful idea. He would take her to New York City to watch the ball drop at midnight in Times Square and also to meet the most important member of his family—his sister, Mim.

My Aunt Mim was eight years old when my dad was born, so of course she took care of him, treating him like one of her dolls. And he adored her. He was the one who first called her Mim when he was learning to speak. Her name was Miriam, but he was unable to say it. Instead, it came out as Mim. And so it stuck. They were very close growing up and remained so even when she left for college. She attended Syracuse University, so she wasn't too far from home and would visit almost every other weekend. He would go and stay with her some too. After she graduated, she moved to the city. She was much further away, so he didn't get to see her as often. She had hoped he would follow in her footsteps and attend Syracuse as well, but he chose Rutgers. Mim always believed it was so he could be closer to her, less than an hour away. He never would admit to it though. He visited quite regularly to begin with. But then he got a girlfriend, so she rarely saw him much after that. She knew he was enjoying college life and time with friends.

Mim was excited when he called, asking to see her on

New Year's. He wanted to take my mother to see a few of the sights, like the Christmas tree at Rockefeller and maybe ice skating in Central Park. Mim declined to join them but suggested they come to her apartment later. There was a great Italian restaurant not too far from where she lived, and they could have dinner there. My mother was excited too. As close as she lived, she had never been to the city. She was also excited to meet his sister. She had heard so many good things about her.

The European vacation didn't pass quickly enough. My mother was anxious to get back. My dad stayed at home in Troy for the majority of Christmas break but left with Mim when she decided to go back to her apartment after the holidays. When my mother returned from Europe, he took a train to the university and met her there; and then they traveled back to the city. They were so glad to see each other again after being apart for so long.

They had a wonderful day together. My mother was excited to see everything. A light snow was falling, and the buzz of the New Year was in the air. Times Square was filling up quickly, and they weren't sure there would be room for them later that night. Neither of them cared. They agreed they would both be perfectly happy to watch it on television at Mim's apartment. There would be other chances to come back. Knowing my mother was from a very wealthy family, my dad worried she wouldn't be impressed with some of the aspects of the city; but she happily participated in everything. She ate a hotdog from a street vendor, she ice skated in the park, and she even rode the subway. She enjoyed every moment of it.

Later in the afternoon, they realized it was time to go to Mim's. They hopped on the subway and rode from Central Park to the Lower East Side. My Aunt Mim was an artist and embraced the East Village with all her might. She loved every aspect of it. She displayed her art in a local eclectic gallery and was a professor at New York University. She was happily single and lived on the third floor of an eighty-year-old walk-up. Her apartment was surprisingly spacious for the area, with two bedrooms and a full bath. She had enough room just off the living area for her art, so she didn't have to use the extra bedroom. She liked the light better by the terrace. That's what she called the fire escape. The second bedroom was always reserved for her little brother whenever he

5

decided to stay for a while.

My mother was cautious about the area; and for the first time, she seemed unimpressed with something. Disappointment flickered across her face and quickly disappeared behind a smile. But my dad saw it.

"Are you okay?" he asked.

"Yes," she said, smiling. "Just nervous, that's all."

He smiled, believing her. She was looking up at him happily, her cheeks flushed from the cold and the excitement of the day. He held her hand as he buzzed for Mim to let her know they were there. Squeals of delight came out of the crackling speaker. She buzzed them in, and my dad grabbed the heavy door and pulled it open so they could escape the cold. Inside the entryway was warm and surprisingly appealing for the age of the building. It smelled old but not musty. They ascended the wooden staircase; and at the top of the third floor stood Mim, so excited she could hardly stand it. She threw her arms open as if she hadn't seen him in months when, in fact, she had seen him that morning. My dad stepped a few steps ahead of my mother and embraced Mim on the landing.

"Now Paul, who is this you have with you?" Mim asked, as if it were a total surprise that someone was there. My dad laughed, backing up and making room for my mother to reach the landing and stand with them. When he turned and looked at my mother, she seemed much different. The happy, giggling young woman who had climbed the stairs was now stoic and sullen. Her arms were crossed in front of her, giving Mim the impression that she did not want to be hugged. She stared at Mim and then at my dad.

"Sweetie, this is Mim," he said rather timidly. "Mim, this is Paige."

"Hi there," said Mim, somewhat perplexed. "It's nice to finally meet you. Paul has told me so many wonderful things about you."

"It's nice to meet you too," she said quietly.

Mim and my dad looked at each other curiously, as only a brother and sister could.

"Well, come on in," Mim said, trying to sound more cheerful.

They followed her into her apartment and hung their coats on the rack near the door. The small foyer area led into a small kitchen and then into a comfortable living space. It was a cozy apartment, decorated tastefully with Mim's own art. She directed them to the sofa and asked if either of them would care for anything. My dad asked for a soda, but my mother declined. Mim talked the whole time as she walked from the sofa to the refrigerator, which was only a few feet. While she wasn't looking, my dad grabbed my mother's hand and squeezed it gently, trying to get her to look at him. She stared at the floor. Mim was rattling on about her latest art project she had been working on that morning. Laughing at herself, she told them that, out of frustration, she just threw the whole mess down the garbage chute. She went on and on and on, sensing that she was going to have to do most of the talking. My dad would engage in much of the conversation but was preoccupied with my mother's silence.

"Well," Mim finally said, after talking about everything she could think of, "why don't we hurry down to Bellino's? They get crowded very early."

My dad agreed, and they all got up and headed for the door, putting on their coats. They walked two blocks down 7th, careful of the newly fallen snow. It had gotten much colder since earlier that day. Everyone was bundled up, and my dad noticed that my mother had her hands stuffed in her coat pockets. She wasn't the same carefree girl she was just hours before. She wasn't holding his hand. She wasn't laughing and talking. She wasn't talking at all.

They reached the restaurant and quickly got a table. They ordered according to Mim's suggestions. My dad and Mim talked and laughed, but he was also still very aware of how quiet my mother was. He wanted to make Mim feel comfortable in such an awkward situation, but he was careful not to leave my mother out as well. Mim continued to talk and laugh, seeming not to notice my mother's dour mood. Mim had a little wine in her and continued to entertain, proving that she could—in fact—talk to a wall.

The evening wound down early, and my dad suggested they go back to Mim's to relax, get warm, and wait for the ball to drop. Mim was pleasantly surprised that they had decided not to go to Times Square for the festivities. It was the one night during the year, she told them, that she adamantly refused to make any plans. In fact, she informed them with a humorous tone that they were lucky to have gotten her out of her apartment at all. She and my dad laughed, but my mother snorted mockingly. They stopped and looked at her, shocked.

"You go out?" she asked with a sarcastic tone.

Mim looked at her, then at my dad, and back again at her.

"Well, yes I do. Why do you ask?"

She raised her eyebrows, surprised, and then looked away. "No reason."

It was the only thing my mother had said all night, and it left an uneasy feeling hanging in the air. Within minutes, they got up and left the restaurant, heading back towards Mim's apartment. When they reached her stoop, my mother hesitated. Mim looked at my dad, and he looked back at her. She gave him half a grin and then went inside, leaving the two of them behind.

He looked at my mother and asked what was wrong.

"Paul, if you don't mind, I would rather go."

"Go where? You want to go uptown? We should just watch it here."

"No," she said with an edge of sternness, "I want to go back to campus."

"Back to campus?! Are you kidding me? There is absolutely no way!"

"Why not?" she asked firmly.

He just stared at her. "Well, perhaps because the city is full of people tonight and getting off this island would be impossible. And may I remind you that it will be midnight in a few hours, and I am not traveling all the way back to New Brunswick tonight. I don't even know if a train is running tonight!"

She remained firm but realized she was being unreasonable. "I'm not staying."

"What is wrong with you?" he asked heatedly. "What is your problem? You have acted mad all night; and for the life of me, I can't figure out why."

"I'm not mad."

"Yes, you are, Paige. It's obvious. Now tell me what is wrong."

8

"Listen, I'm going to find a cab, and I'm going back. You can stay if you want."

"No, I will not let you do that. You will not be able to find a cab for one thing, and I will not let you go off on your own. Now come inside!"

My mother realized they were causing a scene. People were passing by, looking at them. She relented and followed behind him as soon as Mim buzzed them in. They were both sulking as they climbed the stairs, her in quiet anger and him not understanding why. He finally stopped and turned to her mid-way up.

"What is wrong? Please tell me what is wrong."

"Let's just go inside, Paul. We can talk about it later."

They entered the warm apartment silently. She went straight to the spare bedroom and never came back out. My dad and Mim sat dejected on the sofa for the remainder of the night. They drank hot chocolate and watched an old movie until just before midnight when it was time to watch the New Year being rung in on television. The mood was somber. When Mim got up to go to bed, my dad grabbed her hand.

"I'm sorry, Mim. I'm not sure what's wrong with her. She has never been like this before."

She smiled down at him. "It's okay. I figure it's jealousy or something. Don't worry about me."

She turned and left him alone, knowing that it was more than jealousy. It was something much more.

***

The next morning, Mim and my dad were finishing breakfast when my mother finally emerged from the bedroom. She was dressed and ready to leave. During the night, she realized how her behavior had ruined the evening. She was still stoic but apologetic.

"Miriam," she said quietly, "I want to apologize for how I acted last night. I have no excuse. I do appreciate you having us in your home."

Mim looked at my dad sideways, knowing that no one had called her Miriam since she was nine or ten years old.

"Well, you're very welcome, Paige," she said, putting down her coffee cup. "I hope you'll come back again."

My mother smiled politely and then looked at my dad, indicating she had said all she was going to say and was ready to go. My dad rose from the table, glancing at Mim. They exchanged knowing looks. My dad knew that Mim had planned a fun day for herself and my mother, if my mother had been different. She planned for them to shop in SoHo and check out the art galleries in the area, as well as other interesting sights that only a true New Yorker knew about. But it was not to be. Sadly, he hugged his sister goodbye and said he would be back later.

He and my mother left in silence and didn't speak until they were on the train in Hoboken. My dad was no longer uncomfortable with the silence. He just wanted to get away from her. My mother kept looking at him, expecting him to speak. Finally, she couldn't take it any longer.

"Paul, are you going to talk to me?"

"The only thing I want to know," he said pointedly, without looking at her, "is what in the world got into you?"

She shifted uncomfortably in her seat. "Just nerves, I guess."

"No, that's not it. I know that's not it. I want a reasonable explanation for why you behaved the way you did towards Mim."

She looked down at her hands nervously. "I don't know, Paul. I was nervous. She's such an important person to you. You idolize her, in fact. I suppose I was a bit intimidated and . . . jealous."

He finally looked at her.

"And besides," she said suddenly, looking up at him, "I was tired. It had been a long day. A fun day but a long day. And," she frowned playfully, "I get cranky when I'm tired."

He hesitated at first but accepted her answer. After a moment, he took her hand; and they sat silently for a few minutes. After a while, she asked about him telling Mim that he would be back later.

"Yeah," he said, "I'm going to spend a few more days with her. I don't have to be back at the dorm until January 6th."

She grew quiet again, not liking his answer. He noticed

10

her silence but ignored it. Finally, she asked why he didn't want to stay on campus and spend time with her. He reminded her that the athletic dorms had been under repair during the holidays and that they were not allowed back in until the sixth. She didn't argue. There was nothing she could do. But she did not like that he would be going back to Mim's.

He drove her to her dorm and told her goodbye, intending to return to the city right away. She was surprised, thinking he would spend the day with her.

"No, I need to get back," he said quietly. "I just want to sleep. I'm exhausted."

She nodded as if she agreed, still knowing she had no room to argue. He kissed her forehead and then left to return to the train station. He arrived at Mim's an hour later and slept for the rest of the day. Mim quietly hummed as she worked on her art in the corner near the terrace. She was happy to have him back for a few more days.

***

My dad spent the remainder of Christmas break just hanging out with Mim and doing their favorite things. He dreaded going back to school. He was still angry about how my mother had acted, and he was having a difficult time reconciling his feelings about that and the feelings he had for her. He didn't share much of what he was thinking with Mim, but she could tell he was upset.

Finally, she spoke up and told him that he ought to focus on how much he loved my mother, how much fun they had together, and how compatible they were. Mim said not to let what happened with her be a deterrent to how he really felt about the love of his life. He disagreed, saying it had everything to do with how he felt. He said that my mother should know how much he loved Mim, how important she was to him; and she ought to respect that, despite her feelings of jealousy. He was not going to allow my mother to mistreat his sister, just as he would never allow Mim to mistreat my mother. Mim relented but told him that she did not want to be the reason he lost the greatest love of his life.

He didn't call my mother when he arrived back at his dorm. In fact, he had not called her since dropping her off New

Year's Day. He still needed time apart to think. Classes started the next day. He knew he would see her because they had registered for many of the same courses. He went in, not seeking her out. She approached him, knowing he was still angry.

"Hi, Paul, may I sit next to you?" she asked cautiously.

"Sure," was all he said.

"When did you get back?"

"Yesterday."

"Oh, I see. I thought you might call."

"No, sorry. I was busy."

His answers were short and without explanation. The professor started the class before she could ask anything else. My dad sat rigidly beside her. After class was over, she followed him out. She knew he was very unhappy with her.

"Paul, I know you're mad. I really am very sorry for the way I behaved."

He looked at her, his mind made up. "I will not tolerate your behavior towards Mim. I don't really know what your problem is; I guess jealousy, but you better get over it because Mim is the most important person in the world to me, and you better respect that."

She was taken aback. "*I'm* not the most important person to you?"

"Yes, Paige, you are important; and you will become more and more important the longer we're together. But I've only known you a year. I've known my sister my whole life."

Inside, she was hurt and seething, furious that she was not already the most important person to him. Outwardly, she softened, trying to gain his forgiveness.

"I know how important she is to you. I do respect that, and I promise I will not behave that way again. Just please forgive me, okay?"

He nodded. "I can forgive you, but I need some time to get past this."

"Sure," she said.

"I'll see you later."

He turned to leave. When he was a few feet away, he turned back towards her.

"Just so you'll know, Mim respects how I feel about you.

12

She told me that if I truly loved you, not to let you go just because of what happened with her."

"And do you truly love me?"

He didn't answer. He turned and walked away.

They had another class together later that day and made a mutual effort to sit beside each other, although they didn't have much to say. They didn't eat lunch together or even dinner. My mother respected that he needed his space.

After a few days, things slowly began to get back to normal. He was still reserved, but my mother knew it wouldn't take long for him to return to his old self. She was cautious but acted extra sweet. Within weeks, everything was fine. They never talked about it again.

Spring training began in late February. Between athletics, classes, and studying, my dad was very busy. My mother would go to many of his practices to watch, just as other girlfriends did. There wasn't much time to date. She was disappointed, but she understood his rigorous schedule.

He had regained his feelings for her, and he felt they were back to normal. He knew, however, there was something missing. It wasn't exactly as it was before. He loved her, though; and that's what he focused on.

Chapter 2

~*April 1977*~

My grandfather's birthday coincided with spring break that year, so my dad saw it as the perfect opportunity to take my mother home to meet his family. They usually had a large celebration with many family members present. He was anxious for her to meet his parents and see what they thought of her. He knew Mim would be there too. He was looking forward to seeing her again because there had not been time to visit since before the semester began. He was also curious to see how my mother would act towards her. He was hoping it would be different this time but was afraid it wouldn't be.

My mother was nervous when she went to meet my dad's family. She was a confident person but knew it was a big step in their relationship. Classes ended that Friday, so their plan was to leave early Saturday morning and drive three hours to Troy. They would stay overnight at his parents' house and go to church with them the next morning.

They arrived before lunch. My dad could sense how nervous she was. He reassured her, telling her that they would love her. And they did. My dad's parents and Aunt Trudy and Uncle William were there to greet them. My mother was beautiful and stylish. She had a warm, shy smile; and they instantly took to her. My dad's mother and aunt were immediately impressed, and his dad and his uncle patted him with eyebrows raised, indicating what a gorgeous girl she was.

They were ushered in and their things were put away.

Everyone wanted to know how college life was. My parents fielded question after question about how they met, where she was from, what classes they were taking, cheerleading, her sorority, his ball team—on and on until my dad finally laughed and said enough. They were all curious about the beautiful new couple, excited about the future they might have together. They certainly seemed perfect for each another.

Later, my dad checked on my mother when she was settling into the guest bedroom.

"So the hard part is over, huh?" he said, smiling. "You've met the parents, and they love you, so it's all downhill from here."

"Yeah," she sighed, smiling back at him. "Now to meet everyone else tonight."

"Oh, I don't think you'll have a problem. Not at all. As long as you have my mom on your side, you're set."

She smiled, looking down. "Yes, your mom is wonderful. I really do like her."

He nodded and then suggested they hurry down and eat lunch. His mother had made his favorite: a special homemade pizza that could make her a millionaire if she would relinquish her recipe. My mother eagerly went, wanting to continue to make a good impression. She was the dutiful guest, helping with whatever needed to be done. My dad sat at the table, watching how well my mother interacted with his parents. In the back of his mind, he was thinking about Mim. Why had my mother had such a horrible reaction to her? She was due to be there that night for the big family dinner. He hoped that maybe my mother would be better since the whole family would be together.

Everyone started arriving at six o'clock. Dinner was catered from a fabulous Greek restaurant in Albany. Everything was perfect, just as my dad's parents always made it. There was a buzz in the air about Paul's new girlfriend. Everyone was excited to meet her. My mother smiled happily and held my dad's hand. She was warm and friendly, just as she always was.

By six-thirty, it was announced that dinner would be served soon. My dad was sitting with my mother on the sofa when his Aunt Grace started asking where Mim was. "It's getting late," she said. "Has anyone heard from her?" He laughed slightly and

15

reminded her that Mim was always running late. "She'll be here," he assured her. My dad thought he could have mistaken it, but when Mim's name was mentioned, he was sure my mother stiffened a bit. They had not discussed her or the incident from New Year's. Both of them had conveniently avoided it.

Mim arrived fifteen minutes later in a flurry of laughter and hugs, apologizing for being late. "It was the weather, you know." And she was sure the train had been delayed by at least forty-five minutes. She was quite the animated person. It was obvious that everyone in the family adored her, laughing at everything she said and hugging her sometimes two or three times. It had been so long since they had seen her. My dad rose immediately to go to her. My mother followed slowly behind. She knew she would need to redeem her behavior, but she lacked enthusiasm.

Mim grabbed my dad and hugged him tightly. "I missed you! I missed you! I missed you!" she said as she rocked him from side to side. He laughed and said he had missed her too. They stood there facing each other, talking and catching up for a few minutes. My dad did not move aside this time to allow Mim and my mother to speak. My mother stood there, not particularly wanting to speak to her but not wanting to be ignored either.

"My goodness, Paul," my grandmother finally said. "Introduce Mimmy to Paige."

"We've already met, Mom," Mim said.

"Oh," my grandmother said with a perplexed look on her face. She did not understand that if they had already met, why Mim wasn't greeting her in her usual manner. My dad moved a little so the two of them could face one another.

"Hello, Paige," Mim said pleasantly enough, knowing this was her family, her territory.

"Hi," was all my mother said in response.

In an instant, Mim was going around the room speaking again to every one of the family members. There were sixteen in all present. She was vivacious with a dry wit that had everyone gasping for breath, they were laughing so hard. Mim was a people watcher and had done quite a lot of it on her short journey from New York City to Troy. Mim, herself, was laughing so hard that she could barely recount the man on the train who was actually using his very large cat as a "scarf," curling the animal around the back of his neck. The cat slept the whole way, and Mim had actually reached the point of wondering if the cat were even alive.

It was becoming perfectly obvious to my mother that Mim was the center of attention in the family. Mim had very much intended for her to learn that. My mother sat there smiling pleasantly and laughing courteously as the humorous stories were told; but inside, she was livid. She was angry because of how she felt to begin with, knowing she would have to hide it; angry about being ignored, knowing it was nothing more than brother-sister manipulation; and angry that my dad would do that to her. My mother had hoped that she would be seen instantly by this wonderful family as the perfect daughter-in-law, if not the perfect daughter. Now she realized that Mim could not be replaced. Everyone adored Mim, especially my dad. So she sat, furious; but no one knew it.

Dinner went well. Mim continued to entertain and everyone continued to laugh, my dad included. He was unaware that he was ignoring my mother. He was so caught up in his sister's antics, he didn't even think about it. Every now and then, he would look at her, laughing, thinking she should be laughing too. At one point, she just glared at him. She had had enough. He regained his composure and sobered up, realizing she was unhappy. He was intentionally cool to her when Mim arrived but had not realized how he had been neglecting her. He sensed she would have something to say about it later.

The gathering ended around ten o'clock that night. My grandparents went straight to bed, leaving my dad, mother, and Mim to themselves. The three of them sat in the den together. Mim and my dad were chatting. She and my mother had not spoken to each other all evening except for the small exchange when Mim arrived. She noticed my mother was acting pleasantly enough—the key word being *acting*. Mim knew it wasn't genuine. She sensed in my mother's demeanor that she was the same as she was New Year's. Mim was very good at reading people.

The conversation wound down between them, and Mim excused herself and went to bed. My parents were left alone together, and my dad dreaded it. He had barely spoken to her that evening, but it was not on purpose. He knew, that until Mim had arrived, my mother had been quite happy and enjoying the attention she was getting. But as soon as Mim showed up, sucking all the oxygen out of the room, everyone focused on her. He knew my mother felt slighted.

They sat in silence for a minute or two before my dad reached for her hand. She was actually in a very awkward position: upset at how the evening had gone but needing to be careful not to show how irritated she was. It didn't matter, however, because he already knew.

"You doing okay?" was all he could think to say, wondering if she was going to express what was on her mind or just ignore it.

"Sure," she said. Such a short answer. He knew she was upset.

"It looks as if my family is quite impressed with you," he said, trying to ignore her mood.

"Yes," she said, "they seem lovely. I'm quite impressed with them too."

"You are?" he tried to joke, hoping to lighten the mood.

"Well, yes. You have a wonderful family. And I'm very impressed with how they seem to adore Mim."

He was somewhat puzzled. He had expected she would say such a thing with a hint of sarcasm, given how she obviously felt about Mim; but instead, she seemed very sincere.

"Well . . . yeah they do. Why does that impress you?"

"Oh, it's just because I believe adoption is such a wonderful thing. Just the thought of someone taking a child into their home and raising her as their own. And to see the whole family embracing that child, as well—even years later when she's an adult. It's just very heartwarming."

My dad sat, perplexed. "You think Mim's adopted? Why do you think that?"

My mother was genuinely surprised. "She's not?"

"No," he answered, still dumbfounded.

"Oh . . . well, I just thought . . ." she said, not sure how to explain herself. "I just assumed . . ."

My dad looked at her, waiting for an explanation. "You assumed what?"

She shifted uncomfortably next to him. She had been

relieved at one point early on in the evening when she concluded to herself that Mim was adopted. She was sure of it.

"Well, Paul," she began, trying to form her thoughts into words. "Well . . . she looks so different from everyone in your family. So I just assumed."

"Different how?" he asked gently but knew it wasn't going to go well.

"Well," she shifted again. "Well, Paul, Mim is just so . . . large."

He looked down at the floor and sighed.

She rushed to complete her thought. "I don't mean to be harsh, but . . ."

"But what?" he asked, sounding slightly irritated.

"Maybe we should talk about this another time," she concluded, sensing he was getting upset.

"No, we'll talk about it now."

"Okay. Well, no one else in your family is that . . . large," she tried to say carefully. "And no one else has dark, curly hair like her. Everyone is so thin, and . . . well, no one looks like her. I'm sorry I assumed."

My dad continued to stare at the floor for a few minutes. He finally spoke. "Is this what the problem was last New Year's?"

She blinked, acting innocent. "What do you mean?"

"You know exactly what I mean. Was this the reason . . . that Mim is overweight . . . was that the reason you acted the way you did?"

"Honestly, Paul," she defended, "I'm not that superficial."

"You're not?"

"No, I'm not," she said emphatically.

"Then what was the problem? And what is your problem now? You hardly said anything tonight, and you did not make one effort to talk to Mim other than to say hello."

"I didn't make an effort to talk to *her*? Maybe *she* didn't make an effort to talk to me. Neither did you, for that matter."

My dad just shook his head and laughed a sarcastic laugh. "Why should she after the way you acted towards her?"

My mother was taken aback. "How dare you!"

"What exactly is your problem?" he persisted. "I would

really love to know. You seem to have it in for her. And at first, I thought it was because you were jealous. Now I'm wondering if that's what it truly is. And do *not* tell me it's because you're nervous. You were not nervous meeting anyone else in my family; or if you were, you certainly didn't show it. And you certainly were *not* as cold to anyone else as you were to Mim."

My mother's anger was rising because of what he was saying. She was upset because he wasn't on her side and even more upset about how the whole evening had gone, how everyone's attention was on Mim and not on her. Certainly that my dad's attention had been as well.

"I think I'm going to go to bed," she finally said, getting up from the sofa.

"No," he said sharply, "you will answer me."

She glared at him. "You want me to answer you? Okay, then I will. I had no idea that *those* genes were in your family. It certainly is a surprise since everyone in your family looks so normal. No one else is morbidly obese. No one else has black, unruly hair. No one else. So forgive me if I thought she might be adopted. I see now that I was wrong."

He stood there, almost speechless. "*Those* genes? What do you mean by *those* genes?"

"I just told you what I meant. Morbidly obese and black, curly, unruly hair. It's disgusting."

"Those are the things you have against Mim? That's all you see when you look at her?"

My mother stood there, not responding. But her silence told him everything.

"I'm going to bed," he finally said, walking past her. He turned and looked back at her when he reached the hallway. She was still standing in the same spot.

"If that's all you see, then I feel sorry for you. Mim is *the* most amazing person I know—that I will ever know. And you are missing out if you can't see that. And if you are so superficial that you can't get past what you see on the surface, then you don't deserve to know her. And you don't deserve to know me."

He turned and walked away. My mother stood there with angry tears welling up in her eyes. She heard what he said but did not take it the way he had hoped she would. All she heard was that

Mim was an amazing person and not her. She was desperate to marry him one day; but at that point, she felt she would never be the most important person in his life. It would always be Mim. Big fat Mim.

***

The next morning, Mim could feel the tension between them. My mother ate quietly and then returned to her room to get ready for church. Their plan was to attend the service and then leave mid-afternoon to return to school. The next day, they would leave to spend a few days with my mother's parents so my dad could meet them. He wasn't sure he wanted to now.

When they were alone, Mim leaned over to my dad.

"Did you two break up last night?"

"I don't know," he said quietly.

"You don't know?"

He shook his head.

"Well, when will you know?" she asked, puzzled.

My dad sighed and sat back in his chair, his eggs barely touched. "I don't know."

"You don't know what?"

"I don't know what I want anymore." He paused, and she let him sit there and think. "I do love her . . . I just don't know. You know what the problem is, don't you?"

She looked at him and nodded. She had known the moment she met her. And she knew the dilemma he was facing. Sometimes, only siblings can know the things that are thought and felt without having to utter a word. Mim felt deeply for him. She understood what he was going through.

"Listen," she said, gently touching his arm, "I've told you, don't worry about me. If all of this is about me, then don't let it get in the way. If you truly love her, none of this will matter."

"That's not true," he said. "Right now, you are the most important person in my life. There is no way that I can marry someone who can't see what I see in you and who doesn't love and respect you. *And* who doesn't respect how much I love you. I've told you that before."

"Paul," she said in almost a whisper, "it doesn't

matter if she loves me or not. All that matters is that she loves you and that you love her. You need to figure that out. You need to examine your heart and decide how you feel about her—how much you really love her. Then you need to know for sure how much she loves you. That's all that matters in life. Do you understand?"

He nodded.

"Okay then," she concluded. She started to get up from the table but then sat back down. "And listen," she said, pausing and looking at him, "I am important in your life, and you're important to me; but I shouldn't be the *most* important person in your life. That should be your future wife, whoever she may be. Whether it's Paige or someone else. Okay?"

He nodded again, knowing she was right. Mim got up and left the kitchen. She would have to hurry because, as usual, she was running late. My dad sat there for a few more minutes and then went to dump his food in the disposal and put his dishes in the sink. He stood at the counter, lost in thought. He turned when my mother came into the kitchen, dressed for church and looking stunning. She approached him timidly.

"Paul, I—" she began to say, but he interrupted her.

"Listen, Paige," he paused, "I'm sorry about last night. It was wrong of me to ignore you like I did. There's really no excuse, but I'm really struggling here. I love you. I really do. And I guess it might seem strange that I'm so protective of my sister, but we're close. My parents didn't think they would be able to have children. And because of that, we're just extremely close and, well I guess, extremely protective of each other. And I just don't get your attitude towards her. Is it just her weight? Is it a jealousy thing? But regardless, I think it's ridiculous."

"Paul—" she tried to interrupt, but he stopped her.

"I think I need some time, Paige. Just some time to sort out my feelings with all of this. I think we're perfect for each other, really I do. But I don't like this side of you, and I keep trying to figure out which one is the real you."

"You know the real me," she insisted.

He shook his head. "No, I'm not sure that I do. It's only with Mim that I see this coldness, but it's *so* overwhelming. It makes me wonder if that's the genuine side of you and everything else is just, well, fake."

22

Burning tears sprung to her eyes. She nodded. "Fine, if that's all you see. Then fine."

"That's not all I see, but it's confusing. I need to understand what you're feeling and why you act the way you do towards Mim."

She shook her head, refusing to explain. She had already begun to shut herself off from him. He detected it as the coldness returning rather than what it really was, which was her self-protective nature.

"Fine then," he said. "Let's just take a break and figure out what we both want."

She didn't respond. She only stood there. After a moment, he turned to go get dressed.

"If you don't mind," she said quietly, "I don't feel like going. You can go with your family, and I'll be ready to leave when you get back, or we can leave now. I just can't go to church and sit with your family and act as if everything is okay between us."

He thought for a moment. "No, you're right. We should head back now. I don't want to pretend either. I'll tell Mom that we need to leave. I guess I'll just make up an excuse."

She nodded and turned to go pack her things.

Much to the objection of his mother, they left not long after everyone departed for church. She and his dad were sad to see them go. Rather than telling them the reason why, my dad just said my mother's parents needed her to come home earlier than what they had planned.

My parents drove all the way back to campus without speaking. My mother had retreated into her silence, and my dad didn't know what else to say. He dropped her off at her sorority house and then left to go catch up with some guys who were leaving on a beach trip. He had decided at the last minute to go with them. He wasn't sure if she stayed on campus or went back home to spend spring break at her parents' house. For the most part, he didn't care.

He spent the next six months pretty much ignoring her. She didn't bother him, and he was surprised by it. She kept her distance rather than trying to find little ways to stay connected to him. He dated a couple of other girls but never found them as interesting or as much fun to be around as my mother. He found himself comparing every girl to her, but no one measured up.

After a long absence, he began to miss her. He found out through mutual friends that she had dated someone during the summer, and he was surprised at how jealous he felt. He wrestled with his feelings about her coldness, still not understanding it completely. But he remembered Mim's words; and as time passed, his anger about it lessened.

He decided to call her in October of their junior year. He was amazed at how at ease they still were with each other. He had been so nervous about calling; but when she answered, he felt as if no time had passed since they last spoke. She seemed friendly and forgiving, and he was relaxed and laughing within minutes. He felt as though their time apart had been good for both of them. Perhaps, he hoped, she had grown from her immature reaction to his sister; and above all, he still felt that love for her as he had before. They began dating again but took it slowly. Neither of them mentioned Mim or what had transpired between them. When she went home with him to Troy for Thanksgiving, she acted perfectly normal towards Mim. My dad truly felt she had changed. Mim was hopeful but not completely sure. She kept her thoughts to herself, however.

My dad met my mother's parents for the first time that Christmas. It was the only time he had been invited to their home. He found her father to be courteous enough but not overly friendly. Her mother's natural demeanor was distant and cold. She seemed judgmental and critical of everyone and everything. My mother was reticent to share with my dad how she felt about her parents— specifically about her mother. But he noticed how introverted she became around them. She seemed vulnerable and childlike whenever they were present.

Later, she admitted to him what an absentee father she had and how overbearing her mother was. She never felt she could do anything right, and she knew she was a constant source of disappointment to both of her parents. One thing he distinctly remembered from that trip was how she kept saying over and over again that she didn't want to be like her mother. She cried when she said it, in fact. She did not want to be like her.

He felt closer to her after that, wanting to protect her

somehow. She was from an extremely wealthy family, but no one would have ever known it. She seemed so down to earth, never letting on that her parents were worth millions upon millions. She lacked arrogance and entitlement, and he respected her even more for that. He knew she was different from them. He trusted that completely.

He proposed to her that spring. He had decided that he loved her more than anyone and wanted to spend the rest of his life with her. He truly believed with all of his heart that they were the perfect couple and that they would be happy together. He had no doubt.

Chapter 3

~September 1979~

Paul Michael Allen married Paige Anne Martin on September twenty-first, after they both graduated in May of the same year. Mim helped him pick out the ring from a small but well established jeweler in Manhattan. She had reminded him that, as far as anyone was to know, she was not there. My mother never needed to know that he didn't pick it out on his own. Two carat, brilliant cut, perfect clarity, set in platinum. Beautiful. The wedding band was made with another carat of smaller diamonds. It was perfect for her.

According to my dad, something about my mother changed during this time, from proposal to wedding. She was always a Type A person: SGA vice president, cheerleader, sorority member extraordinaire, straight-A student from birth through college, on and on and on. It must have been exhausting. But she was obsessed during her senior year and was trying to plan a wedding as well. My dad said she was like a crazy person, always in a hysterical rush. Another thing happened as well. She became a perfectionist—and not in a good way. Everything had to be perfect. Everything. Almost wasn't good enough. Everything had to be just so, especially the wedding. She planned every single detail. Her mother, my Grandmother Martin, helped as well. Along with being cold and distant, my grandmother was the queen of perfection. In fact, no one could ever please her. Especially not my mother. My dad always believed that was why my mother became obsessed, trying to somehow gain her approval.

My mother was an only child. Her mother was overprotective and domineering, sternly molding her only daughter into what she wanted her to be. My mother dutifully complied, hoping to make her happy. When it came time to plan the wedding, my grandmother allowed my mother to make all the decisions but guided with a watchful eye. Well, more like a hawk. In turn, my mother nervously tried to make everything perfect. And everything was beautiful. The ceremony was held at a charming old Presbyterian church in Alexandria, Virginia. Her gown was slim fitted with a sweetheart neckline and a train that was a tasteful length. My mother refused for the bridesmaids' dresses to look hideous. Instead, she chose a beautiful dress with a flattering cut in a soft shade of cornflower blue. My dad looked handsome in his black tux, as did the groomsmen. It was picture perfect. There was not one detail out of place.

There was, however, one glaring detail that was left out. My mother had not asked Mim to be in the wedding. She definitely didn't ask her to be a bridesmaid. She didn't ask her to serve in any capacity. My dad's family was surprised. Certainly the groom's sister would be in the wedding party, they had thought. He dismissed their concerns, saying it was the bride's decision. But he confronted her and was upset about it himself. She complained that it was her mother's fault because she was demanding that her cousins be in the wedding. My mother, of course, wanted her best friend as her maid of honor. Next, one of her closest friends from her cheer squad and, third, her closest sorority sister. That left three spots, and her three cousins fit perfectly. Conveniently. My dad suggested a seventh bridesmaid, but my mother was adamant that she would not go with an odd number, and a large wedding party would begin to look tacky. He was furious, and it caused many heated arguments, but my mother stood firm.

On the surface, Mim and my mother got along well. They were always pleasant towards one another, but they rarely saw each other. My dad would travel into the city to see Mim, but my mother always had an excuse not to go. So it was mainly during holidays or at some sort of family get-together that they would run into each other. Mim was the only person who wasn't surprised that she was left out of the wedding. She knew my mother was only being nice because she had to. She also believed that her behavior would change after they were married. She had debated with herself—agonized over it really—whether or not to talk to my dad about it. But Mim was not a self-centered person. She wanted my dad to be happy, and Mim truly believed that he would be happy with my mother because she knew how much he loved her. So she continued to reason that if the only problem standing between them was her, she would relent. Just as she had told my dad before, she did not want to be the problem or the further cause of trouble between them. She felt like they would have a wonderful life together, and she would still see her brother at various times, so she said nothing. Instead, she went to him for the third time, knowing the arguments they were having over her not being in the wedding and told my dad she was okay with it. She said she didn't want to invest in a bridesmaid's dress that she would never wear again. Plus, she joked, she was too old to be a bridesmaid. A full eight years older than the bride is simply embarrassing. She laughed her way through it and reassured him she was fine. She was content to sit with the family and watch him get married. He believed her; and feeling he had her blessing, he married my mother. Mim always thought it was ironic that the one person my mother despised most was the one person who could make or break her wedding. My mother, Mim had thought, should have been very thankful she was such a generous person.

***

My parents both graduated near the top of their class. My dad earned a degree in finance and landed a lucrative job as an investment banker. My mother became a pediatric nurse. Within a year after they married, they settled in the affluent town of Greenwich, Connecticut, in a beautiful old two-story on Abbington Lane. My mother loved the charm of the historic area, and my dad loved that the area had held its value throughout the decades. It was the perfect house, in the perfect area.

My dad had briefly discussed staying in New Jersey after graduation; but after four years of college, my mother was ready to leave and live somewhere else. Connecticut was a good choice for both of them. For my mother because of the name and reputation of the area; for my dad because of the location. Greenwich was still about three hours away from my dad's family, similar to when he was at college. But it was much further away from my mother's parents than when she was at Rutgers, five hours instead of three. She preferred it that way. She wanted to be away from her mother's watchful eye. And for my dad, it was only an hour by train into the city where he worked in Manhattan and only an hour away from Mim.

My mother's desire for perfection only increased after she was married. The house always had to be perfect, as if they were living in a magazine. The yard had to be immaculate. Not one thing went unnoticed. Her Type A personality continued. She became a member of the Junior League and then president of it within a few years. She continued her work as a nurse, choosing to work postpartum or labor and delivery at the hospital rather than working in a doctor's office. She preferred the flexible hours. She loved her job and her volunteer work, as well as taking care of her home and her garden. She was never bored.

Despite my mother's increasing need for order and achievement, my dad did not see her as a reflection of her own mother. They were extremely happy the first few years of their marriage, and he was blind to the person she was beginning to evolve into. Her mother visited occasionally; and when she did, my mother would revert to the same vulnerable behavior he noticed in the beginning.

As their fifth anniversary approached, my mother was ready to start a family; and my dad agreed it was time. He was a brilliant money manager and had their whole financial life planned out. The five year mark, according to his calculations, was the right time to have a baby. So with my dad giving her the green light, my mother began to plan. She wanted the baby to be born in May, which meant she would have to get pregnant in August. It was early July, so everything would need to happen fast. My dad disagreed with the frenzy of what was taking place. He wanted to wait a few months and take it at a slower pace. But my mother wouldn't comply, adamantly deciding that the baby must be born in May. Could she explain why? No. All she could reason was that May was the perfect month for a baby. Everything would be green and blooming, a symbol of new life. It would be the cool of the spring before the heat of the summer would roll in. Summer, she believed, was just too hot to be pregnant. So yet again, my dad relented; and on the evening of their fifth anniversary, my mother announced to him that she was indeed pregnant. Despite his initial misgivings, he was very happy. They celebrated the new life they had created and began to discuss names and the possibility of a boy or a girl.

Little did my dad know at the time, but my mother, in all her pre-baby planning, had already decided on the possible names of her future children. Not only would all the names begin with the letter A, but they would also be in alphabetical order. This was the point at which my mother's quest for perfection kicked into overdrive and—although not diagnosed—her need for perfection evolved into a full-fledged obsessive-compulsive disorder.

She had long ago decided that her first daughter would be named Abbigail, Abbi for short. However, they lived on Abbington Lane, so that would no longer work. She knew when they purchased the house that the name would conflict. So she scratched Abbi off her list. She loved the name Amanda, and there was nothing to interfere with that choice. So if the baby were a girl, that would be her name. As far as boy names were concerned, Adam was her first choice. That would be the baby's name if it were a boy. However, if a girl was the first to be born and named Amanda, and then a boy were to be born later on, he could no longer be named Adam. This would disrupt the alphabetical order of birth. Absolute madness! A future son would then be named Andrew. My mother used her charm and wit to get my dad to agree with her final decision without him even knowing it was the final decision. My mother was a master of such things.

My parents also made another decision. They would wait until the baby was born to find out if it was a boy or a girl. My parents both agreed that there were so few surprises in life, and that would have to be the biggest one. The thought of the doctor announcing what sex the baby was when it was born kicking and screaming right there in front of them was so much more appealing than in an ultrasound room with a tech announcing it as she pointed out genitalia on a grainy screen. My mother's years in nursing helped make that decision for her. The only problem my mother foresaw in this plan, however, was planning for the nursery and the layette. She naturally would want everything blue for a boy or pink for a girl, with all kinds of cute clothes already hanging in the closet. But this was the one thing my mother stood firm with herself on. Instead, she decorated the nursery in all shades of soft pastels. The only clothing she registered for was zero to six months so that no one would buy anything beyond that. Six months would give her plenty of time to revamp everything to suit the new baby, be it boy or girl. In fact, she had it done within two months.

~May 1985~

The official due date was May twelfth; and as fate would have it in my mother's perfect world, she went into labor. My parents were excited to meet their new baby, as were all the other family members who had gathered in the waiting room that day. Excitement was in the air. Would it be Adam or Amanda? The nurses were excited as well. They were all friends and colleagues of my mother's. One thing everyone knew was that, whether it be a boy or a girl, it was going to be a beautiful baby. And she was. My older sister, Amanda Lynn Allen, was born at four thirty-five that afternoon, weighing seven pounds, six ounces, and twenty inches long. The perfect size for a newborn baby.

Mim had been waiting for the big event, keeping everyone entertained as usual. Both sets of grandparents were there, as well as various friends and a few aunts and uncles. My mother's parents sat near my dad's parents but still kept a bit of a distance. They spoke some and smiled politely but otherwise remained disengaged from the conversation. They were not amused by Mim in the least. In fact, Grandmother Martin eyed her with disdain. Mim felt her glare without looking and knew immediately where my mother got her judgmental attitude from. When my dad came out holding Amanda and announced she was a girl, everyone jumped to their feet and clapped and cheered. They were all very excited. Everyone ooh'd and ahhh'd over her. She was such a pretty baby. In fact, my Grandmother Martin made a point to say, "Thank God she's a beautiful baby."

For the next two days, my mother's hospital room was a flurry of activity. Family members and friends were coming and going, excited to see the new Allen baby. Amanda was the first grandchild on both sides, so that garnered a lot of attention in itself. All the nurses wanted to see her, hearing how beautiful she was. And she was, of course, Paige's daughter; and they all loved my mother. There were so many pictures taken, my dad said it looked like a press conference. Such excitement! And my mother loved every single minute of it. She loved being the center of attention, and she absolutely loved her daughter being the center of attention as well.

My mother made sure that someone was on hand to video every aspect of Amanda coming home. From leaving the hospital to arriving home, the first bottle, the first bath, laying her in the crib for the first time—everything was documented. My parents were very proud of their new baby and ecstatic to finally have her home.

The next few days and weeks passed by too quickly for my mother. She thoroughly enjoyed taking care of Amanda. She loved feeding her and rocking her. She decided to talk to my dad about not going back to work for a while, just until Amanda was a little older. She didn't want to miss out on such a special time with the baby while she was a newborn. My dad assessed their finances and decided that, with his new promotion, it would work for my mother to stay at home. This made my mother very happy. She enjoyed having time to play with the baby, work around the house and in the yard, and to continue to do her volunteer work. Everywhere she went and whatever she did, she always had Amanda with her. She loved showing her off.

When Amanda was about nine months old, my mother started feeling sick. She was suddenly nauseous and tired. With it being near the end of winter, she was afraid she was getting the flu, but she never ran a fever. Grandmother Allen stayed for a week because my mother feared getting the baby sick. After a few days, the symptoms were still there, so she went to the doctor. She learned that it wasn't the flu but was very surprised to discover what it was. She was pregnant again. This was totally unexpected; and my mother, being a perfectionist, did not like unexpected things. "How did this happen?" she wanted to know. In her perfectly scheduled and planned life, she had no idea how this could be.

As it turned out, she was pregnant with me. So my very first mistake in my new little life was that I was unplanned. Strike one. The second mistake was that I made her deathly ill, something she did not experience with Amanda. And worst of all, because she was so sick with me, it interfered with her caring for Amanda. Strike two.

It was around this time that my dad's grandfather passed away. My dad adored him and was absolutely devastated when he died so suddenly. He was inconsolable, and it wasn't until weeks later that he finally started emerging from his grief. When he did, he had one request of my mother. He wanted to name the baby after him. My dad had a feeling I was going to be a boy. He begged my mother for this one request. Now, one needs to know how this upset my mother's plans. She was a tedious planner. She not only had all of our names picked out but our educational and career paths were decided as well. So to ask for a name change was serious business. She was none too happy. The name she had already chosen for me, believing whole-heartedly that I would be a girl, was Anna Michelle. It was a blend of both her and my dad's middle names. It really should have been my older sister's name, but it would have thrown off the alphabetizing of the names, and that would have been the end of the world. Certainly it would have upset the balance of the universe.

So Anna Michelle was chosen for a girl and Andrew for a boy. It was just after she had decided this that my dad asked her to name the baby after his grandfather. The name my dad wanted? Ronald Franklin Allen. That upset Paige Allen more than anyone could know. She did not like either name in the least. She tried to negotiate with my dad and use Ronald as a middle name. Andrew Ronald Allen would not be that bad. Most people don't even pay attention to the middle name. Sure it would be on important documents—school and various legal forms, but it could be ignored for the most part. My dad was insistent, and he had never been more insistent in his whole life. His grief would not fully be relieved until this was done. My mother, for once in her life, relented and just prayed for a girl.

~November 1986~

I was born in early November. It wasn't May, but I wouldn't exactly call it strike three, seeing as I was unplanned in February. I think such things should be under the same umbrella of mistakes. But I digress. My dad told me that the day I was born was better than any beautiful spring day in May. Autumn was his favorite time of year; and because of that, he remembered that the day I was born was a beautiful, crisp fall day. The trees were dressed in red, yellow, and orange foliage. College football was in full swing. The holidays were around the corner. As far as my dad was concerned, it was the perfect day to be born.

As it was eighteen months before, everyone was anxiously waiting at the hospital. The nurses were all abuzz waiting for the next Allen baby to be born, certain he or she would be just as beautiful as the first. Both sets of grandparents were there again, playing with Amanda and passing her around. She had grown into the most beautiful toddler with blonde curls and big blue eyes, and she was so smart. She was advanced for her age and had already begun to speak clearly. My mother had declared she would be another Type A, just like herself. And definitely a straight-A student. No doubt about that. Amanda had always been a happy baby who never fussed but smiled all the time. She was the perfect child. My Grandmother Martin was most proud of her, continually saying how she was a perfect little version of Paige. She was just as my mother had been when she was a little girl. Mim was trying to play with Amanda and make her laugh; but every time she would get her attention, Grandmother Martin would distract Amanda and make her come over to her. 'Yep,' Mim thought, 'I see where Paige gets it from.'

My parents were in the delivery room, anxious to meet their new baby. I was born at two-fifteen in the afternoon. My mother breathed a heavy sigh of relief when the doctor said I was a girl. She wept with joy. Her prayer had been answered. She would not have to use that horrible name. My dad smiled broadly when he looked at me. I was a screaming, healthy baby. When the doctor held me up for my mother to see, she immediately stopped crying. A cold look crossed her face. My dad sensed it immediately. He had seen it before. What she saw was that I was a bigger newborn than Amanda had been. Petite little Amanda only weighed seven pounds, six ounces. I was ten pounds, four ounces. Not only that, but I was born with a thick shock of black hair that was just long enough to begin to curl. I'm sure I practically looked like a sumo wrestler. What my mother saw was Mim. I was her worst nightmare incarnate. I had inherited the stray gene my mother had

34

feared. Strike three.

My mother was despondent. My dad said it was as if she had gone into a catatonic state. The nurses, her friends and former co-workers, were all confused. They had not seen anything like it before and wondered aloud if perhaps she had suddenly slipped into some sort of deep postpartum depression. No one, however, had seen such a quick onset of it. My dad was the only one who knew what the problem was, and he quickly took charge of me. The doctor had a nurse take my mother's vital signs. After seeing that everything was normal, he gave her a sedative so that she could sleep. Surely she just had a rough delivery and would be better soon.

In the waiting room, there was a strange mix of reactions from all the relatives. All of those on my mother's side smiled cordially and talked about what a healthy baby I was and how dark my hair was—and so much of it. Years later, my dad admitted to me that it was very different from the reaction they had with Amanda. Especially Grandmother Martin. She had nothing to say. My dad's side of the family knew what the problem was. They knew it was because I resembled Mim. Mim herself was overjoyed but cautious. She understood the gravity of the situation. My mother slowly came out of her stupor and began interacting with family and friends. It was strange though. She would talk about everything, but she wouldn't talk about me. I asked my dad once if she ever held me in the hospital. He didn't answer.

Now if matters couldn't get worse, the issue of my name came up. Before my mother saw me but just after she was told I was a girl, she was under the impression that her promise was null and void due to the fact that I wasn't a boy. However, my dad saw it differently. When it came time for him to bring it up, he approached my mother very carefully. I was always surprised he was so brave, given that she was already disappointed that I looked like Mim. So, what next? He still wanted to name me after his grandfather? A name my mother hated? I guess my dad really had been determined. What he didn't realize was that it was yet another curse he was putting upon my head. Strike four, if strike four was even possible.

He cautiously approached my mother. He brought up the issue of the birth certificate and needing to decide on a name. She shrugged. He reminded her about the agreement they had with his grandfather's name. She told him yes, if I had been a boy. He said he had wanted it regardless of the sex of the baby. My mother glared at him.

"What do you want, Paul?" she said through clenched teeth.

He decided to stand his ground. "I still want to use his name," he said adamantly.

"You want to name her Ronald Franklin?"

"No," he said a little more carefully, "I want to name her Ronda Francis."

My mother stared at him with enough anger that, if she hadn't been subdued on medication, she would have thrown something at him.

"Is it not bad enough," she said in almost a whisper, "that she will look like your sister? Do you have to insist she have such a hideous name?"

"It is not hideous!" he shouted, surprising himself.

"It is hideous to me!" she shouted in return.

At that point, a nurse walked in to bring me back from the nursery. She smiled as she entered the room. It was obvious she had interrupted something when she saw my mother recoil and turn away from my dad. He took me out of the hospital bassinet and began rocking me. My mother never turned to look at me. My dad had said I actually was a beautiful baby, but all my mother saw was that I was a chubby newborn with thick dark hair. He had tried to convince her that I would grow and become even more beautiful, but she wouldn't acknowledge it. He sat, rocking me for a long time. After a while, my mother said—without turning to face him—that he could go ahead and name me whatever he wanted. Anna Michelle was too pretty a name for me anyway. He looked at me with tears streaming down his face, realizing he was married to the most heartless woman on earth.

I was taken home without much fanfare. A couple of pictures were snapped but not much more. It was a very subdued event. My mother was happy to get back home to Amanda. My dad decided to take some time off of work until everyone was adjusted. He thought my mother would gradually show an interest in caring for me. Apparently she never did. My dad used the excuse that my mother needed help with a toddler and a newborn so that his mother would come and stay with us for a while. My grandmother was happy to do it. She had always gotten along well with her daughter-in-law, but she did notice a difference in her this time. She talked very little but was always holding Amanda or playing with her. My grandmother would tell my dad later that she never interacted with me.

As if things weren't bad enough, my birth certificate and Social Security card came a few weeks later. They sat within the assorted mail for a couple of days until my dad got around to filing them away. He glanced over my birth certificate and noticed there was an error. A big error. He looked at my Social Security card. Another big error. My name was wrong on both. It wasn't listed as Ronda. No, not at all. It was listed as Roda. A simple typographical error. Some brilliant transcriptionist at the hospital had accidentally skipped that very important *n*. My dad sat there, drained. Another thing had gone wrong in my new little life. How hard would that be to correct? Apparently it's not that difficult, but he was so overwhelmed with life at that point that he never pursued it. So I was stuck with Roda.

I often wondered how and when he broke the news to my mother. Wouldn't that have been more difficult to deal with than simply going to the proper government agencies and getting it corrected? I always assumed she had no reaction because she had already written me off anyway. Growing up, I had asked my dad several times why he didn't have it changed, but he never could seem to remember. When I was nine, he did tell me that he regretted not changing it back, especially since he was so adamant about naming me after his grandfather. But he was the type of person who believed everything happened for a reason, so he let it go. I, myself, always saw it differently. I would rather be Ronda than Roda, but that's life—and life isn't fair.

When I was a few weeks old, he decided to put me in daycare. There was a facility in his building. It wasn't a difficult transition for him, and he enjoyed having more time with me. He would always be the one to bathe and feed me every night. Amanda stayed home with Mother, and Mother cared for her every evening. My dad would often suggest that he take care of both of us at night, but my mother was very protective of Amanda. Daddy later realized that she didn't want my sister interacting with me. I often used to wonder why my dad put up with her behavior. He said at first, it was just to make things easier for her as she adjusted to two small children. In the beginning, he did believe part of it had to do with postpartum depression. He later realized that wasn't quite it. In the early years when they were new parents, he excused much of my mother's behavior; but later on, it caused many problems between them. Later on, he could only wish he had dealt with the problem in the beginning. But he also realized that Paige Allen was who she was, and arguing with her didn't necessarily mean that would change. Her perfect world had a flaw, and she did not like it.

According to my dad and verified by pictures he took, I grew into a very cute baby. I was fussy to begin with but then developed into a contented baby. I lost much of my newborn hair, but it grew back just as thick with loose curls. I had Mim's brown eyes and long dark eyelashes. My cheeks were rosy and round. I was actually an adorable, healthy, happy baby—if I must say so myself. When my dad took me to work, all the women made a fuss over me. The daycare workers were always excited to see me. But in the evenings when we came home, my mother would only greet my dad. He would try to tell her about something new I had done or how everyone at work just adored me, but her only response would be, "That's nice."

When I was nine months old, my mother got pregnant again. I was told she had not been excited about it. Certainly not as excited as she had been when she first learned she was pregnant with Amanda. My dad continued to rationalize it as the baby blues, but deep down he knew why. He tried many things during that time to make her happy. He continued to take me during the day, and he would tend to both me and my sister at night. It was the only time period she allowed that to happen. He would play in the floor with us and encourage her to play too. He would make me laugh so that she could hear the funny giggle that I had, hoping she would look at me and smile or even laugh too. It never worked. If she had energy for anything, it would be to take Amanda up to her room and rock her to sleep.

My sister, Ashley, was born when I was eighteen months old. She looked very much like Amanda when she was born, and my mother sighed and laughed when she saw her. Her joy had been restored. She kissed Ashley and cuddled her as soon as she could. The nurses and the doctor saw nothing unusual; but my dad stood there, speechless. Anger and sadness welled up inside of him, and he had no idea what to do with those feelings. He knew she would never love me. He knew she would never give me a chance. He pretended to go through the motions of a happy new dad, but he was seething within. It was not that he didn't love his new daughter. He did. He was very happy, and he rocked her and cradled her as he normally would. But he looked at his wife in a much different light. Her behavior confirmed his worst fear. It had not been postpartum depression as he had tried to make himself believe. It was much worse than that. It was total disdain for her middle child, which stemmed from total disdain for his sister.

She acted like a proud new mom while she was in the hospital with Ashley. She gladly entertained family and friends who came to visit. She held the baby the entire time, passing her to whomever wanted to hold her next. She talked to the nurses about Ashley and what a beautiful baby she was. Amanda, who had just turned three, would sit on the bed beside my mother and look at Ashley as my mother told her that she was her new little sister. I sat in my dad's lap whenever I was there and was never allowed on the bed.

My mother commented often on how Ashley looked just like Amanda when she was born. She was very proud of her new daughter. My mother made a big fuss when they took her home, making sure pictures were taken of every possible moment. She definitely made sure pictures were taken of Amanda and Ashley together. She did tolerate my dad taking pictures of the three of us, but only a few were allowed.

He had thought later to try to talk to her about all of it in a very rational way. He wanted to understand how she felt and why she seemed to reject me. He wanted to get everything in the open, figure it out, and make it all better. He wanted the family to be complete, and he wanted his three daughters to be close. My dad thought the best way to approach the subject would be to bring up the name I was supposed to be given. He knew it might be a sore subject, but that was the only thing he could think of.

He asked her why, since she loved the name Anna Michelle so much, had she not used it for the new baby. She said she had long ago decided that if there were a third daughter, her name would be Ashley. She believed it was the perfect name for the youngest. He tried to be diplomatic, hoping to soften her so that she would open up to him. She was nice, she was pleasant, but she was very guarded. He acknowledged that he knew she had loved the name Anna Michelle. He apologized for being so adamant about changing it, especially since the mistake was made with my name. He had assumed she would use it for the next baby and apologized for not talking to her about it. She sadly gazed straight ahead the whole time he talked. She was absentmindedly stroking Ashley's head and rocking her as he talked.

He felt as if he was apologizing profusely, yet she was not responding. After a while, she just looked at him and told him that, in all reality, she probably would not have named me that after all. He was confused and asked why. She said because I was not worthy of that name, and I was not the daughter she had hoped for. He felt as if his heart had been ripped out of his chest. He had no idea how to respond. He was stunned. He got up and was walking out of the room, knowing something needed to be said. He turned from across the room and looked at her as she sat cradling their new daughter, a coldness engulfing her. All he could manage to say was, "Roda is a beautiful child, and one day you'll regret utterly rejecting that wonderful human being." She never looked at him. She only looked down at Ashley as she slept and hummed to her softly.

$$\mathscr{Chapter}\ 4$$

~1988-1992~

I grew from a chubby little baby into a chubby little toddler and, subsequently, into a chubby little preschooler. My dad said I loved to eat and loved all kinds of food. I was not the picky eater my sisters were, so at least I excelled at something they didn't. As we got older and sat around the dinner table together, my mother would always eye me critically. She was always aware of how much food I was eating. She could ignore everything else about me, but she paid attention to how much I ate. She would comment on the small portions my sisters would eat, saying how they ate like little birds; but then she would stare at my plate and the mountain of food on it. She would ask my dad, "Honey, do you really need to let her eat that much?" I guess he didn't know how to handle it. He wanted me to be happy, and I was happy when I was eating.

My dad was fully in charge of me. As it started when we were born, so it continued. My mother had Amanda and Ashley, which she juggled very well. A third child would be too much to handle at one time, so she conveniently left it up to my dad. From the beginning, she used it as an excuse to ignore me. She never addressed me directly but issued instructions or complaints through my dad. "Paul, her shoes are untied," or, "Paul, don't let her have dessert." Nothing was ever said to me directly. However, I do remember one specific moment, and I believe it was my very first memory from childhood. I was about three years old, and my mother was sitting on the sofa with Amanda and Ashley, reading a book to them. It was a book I loved that my dad always read to me.

41

I went to the edge of the couch and began to climb up so that I could sit and listen too, but my mother reprimanded me. She told me no, to get down, and that my dad would read it to me later. I'm not sure if I had been hesitant about approaching her before that, but I certainly was after. I remember Ashley looking at me, but she was about two years old and didn't really comprehend it. But Amanda was five, and she glared at me. She inherited my mother's gaze very early.

It was also during this early time in my life that I began forming wonderful memories with my dad. As I said, he began taking me to daycare when I was six weeks old, strapping me to him in a baby sling. There he was in his suit and tie with me attached to him while juggling a briefcase and a diaper bag. I'm sure he looked like a single dad, but he did it happily and it formed a special bond between us. We quickly developed a routine of waking up early before everyone else, leaving as the sun was peaking over the horizon, catching the train to Grand Central, then breakfast at a quaint little diner two blocks from his office. One thing I absolutely loved from a very young age was riding the subway. I loved the thrill of hurrying to get on before the doors shut and the car lurching forward at a high rate of speed. And I loved watching people. I was very much like Mim—always observing others.

And that was another advantage of going into the city with my dad every day: seeing Mim. When she wasn't teaching, she would get me from daycare so we could spend the day together. There were also the occasional Friday nights when we would stay over at Mim's and spend all day Saturday with her. Sometimes we would spend all weekend with her. My mother did not like it. I was very young, and my dad and Mim probably didn't think I understood what was being said, but they would talk about my mother and how she didn't like my dad staying overnight. She didn't care if Mim kept me for the weekend, but she didn't want my dad to stay. My dad ignored her wishes and did what he wanted. They talked about how my mother neglected me, which really upset Mim. Any time something was said in that regard, Mim would instinctively pick me up and hold me close to her as if she were trying to make up for my mother depriving me of maternal nurturing. It was, in fact, Mim who was more like a mother to me and not just an aunt.

It was also during these discussions that I began to gain some understanding about the state of my parents' marriage. Even as young as I was, I knew my dad was not happy. As much as he loved my mother, it wasn't enough. He was outraged at how she ignored me, how I wasn't good enough for her. He was disturbed at how she tried to keep me separated from my sisters; and he knew, as a result, he would not be as close to Amanda and Ashley as he should be. He wanted desperately to be close to them, but he could see my mother shaping them, and he didn't know how to stop it. He had overlooked my mother's behavior when we were born. He didn't like it, but he overlooked it. He had hoped it would change, thinking as we grew we would naturally bond. My mother made sure we didn't. Ultimately, he questioned his decision to take me with him every day. As much as he loved it, he wondered aloud to Mim if it wasn't a mistake to separate me from them. Mim reassured him that it was probably for the best, believing that my mother would ignore me and I would only suffer because of it. My dad was at a loss at what to do. So he kept doing the only thing he knew to do. He kept me with him, and he and I stayed close to Mim.

My mother distanced herself by keeping busy with her projects. She was still a member of the Junior League and worked at the hospital just enough to keep her nursing license active, but her real project was "the girls." According to my dad, she began saying "the girls" when Ashley was born; and he knew I wasn't included. She would say, "Paul, you need to bathe Roda while I feed the girls." Or when we were a little older, she would say, "Paul, I'm taking the girls to the park. What are you going to do with Roda?" She never invited him to go because she never invited me. On the weekends when I was with Mim, he would get to participate. Otherwise, it was just him and me.

As we grew, my mother's attention centered on activities for Amanda and Ashley. With her background in gymnastics, she began working with them when they were very young. When they were a little older, she enrolled them in tumbling classes. They both inherited her natural ability and excelled at every discipline that was introduced to them. My dad insisted that my mother include me in the classes, thinking it would be good exercise for me. She relented and signed me up after the girls had been taking beginning tumbling for a few months. As my parents sat there watching us, it became very apparent to my dad that I lacked the coordination and any hope of agility to be in such a class. He watched as the instructor continually put Amanda and Ashley at the front of the line so that everyone else could observe "how it was done." I was at the end of the line. Girls in the class giggled as I attempted to do even the simplest moves, and Amanda and Ashley were embarrassed and pretended they didn't know me. My mother would glare at me and then at my dad the whole time. He never made me go back.

As soon as my mother realized my sisters' athletic ability, she enrolled them in all kinds of different classes. She had them—not only in gymnastics—but dance, swimming, and ice skating. She felt the sooner they started the better chance they had to excel at an early age. My dad had hoped to coach a softball team when we were little, but the girls were always over scheduled and didn't have time. When I was four years old, he started working with me to see if I had any hint of his talent. He had hoped softball might be a good outlet for me to excel in. It wasn't. As much fun as he tried to make it for me, I lacked the talent. I was too chubby and too uncoordinated. So instead, my dad enrolled me in an art class. He found out very quickly that I had indeed inherited a talent. It was Mim's talent. My art teacher constantly bragged about me, making my dad proud. He was well aware of my low self-esteem, and it thrilled him when someone—anyone—would compliment me. To boost my spirits, he would frame my pictures and hang them around the house and in his office. My mother wasn't too thrilled about my talent. It was yet another reminder of Mim.

I grew very close to my dad during those formative years. My favorite thing was sitting in his lap in his chair. When I was born, he held me all the time while sitting in his chair. When I was a toddler, he would read to me at night. When I was a preschooler, we would sit there while he was teaching me my letters and numbers. Anytime we were in the den, there was no other place that I would sit; and if he wasn't there, I would sit in his chair by myself. Oftentimes, I would climb up in it just to take a nap. I loved my dad's chair, and I loved sitting with him even if

44

we were just watching the news or a baseball game.

I can still vividly remember one Sunday afternoon when my dad and I were home alone, sitting in his chair reading a book. He tried to sound excited when he told me I would be starting kindergarten in the fall. He said I was getting to be a big girl, and it was time for me to start big school. I didn't understand because I liked the school I was at. I loved going to work with him every day, and I didn't want to go anywhere else. I asked him questions. Where was this school? Why couldn't I go to a school near where he worked? He told me I would be going to the same school Amanda went to. This upset me, and I started crying. I didn't like Amanda. She had just turned seven, and she was mean. She was the perfect image of my mother. She was tall for her age, very slender with long blonde hair and clear blue eyes. She had learned to treat me just as my mother did but even worse. She was very aggressive and would push me out of the way if I ever got near her. She would snatch things away from me if she didn't want me to touch something. My mother would see her actions but would never reprimand her. However, Amanda was always careful not to treat me badly in front of my dad. So the thought of going to school with her scared me. I had been under my dad's care and protection every day, and now that was about to change. I think I cried myself to sleep every night the entire summer.

He was just as upset as I was and even more so after seeing my reaction. He enjoyed our time together and didn't want it to change either, but there was nothing he could do. He had looked into a few private schools in the city, but they were outrageously expensive. It wouldn't have mattered though because my mother would have been furious. She always focused on the appearance of things; and even though Greenwich had great public schools, she had hoped that the girls could go to a private school. She desired the prestige of it. My dad had said no, they couldn't afford it. They especially couldn't afford for all three of us to go. He knew there was no way he could get away with just sending me. So we resigned ourselves to the fact that our mornings together would end, and our train rides home in the afternoon would as well. Another big change would be not seeing Mim as often. We spent the last weeks of that summer too sad to enjoy our time together.

I still remember the very last day before school started. I cried the moment I woke up. I cried on the train the whole way there. I cried during our last breakfast at the diner. I cried the whole time I was in daycare. I even cried when we met Mim after work. That was the worst day ever. My dad and Mim were upset too, and there was nothing they could do to cheer me up. We spent the night with Mim; and the next day, they took me to buy a few more outfits for school and some other supplies. It just made me sadder. Anything to do with the thought of school made me sad.

My dad and I spent the rest of the weekend just sitting in his chair. We were both depressed. He kept trying to think of things to cheer me up. He said, since I was getting older, I would have homework; and he would help me with it every night. That didn't sound fun. He said that he would still fix my lunch every day. That helped a little. He said he had arranged with his office to go in a little later for the next couple of weeks so that he could take Amanda and me to school instead of us riding the bus. It helped knowing I would still get to see him in the mornings. He also decided that I was getting too big for the books we had been reading together, so he was going to the bookstore that Monday morning and surprise me with something new that night. He knew that would give me something to look forward to.

My dad starting doing something new on my very first day of school. He began putting messages on strips of paper under my pillow so I would see them when I first woke up. He never admitted it was him but instead would say the "message fairy" had come. I was so little that I believed him at first. I was too young to read, so he would have to tell me what they said. The very first message on the very first day read, *You are a big girl now, and you are going to learn lots of new things.* I remember smiling, wondering what the message fairy knew I would learn. It became an adventure. With that and with the anticipation of what book my dad would bring home, I began to look forward to the day.

My dad actually took the day off and told my mom to sleep in. He got us both up and ready, cooked our favorite things for breakfast, and drove us to school. Amanda ignored my presence the whole time. And when she talked to Daddy, she tried to sound very grown up. She was starting second grade and was mature for her age.

When we arrived at school, Amanda got out of the car and walked on ahead of us. She was obviously well liked because everyone she passed said hello to her. My dad smiled at me, held my hand, and walked me to my class.

My teacher was Mrs. Tucker. She was the perfect kindergarten teacher. She was friendly and affectionate, and she had the prettiest smile. It was her first year teaching, and she was full of new ideas. She had the most fascinating room and all kinds of interesting things to play with. As I looked around, I overheard her telling my dad how she and her husband had spent all summer decorating her room. She had a reading loft with pillows and stuffed animals to lie on. Underneath was a kitchen with little stools to sit on. I couldn't wait to play on it. I stood there with my dad until she told me which cubby was mine and to go put my things away. Then she told me what desk to sit at. It was the one closest to her desk, so I was happy about that. My dad could see how excited I was. After a few minutes, he decided to leave. He smiled, hugged me goodbye, and reminded me that he was going to surprise me with a new book after school. He told me he would be back to pick me up, and we would go get a special treat. Probably ice cream.

Amanda decided to ride the bus home with her friends, which was fine with me. My dad and I went to Katie's Bakery, one of our favorite places. So it wasn't ice cream but a doughnut instead. My mother would be furious either way. She was constantly counting my calories.

I had a wonderful first day at school and was telling my dad every detail in between bites. I told him all about how much fun I had in the reading loft, what we did on the playground, how much my teacher loved the drawing I did for the book she read us, and how much I liked eating in the lunchroom instead of in the classroom like we did at daycare. It was a very good first day, and my dad was glad to see I was so happy. He felt that maybe it would be an easy transition for me after all.

When we were driving home, he asked if I wanted my surprise then or at bedtime. I had forgotten all about it! A big smile crossed my face when he mentioned it. I thought about it but couldn't decide. So I asked what he thought. He thought for a minute and then said we should wait until bedtime. So I agreed.

My mother was preparing dinner when we got home. She acted indifferent when we came in. She saw that we were laughing and in a good mood. She didn't seem to like it. Amanda had been home for over an hour, so my mother wanted to know where we had been. My dad lied and told her the bookstore. He knew she would be upset if he told her we went to the bakery since she was cooking so early. He had forgotten that during the school year my mother wanted us to eat earlier since we had to go to bed so soon. My dad tried to keep the mood light. He smiled at me and said, "Roda, tell Mom about your first day." He was hoping my mother would be interested. She wasn't.

"Paul, I'm trying to get dinner ready," she said flatly.

"She had a really good first day," he said, encouraging me. "You should hear about it."

She put the spoon down and turned to look at him. "Why don't you ask Amanda how her day was?"

My dad was surprised. "Well, I would love to hear how Amanda's day was," he said, smiling at my sister while she sat at the kitchen table, already working on her homework. She looked at him but didn't smile.

"Well, perhaps if she knew you were planning to take Roda to the bookstore, she would have gone too, and she would have told you about her day. On your little trip to the bookstore, did you bother getting Amanda a book? Or one for Ashley?"

My dad stood there. "No, I just thought Roda needed a reward for being so brave on her first day."

"A reward?" she asked in exasperation. "Does she need a reward for *everything*?"

My dad didn't like to argue in front of us. He didn't want to engage her, and he knew the exchange had already begun to ruin the excitement of the day for me. Amanda had finished her homework and was gathering her books to go to her room. Ashley was sitting on a stool in the kitchen, helping my mother cook. So Amanda helped her down and took her upstairs. My dad looked at me and told me to go too. I carried my Hello Kitty book bag up to my room and sat on my bed. I could hear my parents arguing. They

48

were always arguing about me.

"Why can't you show even the slightest interest in her?" he yelled.

"And why can't you show even the slightest interest in your other two daughters?" she yelled back. She was always trying to turn the argument around on him and ignore her own behavior.

"I wanted Amanda to ride home with us! She wanted to go with her friends!"

"Well, perhaps if you had bribed her with a gift, she would have gone too!"

"Bribe??!! I did no such thing! Roda was scared, and I promised her a book to give her something to look forward to!"

"Oh," she said calmly, "*Roda* is always scared, isn't she? *Roda* always needs encouragement, doesn't she? That's always your excuse for favoring her." She said my name as if it were disgusting to her.

My dad had enough. He turned to leave the room to go upstairs. "I have to favor her because you completely ignore her. You always have. And now you're teaching Amanda and Ashley to ignore her too."

He left her alone to finish dinner and came upstairs to talk to Amanda about her day. She was sitting on her bed, coloring with Ashley. It was sad that my dad didn't have a close relationship with them, and I know it really bothered him. I would see him trying to make an effort, but they were always guarded. Especially Amanda since she was older. My bedroom was next to Amanda's, so I could hear my dad talking to them.

"Hey girls," he said. I could tell he was smiling. "Can I color too?"

"Yes, Daddy," Ashley said, handing him a crayon. "You can color the pony."

"You want me to color him blue?"

"Uh-huh," she nodded.

He laid on the bed and began helping Ashley. "Well, tell me about your day, Manda. How does it feel to be a big second grader?"

She shrugged.

"Manda, I really want to hear how it went. I really wish you would have ridden home with us today."

She shrugged again and started helping them color. "I just wanted to ride with my friends."

"Well, I can understand that. You're getting older now, so that's not surprising. But listen, I've decided to take off all week, and I would really like it if you would ride home with us. You can ride with your friends next week when I go back to work. Okay?"

Amanda thought for a second and then said, "Okay."

"Can I ride too, Daddy?" Ashley asked.

"Well of course you can!" he said, thrilled that she suggested it. "Do you want to get up early and go too, or just go after school?"

Ashley paused from her coloring to think. "Ummm . . . I may want to sleep. So maybe in the afternoon. Can we go get ice cream?"

Daddy nodded. "Yes, of course!" He and Ashley laughed. He turned his attention back to Amanda. "So? Anything great to report about today?"

She shrugged. "I have Mrs. Butler. I really like her. And Sidney is in my class this year . . . *finally*."

"Finally?" my dad asked. "She's never been in your class before?"

"No."

Sidney was on Amanda's gymnastics team. She and my sister both made pre-team when they were six years old. Such natural talent. Ashley was just as good, and my mother was sure she would make it in another year or two as well.

"So, what else? You learning algebra yet? Studying Shakespeare?" he tried to joke. Amanda didn't laugh. "Alright," he sighed, "my seven-year-old is turning into a teenager already."

He finished coloring the page with them and then got up. "Okay, you two. Dinner will be ready soon. Oh hey, Roda and I bought a new book, and we're going to read it tonight at bedtime. Do you two want to join us?"

Amanda answered right away. "I'm sure I've already read it."

"You don't even know what it is," he said, frowning.

"I'm sure I've already read it," she said again. He knew it was her way of saying no. He could see my mother in her. He could see her slipping away, conforming to the image my mother intended.

"I want to, Daddy!" Ashley said excitedly. He smiled, knowing there was still hope for her but realizing it would be inevitable that she would be like Amanda.

"Okay then, Ash, we'll do it after bath time. It's a date."

Ashley smiled and then turned the page and started coloring a new picture.

My dad walked into my room. I tried to look busy with my dolls, as if I hadn't heard the conversation. He picked up my brown bear, Mr. Cocoa, and started talking to Miss Giggles in his funny Mr. Cocoa voice. I laughed. He sat on the floor next to me.

"What book are we going to read, Daddy?"

"You don't want to wait for the surprise?"

"No," I said, shaking my head.

"Alright, I'll tell you. It's *Charlotte's Web*. Have you ever heard of it?"

I shook my head, my eyes wide with anticipation.

"Well, don't worry," he said, "you'll love it. Lots of different characters. Lots of different voices." He smiled, teasing. My dad had the best voices for every character in a book and for every doll and stuffed animal I had. He had a way of making all of them come to life. I couldn't wait for bedtime that night.

Dinner was uneventful. My mother sat, not speaking. She never asked about my day. My dad carried the conversation, trying to get Amanda to talk. Ashley was her usual chatty self. She and my dad were practically the only ones talking. I remained quiet, as usual.

It was during dinner that Ashley brought up reading the book later. My mother shot my dad a look. He ignored it but knew it would lead to an argument later. And it did. They argued in their bedroom for an hour after dinner. Amanda got her shower first and then bathed Ashley. Surprisingly, she ran my bath water so the temperature would be just right. I was never sure what prompted that.

After emerging from their bedroom, my dad came upstairs. He looked tired. It was only seven o'clock, so he was surprised we were all bathed and in our pajamas and in bed. He

51

went into Amanda's room first and thanked her for taking charge and making sure everyone was ready for bed. He knew she was responsible for that, and he was glad to see that she had helped me as well. He stayed in there for a little while just talking to her, catching up with her and learning more about her day. He had to ask all the questions at first, but then she began to open up and share some things on her own. When he got up to leave, he asked if she would come join us while he read to Ashley and me. She was a little less hesitant than before but still said no. She told him she was tired and just wanted to go to sleep. He smiled and said okay.

When he walked into the hallway, he announced in an enthusiastic voice, "Ashley! Come to Roda's room! We need to see what this little pig named Wilbur is up to!"

Ashley bounded out of bed where she had been having a conversation with Barbie about her new outfit. She ran down the hall into my room and jumped on the bed. She was always happy, but I don't think I had ever seen her so excited. My dad picked up the book that had been sitting on my nightstand. I had been looking at the pictures earlier but couldn't decipher any of the words. When we had all found a good spot and we were all comfortable, he opened the book dramatically and began reading aloud the adventures of Wilbur, Charlotte, Fern, and Templeton. And without fail, he told it in the most amazing voices. Ashley and I looked at each other often and laughed. Even though we couldn't read yet, that was the moment we both began to love chapter books; and we both wanted Daddy to read to us every night, no matter what. Even though Amanda said she was going to sleep, my dad still left the doors open just in case she was listening.

My mother never came upstairs to say goodnight.

***

I think my dad decided that night to make more of an effort to be closer to Amanda and Ashley, and to make sure they somehow bonded with me. I think his hopes were high, but he was unaware of the power my mother actually had. She knew she had Amanda on her side. She knew Amanda was just like her; and she knew that, besides her influence, the influence of school friends would keep my sister from wanting to get close to me. Ashley would be more difficult. My mother knew she could do it but it wouldn't be as easy. Ashley's personality was different from Amanda's. She was always smiling, always friendly, and always ready for an adventure. My mother knew my dad would be able to shape her, and she could see that Ashley did seem to like me. So my mother knew she would have to be underhanded about it.

The second day of school was much like the first. My dad drove us to school, and he walked me to my class. Amanda got out of the car and barely waved as she ran to catch up with her friends. I had fun in Mrs. Tucker's class and was excited to see my dad when he picked me up that afternoon. Amanda did ride with us, but Ashley wasn't with him. We had planned to get ice cream, just as she requested, but she didn't come. Amanda seemed indifferent, but I asked where she was. My dad said she didn't feel like coming. He said she was playing with her dolls and was going to help Mother with dinner, so she decided to stay home. I could tell my dad was upset about it. He was very quiet. I'm not sure if he realized it, but I knew the real reason she didn't come. My mother had gotten to her. She was manipulative, and she would stop at nothing to get her way. The optimism my dad felt the night before was gone.

Everyone was quiet at dinner. Ashley talked some, but mostly she hummed to herself. Amanda seemed bored, as usual. My dad seemed lost in his thoughts while my mother seemed a bit smug. I just looked around, watching everyone; and I ate.

Amanda excused herself first so she could finish her homework. My mother took Ashley upstairs to bathe her, and my dad and I cleaned up the kitchen. That was our usual chore, and we enjoyed doing it together. He still didn't say much, not even to me. After a while, I asked if we were going to read again that night. He smiled and said, "Of course we are."

By the time we finished the dishes and went upstairs, my mother was in Ashley's room, curled up with her on the bed and reading her a book. My dad's jaw clenched. He looked down at me and told me to get my pajamas out and that he would run my bath water. While it was running, he looked in on Amanda. She was sitting in her overstuffed chair, talking on the phone to one of her friends. She looked up at him and smiled but continued to talk.

She was off the phone when I was getting out of the

bathtub, so he went back into her room and talked to her for a while. He had decided to spend time with her every night because he knew she was slipping away. He wanted all of us to spend time together, but he knew Amanda would resist it. He stayed in her room for almost an hour. They talked, and he looked over some of her homework. I was playing in my room while I was waiting for him, and my mother was still spending time with Ashley. After she tucked Ashley into bed, she turned off the light and told her goodnight. Then she went to Amanda's room. She didn't say anything to my dad but kissed Amanda on the forehead and told her goodnight. She left and went downstairs. She never came into my room.

My dad told Amanda goodnight and then walked to Ashley's room. He was irritated that my mother had put her to bed and turned off the light. He stood in her doorway and happily said, "Ash, you ready to find out what happens next?"

She turned over in bed to face him. "I do," she whispered, "but Mommy said not to get up."

"Nonsense!" he exclaimed excitedly. "We have to find out what happens next! And we have to do it together!" But he sensed how timid she was, believing she would get in trouble. He smiled. "Okay, how about this . . . Roda!" He shouted for me, and I ran into the hallway. "Ashley is apparently restricted to her bed for the night. So how about we go in her room this time?"

I was excited because I was rarely allowed to go into Ashley's room, and I was never allowed in Amanda's. I ran to my bed and grabbed Mr. Cocoa and Mrs. Giggles so they could hear more of the story too. I skipped down the hall to Ashley's room and settled on the bed, asking Ashley if she wanted to hold Mr. Cocoa again that night. She did. We snuggled up next to Daddy as he began to read the next chapter. I loved little Wilbur, and I loved how Fern loved him even though he seemed worthless.

We were two pages in when my mother came upstairs and stood in the doorway with her arms crossed. She stared at my dad as he continued to read, ignoring her. I looked towards her but didn't make eye contact. Ashley shrunk down further into the bed, hoping she could disappear under the covers.

"Paul," my mother finally interrupted.

He paused and looked up at her in a very blasé manner.

"Yes, Paige?" he said flatly.

"Ashley has already been put to bed for the night, and I have already read her a book."

"Yes, *you* have read to her, and *you* have tucked her in, but now it's *my* turn."

She stood there, adamant. "Why are you defying me?"

"I am not defying you. We did not discuss *who* puts her to bed. We can *both* spend time with her before she goes to sleep."

"I have already put her in bed!" she said through clenched teeth.

"Well," he said matter-of-factly, "from now on, don't bother until I have read a book to her. *We* are going to read this book every night. And then after this one, there will be another one. If *you* want to read her another book, that is fine. But *we* are going to read this one also."

He emphasized the words, knowing it would irritate her even more. She glared at him and then turned and left. He smiled, gave us a reassuring squeeze, and continued reading. Ashley still enjoyed the story but seemed very unsure and even scared. I knew Mother had said something to her that day, but I had no idea if she tried to gently persuade her or just outright threatened her. I had a feeling that my mother might resort to threats if it was necessary to get her way.

When the chapter was over, we begged him to read just a little of the next one. He laughed and said, "No, no, no. You will both have to wait until tomorrow night." He was hoping to build anticipation, and it was working. We couldn't wait. He really hoped the tactic would continue to work on Ashley, knowing that my mother would try her best to discourage her from spending time with us.

Amanda had already turned her light out when we passed by her room. Daddy stood at her door and said goodnight, but there wasn't a response. He tucked me into bed, told me goodnight, and then went downstairs. My mother was waiting for him in the den, and they immediately began arguing. He ushered her into their room and closed the door, not wanting the sound to drift upstairs. But they were yelling so loudly that they could still be heard, although I couldn't make out everything they said. They were arguing over Ashley. At first I was somehow relieved, thinking at least it wasn't about me that time. Then I realized that in an indirect way it was because of me. It was because my mother did not want Ashley to spend time with me.

My dad apparently won the argument. For the rest of that week, Ashley was with him when he picked us up; and he read to us every night. After we finished *Charlotte's Web,* we learned about the adventures of Stuart Little. Then we heard how Mary, Colin, and Dickon transformed things in *The Secret Garden.* Next came Mrs. Whatsit, Mrs. Who, and Mrs. Which in *A Wrinkle in Time.* I swore that even when I learned to read, I would still want my dad to read to me every night. And we both hoped Ashley would too, but I think we both knew it was inevitable she wouldn't.

Chapter 5

~September 1993~

Kindergarten had been a fun year, but first grade was a different story. Whatever cuteness I had was gone. I gained twelve pounds and—at six years old—wore a girl's size ten. Not good. Pants were the biggest ordeal. I had to resort to wearing boys' husky jeans. My sisters both wore sizes below their age until they started getting so tall they had to wear slim fit. That just wasn't fair.

School was horrible. I had been fortunate in kindergarten to get a brand new teacher, a teacher who never knew who Amanda Allen was. I wasn't so lucky in first grade. My teacher was Mrs. Sanders, and she had the pleasure of teaching my perfect sister. I believed, without a doubt, that she found Amanda to be brilliant; so advanced for her age, as others had said.

My dad, once again, took the week off from work so he could take us to school and pick us up. He and I walked Ashley to her class. She was excited to start school, and I was excited that she got Mrs. Tucker. I told her all the wonderful things she had to look forward to. After we dropped her off, my dad walked me to my class. I was filled with dread.

Mrs. Sanders remembered my dad and smiled as if she were surprised to see him. I appeared from behind him where I had been hiding. Her smile dropped, and she looked confused.

"This is my daughter, Roda," he said, pulling me forward. "She's in your class this year."

"Well, yes of course," she said, trying not to sound as perplexed as she looked. "I guess," she paused. "I guess I didn't realize she was your daughter. I remember her from Mrs. Tucker's class, but I just didn't make the connection."

She looked down at me, smiling; but I detected the condescension. I was perceptive like Mim, even at an early age. "So you're Amanda's sister?" she asked. That was the first time out of hundreds—maybe thousands—of times that I would be asked that simple question.

"Yes, ma'am," I said politely but quietly. If I had any hope, maybe she would at least think I had good manners.

Her smile was stiff. She motioned me to a desk. "You may sit right over there, dear. It already has your name on it."

I hugged my dad goodbye, wishing he didn't have to go. He promised the day would fly by and that he would be back to get me. I nodded sadly. He walked to the door and then looked back and smiled at me. I was just standing there by myself, feeling very alone. When he was gone, I sat down in my seat. I looked around at the other kids. I remembered most of them from kindergarten, but they hadn't been in my class. They had either been in Miss Kelly's class or Mrs. Reynold's class. There were two kids who had been in my homeroom the year before, but they were boys. I had not made any close friends in kindergarten, but we had all gotten along. It seemed different this year, as if everyone had broken into groups. There were three different groups of girls and two different groups of boys. The girls were either in the Amanda-girl group—the popular girls who acted like my sister; or they were a bit tom-boyish and athletic; or they were the smart girls. I didn't fit in with any of them. So I sat quietly at my desk and waited for the bell to ring.

The day didn't improve much. We went to lunch, but I didn't have anyone to sit with; so I sat on the end next to one of the smart girls. At recess, I didn't have anyone to play with. I saw a couple of girls from kindergarten, but they had made friends with other girls in their class. I tried to talk to them, and they spoke briefly but then ran away to join their group. It was almost as if they had forgotten who I was and that somehow all of the other kids had remained friends over the summer.

We were about to line up to go inside when I saw Ashley's class coming to the play ground. I ran over to her, and she smiled and spoke to me. She was having a fun first day. Her new friends were insisting she play on the swings with them, so she waved goodbye to me. I went to the back of the line and looked over at her. She was surrounded by girls all wanting her attention. She was going to be just like Amanda. I wondered how it must feel to be like that, when everyone wanted to be your friend. I thought about how it was in kindergarten when all of us girls just gravitated towards each other, and there didn't seem to be just one girl we flocked to. And I didn't feel intimidated last year. I didn't feel scared to go up and try to talk to someone. This year it was different. This year everyone was centered on someone within their group. The Amanda-girl group was led by a girl named Allyson. Oh, and how perfect that her name started with an A. She fit right in as the leader of that group. My mother would have been proud. If she ever met Allyson, she would swear that we were switched at birth. There were two other girls in Allyson's group, and the three of them stood there as if they were miniature models.

The next group was the athletic girls. They were led by a girl named Kelsey, who was a softball prodigy at the tender age of seven. She seemed nice enough, but I was still intimidated. I wasn't athletic at all, so I was sure I would be rejected. There were three other girls in her group who either played softball, as well, or soccer. They had the privilege of either staying among their own group or playing with the boys. The boys always respected the athletic girls. Unless there was one popular boy, the Amanda-girls wouldn't pay attention to them. But the boys always knew the athletic girls would play.

The third group was the smart girls, led by Emma. There were three of them and they seemed friendly, but they were always whispering quietly to each other and giggling. It seemed like it would be difficult to get to know them.

Another thing I noticed was that these three groups interacted with other similar groups from the other first grade classes. All of the kids seem to know each other, so they could either stay in their small groups or join a larger group on the playground. I had looked around while everyone was playing to see if there were other stragglers like me with no one to talk to. There weren't any. Just me, so I was the odd one out.

This was my first year to have actual school books. Everyone else in the class was buzzing with excitement about their text books. They had graduated from the baby class of coloring books with numbers and letters, and now they possessed actual text books! Certainly an important rite of passage. I myself was not as thrilled. I could already tell from the very first day that it was going to be hard. Mrs. Sanders had given us a math worksheet with ten addition problems on it. One plus one, two plus two, three plus two. All very simple for some. Then she told us she was going to time us. She would give us one minute to complete the worksheet. She called this a speed drill. Oh, that sounded fun. I slowly picked up my Hello Kitty pencil and looked around, noticing that everyone else was on the verge of excitement with their pencils ready as they anxiously awaited Mrs. Sanders to say, "Go!" When she did, they took off with such speed that almost all of them were done well before she said, "Stop!" Except me. I was still on my second problem, counting three plus three on my fingers. I decided right then that I hated math.

Later, she had us turn to the first story in our reading books. She divided it up into twenty-three parts and assigned us all a small section to read. I was so nervous waiting for my part and so in awe at how well everyone else could read that I was completely lost when it came my turn. If no one had noticed me before, they certainly noticed me then. I flipped back and forth through the pages, hoping something would jump out at me and tell me where in the world to start. I was a very noticeable shade of red. Mrs. Sanders sighed quietly and got up from the stool she had been sitting on at the front of the class. She stood over me as she flipped to the correct page and then pointed with her long, red fingernail to the section I was assigned to recite. It was then that I realized I couldn't read. I recognized some words like *the, and,* and *at*; but I had no idea what almost all of the other words were. Mrs. Sanders verbally prompted me. "Please begin to read, Roda." I sat there, frozen, staring at the page. I looked up as she sat squarely back on her stool. She must have realized by the sheer panic on my face what the problem was. A brief look of concern crossed her face, and then she began reading the passage for me. I looked around sheepishly to see if anyone was looking at me. They all were. Some were giggling. I'm quite sure I hadn't made any points with the smart girls. Next was Allyson's turn, of all people. She quickly picked up where Mrs. Sanders left off, and she read without fail.

Stupid show off.

Feeling defeated, I was ready for the day to end. I packed up all those wonderful text books and waited anxiously for the dismissal bell to ring. I was ready to see my dad. I sat there, bored, while everyone else talked around me. The Amanda-girls were talking about Allyson's strawberry lip gloss, the athletic girls were discussing the practice they would have after school, and the smart girls were whispering excitedly about having actual homework. Which reminded me that I had forgotten to write the assignment down. So I dug my pencil and my notebook out of my backpack and looked at the board. I squinted my eyes so I could see the assignment better. It was a little fuzzy. Great.

My dad was waiting in the car when the bell rang. I was the first one to get there, and I burst into tears the moment I saw him. Concern overwhelmed him. "What's wrong?" he asked the second I opened the door. I couldn't answer, I was crying so hard; but I knew I would have to stop because Amanda and Ashley would be there soon. I tried to catch my breath while my dad gently patted my back. How I wished that it was just him and me going home. How I wished Amanda and Ashley would just ride the bus. No such luck. Ashley made it to the car next, smiling broadly and talking non-stop about how much fun she had, how many friends she had made, and everything she had learned. Amanda finally tore herself away from her adoring friends to come to the car. She didn't say anything about how her day had been, but she was a third grader now which meant she was practically an adult. She sighed when she got in the car, indicating her disapproval of me sitting in the front. My dad told her I wasn't feeling well and that she could sit in the front the next day. I was glad to be up there so they couldn't see I had been crying. But they never paid attention to me anyway.

As soon as we stepped inside the house, I ran upstairs. But I was not out of earshot before I heard my mother ask, "How was the first day of school for my girls?" She said it with such excitement that I thought I might vomit. Ashley immediately began the same enthusiastic explanation she recited when she got in the car. Amanda sat at the table and just shrugged. She was too cool to gush about the first day of being queen of the third grade.

My dad lingered in the kitchen for a few minutes, listening

to Ashley again. My mother was excited to hear that her youngest daughter was destined to be just as popular as her oldest. That was of utmost importance to her. He motioned to my mother that he was going upstairs to check on me, but she wasn't concerned. She continued to ask Amanda and Ashley questions about their wonderful day.

I was lying on my bed, sobbing, holding Mr. Cocoa and Mrs. Giggles for comfort. When my dad walked in, I pushed them aside and clung to him. We were never allowed to close our doors, but my dad closed it when he came in. He knew I wouldn't want my sisters to hear. He didn't want them to hear either. He would stick to the excuse that I didn't feel well. He rocked me for a long time until my sobbing began to subside. When I was calm, he asked me to tell him what was wrong. So I told him everything, even about how the blackboard was fuzzy. I asked him if I was going to need dumb glasses. He let out a soft sigh and rubbed my arm as he embraced me, trying to figure out a solution to it all. He had been concerned about me making friends but hadn't been too worried since I had been there the year before. He was amazed at how quickly the social dynamic could change from one year to the next, specifically how children so young could be so cliquish. He expected it in middle school and definitely high school but not elementary. He never remembered it being that way when he was younger. But he was a guy, so maybe girls had been different. He was very concerned with my academic performance. We had read books together, and he thought I was on track with reading, but apparently I wasn't. What he slowly began to realize was that we had read many of the same books over and over again, so perhaps I had memorized them.

My dad began to formulate a plan, and he knew I always felt better when he had a plan. He said we would eat dinner, and then he and I would work on my homework. We would practice a few math problems and do a little reading. Then the next day, while I was at school, he would pick up flash cards for us to work with every night. "We will catch up," he promised. The problem was, I was already so far behind that I didn't feel I would ever be able to.

"When did first graders learn how to read?" he wondered out loud. "I thought that was *when* kids learned to read. And how did they know math already?"

I concluded that I was the only dummy in a class full of brilliant kids. Just great. I knew my dad was surprised, but I guess he really never paid attention before. Amanda was brilliant. She had learned to write her own name when she was three and was reading by the time she was five. I'm sure she could have done algebra in first grade if it had been introduced to her. And Ashley was going to be just as smart—if not smarter.

"Daddy," I asked as we got up to go eat dinner, "will we have time to read tonight?"

"Well of course!" he exclaimed, excited to see me attempting to return to normal.

"Which one did you buy today?" I asked, since we had established the tradition last year that he would surprise me with a new book on the first day of school. He loved the classics, so I expected him to say *Treasure Island* or *Little House on the Prairie*, but I was wrong.

"Oh," he said, smiling, "I am going to introduce you to a little girl named Ramona Quimby!"

"Ramona?" I asked, my eyes getting big. "Her name is almost like mine." I was in awe.

"Yes, I know," he said as he winked. Then he bent down and whispered. "And she's got a mean big sister named Beezus. Isn't that just the worst name in the world?"

I nodded. "Yeah, that's awful."

***

Dinner was ready when we got downstairs. My mother had made spaghetti in honor of Ashley's first day of school. Spaghetti was Ashley's favorite. My mother didn't make my favorite last year, but it didn't matter because I loved everything.

For the first time that day, I was starting to feel a little better. No one mentioned us being upstairs or that my face was red from crying. Mother and Ashley just rattled on about the first day of kindergarten. Daddy joined in on the conversation, and I just kept stuffing my face with the delicious spaghetti and looked around at everyone as they talked, my feet swinging as I chewed. Amanda wasn't talking at all, of course. Surprisingly, Ashley asked me a direct question. She never asked me direct questions in front of Mother.

"Don't you like that alphabet game Mrs. Tucker teaches?"

I nodded, swallowing a bite of my garlic bread.

"*Ah, ah,* A . . . *buh, buh,* B . . . *kuh, kuh,* C," we recited in unison. "*Duh, duh,* D . . . *eh, eh,* E—"

"Ashley," my mother interrupted, "you need to finish your dinner."

We looked up to see Mother staring at Ashley. Amanda was staring at me like I had just gotten weirder. My dad had been smiling, listening to us. "Let them finish, Paige," he said, overriding her command. But we didn't finish. I supposed that maybe we would later. Ashley looked sheepishly at Mother, acting as if she had been reprimanded. She took a few more bites of her dinner.

Ashley was the type who liked to talk. So when she wanted to talk, it was hard for her to be quiet. She looked up at me and said, "Roda, I have six new friends. How many new friends do you have?" As soon as she uttered the words, Amanda laughed. It was a sarcastic snort of a laugh, and she just glared at me. My mother suppressed a smile. The happiness that I had allowed myself to feel quickly drained from me. I stared down at my plate, just wanting to disappear. Ashley was confused. She didn't understand Amanda's reaction to her question. My dad rubbed his eyes. He had worked hard after school to lift my spirits, and now Amanda—and even my mother—had crushed them in an instant. Daddy looked at Amanda and ordered her to leave the table and go to her room. This had never been done before. Amanda was shocked, and my mother was livid.

"She does *not* have to leave the table," my mother demanded.

"Yes, she does," he directed back, "and she will." He looked sternly at Amanda. "Now go."

Normally, she would listen to Mother. But he said it with such authority and such anger that she got up and left. My mother glared at my dad, and he glared right back. Ashley started to cry because she felt she had done something wrong but didn't know what. I knew an argument was about to start, so I looked at her and subtly motioned for her to follow me. We quickly went

64

upstairs just as my parents began yelling.

They always fought, mainly about me. But in the beginning, or as far back as I could remember, they tried to hide it from us. They would go behind closed doors or argue in whispers. But the older we got, the more vocal they became, and the louder they got. By the time Ashley and I had reached the top of the stairs, they were yelling at the top of their lungs. Amanda shut her door as we passed by. Ashley and I went into my room and closed the door also. They were yelling so loudly that we could still hear them, but we couldn't understand everything they were saying.

Ashley cried softly. "Why are they fighting, Roda?"

"Because of me," I said, looking down.

"But why?" she wanted to know.

I thought for a second. "Because I don't have any friends."

Ashley looked at me sadly. "You don't?"

I shook my head and tears fell down my face. We stayed in my room and waited for my dad to come up. When he finally did about thirty minutes later, he looked spent. He was exhausted from screaming. He told Ashley to get Amanda to help her with her bath so she could get ready for bed. She could watch a little television in Amanda's room and then join us later to read the new book. She got up to leave the room and timidly hugged Daddy as she passed by him. She got to my door and then turned around. She quickly ran back to me, hugged me, and said, "I'll be your friend, Roda." I watched her as she ran away, and I thought, 'For now you will be.' I knew eventually she would grow up and become just like Amanda.

That night, my dad and I followed his plan. We worked on my homework and went over math and reading, but we didn't spend much time on it. We knew our nights would be filled with playing catch up, so we decided to focus on something fun. I was anxious to hear about this Ramona girl, and he and I both perked up when it came time for him to read. He called Ashley to come listen too, and she happily joined us. He had asked Amanda if she wanted to listen, but she said it was a baby book. He never failed to ask her, though, just to try to include her. My mother never came upstairs for the rest of the night. My dad stayed with me while I tried to fall asleep. I began to cry as night came to a close and the thought of going back to school became all too real. I did not want to go back. My dad laid there with me, trying to comfort me.

"You should try to talk to those quiet girls," he encouraged. "I'm sure they're very sweet."

"They won't like me," I concluded. "I bet they think I'm the dumbest girl ever."

He rubbed my back. "Well, you should at least try."

I could tell he was worried. I could tell it bothered him just as much as it did me, but he didn't know how to make it better. He promised again that we would work hard to catch up. He tried to tell me all kinds of encouraging things, but none of it really mattered because I knew it wouldn't get better.

"Nobody likes me, Daddy. Nobody does."

"That's not true," he tried to reassure me, but it was true.

I laid there wishing I was that stupid Allyson because everyone would like me, and my mother would be proud of me and love me too.

Chapter 6

My dad surprised me that Friday after school by announcing that he and I were going to Mim's for the weekend. I was actually so excited I thought I might burst. He had our bags packed and loaded in the car when he picked me up. Amanda and Ashley already had plans to spend the night with friends, and they were riding home with them. So my dad and I left for the train station straight from school. I had seen Mim the week before school started because I had continued to go with my dad into the city during the summers. Mim had coordinated my schedule according to the summer programs offered by the different colleges in the Manhattan area. My dad had liked the idea of enrolling me in continuing education classes, and I enjoyed the art classes.

We arrived at her apartment by six o'clock. She met us at the top of the stairs in her usual manner of shrieking with delight and hugging us tightly, as if it had been forever since she had seen us. "Come in, come in," she said, ushering us into the apartment. She had timed our arrival perfectly with the removal of her famous chicken tetrazzini from the oven. There's nothing like dinner being ready the moment you walk through the door. My peanut butter and jelly sandwich was long gone from lunch, and I was starving. I devoured the chicken and pasta that was bathed in Alfredo sauce and mushrooms. The garlic bread was smothered in melted butter, and her homemade Italian dressing on the garden salad was absolute heaven. Mim knew the importance of good food.

They laughed in surprise, watching me eat as if I hadn't eaten in days. Mim patted my hand and lovingly said, "Honey, slow down. You'll get a tummy ache." But I couldn't help it. Her cooking was too good. Surely she should have opened a restaurant rather than teach art history. She definitely missed her calling in life.

I had been so enraptured with eating that I didn't pay attention to anything they had been talking about. When I finally slowed down, I realized he had been catching Mim up on the events of the week. I realized this because, when I looked up from my empty plate, I saw Mim looking at me sadly. Suddenly, to compensate, she smiled. "You get more beautiful each time I see you," she told me. A tiny, unbelieving smile crossed my lips, and I cast my eyes downward. I knew she believed what she said, but I didn't believe it about myself.

"I have a surprise for you," she said.

"You do?" I asked, not expecting it.

"Yes, I do. But first, let's clean up this mess and then get all cozy on the couch. How 'bout it?"

I sprung from my seat, wanting to get it all done as quickly as possible. Mim was always good about cleaning up as she cooked, so there wasn't much to do. We were done in no time. My dad and I settled down on the sofa. One thing I always noticed about him when we were at Mim's was how relaxed he was. He seemed like a different person. He wasn't stressed from work or my mother. He could just relax and breathe and enjoy the calmness.

I snuggled up next to him as Mim went to retrieve my surprise. A thousand thoughts went through my head. What could it be? A new stuffed animal to hold? A new book to read? I could hardly wait. I closed my eyes until she was standing in front of me and said, "Okie dokie." When I opened them, I saw it was a sketchbook and a small set of charcoal and graphite pencils. I reached my hands out to take them as if she was giving me a precious gift. I was in awe. I had seen my aunt sketching many times before, and I was fascinated by drawings that were born out of shadows of charcoal. Now I had my own set.

"Can I draw something?" I asked in almost a whisper.

"Well, of course you can, honey," Mim encouraged. She loved that I had such a strong interest in the arts and that I had budding talent. She opened the box and started to hand me a graphite pencil, but I wanted the charcoal. She smiled and handed both to me.

"Show me something great," she said.

I took the pencil as if it were a key to another world, and I smiled at my dad. "What should I draw?" I asked.

"Draw something you love," he said.

I sat in the corner of the sofa as Mim and my dad relaxed and watched an old movie on television. I began to sketch immediately, but I wanted it to be a surprise to them. I decided, after all, to start with the lighter graphite pencil to draw the overall picture. But I was anxious to use the darker, rougher charcoal to shade things and give them depth. My art class had not been introduced to this method yet, but I had observed enough and felt I had an eye for it, so I tried my best. I worked for an hour, and what slowly began to occur to me was that I *had* been given a key to another world. I paused to flip through the blank pages of the book, imagining all the things I could draw. This could be my escape from the world around me. I smiled to myself and thought of all the possibilities.

I was just finishing when the movie ended. My dad turned to me and suggested that I get ready for bed. I closed my sketchbook and replaced the pencils in their box.

"Are you finished with your drawing, sweet pea?" Mim asked as I walked towards the spare bedroom.

"Yes, ma'am," I said casually over my shoulder.

"Well," she laughed, "do we get to see it?"

I laughed in return. "Maybe when I get back."

Mim looked at my dad and chuckled. "She's like a little adult, you know?"

He laughed and nodded.

When I got back, Mim seemed to be sitting on the edge of her seat, waiting to look at my drawing. I nonchalantly handed it to her as if it were no big deal. I was actually surprised at myself because normally I would be so anxious for affirmation. But somehow, because it was my dad and Mim, I didn't feel that way. I knew they would love it even if it were the worst drawing on earth. When she opened the cover, she let out a small, barely audible gasp; and her eyes widened. She blinked and stared at the detail of the picture.

My dad was suddenly more curious. "Well, are you going to let me see?" he asked, smiling.

She looked up at him and then looked at me. "Roda . . . I'm . . . I'm amazed. It's beautiful."

My dad reached out and took the book. He was suddenly as entranced as Mim. "You drew this?" he said in awe.

I giggled. "Well, yeah, Daddy. Who else do you think would have? The tooth fairy?" Signs of my sarcastic humor were evident at an early age.

Mim sat next to my dad on the sofa. "The detailing is amazing for her age," she said while he studied it. "I can't believe she drew it so quickly." My dad nodded in agreement. "The shading is exquisite as well," she continued, as she pointed to some areas. "Amazing for a six year old."

I was intrigued by their fascination. "So, is it good?" I asked, genuinely wondering what they thought.

They both looked at me. "Roda," my dad said, "it's beautiful." I smiled and looked again at the picture I had drawn. It was of Mim's living area with her and my dad sitting and watching television. I had even captured a picture of the movie on the television screen. I thought it was okay. I shrugged and then asked if I could have dessert before I went to bed. Yummy chocolate cake. Delicious.

My dad was so happy when he tucked me in that night. We were always so happy at Mim's. Her home was our sanctuary. I always felt a peace envelop me. I loved the hum of the air conditioning units in the summer and the clinking of the radiator in the winter. I loved the sirens passing on the street below. I loved how Mim hummed when she worked. And I loved when she would give me a great big warm hug.

"Daddy," I said as he was about to turn out the light, "I wish we could stay here. I wish we never had to leave."

"You do?" he asked sadly.

"Uh-huh," I nodded.

He sat back on the edge of the bed. "Yeah, I do too."

"When I'm here, I pretend Aunt Mim is my mommy. I don't tell her that, but I do." He caressed my hair and smiled sadly.

He thought for a moment. "You know," he said slowly, "Mim might like it if we came every weekend. What do you think of that? Should I ask her?"

"Yes!" I said sitting straight up in bed, causing Mr. Cocoa and Mrs. Giggles to fall off the side. I hugged my dad tightly. He promised we would talk to Mim about it the next day, but he felt certain she would love the idea. He reached down and picked up my friends and tucked them safely back under the covers with me. The thought of spending every weekend with my aunt was absolute bliss. With that to look forward to and having my sketchbook, I knew I would be able to survive every week that was ahead. I was so excited that it took me a while to fall asleep.

The next morning, I awoke to the smell of pancakes and bacon. I bounded out of bed, ready to see if Mim would let us come every weekend. I didn't even have to ask. She was at the stove flipping pancakes when I skidded to a stop at the table. She looked at me with a big smile on her face.

"Good morning, honeybee!" she sang. "I hear we get to see each other every weekend from now on!"

"So it's okay?" I asked, about to burst.

"Well, of course! I would love that!"

I ran to her and hugged her. She laughed, hugged me back, and patted my bottom. "Now sit. You are just in time for breakfast."

I turned and hugged my dad too; and then I sat, waiting for Mim to hand me my plate.

We spent the majority of the day in the park. It was a beautiful day in September, and the heat of summer was finally giving way to the feeling of fall. Later, Mim decided we should go to an art gallery that she frequented. Some of her art had even been displayed there. I was fascinated by all the sketches and paintings and photographs that I saw. She looked at me and said that she wouldn't be surprised to see my art hanging there one day. I smiled at the thought.

***

The weekend passed by much too quickly. Before I knew it, we were on the train back to Greenwich. That dreaded Sunday feeling came over me. The end of the weekend; the beginning of the week ahead. We were silent the whole way back home. The happiness we had at Mim's quickly turned to quiet sadness as we approached.

We pulled into the driveway around five o'clock. Amanda and Ashley were in the backyard jumping on the trampoline. My dad went over and spoke to them, asking how their sleepovers were that Friday night. Amanda acted aloof. No surprise. Ashley seemed sad. When we walked away, she jumped down and ran over to Daddy.

"Daddy, why didn't I get to go with you too?"

He knelt down to look at her face to face. "Sweetie, you had that sleepover with Elizabeth. You can go next time though. How about that?"

She nodded. "Yes, Daddy! I want to!"

We turned and saw my mother standing on the back porch, staring at my dad. He walked past her as if she wasn't even there, and so did I. She followed him into the house, fuming.

"Are you not even going to speak to me?" she demanded.

He turned to face her. "I would love to speak to you, Paige. But you're mad, and I'm not going to engage you when you're mad."

"What makes you think I'm mad?" she asked.

He glared at her. "Really, Paige? You have no idea *why* I think you're mad. You're always mad. That's how I know. And simply by the way you were just standing out there looking at me. That's how I know."

"Do you even care to know why I'm upset?" she asked, trying to gain sympathy.

"I know exactly why you're upset. You're upset because I spent the weekend at Mim's. That always upsets you."

"Then why do you do it?"

He was trying to remain calm. "I am so tired of arguing with you. I really am. You know why I do it. She is my sister, for one thing. I want to spend time with her, and I want Roda to spend time with her. And frankly, sometimes we just need to get away from you."

"Get *away* from me? Is that what you said? You need to get away from me?" she asked indignantly.

"Yes, Paige, I need to get away from you. Sometimes I want to get as far away from you as possible."

She was speechless. She stood there, dumbfounded. He had always told her it was to see Mim or to have me spend time with her, but he had never actually said it was to get away from her. That was a new revelation. She was standing there, holding onto a chair at the kitchen table. She was trying to catch her breath, and I thought she might actually start crying. Deep within him, he felt sympathy for her. Something within him from somewhere long ago flickered inside of him. He suddenly felt bad for saying what he had said.

"Paige, honey," he said more softly, "why do you keep doing this? Why can't we just be a family and all of us do everything together? Why do you keep putting all this distance between us and getting upset about everything I try to do?" He stepped towards her, wanting to embrace her, hoping there was some compassion there. But she backed away, and she looked at me. I knew she blamed me, as if I were the instigator to all the troubles within our family.

"You can take her," she said, furious, "but you will *not* take Ashley. I will not allow it."

His anger returned. Whatever he felt just moments before quickly left him, but he continued to remain calm in front of me.

"I will take Ashley," he said in a measured tone. "If she wants to go, I will take her."

"She is too busy to be gone for an entire weekend!" she shot back.

"She is in kindergarten. Life is *not* too busy or too complicated when you're in kindergarten."

"Have you seen her schedule?" she asked, motioning towards the calendar hanging on the refrigerator. "She has something every weekend."

He walked over and reviewed it. The Amanda and Ashley social calendar had been created when Amanda was born. In the beginning, there had been diaper changes and feedings posted on it, as well as doctor's appointments and medication schedules. Later, play dates and tumble class schedules were posted for both of them, as well as their other extracurricular activities. Now it had birthday parties and spend-the-night invites listed, as well as every single gymnastics class during the week. Practically every day was filled.

He pointed at it. "*This* is ridiculous."

She was incredulous. "What, exactly, is that supposed to mean?"

"I mean it's ridiculous. There is absolutely no reason why girls this young need to be so over scheduled. You need to be very selective about their activities."

"The girls are very well liked," she said proudly. "I will not hinder their social lives."

"Well, if the girls are so well liked, I'm sure everyone will understand if they don't show up every now and then," he said, marking through the birthday party Ashley was to attend the next Saturday and the movie date scheduled for Amanda with one of her best friends.

My mother nearly came unglued. "How *dare* you!" she shouted. "You will not say that they cannot go!"

"I will so."

"You cannot dictate these things! If they want to go, they will go!" she yelled.

"Ashley has already said she wants to go to Mim's the next time we go," he said smugly.

My mother suddenly put it together. "You're going to Mim's again next weekend?"

"We sure are, and Ashley is coming with us. And Manda too, if she wants to."

My mother was absolutely seething from within. I was sitting there, literally waiting for her entire body to explode from anger. If she were a violent person, she would have begun to throw things; but then her perfect house would be damaged, so she contained herself. She stormed off to her bedroom and slammed the door. She began screaming in such a way that Amanda and Ashley ran in to see what was wrong. My dad completely ignored my mother's tirade and asked if they wanted to order pizza for dinner. That Sunday turned out to be not so bad after all.

***

My mother never came out of their bedroom that night. My dad decided to pre-empt my mother's influence by asking Amanda and Ashley if they wanted to go to Mim's the following weekend.

"I do! I do!" Ashley squealed.

My dad laughed. "You do? Are you sure? Are you really, really sure?"

She nodded excitedly.

"But what about Emily's birthday party Saturday? You would miss that," he said casually.

Ashley shrugged, unfazed. "I don't really care. I don't like her that much anyway."

"Okay then," he said happily, "it's your decision." Ashley nodded in affirmation. Then he looked at Amanda. She had not reacted. "Do you want to go too, Manda?"

She thought for a moment. He and I were both surprised she was actually considering it.

"Well, I'm supposed to go to a movie with Hannah."

"Can you go to the movie another time?" my dad asked.

"Maybe. I don't know," she said slowly. She was thinking, and I believed she was wondering more about how Mother would react rather than if she could reschedule with her friend.

"Well, okay," my dad said reassuringly. "Just think about it and let me know. And if you can't this weekend, you can go another time."

Amanda looked worried. "Dad, why are you going back next weekend?"

The look on Daddy's face revealed that he had not considered how my sisters would react to us leaving every weekend. He knew it would upset Amanda. Ashley would be sad, but Amanda would be very upset. He thought for a moment before answering. Just as he was about to say something, I interrupted.

"I want to go to Aunt Mim's every weekend," I announced, knowing Amanda would be glad to see me go. "And sometimes Daddy is going to go with me, and sometimes he's going to stay here."

Amanda just looked at me. She didn't glare or sneer, she just looked at me.

"Dad," she asked sadly, "are you going to leave us?"

"No, honey," he said quickly. "Absolutely not. I would never leave you. It's just that Roda wants to spend more time with Aunt Mim," he said, looking at me, thankful I had given him a way out of upsetting Amanda. "And she's too young to always go by herself. But I will be here to go to your gymnastics meets and do other stuff with you and Ashley."

"What about Mommy?" Ashley asked. "Do you want to do anything with her?"

He smiled at her. "Of course, honey," he lied. "I want to spend time with all of you." Both of them seemed to accept his explanation. I knew at that point, he would not be able to go every weekend.

"But listen," he added quickly, addressing Amanda, "I want you and Ashley to go sometimes, okay? She's my sister, and I want the two of you to get to know her as well."

Ashley nodded eagerly while Amanda nodded slowly.

"Won't Mommy go sometimes too?" Ashley asked innocently. Before my dad could answer, Amanda looked towards her and quietly said, "Mom doesn't like her."

"Doesn't like who?" Ashley asked.

"Aunt Mim," she said, embarrassed that she had actually said it in front of my dad.

"But why not?" Ashley continued to inquire.

"Manda," my dad said kindly but with a hint of sternness. "Just because Mom doesn't like her doesn't mean that you can't like her. Do you understand?"

She nodded.

"And if you're afraid Mom will be mad if you go," he continued, "don't worry about that. You let me worry about it. I mean," he said, thinking, "even if we have to make it look like I'm forcing you to go, we will do that."

Amanda nodded and said, "Okay."

And that's exactly what he did the next weekend. My dad made it look as if he was cancelling their plans and making them go with us. He fully expected to incur my mother's wrath. Instead, she remained completely silent, closing herself off in anger. I knew within that anger, she would plot her next move, as if their marriage had become nothing more than a strategic game of chess.

***

My dad had been taking me into the city since I was a few weeks old, so I never had that sense of awe that a person feels

76

when they encounter it for the first time. But I could clearly see it on my sisters' faces the moment we departed the train and entered the concourse at Grand Central. They were amazed at the size of it and of all the people bustling about. My dad had wanted to show them everything right away, but it was rush hour on a Friday, and he knew better than to take three small girls out on the street in the midst of an enormous crowd and frantic traffic. In fact, he made sure we all held hands so no one would get lost. We took the subway to Mim's, and my dad promised all the great things we would see the next day. They happily agreed. All of it was new to them, and they seemed to be enjoying the experience. When we got on the subway, I smiled broadly and said to them, "Hold on! It goes fast!" We all giggled when the train took off. My dad smiled, seeing how well the three of us were getting along.

As usual, Mim had dinner ready the moment we got there. She didn't greet us at the top of the stairs in her cheerful manner. Instead, she was more subdued so as not to startle my sisters with being too happy. She knew they were more like my mother, so she wanted to be careful. She had opened her door and stood there waiting for us. The smell of spaghetti wafted out into the hallway; and before we reached the landing, Ashley cried out, "Daddy, I smell 'paghetti!" She and I reached the top first, and my dad and Amanda came up behind us. I ran to Mim and hugged her, and then Ashley hugged her too. She reached out to hug Amanda and my dad.

"I'm so glad all of you are here!" she said excitedly. "Come in and eat. I know you must be starving."

We put our bags away and got cleaned up for dinner. Mim was already serving our plates when we got to the table. I wasn't sure who was more excited that we were all there, but I was thoroughly enjoying it. I felt as if Amanda and Ashley were in my world, and they seemed to like it. Ashley was always happy, but I was watching Amanda in particular, and she seemed much more relaxed. She seemed happy. I watched how she reacted to Mim. I was afraid that since Mother didn't like her then neither would Amanda. She was very nice towards Mim, and I was glad. In fact, she laughed at everything Mim said. I had wondered if she would sulk all weekend since that's how she acted at home.

The spaghetti was delicious, but I tried not to devour it like

I normally would. I tried to eat at the same pace as my sisters. One thing I noticed was how much they ate. They ate a lot! I don't think I had ever seen them eat that much in my life, and I think my dad noticed it too. I concluded, as did he, that they ate very little at home because that's what Mother wanted them to do. It was also obvious to my dad and me how different they were without my mother around. Especially Amanda. It was heartbreaking the amount of influence Mother had on her.

After dinner, we settled on the floor in the living area to play a board game. Mim made us hot chocolate with miniature marshmallows and put a Disney video on for background noise. She knew how to make everything comfortable. Later, we settled on the sofa and talked about everything we were going to see the next day. It was all the touristy stuff. I was excited when Mim said she was going with us. I hadn't expected that. She never wanted to see all that stuff. But she wanted to spend time with us; and of course, my dad needed help navigating the city with three girls.

"Roda," Mim said, "how could I forget? Did you bring your sketchbook? I want to see what you drew this week."

I nodded and ran to get it out of my book bag. I had taken it to school every day and sketched during recess. I had drawn the playground, trees, and some flowers that were on the ground near the fence. I enjoyed the escape it gave from the world around me. I was constantly thinking of what I could draw next or how to add more detailing to what I had already sketched. It kept me from worrying about the people around me who were ignoring me. I ran back to the sofa and gave it to Mim. She quickly began to flip it open. She was just as astounded as she had been the week before.

"Roda, honey, your detailing is amazing," she said, placing her hand lightly over her mouth. "Just amazing."

Neither Amanda nor Ashley were aware of my sketchbook. They looked over at it curiously and then seemed surprised themselves. They looked carefully over each detail as Mim turned the pages.

"Wow, Roda," Amanda said, "you can draw really good." Ashley looked at me and nodded in agreement. I smiled at them, glad to have some kind of talent they could appreciate.

"Can I draw a picture?" Ashley asked, looking hopeful. I didn't like the thought of wasting a sheet, but I told her she could. I didn't want her to use my art pencils though. Mim had the same concern, so she went and got her a regular pencil instead. Ashley would never know the difference. She laid the book in her lap and thought for a second, and then she began to draw. She drew a picture of a puppy and a dog house under a tree. It was a typical picture that a five-year-old would draw, but it was good. When she was done, I asked Amanda if she wanted to draw something. She thought for a moment and then said yes. So I handed her the book and the pencil. She asked Mim if she could use her colored pencils instead. "Well, of course, honey," she said as she got up to retrieve them. Amanda was actually a good artist herself. She drew a very detailed picture of a red barn with a horse standing outside. There was part of a fence with a tree and flowers next to it.

"Manda," my dad bragged, "that is really good! You need a sketchbook of your own."

"Oh, I've got an extra one she can have," Mim said, hopping up. "And you can keep those pencils if you'd like." Mim had plenty of art supplies. Amanda smiled. She really seemed excited. When Mim returned, she had two sketchbooks. She handed one to Ashley.

"I get one too?" she squealed.

"Oh, of course you do! I wouldn't have it any other way." She handed her a set of colored pencils as well. Ashley immediately began to draw.

After a while, the three of us began to get sleepy. Daddy suggested we go to bed since we had such a big day ahead. He would sleep in the extra bedroom so that we could all sleep on the pull-out sofa in the living room. Mim brought in sheets, blankets, and pillows; and made it very warm and cozy for us. We snuggled under the covers, Amanda and me on both sides and Ashley in the middle. Mim was the first to kiss and hug us goodnight, saying again how much she enjoyed us being there and all the fun we would have the next day. My dad spent a little more time with us, lying at the foot of the bed, talking to us. I could tell he was overjoyed at having his three girls together like we were.

When he left and went to bed, the three of us laid there in the dark. The only light shining was a nightlight in the kitchen and the street lights glowing from outside. I told them not to be scared of all the noises outside, especially if a siren went by. They promised they wouldn't be afraid. We laid there and talked and giggled for a while until we finally fell asleep. And I remember, as I fell asleep, I was thinking that night was the best night of my life.

We awoke early the next morning and ate a quick breakfast of toasted bagels and cream cheese before heading out. It was another beautiful fall day, perfect weather for sightseeing. We started on the south end and worked our way up. A ferry ride to Ellis Island and the Statue of Liberty were first on the list. We were all too young to appreciate the historical aspect of the island, but we thought the statue was cool. My dad's office was in the financial district. We made a quick stop there so my sisters could see where he worked. They had never been there before, and they were quite impressed. His office was decorated with our pictures and some of my art work. He told Amanda and Ashley he expected them to draw him a few pictures so he could add them to his art collection. They both laughed and promised they would.

Next, we hopped on the subway and traveled uptown to midtown Manhattan. My dad thought the best place to start would be the Central Park Zoo, which was fun. We spent hours there. When we were done, we grabbed a few hotdogs from the vendor just outside the park and had an early lunch. Afterwards, we played in the park while my dad and Mim relaxed. The three of us had the best time playing on the swings and the monkey bars. At one point, I ran over to my dad and hugged him tightly and told him that it was the best day I had ever had. He smiled, knowing how happy I was. I quickly ran back to my sisters as they were climbing the ladder on the big wavy slide. It was hard to believe that my sisters actually wanted to play with me. Not so much with Ashley, but it was definitely hard to believe with Amanda. It was like she was a different person.

When we left the park, we went to FAO Swartz. Daddy let each of us pick out a toy and get a bag of candy. We all thought that was the best thing out of the whole day. Next, we went to Macy's on 34th Street. Mim showed us something really interesting. It was the original wooden escalators from decades ago when the store first opened. They weren't like the ones now that are wide and run smoothly. They were very narrow with wooden sides and railings. They were still in working order, but they creaked as the mechanics moved them forward, upstairs and down.

She let us ride them, but she told us to come back down quickly so as not to disturb the employees who worked in customer service near the top of the escalator.

After that, she took us to the area with all the jewelry and said she wanted to buy a small piece for each of us. She said we could choose whatever we wanted. I chose a small gold bangle bracelet with tiny pink flowers intricately designed on it. Ashley chose a ring that matched my bracelet, and Amanda chose a gold necklace with the initial A on it.

Next, we walked to Rockefeller Center. It was an amazing place to see, especially at Christmastime. It was a month before it opened for the season, but my dad showed Amanda and Ashley where the ice skating rink was and promised to take us back soon. "It would be better to do it," he told us, "when it was closer to Christmas and the tree would be up as well." Since both of them had taken lessons, they were anxious to skate. I was afraid I wouldn't do well, but I was willing to try.

We sat in the plaza for a while, eating soft pretzels and talking. Everyone was so happy. Ashley was sitting on Mim's lap giggling about something, and Amanda was snuggled up next to Daddy. She looked so much like Mother, like a tiny version of her. My dad just looked at her and smiled, and he was reminded of a day long ago when he was there with my mother for the first time. He remembered how happy and excited she had been, and he could see it in Amanda. I overheard him telling Mim later, that sitting there watching Amanda smile and the excitement in her eyes was actually heartbreaking for him because it wasn't Amanda that he saw. He saw my mother, the way she used to be. And it reminded him of something that once was and would never be again.

When we were done, we walked over to St. Patrick's Cathedral. It was absolutely breathtaking. We were too young to appreciate the magnificent architecture, the statues that lined the walls, and the beautiful stained glass windows; but we were in awe. We walked around, very respectful, not touching anything but only looking. We lit candles in remembrance of our loved ones. I especially lit one for my dad's grandfather, for whom I was named.

When we left, we went to the top of the Empire State Building to observe the city from high above. Ashley wasn't too impressed. She swore that Daddy's office building was much taller. He laughed and said, "Well this building is important nonetheless." Finally, we ended the day in Times Square. My dad specifically waited until it was nighttime to take us there because it could only be truly appreciated at night when everything was lit up, blinking and glowing. Amanda was most captivated by it and said in almost a whisper, "It's magical."

That night, we picked up a pizza at Bellino's and collapsed on Mim's sofa. It had been a fun day but exhausting. We felt as if we had walked over a hundred miles, but we were so excited about everything that we didn't notice how tired we were until we stopped. After we ate, Daddy told the three of us to take our baths and get ready for bed. When we were all done and comfortable on the pull-out bed, we each took our sketchbooks and drew pictures of our favorite things from the day. I drew a collage of pictures that included the flickering candles at the church, the three of us swinging in the park, and a tiger at the zoo. Ashley took her pencil and traced the outline of her hand and then drew the ring Mim bought her on her finger, and I told her she could draw my bracelet too. Amanda drew a beautiful picture of Times Square.

We fell asleep very quickly; and the next morning when we woke up, Mim was preparing a big breakfast for us. Since the day before was so busy, we were going to take it easy and hang out at the apartment. We worked on whatever homework we had and played board games. Mim set her art easel up near the terrace and let us each paint a picture. It was a lazy Sunday. The later the day got, the sadder I began to feel. I knew we would be going back soon, and I saw that my sisters felt it as well. Everyone grew quieter as the day went on.

By four o'clock, we were preparing to leave. Mim hugged us all goodbye and promised that next time we would go to a Broadway show, something fun we all would like. She told Amanda and Ashley that she wanted them to come back very soon, and they promised they would.

No one spoke on the train ride home. I couldn't quite understand why Amanda and Ashley would be so sad. They always seemed to enjoy being at home. Maybe the excitement of the weekend coming to an end was the cause.

We got home around six o'clock; and when we walked in the back door, my mother wasn't in the kitchen like she normally would be. She was in her room reading a book. She didn't greet us or even speak. She just stayed in there. My sisters seemed very nervous, especially Amanda. She timidly walked to the bedroom to say hello. My dad started looking through the fridge in order to cook us something for dinner. Amanda still seemed worried when she came back into the kitchen. Ashley looked at her and then slowly walked to the bedroom. Neither of them stayed very long before coming back to the kitchen. The three of us helped Daddy cook tacos; and then after we ate, we helped him clean up. My mother never came out of the bedroom.

After dinner, we got ready for bed. We seemed to suddenly slip into the same routine as before. We were all doing our own thing, all doing it separately and quietly. There was a sense of dread that had come over all of us, and it was unlike the dread I normally felt on Sundays. It was as if we weren't allowed to talk or laugh or even smile. My mother had retreated into her silence. It was her way of punishing us, especially my dad. Especially Amanda. It was as if joy was not allowed and any sense of normalcy was completely taken from us because we had dared to disobey her. I fell asleep that night knowing that the memory of the weekend had crystallized in my mind as the greatest weekend of my life, but also knowing that it would never be that way again.

Chapter 7

I would like to say everything changed for the better, but it didn't. It got worse. The power my mother had over my sisters was evident. I had always sensed it, but I had not fully realized to what extent that power reached until we returned from our trip. When we were away and they were removed from Mother's watchful eye, Amanda and Ashley were completely different. But when we returned and faced Mother's wrath, they became locked down in her silence. She didn't speak to any of us the whole week, and it wasn't until the following weekend when my sisters didn't go back to Mim's that she began to acknowledge their presence. When they stayed home the weekend after that, she began to speak in short, direct sentences to them. It wasn't until a full month later when she returned to normal with them, yet there was still a briskness about her. She no longer trusted them. My dad had been careful to make it look as if it were his idea they go, but she was still not completely sure that they didn't enjoy themselves.

Amanda became calm, poised, almost zombie-like. She threw herself into her schoolwork and gymnastics and stayed solidly focused on that. She stuck to her schedule of dates with friends and birthday parties. She never deviated from our mother's wishes. She sat at the dinner table and ate quietly, always picking at her food as if she were never hungry. She and I always sat diagonally across the table, and it had never been unusual for her to glare at me or act bored. Now she just looked down in quiet submission. Ashley was old enough to understand how she should act but too young to be quite so submissive. She wanted to talk. She always had so much to say. So at dinner, she would sit there and fidget.

My mother's new rule for them was to tell her everything as soon as they got home. They were to report their grades, what they were learning at school, what they had for homework, what happened with their friends, and what invites they got. Everything pertinent was entered on the calendar immediately. On the nights they didn't have practice, they could choose to help Mother with dinner or go to their rooms. Talking was not allowed at dinner. That wasn't a problem for me since I never talked, and it wasn't a problem for Amanda either because she didn't talk unless Daddy engaged her in conversation. But when no one spoke, it made everyone uncomfortable. My dad did not comply to begin with. He would ask them questions, expecting an answer; but they would glance at Mother, and then continue to focus on their food. Ashley was the only one who would give Daddy a quick glance as well.

"What's going on here, Paige?" he asked. She didn't answer. She wasn't speaking to him. "Paige, answer me," he demanded, but she ignored him.

He looked sternly at my sisters. They sank further in their chairs, feeling completely trapped in between our parents. He sat there, frustrated, resigned to the silence. He understood what was happening, but he was helpless to do anything at that moment without Amanda and Ashley being caught in the middle. So he waited.

He didn't bother talking to my mother. It really was like talking to a brick wall. A stone silent brick wall. He went to Amanda's room at bedtime. He was becoming even more alienated from his daughters, and he wanted to know why. He closed her door and sat on the bed.

"What's going on, Manda?" he asked with concern.

She seemed afraid to talk, as if paranoid that Mother was listening. "Nothing, Daddy," was all she would say. She hadn't called him daddy since she was five.

"It's just you and me, sweetheart. You can tell me."

She looked at him and then looked at the door, afraid that Mother might come in at any minute and find them talking. He just nodded, sensing what she was feeling. "Okay, we'll talk about it later." He sat there a little longer, asking about her day and spending a little time with her before he said goodnight. When he opened her door to leave, they both held their breath, wondering if

Mother would be standing in the hallway. She wasn't, surprisingly enough.

He went to Ashley's room next, but he knew there was no sense trying to talk to her either. Amanda wouldn't talk and neither would she. He spent a little time with her as well, asking about her day and playing Barbie and Ken with her.

"You okay?" he asked her after a while.

"Umm-hmm," she nodded without looking at him. He scratched his head.

"You ready to come into Roda's room and read some more with us?"

She thought for a moment. We had not read since we got back from Mim's that weekend because of what was going on with Mother, but Daddy decided it was time to start again. He let her think it through; and finally, she said no.

"Why not?" he asked. "You love when we read together."

She seemed afraid to talk but finally whispered, "I'm too scared to."

"What are you afraid of?" he whispered back, his heart sinking for her but his anger rising towards my mother.

"That Mommy will be mad."

He nodded. "Has she told you not to read with us?"

She nodded but didn't say anything else. He nodded, indicating he understood. "What if I said it was okay?" he asked. "Would it be okay then?" She shook her head. He realized very quickly that his parental influence had been usurped. My mother had closed herself off in silence, mentally threatening their two daughters and taking away his power to argue or even dictate what they could do because now Amanda and Ashley were too afraid to comply.

He was furious, and Ashley sensed it. "Daddy," she whispered, "please don't say anything to Mommy. I'll get in trouble."

My dad was ashen when he came into my room. He sat on the edge of my bed, stunned. Until that moment, he had no idea of the psychological depths Mother's hold had on them. He stayed there for a few minutes, trying to figure out what he should do. He tucked us all in and told us goodnight and then went downstairs. My mother was in the bedroom, reading. She had a very smug look on her face. He went in and closed the door behind him. He sat on an ottoman near her side of the bed and just looked at her. She casually looked at him and smiled.

"Paige," he started, "we need to fix this."

"Fix what?" she asked innocently.

"We need to fix this family," he said, ignoring her aloofness, "because I will not tolerate this silence. I will not tolerate my girls being too afraid to talk."

"*My* girls?" she repeated, mocking him. "Are they only *your* girls?"

"Right now I feel like they are. I feel like they're your girls and my girls. I don't feel like they're *our* girls. And you certainly don't act as if Roda is yours. You completely ignore her like she doesn't even exist."

My mother kept the smug look on her face and continued to flip the pages in her magazine.

"Are you listening to me at all?" he asked, annoyed by her indifference.

"Well, of course I am, Paul," she said coolly.

"Did you hear what I just said about Roda? Do you not realize that this is the root of everything that is wrong?"

She nodded. "Of course it is."

He sat there for a moment just looking at her. "Well, what can we do to fix this?"

"I don't know," she sighed.

He glared at her. "Do you love Roda at all? Do you even care about her in the least?"

"I told you how I felt when she was a baby," she stated matter-of-factly.

"What? That she wasn't the daughter you had hoped for? Is that it?" he asked, his temper rising.

"Yes, Paul, that is exactly it. I have two wonderful daughters, and it would have been nice to have a third that I could be proud of, but Roda is different."

"And you don't like different, do you?" he charged.

She finally looked straight at him. "No, I do not."

His anger was beginning to get the best of him. He really wanted to stay in control and be reasonable, but my mother was not rational. He got up and started pacing the floor, trying to remain calm when all he wanted to do was lash out at her.

"You don't see what a wonderful person she is?" he asked, catching his breath and trying to reason with her. "You don't see it at all?"

"No, Paul," she said, closing her magazine but keeping her fingers in between the pages to mark her place, "I do not see what you see. I see an overweight girl who has no motivation to make herself better. She is sloppy and stupid. She lacks talent, and she is an utter embarrassment. I pray to God every day that teachers and kids at school never realize that I am her mother; and I am thankful that, if and when they do, they have enough discretion to ignore it."

My dad was so overcome with disbelief that he sat back down.

"You do realize that you gave birth to her, don't you? You do realize she is part of you? How can you say such horrible things about someone who grew inside of you? Are you really *that* heartless?"

My mother stiffened. "I am not heartless."

"You have absolutely no compassion for her," my dad accused.

She thought for a moment. "No, I have no sympathy for her."

"You have *none*?" he asked, his voice rising.

"No, not at all."

"Not even the slightest concern about how she struggles in school or how she doesn't have any friends?"

"No, Paul. Like I said, it's more of an embarrassment."

He glared at her, all of his rage coming to the surface. "You are an absolute cold-hearted BITCH!!!" he yelled. "YOU, *YOURSELF*, ARE AN EMBARRASSMENT, PAIGE!!! YOU ARE!!! AND YOU DO NOT DESERVE TO BE HER MOTHER! YOU DON'T EVEN QUALIFY TO BE HER MOTHER!"

She opened her magazine calmly, ignoring his tirade. "I'm just being realistic, Paul. Every mother would be embarrassed by her. Wasn't your mother embarrassed by Miriam?"

He rushed towards her, snatched the magazine out of her hands and threw it across the room. "How DARE you say that," he charged. "How DARE you denigrate my sister," he said, lowering his voice. "She is an amazing person, and she is SO much more accomplished than you will ever be. YOU are just a bored, superficial housewife with nothing more to do than judge others, and I am SICK of it."

"Paul," she sighed, "it doesn't matter how accomplished you are if you're a fat slob."

My dad was not a violent person. He was the gentlest person who ever lived. But when my mother said that, he grabbed her and shook her and slung her across the bed.

"I AM SO DAMN SICK OF YOU!!! I AM SO DAMN SICK OF HOW TRANSPARENT AND SHALLOW YOU ARE!!!" he yelled at the top of his lungs. "I WILL NOT TOLERATE THIS ANY LONGER!!! I WILL NOT TOLERATE YOU BRAINWASHING AMANDA AND ASHLEY AND MAKING THEM AS HEARTLESS AND HATEFUL AS YOU ARE!!! AND I WILL NOT TOLERATE YOU ISOLATING RODA AND MAKING HER FEEL LESS THAN HUMAN!!!"

My mother sat up, unfazed. "And what are you proposing, Paul? Tell me, what you are going to do to change any of it?" she asked calmly.

He glared at her, realizing there was not one ounce of humanity within her. "I am going to leave you, Paige. That is what I am going to do."

"Are you now?" she asked, amused. "Are you certain of that?"

"Yes," he said. "I have thought about it for a while now, and I think we would be better off without you."

"Without me?" she laughed. "How do you expect to accomplish that?"

He stared at her. "I'm going to divorce you. I'm going to take Roda, and we will gladly live somewhere else. And we will work out custody arrangements for Amanda and Ashley."

She smiled. "No," was all she said.

"No?" he asked, cocking his head to the side.

"No," she repeated.

"What do you mean no?"

"No, you will not divorce me," she said matter-of-factly.

"Oh, really, Paige? And why not?" he asked dryly.

"Are you forgetting that my father is Edward Martin, top

D.C. litigator? Have you forgotten that, Paul?"

My dad didn't respond.

"So, no, you will not divorce me or I will make your life a living hell. I will have the best lawyer money can buy. My parents will spend *any* amount it takes, believe me. And when I get done with you, you will regret the day you ever entertained the idea."

"Regardless," he pressed on, "I will have joint custody, and the girls will stay with me apart from you. That's what I really want."

"The girls? Does that include Roda?"

"Roda will be with me. I will have custody of her."

"No," she said.

"NO?!" he yelled. "WHAT IN THE HELL DO YOU MEAN NO?!"

She smiled. "There is *no* judge who would take a child out of her home. There is *no* judge who would rule to separate three sisters. There is *no* judge who would take a daughter away from her mother." She smiled a devious smile and delivered the final blow. "I will ask for Roda, and I *will* get Roda. You won't stand a chance."

"You don't even want her!" he yelled in a more subdued tone. "You don't even want her now! You do not even care about her!" He could feel that he was beginning to plead with her.

"I know *you* want her. That is why *I* want her. And I *will* get her. You will *not* have any control over it."

"You wouldn't do that," he tried to say calmly. "You would *not* do that."

"Oh," she smiled, "but I would."

"You unimaginable bitch!" he yelled in defeat. "You are a miserable excuse for a human being!"

She smiled at him, knowing she had him trapped. He was utterly and completely trapped.

He looked at her in disbelief. "You would do that? You would use Roda as a pawn in your sick, twisted game? And you would want to stay in an empty marriage, knowing I don't love you anymore? Knowing I despise you?"

"Paul, honey," she said sweetly, "we have such a good life. Why would we mess that up?"

"You are unbelievable."

She smiled.

"I want Roda," he said firmly.

"No," she said adamantly. "Roda is mine."

I sat listening outside the closed door. Tears were streaming down my face as I hugged my knees to my chest. I was unwanted and unloved by my mother. The only thing I was useful for was leverage. My dad was miserable, and we were trapped in her web, and it was all my fault.

***

To the outside world, Paige Allen had the perfect life. Everything seemed flawless. She was absolutely beautiful and she had a handsome, successful husband who everyone believed adored her. She had the perfect home, and everything she possessed was envied by others. She had two beautiful, smart, athletic, popular daughters who always captured everyone's attention. To the outside world, she seemed like the perfect wife, the perfect mother. She kept the flaws well hidden. She was very protective of the facade she had created, and she was determined to keep it that way.

My mother had intended to go back to work part time when the three of us were in elementary school. But when the time came, she changed her mind. She decided to take another path, one in which she could hover over her perfect daughters and guide them according to her will. She did so quite deftly with the perfect blend of kindness and manipulation.

She became a room mother when Amanda started kindergarten. The following year, she joined the PTA and quickly became an officer. The next year, she was vice president; and president the year after that. She had been president of the Junior League, so president of PTA was small stuff. She organized fund raisers and led membership drives. She was very successful in those two endeavors, having higher percentages than any president before her. She was a liaison between the teachers and the administration. Everyone knew her. Everyone adored her. The teachers who taught her perfect daughters were thrilled to have them in their class. Those teachers who were grades ahead all hoped to have the honor of teaching them.

Their coaches were just as enthralled with them and even more impressed with my mother's own gymnastics training. They would often consult with her about technical moves and the execution of those moves by team members. She was always thrilled when other moms would overhear the conversations. She wanted them to know she was an expert without having to tell them directly. That would be considered in poor taste. After a while, the other moms would even approach her about advice on their own child's training. My mother was always careful to express her opinion but still give full credit to the coaches. She didn't want to make enemies.

She enjoyed her perfect life. She enjoyed being the center of attention, and she enjoyed her girls being in the spotlight as well. She wouldn't have it any other way. But then there was me. I was the flaw in her flawless world, and she made sure to keep me at a distance.

When she was a PTA officer—even when she was president—she was still the room mother in my sisters' classes. She was never the room mother for my class. She attended every party and every field trip that Amanda and Ashley had, but she never came to any of mine. She consulted with their teachers often, enjoying every compliment about how intelligent they were. She never talked to my teachers about me because she wanted to remain oblivious to my problems and my struggles. Instead, my dad stepped in. He was at every class party, and he went on every field trip. He was in constant communication with teachers about my grades and the specific areas I needed to focus on.

I ended up having almost every teacher that Amanda had throughout elementary school. Every teacher, even the ones Amanda didn't have, knew who my mother was, and they knew who my dad was; but just as my mother ignored that I was her daughter, so did they. When Ashley came along the following year after me, the teachers gladly acknowledge that she was Paige Allen's daughter.

Both of my sisters were teacher's pets. I never was. Just as Mrs. Sanders had smiled at me the first day with an air of condescension, so did all my subsequent teachers as well. I was pegged early on as a below par student, a student who struggled rather than excelling. I was below average while everyone else in my class was brilliant. My teachers seemed to prefer the brilliant students. It made their job that much easier and enjoyable. They could teach with little effort and feel good about the fruits of their labor. But throw me, a child who struggled, into the mix and you might find a teacher who resented having to make the extra effort. Surely, they must have concluded, it was my inability to learn as opposed to their inability to teach. Or perhaps, such a child as myself is wired differently and the approach to teaching must be different. Too time consuming for a classroom, so it must be done at home. Some teachers didn't want to spend time trying to unlock my mind and gain the satisfaction that comes from that. They wanted my dad to figure it out.

As I said, all of those teachers adored my sisters but not me. After I had left their class and moved on to a different grade, they would act as if they didn't know me. I would be standing in line with my class and a former teacher would walk by. She would say hello to other kids but never to me. All of my former teachers would act as though they didn't see me or just didn't remember me. I assumed it to be intentional; or perhaps, I just wasn't that memorable. However, even Mrs. Tucker—my sweet, friendly kindergarten teacher—stopped acknowledging me when Ashley was in her class and she learned who Paige Allen and Amanda Allen were.

My sisters were the center of attention at school. Even kids who weren't in their grade knew who they were. The older Ashley got, the more she became aware of it. I had hoped that after our weekend at Mim's the three of us would somehow find a way to stay close despite the efforts of my mother to keep us apart. But her intimidation worked, and they began to grow more and more distant soon after we returned. They complied with her wishes of not doing anything with Daddy or me. They would speak to him only if absolutely necessary, but they never spoke to me. At first, it was as if they thought my mother could hear them even if she wasn't there. Later, it just became commonplace. When my dad went to gymnastics meets, my sisters and my mother would act as if everything were normal; but when it was just the four of them together, they would sink back into the reality that was dominated by my mother's silence.

As expected, when Ashley was in first grade, she made the

gymnastics team and quickly advanced levels in a matter of a year or two. She surpassed where Amanda had been at her age; and even though Amanda was three years older, Ashley quickly advanced to just one level below her. Mother took notice of her ability and her competitive spirit. She also noticed that Ashley consistently made better grades than Amanda. Amanda always made low to mid A's. Ashley always made perfect scores. Always. It happened very subtly, but Mother began to favor Ashley over Amanda. Amanda had always been a little clone of my mother in every way: her appearance, her temperament, her smug personality. It had required very little effort for Mother to mold her. Ashley had indeed been harder to shape to her will. She was too friendly, too kind. But as she grew older, little by little, she grew more conceited. My mother took full advantage of her change in disposition. She groomed Ashley to be just like her. A Type A with perfect grades, perfect friends, and the perfect life. Amanda noticed that she no longer held Mother's attention the way she used to; and I noticed that my sweet, friendly, funny little sister slipped away and became someone I did not recognize.

Chapter 8

My dad was always family oriented. He grew up in a wonderful environment full of love and laughter. He was the baby, and Mim was his only sibling. His parents struggled to have both of their children; and because of that, they loved and cherished them more dearly than most. Mim was born ten years after they were married, after trying desperately for seven years to have her. My dad was born eight years later and was a bit of a surprise. They had tried for six years but gave up, resigned to the fact that Mim would be their only child. Through all the tears and all the heartache, they knew the value of a child. And because both of their children's lives began with such struggle and prayer and thankfulness, my grandparents were ferociously protective of Mim and my dad. Therefore, my dad and Mim were ferociously protective of each other. Mim truly was a second mom to my dad, and he worshipped her.

Even though Mim was always large for her age, she was very well liked. She had an amazing personality, and people always gravitated towards her. She was popular in school, and she was extremely smart. I'm not sure my mother ever knew that about her, since those were the qualities she looked for in a person to determine if they had any worth. The only area Mim struggled with was her appearance. Sometimes people would judge her before they really got to know her, and that was where my dad's protective nature emerged from. If someone made fun of her weight, he was always quick to jump in and defend her. When he was in sixth grade, he punched one of his best friends for making fun of her in a bathing suit. He would not allow anyone to disparage her. That was his nature.

She was protective as well, in a motherly way. She was always afraid he would get hurt. He was a rambunctious, athletic boy; and she always worried he would get a black eye or a broken bone. She was more worrisome than their own mother. But Mim loved how cute and funny he was. He could make her laugh just by looking at her. They truly were closer than any two siblings could be. He was her advocate, and she was his advisor. If Mim said don't do it, then he wouldn't do it. That's why, when it came to my dad deciding to marry my mother, Mim's opinion was the only one that mattered. At the time, Mim honestly believed she was the only problem they had, the only thing that was wrong between them. She knew they were perfect for each other. She could see it. She knew it from how he talked about her. But he was protective of Mim, so he would not marry her if Mim didn't advise it and precisely because it involved her.

All she wanted was for him to be happy; and aside from her, she honestly thought he would be. But when I was born, she realized what a mistake it had been. She knew my mother would always be that way towards her, but she never dreamed they would have a child who my mother would soundly reject. The moment she realized it in the hospital and every time afterwards when my dad told her how my mother treated me, she cursed herself for ever believing Paige Martin Allen could make my dad happy. In fact, she made him miserable.

When he married, my dad always wanted to have the kind of loving family he grew up in. He wanted his children to be as close to each other as he and Mim were. He wanted to take fun family vacations and sit around together on Friday nights watching movies and playing games. He dreamed of a big family and always worried that he might have the same problem conceiving children that his parents endured. So each time my mother got pregnant, he was so thankful and valued each of us before we were ever born. When he first saw my mother's reaction to Mim, he was very hurt. He loved both of them very much and had wanted them to be close. He knew Mim was open to a close relationship, but realizing that my mother wasn't saddened him. It wasn't until later that he realized the superficial nature of her first impression of his sister, and it angered him. He had considered not marrying her because of it. It wasn't that he was choosing his sister over his girlfriend, but something about it bothered him in a profound way. He never could quite put his finger on it, but her superficial nature was off-putting. And with it being directed specifically towards his sister, it made it worse. But because Mim had given her approval, he felt it would be okay to marry her. He loved her deeply and wanted to marry her; but even with Mim's blessing, there was still a twinge of doubt. But he chose to ignore it.

The early years of their marriage had been wonderful. They were happy and in love. When my dad's family got together, my mother was pleasant enough towards Mim but never made an effort to get close to her. My dad would visit Mim periodically while working in the city. It all worked well, and Mim was fine with it; so therefore, my dad was too.

My dad hadn't noticed early on how she was slowly turning into her mother; but after we were born, he began to realize it—especially with the way everything had to be just so. She had always complained to him about how her mother was and said she was determined not to be like her, but slowly the process began. At the beginning of college, my mother had been a vivacious person, always laughing and always happy. By the time she graduated, she was calm and very controlled. When Amanda came along, she was very organized and scheduled. And when I came along, she slipped into a dark place in which my dad did not recognize her. He had no choice but to remain in the marriage, knowing I would be the sacrificial lamb if he didn't. And as bad as life was with her, it would be absolute hell trying to get away from her.

My mother became a monster. A controlling parent whose favorite children were scared of her. A competitive parent whose daughters felt they had to battle for her attention and approval. A hateful, superficial parent who ignored the imperfect daughter. And the manipulative wife who trapped her husband in an empty, loveless marriage. Any ounce of happiness was drained from her, and the only thing that replaced it was the satisfaction of her two daughters' accomplishments. She lived her life vicariously through them. When they succeeded, she succeeded. They were popular; therefore, she was popular. When they made straight A's, she relived the feeling of making straight A's. When they won an award, she won an award. She was completely consumed by their progress and expected them to excel. She actually demanded excellence because she was furious if either of them made the slightest mistake. If a small mistake was made during a gymnastics routine or if an A was too close to a B on a test, she would lecture them for an hour about the importance of being perfect. If it were a big mistake, she would simply ignore them because she couldn't tolerate failure. If they made a mistake, she made a mistake. And she did not like making mistakes. Sometimes I was glad she rejected me.

~March 1996~

It was a big decision for Amanda to try out for cheerleading when she was going into the sixth grade. My mother had pushed her in gymnastics in an obsessive way. But because she was never allowed to quit gymnastics and try out for cheerleading when she was younger, Mother allowed Amanda to choose for herself which one she would do. And besides, my mother believed Ashley was the one who really excelled at gymnastics, so it wouldn't be a waste if Amanda gave it up.

We went to watch her tryout on a Friday after school. She had been at cheer camp every day after school learning the routines, and she would come home every evening and practice in the back yard. She was very good. Because of her gymnastics training, she was one of only a few who could actually throw a back handspring, and her jumps were phenomenal since she was so flexible. I was so jealous. I watched her in the gymnasium as she performed flawlessly. Her blonde ponytail was bouncing, and a huge smile never left her face. She was the ultimate cheerleader, and I had no doubt she had made the squad. My mother fretted while she performed, scrutinizing every move. She was very disappointed in her performance. I leaned towards my dad and whispered, "I think she'll make it." He looked at me and smiled and said, "I think so too." And sure enough, she did. My mother was pleasantly surprised but surprised nonetheless. After seeing Amanda's perfect execution, I wondered if my mother could ever be pleased.

My mother immediately became the ultimate cheer mom, getting to know the cheer coach on a first name basis. She became the team mom, of course; and all the other moms gravitated toward her. Just as with gymnastics, she was the expert since she had been a college cheerleader. The other moms were in awe because that was such a difficult level to achieve. My mother gained a lot of satisfaction out of her daughter being a cheerleader. She quickly realized the enhanced popularity it provided. She began to grow bored with gymnastics, and her attention to Ashley began to wane. Ashley noticed very quickly and waited impatiently to be old enough to try out herself. My mother would, no doubt, be pleased with that decision because she knew it would extend her own cheer status three years beyond Amanda.

It wasn't long after Amanda made the squad when Grandmother Martin came to stay with us for a few days. My grandfather was away on business, and she didn't want to stay by herself. My mother always seemed nervous when my grandmother was around. The one who could never be pleased couldn't even please her own mother. The house was never clean enough; dinner was never good enough. My mother struggled to make everything absolutely perfect, only to be told it wasn't. My grandmother would complain about the littlest things being wrong. If it was something big, she wouldn't speak at all. She would only raise her eyebrows. My mother was definitely a mirror image of her own mother. The uncomfortable silence of disappointment was the worst kind of punishment.

When I was little and Grandmother Martin would visit, I would always hide. My mother wanted me out of sight anyway, but I was always scared to death of my grandmother. She, like my mother, never spoke to me. She eyed me with the evil eye of disappointment, her eyebrows raised to maximum arch. She was the matriarch: tall, blonde, slim, and regal. My mother was her clone. Amanda and Ashley had inherited their good genes. I was not so lucky. Not fitting the mold meant I was not a part of the bloodline. The one thing my mother and I always silently agreed upon was that both of us wished I was at Mim's when my grandmother would come to visit. She didn't want me—a constant reminder of a mistake she had made—to be around for her mother to see. And I didn't want my grandmother to see me either. I was used to being awkward and ugly around my mother; but when Grandmother Martin was there, I felt even more awkward and uglier than usual.

I wasn't able to go to Mim's when my grandmother came to visit after Amanda made cheerleader. She was away at a teacher's convention. It wouldn't have mattered anyway because my grandmother stayed for an entire week. An entire week! Everyone was uncomfortable. It wasn't just me. Not long after my dad realized he was trapped in the marriage, he simply chose to start sleeping in the guest bedroom. But when my grandmother was there, he had to sleep with my mother. Not only because my grandmother was to sleep in the spare bedroom, but also because my mother insisted that he make everything look normal. That's all she cared about: the appearance of things. He complied, knowing she would make life even more miserable if he didn't. Amanda and Ashley were always somewhat at ease with Grandmother Martin, but now Amanda was on edge because of quitting gymnastics.

Not long after she arrived, Grandmother Martin set her heavy gaze on my sister. "Amanda, darling, did you really quit gymnastics?" she asked.

Amanda replied in a nervous, quiet voice. "Yes, ma'am."

"And you gave it up, why?" she asked icily.

"Because I wanted to be a cheerleader," she replied cautiously.

"A cheerleader?" she asked, her eyebrows raising a bit more.

"Yes, ma'am. I can show you my uniform if you—"

"No, that won't be necessary," my grandmother interrupted rudely, waving a dismissive hand. "Paige, is this your influence?" she asked, glaring at my mother.

"Well . . . no, Mother. She decided for herself." I had never seen my mother be as submissive as she was when she tried to answer her mother's pointed question.

"You let *her* decide? She is far too young to make such decisions," Grandmother said with an air of contempt.

My mother didn't answer. She didn't know what to say.

"Paige! Answer me," she snapped, as if my mother were ten years old.

"She wanted to, Mother; and I let her."

The room grew quiet. I was silently observing, as usual. My mother looked like a child who was about to be reprimanded. Amanda's head was bowed, knowing Mother was in trouble because of her. Ashley looked around nervously, hoping that Grandmother's attention wouldn't focus on her. No such luck. Grandmother looked directly at her.

"Ashley, darling, are *you* going to decide to be a cheerleader as well?"

Ashley shifted in her chair. "I love gymnastics, Grandmother," she said, avoiding the direct question. Surprisingly, Grandmother allowed her to get away without a yes or no answer.

"That's good, dear," she smiled. "I know you're the real star anyway." As she said that, she turned and looked directly at Amanda to see her reaction to such a cutting remark. Amanda kept her head down, careful to avoid Grandmother's burning glare.

Daddy had been standing in the doorway listening to the conversation. "Catherine," he said kindly. Everyone turned, not realizing he was there, "both of my girls are beautiful gymnasts, and," he said, smiling at Amanda as she looked up at him, "Amanda is the most beautiful cheerleader I've ever seen." Amanda smiled a thankful smile at him. My mother looked at him with hurt in her eyes, wondering if he no longer considered her the most beautiful cheerleader he had ever seen. "And," he continued, "if Ashley wants to cheer also, then we will let her." Ashley smiled too.

My grandmother rolled her eyes, offended. "Such poor parenting decisions," she said. "Children should *not* be allowed to make their own decisions. They will only make foolish choices."

"I disagree," my dad said firmly. "Children need the freedom to make some of their own decisions—with parental guidance of course. But if they don't learn to make decisions now, how will they ever learn?"

Grandmother was not used to being challenged. People were never brave enough to stand up to her. She ignored the question and asked my mother for more tea. My mother quickly complied, and she and Grandmother started discussing the need for new drapes in the dining room. I was nine years old, and my dad had just taught me a profound lesson. If you stand up to those arrogant people who belittle you, they will have no choice but to back down. It was a spark that ignited within me. I looked up at him and smiled, and he smiled back.

Later that night, I overheard my dad talking to my mother

about what happened with Grandmother.

"Paige, don't you see how your mother is? Don't you see how mean and hurtful she is? Don't you realize you treat our girls the exact same way?"

My mother was quiet but defensive. "I am not that harsh. I most certainly am not."

"Yes, you are. You just don't realize it. Don't you see how your mother makes you feel? You make the girls feel the exact same way."

"Paul, I'm tired. I want to go to sleep."

"Admit it, you do," he persisted.

"I will admit no such thing," she hissed. "Now goodnight." With that, she turned over to go to sleep. She would have no further discussion about it. But then she turned half way back and said, "Oh, and from now on, my mother wants you to call her Mrs. Martin."

"The hell I will," he responded, jerking the covers away from her.

My dad couldn't fall asleep, especially not beside her. So he grabbed his pillow and went into the den. I hurried to the sofa so I wouldn't be caught eavesdropping. He was surprised to see me there. "What are you doing down here, pumpkin?"

I yawned. "I couldn't sleep. I just came down here. I was thinking about watching some television."

"Oh, you were?" he laughed. "Well, I was thinking the same thing. What should we watch?"

"I don't care. Whatever you want to watch," I smiled.

We settled on the sofa together, watching a game show he found; and we quickly fell asleep.

***

The next morning, I decided to try something new. I decided to stand up to my mother. I decided to make her talk to me. One thing she didn't know about me was that I, by the young age of nine, had become a very good cook. I had learned from helping my dad in the kitchen and by spending weekends with Mim. She loved to cook and had taught me so many things. I was awake early and went straight to the kitchen when I heard my mother in there. She always prepared a big breakfast on Saturday mornings. When I walked in, she already had out mixing bowls and eggs and pancake batter.

"I want to help cook," I announced. She turned and looked at me with utter surprise. I think that was the first time in my life I had actually spoken to her directly. She had no choice but to respond.

Her back stiffened. "Roda, I don't have time for this."

Nonsense, I thought. She always let Ashley help.

"It won't take long," I insisted as I perched myself upon the stool and started cracking the exact amount of eggs needed. "I'll do the pancakes and you cook the bacon. Should we scramble some eggs too?"

My mother just stared at me. I detected the slightest hint of awe, believe it or not. She had no choice but to comply. My dad overheard us and came into the kitchen with a look of amusement on his face. From that moment on, my dad and I had a plan. We would choose our moments and insist on doing whatever we wanted in the nicest way, and she would have no alternative but to abide by our wishes.

When Grandmother came in and saw us working side by side, she was taken aback. "What is going on here?" she asked rudely.

"Breakfast," I said, as if she had just posed the stupidest question ever asked. "Would you like pancakes or eggs, Grandmother?" That was definitely the first time I had ever spoken directly to her and addressed her by name. She was indignant.

"I will have neither. I prefer wheat toast. Dry, no butter, with black coffee."

I happily jumped to her request as if I were a short order cook. I remembered from her visiting before that she loved fresh fruit, so I served her a small bowl on the side. One important aspect of cooking that Mim had always taught me was the aesthetics of it. Any true artist would know this. How food is presented adds to the beauty and enjoyment of it. So I carefully took out my mother's china—ignoring her objections, and I served my grandmother in a style that only she could appreciate. The rest of us followed suit. We ate our pancakes, bacon, and eggs on fine china and sipped our milk from tea cups. My dad was absolutely amused at me taking over the kitchen. My mother seemed impressed by my cooking, but she tried to hide it.

Amanda and Ashley were devouring the pancakes, completely forgetting that they were supposed to eat like birds. In between bites, Amanda asked, "These pancakes are so good, Roda. What did you do to make them taste like this?"

I smiled. "I added a little bit of vanilla and some cinnamon sugar and nutmeg too. It's Aunt Mim's recipe." My mother just looked at me, forgetting that Amanda was not supposed to speak to me.

My dad got up to refill his coffee. "Catherine, would you care for some more?"

"No, thank you," she said, refusing his offer even though she did want more. "Paige," she said, turning her laser sharp attention towards my mother, "did you forget to tell Paul how to address me from this day forward?"

My mother swallowed and cleared her throat. "Yes, Mother, I did, but—"

"Oh, Catherine," my dad interrupted, bending down to embrace my grandmother around her shoulders, "of course she did," he laughed. "But now, why would I do something like that? We're family. We should be on a first name basis."

My grandmother was speechless. My mother's mouth hung open in disbelief. To divert matters, she jumped up to refill Grandmother's coffee. She had anticipated that she wanted more. My dad and I smiled at each other. We were both very proud of ourselves. We had figured it out. We had stumbled upon a way for us to be happy and to interact within our family despite my mother's objections. All we had to do was ignore her intimidation and just be ourselves.

***

Not long after our epiphany of usurping my mother's power, my dad had a wonderful idea. He invited Mim to stay with us one weekend. Rather than us going to her, she would come to us; and she would be able to spend time with Amanda and Ashley as well. I was so excited I could hardly wait. My dad and I decided we would all have pizza on Friday night when Mim arrived, and we would watch old movies. That was always a tradition with Mim. The next night, we planned a big family meal in which we could all join in and cook. My dad made sure to schedule it for a weekend when Amanda and Ashley didn't have prior commitments—which was rare. My mother was furious that he did it in the first place and even more so because he told her at the last minute. She had planned on finally having a quiet weekend. She did not want company. My dad told her to feel free to join us, or she could do her own thing. He didn't care.

When Mim arrived late that Friday afternoon, she entered our home with such excitement it was comical. She really outdid herself with her enthusiastic greeting. Judging by my mother's reaction, Mim's squeals of hello were ear piercingly annoying. But Mim ignored her reaction and hugged her lovingly along with the rest of us. Mim acted completely oblivious to the fact that my mother despised her, and that irritated my mother even more. Amanda and Ashley tried their best not to act excited about her being there, but they were taken in by Mim's magnetic personality. She caught up with each of us: asking me what I had drawn that week, asking Ashley about her gymnastics meet the weekend before, and asking Amanda about her new cheer squad and wanting to see her uniform. Amanda quickly ran upstairs to retrieve it to show Mim. Mim was so excited for her and told her she would come to a game in the fall to watch her cheer. With that, my mother was so irritated she finally left the room. Mim knew what she was doing, and she meant to do it. She knew how to push my mother's buttons.

That night, we all settled in the den for a fun family night of pizza, games, and movies. My mother kept to herself in her bedroom. I wondered the whole time what consequences Amanda and Ashley would pay for participating in the fun, but neither of them seemed to be concerned. It amazed me how different my sisters were around Mim, as if they were under some sort of spell she had cast. I could only wish to have that kind of influence over someone.

My mother carefully observed how they interacted with Mim, and she did not like it. She tried at various times during the weekend to divert them from the activities, but she was unsuccessful. Mim would always have a quick excuse to keep them involved. A spur of the moment invitation came up for the girls to go play, and my mother tried to get them ready to go. Mim laughed and said in her nicest voice, "Oh, don't be silly, Paige. They can go play anytime. I don't get to visit that often. Let them stay here, will you?" Mim was so adept at such manipulation that it wasn't even a question but more of a command. My mother had no choice but to comply. She resented, however, that Mim was able to come into her home and take over in such a way that she had no control. She was outnumbered and completely surprised that Amanda and Ashley were not concerned about the repercussions of their behavior. But Mim was full of love and laughter and hugs, and no one could reject such affection.

Mim was a perceptive person, and one thing she knew about my mother from the very beginning was that she was a coward. She could control and manipulate those closest to her, but those beyond her control frightened her. What came off as cool and indifferent towards others was actually fear. Mim knew my mother would never be able to confront those she feared; and if confronted herself, she would cower. She carefully observed my mother all weekend and went out of her way to be pleasant towards her. My mother did not return the pleasantries. She continued to act aloof, waiting for the weekend to end so she could punish her girls with silence.

Mim had never confronted my mother, but she was ready to do so. She had sat back for years not saying anything, and she was tired of observing from a distance what my mother was doing to her family. So she waited for the right moment Sunday afternoon to say something. Upon Mim's suggestion, my dad was running a few errands with Amanda and Ashley, and I stayed home to work on finishing a drawing for her. She and I were sitting at the kitchen table when my mother walked in to make herself a cup of tea. Mim got up and casually strolled over to her.

"So Paige," she began as she leaned on the counter near my mother, "I wanted to let you know how much I've enjoyed spending the weekend here with all of you."

My mother barely responded except with a small grunt. But Mim continued, ignoring her non-reaction. "You really do have such a lovely home. You have done an amazing job with it."

"Thank you," she said quietly but with a sense of obligation

106

to respond.

"And you have such a wonderful family," she said, moving closer to my mother. "Are you aware of that?"

For the first time, my mother looked up at her. "Well, of course I do," she said carefully, her defenses beginning to go up. This caught my attention, and I paused from sketching to look up at them.

"Then why," Mim asked, moving closer and eyeing her intently, "do you treat them the way you do?"

"I don't know what you mean," she said, looking down at her cup and backing away as Mim advanced.

"Oh, I think you do know what I mean," Mim said, smiling slyly as she backed my mother into the corner of the counter. Trying not to feel intimidated, my mother looked up at her with a smirk of contempt.

"Do you realize," Mim continued, inching closer to her, "that if it weren't for me, you would not have any of this?"

"Oh, really?" she asked sarcastically. "And how is that?"

Mim smiled pleasantly and moved closer until their noses were inches apart. "Because if I had told Paul not to, he would have *never* married you. In fact, I think he was hoping I would tell him not to."

"Really?" she asked, trying not to seem completely intimidated.

"Yes, really," Mim replied, smiling.

"And why do you think that, Miriam?"

"Because he was beginning to see through you, and he knew that I *could* see through you. He was beginning to see how superficial and shallow you truly are."

Mim paused to let the words sink in. "The only mistake I made was believing that it was only about me. I believed that you two would be perfectly happy if I stayed at a distance, but now I see that I was wrong. Now I see it wasn't so much about me but about you and the kind of person you really are. You *are* superficial and shallow. And you are judgmental and hateful. All you care about is how things appear. How the perfect image you've created *appears*, while all along your family is suffering because of your selfishness."

My mother started to speak, but Mim kept talking. "You

have rejected and ignored that precious child," she said, pointing to me. "You have alienated her from her sisters and made her feel as if she were worth absolutely nothing. You pit Amanda and Ashley against each other to see which one wins in the little game of impressing you and gaining your favor. And," she continued, moving so close that her large body pinned my mother in the corner, "you have trapped my brother in a marriage that he no longer wants by threatening to take everything away from him— including Roda." She took a breath. "How *dare* you do all of this to them. How *dare* you lord over them and keep them in fear of even speaking to each other. How *dare* you use intimidation on those you are supposed to love and nurture. I will guarantee you that you will end up old and alone one day. You may have everything you want right now, but I guarantee that one day you will have nothing."

And with that, she pushed off from the counter and away from my mother, who stood there stunned. Mim sat back down at the table with me and smiled as if nothing had just occurred. My mother waited for a moment before slowly picking up her tea and walking out of the kitchen in such a way that it looked as if she might ask Mim for permission to leave. I was in awe of my aunt. Simply in awe. She was the nicest, sweetest, most good-hearted person who ever lived; but that day, I realized how she could rip someone apart without even raising her voice. Armed with her conviction and a smile and her deep sense of maternal protection for both my dad and me, she stood up to my mother in a way that no one else could. To everyone else, my mother was a tough woman who you dare not cross. But to Mim, she was weak; and she felt it was long past time to confront her.

Mim left later that afternoon. We were sad to see her go, but we knew she would be back. We talked about her visiting at least every other month. She told Amanda and Ashley to come stay again one weekend, but she knew it would most likely never happen. We all knew Mother would never permit them to leave and go see her.

We were down the rest of the evening without Mim's laughter filling the house. We ate dinner and watched television, feeling very depressed. My mother never came out of her bedroom after Mim's verbal lashing. She barely spoke to anyone for a week, but we tried to remain normal. I continued to go to Mim's every weekend, and she came to visit us too. And when she did, Amanda and Ashley would always engage in the activities; but otherwise, they would sink into their normal silence. They were never hateful towards me. They just ignored me, which sometimes could be much worse.

Chapter 9

~September 1998~

We all reach a certain point in our lives where who we are crystallizes within our psyche, and we are helpless to change it. That point for me was when I was almost twelve years old. I started middle school that fall, and I still remember the outfit I wore on the first day. I was too big to wear cute clothes like my sisters, so I wore dark jeans that didn't fit right at all and an oversized t-shirt with NYU emblazoned on it. I realized much too late that, even if you had grown up with the same kids in elementary school, what you wore the very first day of middle school made a lifelong impression. My dad, being a guy, had no idea how unflattering my clothes looked, so he was useless to advise me. In my mind, I thought the shirt was cool since Mim taught there and because it was a popular university in the greatest city in the world. But to all the kids at school, it was lame. On a few occasions, some of the girls would just look me up and down and laugh. They all dressed in trendy, slender clothes while I trudged around in a t-shirt and jeans every day. My hair was unruly—as usual, and my skin was showing signs of budding acne. I was a mess, and that was how I saw myself from that day forward.

My transition from elementary to middle school was less than desirable. There was something to be said about the safety of elementary school where you are told where to go, what to do, where to sit, and everything is done in a group. When you enter the world of middle school and high school, you no longer have the security of being grouped together. You are an individual on your own for the most part, allowed to gather with whomever you want.

It's an epic event for someone like Amanda; but for me, it was like being thrown into a shark tank. For Amanda, it was cheering at pep rallies and football games, comparing class schedules with friends, gathering at the lockers, and finally getting to sit with friends at the lunch table. For me, it was navigating through a lonely world of haughty stares and cold shoulders. I did not have one friend. Not one. No one to walk down the hall with between classes; no one to sit with at lunch; no pictures of friends to hang in my locker. While Amanda enjoyed going into each new class and gathering with her friends, I entered each class dreading the loneliness. I used to compensate by drawing; but even though I had won several art awards and competitions, by sixth grade I was known as the weird girl who drew all the time. So I thought it best to bury myself in a book instead. I often wondered why I could never be myself. I was a totally different person when I was at Mim's. I was confident and funny. When I was at home with my dad, I felt embolden by our attempts to undermine my mother's authority. I was still ignored for the most part, but I somehow felt bold. At school, I felt empty. Like a complete failure. Like a complete nobody.

Allyson, my nemesis from elementary school, was in almost every one of my classes. It was amazing how someone like her could focus like a laser on the weaker students. Specifically me. She was relentlessly rude to me every chance she got; and when others would have naturally ignored me, she encouraged them to take notice of what a loser I was. She would snicker if I said or did something wrong in class. She would eye me amusingly and laugh when she saw me walking or sitting alone. I often wondered how it was that she was not genetically related to my mother.

And of course, Allyson made the cheer squad and pranced around every Friday in her uniform. Stupid show off. And of course, because she and Amanda were both cheerleaders, they became friends. Amanda was two grades ahead, so she was more of a mentor; but Allyson was allowed to sit with her at lunch, and they both had pictures of themselves together hanging in their lockers. All the cheerleaders traveled in a pack. It didn't matter their age or their grade. They referred to themselves as big sisters and little sisters. Amanda had insisted that Allyson be her little sister even though she was two grades below her. And I overheard her say one time that Allyson actually could be her sister since they looked so much alike.

~*October 1999*~

It was no surprise when Ashley made the cheer squad the following year. She had been anxiously waiting for three years. By that time, Amanda had moved up to high school where, of course, she made cheerleader as well. And it was no surprise that Ashley and Allyson became instant and inseparable best friends. Just my luck. They practically lived at each other's houses every weekend, and Amanda would be included in the slumber party fun whenever she was available. Fortunately for me, I was gone every weekend to Mim's, so I didn't have to endure the love fest. My mother was practically giddy at the thought of Allyson. It was as if her long lost daughter had found her way home. It was surreal to sit there and listen to her talk endlessly about this girl who wasn't even related to us and even more surreal when Allyson was adopted into my mother's little circle as one of "the girls." When my mother would talk about taking them to the mall the coming weekend, she wouldn't say, "I'm taking the girls and Allyson to the mall." She would simply say, "I'm taking the girls to the mall." And I could clearly see how my sisters were being sucked into the vortex of my mother's manipulation as she created this pseudo-family for herself. Amanda and Ashley were completely lost in the sisterly trifecta with Allyson.

There was one weekend in particular that my mother was extremely excited about. Allyson's parents were going away for the weekend, and she was going to stay at our house. My mother would have that beautiful, angelic creature for the entire weekend. The heavens were opening and the stars were aligning. It was fate. She had insisted my dad stay home that weekend since they would have to take the girls to a cheer exhibition on Saturday morning. My mother wanted it to be the five of them so she could have some sort of fake family time together. She imagined in her mind how it should have been, and she wanted to live it. My dad knew what she was doing and didn't like it, but what could he do? It was a bitter thing to face because I felt invisible, thrown away for something better. But regardless, I was ready to go to Mim's that Friday afternoon to escape the madness of my life.

Unfortunately, my dad called the school and left a message for me to ride the bus home instead. Mim was sick, possibly the flu; and I would need to go home. I was absolutely crushed knowing I would have to face the charade of happy family that would take place. But I knew, I knew more than anything, my mother would be absolutely livid.

My mother's main goal in life was to keep me hidden from the world—at least her world. As far as I knew, Allyson had no idea that I was Amanda's and Ashley's sister; and just like my mother, I'm sure they wanted to keep it that way. I was nervous as I walked to the bus because they would know what was happening as soon as they saw me. When I got on, they were nowhere in sight. I realized right away that my mother must have picked them up. I was sick to my stomach the whole ride home. If I could have gone somewhere else, anywhere but there, I would have.

When I approached the back of the house down the driveway, I could hear the three of them in the backyard. They were practicing cheers and tumbling. Rather than going in through the back door, I went back around to the front and let myself in. I tried to be quiet. I thought that if I could be really quiet, I could sneak up to my room and stay there and never be seen. That didn't happen. My mother heard the front door open and came out of the kitchen to see why. The look of horror on her face was indescribable. "What are *you* doing here?" she hissed. I was too scared to speak. I just started crying. I had no control over it, and I hated that I didn't. I was at my lowest point ever. Not only did my mother not want me, but she wanted another child in my place—a more perfect child. And on top of that, the child she wanted actually existed and was living and breathing and in my house; and my mother was deathly afraid that she would see me.

"Get up to your room," she hissed again, "before the girls come in here."

Too late. They had come inside and heard me crying and came around the corner to see what was going on.

"What is *she* doing here?" Allyson asked in hateful disbelief.

I tried to stop crying. I tried as hard as I could, but it just wouldn't stop. I was frozen there in front of them, paralyzed with

113

fear.

"*Why* are you *not* at Mim's?" Ashley hissed.

"She did this on purpose, Mom," Amanda complained. "She did it just to embarrass us."

I stood there shaking my head, trying to argue; but nothing would come out. Only big fat blubbering tears.

"Why is she here?" Allyson continued to ask. "What is she doing here?" She finally just looked at me as if I was an intruder and said, "Nobody invited you here, *Roda*. You can't spend the night with us. Now go home!"

She said my name with such utter disdain that even my mother couldn't match. Something within me began to well up and rise to the surface. It was anger. I don't think I had ever felt such anger in my entire life; but at that moment, it rose to the top and burst out of me like a cannon. I threw my heavy backpack directly at Allyson, knocking her down. She looked up at me in disbelief as I bent down and yelled at her through angry tears. "I LIVE HERE, YOU STUPID IDIOT!" And with that, I ran upstairs and locked my door. I hid in my closet, hoping my mother wouldn't come after me with a belt.

I stayed in my closet until my dad came home about two hours later. I really wanted to sit at the top of the stairs and try to listen to what was being said about me, but I was too afraid. I could only imagine what my mother said to my dad when he got home. When he got there, he immediately came up to my room. He called my name when he didn't see me, and I cracked the closet door open. He squatted down in front of it and opened it the rest of the way.

"Whatcha doing in there, peanut?" he asked softly.

"Hiding," I said with my head tucked down on my knees that were folded into my chest.

He rubbed the top of my head. "You okay?" he asked.

"No," I replied.

"Well, why don't you come out of there, and let's go eat," he encouraged.

"I don't want to go down there and eat with them," I said adamantly.

"They're not here. They went out to eat. I thought you and I could go do our own thing. Where do you want to go?"

"Can we go get pizza?" I asked hopefully.

"Well, of course we can. And how about ice cream after?"

I nodded excitedly and jumped out of the closet. Then I remembered what I had done wrong.

"Did Mother tell you what I did?" I asked timidly.

He smiled. "No, she's not speaking to me, which is actually a good thing," he laughed. "But Ashley told me."

I frowned. "Oh." Well, of course Ashley would tell. Stupid tattletale.

"Am I going to be punished," I asked, looking down.

"Well, I'm sure your mother wants me to punish you," he said in a serious tone. But when I looked up, he was smiling down at me.

I crinkled my forehead. "Are you not going to?"

"Of course! I'm going to tell your mother that I gave you a firm talking to, and then I took you to Jackson's Café and only allowed you to eat vegetables!" He said it with such dramatic flair that I laughed.

"That would be a lie, Daddy,"

"Would it?" he asked innocently.

I nodded.

"Hmm . . . well, okay then. I will take you to dinner, and we will discuss the incident. That will take care of the first part. Then," he reasoned, "maybe she just won't ask were we ate."

"And maybe she won't ask if we got ice cream?" I asked, smiling.

"Let's hope she doesn't," he said as he winked.

I nodded. "Yes, let's hope."

"But I do want to tell you one thing," he said in a more serious tone.

I looked up, thinking he was about to tell me how wrong I was to do what I did.

"I'm proud of you for sticking up for yourself. That was a brave thing to do."

"Really?" I asked. "It was brave? Even though I knocked her down and used bad words?"

"Well, that part was not so good; but sticking up for yourself when someone is mean is very good."

I sighed, wishing I could always be so brave and do it

115

without my temper getting the best of me.

"You'll learn, Roda," he encouraged me. "It just takes time."

When my dad and I returned, they were already home. The four of them were sitting in the den making beaded bracelets and watching a movie. They were laughing and talking when we came in, but they suddenly got quiet. I wanted to run upstairs and hide again, but my dad had already told me what I needed to do. It was humiliating, but I knew it would help my dad look better to my mother so she would believe he was punishing me. I followed him into the den and instinctively stood behind him.

"Hi there, girls!" he said in the happiest voice he could muster.

"The girls" looked up at him and smiled and said hello. My mother never acknowledged him. I could see Allyson staring at him. It was obvious she thought he was good looking.

"So what are you girls doing?" he asked.

Allyson laughed. "We're making bracelets. Can't you tell?" She sounded flirtatious. Gross.

"Ah, okay," he smiled. He avoided asking where they went to eat so that he would not be asked where we went.

"Well," he said, pulling me out from behind him, "Roda has something she would like to say."

Well, I wouldn't *like* to say it, I thought. But in order for it to look as though my dad had reprimanded me, he and I agreed that I *should* say it. I stood there timidly while the three of them stared at me with daggers. My mother never bothered to look at me. I guess she was in her own little world, pretending I wasn't there.

"Umm," I started, looking down to avoid eye contact, "I wanted to say I'm sorry about throwing my backpack at you and knocking you down."

"You do know that you could have broken my nose or something, don't you?" Allyson asked in a hateful tone.

Oh, if only that had happened, I thought to myself. "Yes, I know," I agreed, "and I'm very sorry about that." Not really.

"And what else?" she demanded, after a long awkward pause.

I looked up at her, clueless. "What else?" I asked stupidly. At that point, my mother looked up at me with piercing eyes. My mind went blank. What was I forgetting? Why was I not remembering what else? I knew there was something else; but with everyone staring at me, I couldn't remember.

"Well, look who's the stupid idiot now," Allyson mocked, and Amanda and Ashley laughed.

"Oh, yeah," I said slowly, "I'm sorry about that too." Never mind that you actually are a stupid idiot, I thought. And never mind that you provoked me by yelling at me that I wasn't allowed in my own home. Stupid idiot.

My dad smiled a fake smile at the girls and then put his arm around my shoulder. I already knew he wouldn't ask Allyson to apologize to me. We had already discussed it. He had said that— sure—it wasn't fair; but when dealing with such arrogant people, it's better to just let it go than to provoke them further. But I wondered if that made me a coward. Is it better to acquiesce rather than to stand up for yourself? If you're weak, wouldn't it make you look weaker? But I was doing it for my dad, so I relented.

The girls went back to their project, completely ignoring me. Sensing I wasn't wanted there, I turned to go upstairs. My dad sat on the sofa and looked at all the stuff they had made, trying to make an effort to interact with Amanda and Ashley. My mother left the den and went into her bedroom while my dad was in there. He and I both knew we had ruined her weekend. Well, actually Mim had by getting sick; but Mother wanted to make it clear that she was not happy.

The next morning, my dad insisted that we all go to the cheer exhibition in the park. My mother argued that I was old enough to stay home by myself, but my dad wouldn't leave me. So instead, he and I drove together and my mother took the girls. There was an arts and crafts festival going on in the park as well, so he and I walked around looking at the different booths, and we ate popcorn and caramel apples. The exhibition was scheduled at one o'clock, so we were sure to be at it a little before time. My mother had stayed with the girls the whole time, chatting with the other moms and helping the cheer coach with whatever she needed. She had hoped to have her good looking husband by her side for the other women to be jealous of, but I had ruined that plan. My mother completely ignored us when we walked up. She wouldn't even sit beside us. She sat with the cheer coach instead.

***

Life got worse at school. When Allyson found out that I was the secret Allen sister, she decided to make my life miserable—even more so than usual. Instead of Amanda and Ashley being ridiculed for having me as a sister, I was taunted for being the unwanted sister. They had always been afraid other kids would realize I was related to them; and if that had ever happened, they would have been thoroughly embarrassed. So now that Allyson knew, the plan was to make me feel as low as possible for being rejected by my own family.

I was sitting at the lunch table the following week, and I noticed Ashley's group looking over at me and giggling. After a few minutes, Allyson walked over to my table and sat down across from me. She looked around at the other rejects: a Japanese girl who barely spoke any English, but was smart as a whip; a tall, emaciated boy with freckles, glasses, and braces who was constantly at work on his scientific calculator; and an overweight African-American boy who was so engrossed in his food he never looked up. We all sat scattered around the table, and no one ever tried to talk to the other. That was the true sign of the reject table: to be such a reject that not even the other rejects would talk to you.

"Cool group," Allyson said sarcastically. "So," she began, focusing on me, "how's it going?"

"Fine," was all I said, looking down at my ham and cheese sandwich.

"I guess since you're Ashley's sister, we actually should invite you to sit with us, huh?"

As perceptive as I was, I could tell from her tone that she was setting me up, hoping to disappoint me. "No, that's okay," I said, looking up at her and smiling. I could see a hint of disappointment in her eyes, knowing she wouldn't be able to pull the rug out from under me.

"Well, okay," she said, covering it with a sly smile. "So tell me," she started again, "how hot is your dad?"

I wasn't quite sure where she was going with this. I shrugged. "Yeah, he's cute I guess."

"Cute? Are you kidding me? He's drop dead gorgeous."

I shrugged again. "Okay."

118

She got this dreamy look on her face. "And your mother is absolutely stunning."

I nodded. "Yes, she is."

Then she looked at me pointedly. "I wonder, then, if you can tell me."

I waited for her to continue but responded when she didn't. "Tell you what?"

She smiled a mean, sly smile and leaned in closer to me and narrowed her eyes. "I wonder if you can tell me how such an amazingly beautiful couple can have such a God-awful ugly daughter like you?"

I tried to remain composed. How was it that I had not expected that? How did I not see that coming? It felt like a punch in the stomach, so hard that it caused physical pain and prevented me from even being able to catch my breath. I just looked back down at my sandwich, willing the tears not to come. I knew she was trying to hurt me. Not only that but to provoke me, hoping to see me lash out in anger again. I took a deep breath and looked up at her.

"You have to be adopted, right?" she kept prodding. "That's the only explanation. And isn't it funny how I look so much like Amanda and Ashley?" she said as she smiled whimsically and looked off in the distance. Then she looked straight at me again with the same sly smile and narrowed eyes. "Or perhaps we were switched at birth. That could explain it." She paused, hoping the ludicrous possibility would sink in. Her eyes narrowed more and she smiled more slyly. "You do know, don't you, that your mother wishes I was her daughter? You do know she told me that, don't you?" She wasn't telling me anything I didn't know, I reasoned to myself. I already knew that, so there was no sense crying over it.

She sat back in her seat with that stupid whimsical look again. "Yes," she cooed, "we were at the mall and she bought the three of us matching shirts and she said, 'Oh, Allyson,'" trying to mimic my mother's voice. "'Dear, sweet, beautiful Allyson, how I wish you were my daughter. You fit in so perfectly with us.'"

Her eyes narrowed again and focused on me, waiting to see my reaction. It was nothing I didn't already know, I kept telling myself, trying to remain calm. But all I felt was numb. It was one thing to think it but quite another to actually hear it. With all my might, I remained calm. I was not going to allow her the satisfaction of seeing that she had any effect on me.

I just looked at her and smiled as if I were totally ignorant about what she had just said. "My mother is very superficial. I can imagine she would want yet another daughter like you. As for me, I take after my Aunt Mim, and I'm very proud of that because my Aunt Mim is the most extraordinary woman I've ever met, and my superficial excuse for a mother has always paled in comparison to her. And she knows it."

I'm not sure where those words came from. They sounded very grown up, and I was proud of them. I did not have the slightest fear that she would tell my mother what I had said. I was hoping she would. She tried to recover quickly and regain the upper hand.

"Well from what I hear, your *Aunt Mim* is so fat she can barely get out of her apartment. And from the way you look, you have no other choice but to be proud that you at least take after someone." And with that, she got up and left. She must have had some sort of expression on her face because all the kids at her table burst into laughter, including Ashley. They had all been sitting there waiting for me to break down into tears, but I had stolen that moment from them. I kept my eyes fixed on Ashley the whole time she was laughing; and when she finally looked at me, there was no shame in her eyes.

***

I didn't tell my dad about the incident. I don't know why I didn't. I should have told him about Ashley participating in it, but I knew it would break his heart. He always worried about me, especially when I started school and had to deal with mean kids. But it was getting so much worse, and I just didn't have the heart to tell him. I would confide in Mim, but I would make her swear not to tell my dad. She promised she wouldn't, but she must have relayed my pain to him somehow because of the way he would look at me. And once, he just looked at me and asked, "Allyson is not a very nice person, is she?"

I looked up at him and shook my head. He thought for a

120

moment and then asked, "Has it gotten worse since she found out who you are?"

I nodded slowly. "Yes, Daddy, much worse." He looked very sad and just nodded in agreement.

He could see what was happening. He could see it at home when Allyson was over or any time either my mother or my sisters talked about her. He knew what they were doing. And while my mother and my sisters were mean, they were—in all reality—the cowards Mim always said they were. They could be hateful and manipulative, but they avoided direct confrontation. Allyson was different, however. She loved going toe-to-toe with someone who she felt was beneath her and making them feel as small as she possibly could. She was as mean as a snake, and she got a thrill out of making others feel worthless. He could see that my mother and sisters desperately wished they could magically replace me with Allyson, and he could see that Allyson thoroughly enjoyed torturing me with that fact.

I think my lowest point was when my mother hung a picture of her "girls" on the refrigerator. It was a close up of the three of them in the backyard in front of my mother's rose bushes. I hated to admit it, but it actually was a beautiful picture. Amanda was on the left, Allyson was in the middle, and Ashley was on the right. It was as if my mother had posed them in birth order. I was amazed at how much they all looked alike. When I was alone, I just stared at it in disbelief. It was the most surreal moment I had ever encountered. I stared at it so intently that it almost felt like an out-of-body experience.

Imagine how it would feel to realize there's a better version of yourself out there, and that your own mother finds that version more valuable than you. How it would feel to see someone you should have been. How it would feel to wish to God, even more than your own mother did, that you could be that person. Now given all of that, imagine the person you desperately wished to be is someone you despise more than anyone else on earth. I have no idea how long I stared at that picture or what broke my concentration, but I vividly remember it was the moment every last minuscule amount of self-esteem drained from me. I was completely empty. I honestly believed I was worth absolutely nothing. I felt like a zombie. I felt numb and without direction. My dad noticed this and instinctively knew why. He knew that picture was meant to be a knife to my heart, and he knew Allyson would have yet another reason to taunt me. Not long after, he took the picture off the refrigerator and told my mother to go put it in her room. She objected, of course; but my dad demanded she put it away, saying, "I will not have this hanging here for Roda to look at every day."

My mother sighed. "And why not? What exactly is the problem?"

He looked at her as if she were the stupidest person on earth. "The problem," he sighed, "is that you make it more than obvious that you are substituting Allyson for Roda just to fulfill some insane longing for the middle daughter you always wanted."

"Nonsense," my mother said in a hollow tone.

"Nonsense? Really? You haven't actually told Allyson that you wish she was your daughter?"

My mother hesitated. "I don't remember saying that," she insisted.

"Well, supposedly Allyson has been constantly baiting Roda with that fact since you told her such an asinine thing. How do you think it would feel to have your worst enemy constantly telling you that your own mother wishes she were her daughter instead of you? Do you have *any* idea how that would feel?"

My mother didn't respond. She just continued to cut the vegetables she was preparing for dinner. "Paul, I have work to do," was all she said.

"Well, that is fine, Paige. But I am either going to rip this picture up, or you are going to put it away."

My mother wiped her hands, took the picture from my dad, and marched to her bedroom. Later, when no one was home, I went into her room and saw that she had framed it and put it on the nightstand beside her bed. Lovely. Her argument to my dad was that it was in *her* room and anyone who didn't want to see it should not go into her room. It really didn't matter to me because the damage had been done. I believed it was her intention all along to make me look at it. To make me face it. That was just the kind of vicious mother she was.

Chapter 10

~May 2001~

Little did I know that throughout my whole miserable eighth grade year, my dad and Mim had been plotting to find another school for me to attend. They had been helpless to do anything when I was in elementary, and they saw that middle school was a bad transition; but when Allyson's bullying began, they knew they had to do something. There was a variety of private prep schools in the city, but neither Mim nor my dad thought I would be better off socially. They felt as though I would still endure the same conceited attitudes but just from different kids. Plus, the expense of private school was still worrisome for my dad. If he could have controlled my mother's spending habits, he might have been able offset the cost; but that was impossible. He was no longer concerned with my mother insisting that Amanda and Ashley go to private school if I went. They were well established with friends and extracurricular activities, and he knew she wouldn't want to uproot them from that.

Apparently, fate intervened midway through the school year. Mim learned that a new charter school would be opening the following fall. She knew it had been in the works for years but never knew if or when it would come to fruition. But donations came through, and a building was found, so the project was on track. Mim was a professor at New York University, so she was asked to be on the Board. Because of that, I had a space available to me; and my dad took full advantage of it. I was enrolled before I even knew it.

It wasn't until the last day of school that I learned about it. My dad and Mim surprised me by picking me up, and the three of us went to Mario's Pizzeria—my very favorite restaurant. We had an early dinner and then ice cream for dessert. I was happy that they had surprised me, but I also thought it was highly unusual. Mim was so excited the whole time; I thought she was going to pop. When we finished our ice cream, I found out why.

"Honey, guess what?" she asked with bright, beaming eyes as she pushed her empty bowl aside.

"What, sweetie?" I asked, playfully mocking her term of endearment.

She looked at my dad, and then she looked at me. "You're going to go to a new school next year!"

I looked at her and then at him and said flatly, "Yeah . . . I know. High school. Yay me."

Mim laughed. "No, honey, not just high school. A completely different school. In the city."

I was confused, not fully believing what I was hearing. I looked at my dad. He was smiling at me. "What school?" I asked.

"It's a new charter school that's opening in the fall," he explained. "They want to eventually expand it to be middle school through twelfth, but right now it's just high school, starting with ninth grade. That's perfect for you! Perfect timing, huh?"

I nodded in disbelief. "Yes, it is." I was stunned. "What kind of school is it? What's it called?"

"The Board met, and we officially decided to call it The McKinley School of Arts and Sciences. It will be a direct feeder school into NYU. Meaning, if you attend there and do well, you'll have a much higher chance of getting into the university."

I was beside myself at that point. My dream was to go to NYU, but I wasn't sure I would ever be smart enough. By going to McKinley, I could focus on my art; and hopefully that would be my way in. Plus, I could finally get away from Allyson and my sisters. And even better, I would get to travel into the city everyday with my dad like we used to do! I was so excited, I broke into tears. "Daddy," I said, "I'll get to ride with you again!"

He smiled broadly. "Yep, that's the plan."

I looked back at Mim. "Will I just be doing art?"

She laughed a deep laugh. "No, honey. You'll have the basic core curriculum, but you will have art classes. A variety of them, in fact."

I think that was absolutely, positively the best day of my life. It really was. We celebrated further by going to the bookstore and getting a few art books that Mim thought would be helpful to me since she was fully aware of McKinley's art program and its requirements. The more I thought about it, the more excited I got. I would finally be away from my sisters and their horrible friends. I would meet new people and maybe even have a real chance of finding a friend. There would be other like-minded artistic type kids there, so maybe I wouldn't seem like such an outcast anymore. It was a liberating feeling. I felt as though I was somehow embarking on a new life, and I saw the beginning of this new and wonderful school as a new birth within itself. And it was exciting to know I would actually be a part of its very first freshman class ever. Something about that made it even more special. My dad was right, the timing was perfect.

My mother and my sisters were in the den when we got home. I was so excited, I rushed in without even thinking how they would react, and I announced the big news. "I'm going to a different school next year!" I shouted with such glee, their mouths fell open. My dad and Mim came in behind me, and my mother went from pure shock at my news to disdain at the sight of Mim. It was a Thursday night, and my dad had not informed my mother that Mim would be staying for a long weekend.

"Paul," my mother said, still eyeing Mim, "what is she talking about?"

My dad had also not informed her of their plans for finding me a new school. He downplayed it quite deftly, acting as if the opportunity had just suddenly arisen. My mother was not that naïve, however. She knew he and Mim must have been plotting it for some time.

She looked suspiciously at my dad. "What's this about, Paul?"

"Well, Mim knows of this new school that's opening in the fall, and there's a spot for Roda," he said, trying to give her the least amount of information as possible.

"And *how* was she able to reserve this spot? She is not Roda's parent." She asked in such a hateful tone that I quickly regretted announcing it to her. Maybe I should have let my dad tell her instead. He didn't seem the least bit concerned though.

"I'm on the Board," Mim interjected, causing my mother to focus her deadly stare on her. Not only did she want to offer my dad an out, but she wanted to remind my mother how much more accomplished she was than her. "I had the spot reserved for her," she continued. "Roda is a gifted artist, and this program will allow her many opportunities in the future."

My mother glared, not speaking.

"It's a new start up school," my dad began to explain further. "Mim took it upon herself to do this as quickly as possible so as not to lose the spot. I think it's a wonderful idea. Don't you?"

My mother looked directly at me. All my excitement had faded, and I stood sheepishly between Mim and my dad.

"I would have appreciated being *asked* before Miriam made such an important decision," she said, trying to control her anger. Then, looking at my dad, she asked, "And just how are we going to afford this?" My mother had *never* in her married life asked my dad how they were going to afford something. She always took great liberty in spending money as she wished, never concerned with finances.

"It's not a private school, Paige," my dad said, already anticipating it would be her first argument. Either that or Mim's effort to usurp their parental decision.

"It's a charter school," Mim explained. "The university has been instrumental in obtaining funding, recognizing the artistic talent in the area. Not only that, but they will have a strong math and science program as well. It will definitely be a feeder school into the university."

My mother ignored Mim. She knew she didn't have an argument there, so she went back to her objections on parental involvement. She refused to believe that my dad knew nothing about the plans ahead of time.

"I want to know why I was not informed about this. I have a right to know, *and* I have a right to be involved in the decision making. I'm not even sure I'll agree to this. So don't get too excited because my say must be taken into account."

"No, Paige," my dad said firmly, "you will not have a say. And do you know *why* you will not have a say?"

My mother jumped to her feet, indignant. "You *will NOT* decide this on your own! You will NOT!"

126

"Yes, I will," my dad said calmly. "I have already decided, she has already been enrolled, and you will *not* do anything to stop it."

There really wasn't anything my mother could do, and she knew it. She wanted to lash out, but she kept her composure with great restraint. She was very much like a wild animal when it came to her temper. And just like a wild animal, she was more vicious when trapped.

"I do not like this one bit," she said, standing in front of my dad. "I do *not* like that you and Miriam conspired without my knowledge; and I know that you did, Paul Allen. I do *not* like that you didn't include me in the decision making process. I have a right to be heard on this."

My dad chided her as if she were a child. "What do you not like, Paige? Do you not like that you don't have any say? Do you not like that you don't have any control? Do you not like that Roda may actually have a chance to make something of herself with this amazing art program? Do you even know how talented she is? No, you don't because you've never bothered to pay attention. You know," he said as he narrowed his eyes at her, "I bet I know what you don't like. I bet you don't like that she won't be under your oppressive thumb anymore. For years, you've been embarrassed that she even existed at school. You tried at all costs to distance yourself so that no one would have *any* idea she was your daughter, but now I bet it thrills you that she is so miserable. I bet it *thrills* you that Allyson torments her daily. I bet you secretly love that. But guess what? I *don't,* and I will no longer stand for it. So Roda *will* go to McKinley no matter *what* you say. Do you hear me?"

My mother stood there, so angry she was about to burst. She shoved my dad backwards and stormed off to her bedroom, slamming the door. I had been so transfixed by the confrontation that I hadn't realized I started crying. Mim instinctively pulled me close and held me to her. My parents hated each other, and it was all because of me. Even something as wonderful as me getting accepted into an amazing program could cause a vicious argument. Their marriage had become nothing more than a power struggle. That's all it was, and it was all my fault.

Amanda and Ashley had been sitting there watching the

exchange. Ashley was staring at me with daggers, no doubt because I had caused another blow up between our parents. Amanda was just looking at me. I couldn't quite read her expression, but there was something sad about it. My dad reached out and hugged me, trying to comfort me. I had done it again. I had ruined another night.

Mim took me upstairs to my room while my dad stayed with my sisters. It had become harder for him to talk to Ashley in the past few years. She had become so conceited, and her emotional distance was a result of my mother's brainwashing. He tried to apologize for the outburst. It had become so commonplace for them to argue that he sometimes didn't pay attention to who was around to hear it. Ashley rolled her eyes and acted like she wasn't listening, but Amanda had a look of concern on her face.

"So, Roda will start in the fall?" she asked.

My dad was a bit surprised. "Yes," he answered. "It really is a great opportunity for her."

Amanda nodded. "What school is it? Did you call it McKinley?"

"Yes, McKinley. It's The McKinley School of Arts and Sciences, actually. It's a charter school. It will be in midtown Manhattan."

Amanda nodded again. "Do you have to be a really good artist to get in?"

"Well, no," he said, "it isn't just an art school. They'll have a strong curriculum in math and science for kids who might be interested in the medical field. But, yes, Roda got in because of her art."

Amanda hesitated, looking at Ashley out of the corner of her eye. "I like art," she said quietly. "I think I'm pretty good at it."

My dad's mouth opened a bit, realizing what she was hinting at. "Honey . . ." he started to say, but Ashley caught on quickly to what Amanda meant, and she butted in. "Oh, you *cannot* be serious! You don't want to go to that nerd school, do you?"

"No, of course not," Amanda denied, knowing that Ashley would tell Mother.

"Then why did you say that?" Ashley prodded.

Amanda sighed. "All I meant was that I like art. That's all." She was growing frustrated with Ashley, but my dad understood the truth. He knew why she said it, and he suddenly felt bad for never realizing she might have an interest in the art program as well. He knew though, in all reality, my mother would never allow Amanda to go. She would *never* allow her to give up cheering and her friends to go to such a school. It was impossible, and Amanda knew it too. But my dad could see in her eyes that she wished she could go, and that was the sadness I saw as well.

Chapter 11

~*June 2001*~

I spent a lot of time at Mim's that summer getting ready for school. She had decided not to teach a summer course at the university so that I could travel into the city every day with my dad and stay with her while he was at work. We would often eat lunch with him, and then she and I would shop for school and art supplies. I also needed school uniforms. McKinley required its students to wear them. To someone like Ashley, that would be the end of the world. School uniforms as opposed to cute trendy clothes? Tragic. To me, it didn't really matter. I didn't look good in anything, so at least I would blend in with the rest of the student body.

I remember the day Mim and I bought the uniforms. My dad wanted me to model them for him when we got home. I was so excited to show him. Not that I thought I looked any better, but there was something about having a uniform that I liked. Maybe it was because I was never on any sort of team with a uniform to wear. I wasn't completely sure as to why, but it was exciting nonetheless.

My mother was cooking in the kitchen, and Amanda was at the table looking at a magazine when I went upstairs to change. My dad was standing there talking to Amanda while he waited for me to come back down. Ashley was over at Allyson's house. The first outfit I wanted to show him was my favorite. It was a pleated skirt with gray, red, and navy plaid. I paired it with a white oxford button-down and a red cardigan. I didn't think I looked great, but I thought it looked very smart. I bounded down the stairs and smiled broadly at my dad. I glanced at Amanda, and she actually had a small smile on her face. I had wondered if she would like it or think it was lame. My dad had a big smile on his face and was about to compliment me when my mother started laughing. It was the same kind of shallow, conceited, selfish laugh that Allyson would always have when she looked at me. My heart sank to the floor. How was it that she could always have such an effect on me? How was it that she could crush my spirit with just a glance, let alone a haughty laugh? I *hated* that she had that kind of power over me. I absolutely hated it.

My dad was instantly furious. "PAIGE! SHUT THE HELL UP! JUST SHUT UP!"

My mother was laughing too hard to stop, but she was able to take a breath and speak. "I can't help it," she said, doubling over. "She looks absolutely hideous!" she said before laughter engulfed her again.

I stood there, stunned. I had never experienced it before. I thought my mother's silence was unbearable, but this took me completely by surprise. What kind of a mother laughs at her own child? What kind? She was the lowest excuse for a mother, if she could even be described as one. As for me, that was the moment I decided she was no longer mine. From that point forward, she was no longer my mother.

As I have said, my dad was one of the gentlest souls on earth, but I could tell he wanted to strike her. He was so furious his face turned dark red and veins were popping out of his neck. He knew better than to hit her, understanding the legal weight she could bring down upon him. So instead, he grabbed her by the arm and ushered her into the bedroom. He slammed the door and began a vicious argument that lasted almost an hour. Amanda looked at me in horror after Paige (no longer my mother) began laughing at me. I was surprised by her compassion. I never realized Amanda possessed it. When my dad removed Paige from the room, Amanda jumped up to take over the cooking so it wouldn't burn. I ran upstairs and collapsed on my bed, crying my eyes out. 'Why is this my life?' I thought. '*WHY* is this my life? Everyone would be better off without me, especially Daddy.'

My dad left the house after he emerged from the bedroom. Amanda had finished cooking dinner; but supposing no one would eat, she put everything away in the refrigerator. I was surprised that my dad left without checking on me. Somewhere deep inside, I feared that he had grown tired of having to deal with me too. I was the constant irritation in my family, and maybe he had grown tired of it all.

I heard a noise at my door and sensed someone's presence. I propped myself up and turned to see Amanda standing there. There was not one moment in my entire life when she had ever come near my room, and I wondered why she had decided to now. Perhaps my dad had told her to check on me since he left like he did. Perhaps she was going to scold me for causing yet another fight between our parents. I had no idea, but she had a very soft look on her face that was hard to read.

I could tell she wanted to speak, but she couldn't think of how to say it. "Roda," she finally said, "I think your uniform looks really good. I really like it."

"You do?" I asked, perplexed.

"Yes, I really do," she nodded. "How many other pieces do you have?" She walked into my room.

"I have four more shirts," I said as I got up and began to pull my new clothes out of the shopping bags. "A blue oxford button-down, a navy pullover shirt, a red pullover, and a white pullover. Then I have two pair of khaki pants and two khaki skirts." I laid them out on the bed as I announced them. "I think I may need a couple of other things."

"No, you don't," she said, looking at each one. "You can mix and match them and make several different outfits. Do you want me to show you?"

"Sure," I said, surprised she was offering. "Oh!" I said, remembering one more item. "I also have this hoodie." I pulled out a gray hooded sweatshirt with *McKinley* printed in navy across the chest. I was most proud of it. Amanda just looked at it for a moment, running her hand across the lettering. A distant look crossed her face. "I like that," was all she said after a moment.

She spent about an hour in my room, showing me the best way to put everything together. She really was quite good at it. I was surprised she was in my room at all and very surprised she stayed so long. She didn't seem to fear Paige coming up and catching her being nice to me. When she was leaving, she looked back and smiled. "You've got a lot of good stuff."

132

I smiled back. "Thanks," I said. "And thanks for helping me."

"You're welcome."

Not long afterward, Amanda's boyfriend picked her up, and they went to see a movie. Ashley ended up spending the night with Allyson, and Paige never came out of her room. My dad came back home three hours later. When he came up to my room to check on me, he was surprised to see me smiling.

"You look happy," he said. "What's gotten into you?"

"Daddy, Amanda helped me with my clothes!"

"She did?" he asked, a confused smile crossing his face.

"Yes! And here's what she told me to do," I said as I pulled everything out and showed him what should go with what. "I think I have about twenty different outfits!" I laughed.

He sat on the edge of my bed and smiled. He looked tired, drained. "That's great, sweetie," he said, trying to sound enthusiastic.

He stayed in my room for a while longer, talking about what happened and how I felt about it. He apologized for leaving without checking on me, but he was glad Amanda jumped in and made me feel better. He was very surprised about it but very proud of her also. I told him I understood that he had to leave because he was so angry and needed to cool off. I was just glad he wasn't trying to get away from me. After about an hour, he left and went to bed. He was exhausted. I stayed up reading for a couple of hours and sketching some. I was glad for the quiet. I was glad Ashley was gone for the night, and I was especially glad Paige stayed in her room. I didn't want to hear her voice.

***

~September 2001~

McKinley started earlier than most other schools. The first day was the Thursday after Labor Day in early September. I was anxious to get started because I had been very impressed when my dad, Mim, and I went for orientation. The building was quite old but newly renovated from a school that had been closed years before. It was located at the edge of midtown near Chelsea, a quick subway ride from Mim's apartment. It was fairly spacious with three levels and hardwood throughout. It felt different from my other school. It felt warm and inviting, like a safe haven. Like a sanctuary.

I jumped out of bed early on the first day of school. My dad and I had decided to leave a half hour earlier than usual, so I was awake before dawn. Amanda and Ashley weren't starting school until the following week, so I was careful not to wake them. I was almost ready and had just gotten dressed when someone knocked on my door. I assumed it was my dad; but when I opened it, Amanda was standing there.

"Hey, can I come in?" she whispered.

A little surprised, I opened the door further and stood back. "I didn't wake you did I?" I asked.

"No, not at all. I was hoping to see you before you left. I wanted to check out what you were wearing."

I stood back, held out my arms, and shrugged. "I guess this," I said. It was the same outfit I had put together for my dad to see the day we bought uniforms.

"I really like it, Roda. It looks really cute on you," she smiled. It was a genuine smile. "May I make a few small adjustments?"

"Sure," I said, grateful for any good advice.

She adjusted my skirt a bit lower and had me tuck in my shirt a bit straighter. We both thought it looked better to have the cardigan unbuttoned. It would be too confining otherwise. She unbuttoned my shirt collar and flipped it up in a very preppy manner and then adjusted the cardigan around it. She pushed the sleeves of my sweater up, unbuttoned my shirt cuffs and rolled them up. She stood back and looked at her work. "Almost done," she said thoughtfully. She unbuttoned my top button and spread the collar a little further apart. Her eyes got wide. "I have just the thing! Be right back," she whispered. When she came back, she had a short strand of fake pearls she had worn to Homecoming. She hooked the necklace around my neck and then stood back admiring her work. When I looked in the mirror, I had to say it was a big improvement.

She approved that my hair was down rather than up in a ponytail. It looked pitiful either way. Then, looking at my feet, she said, "Roda, you need flats, not sneakers. Sneakers are only for gym." Ah, a secret I was not aware of until then. No wonder people laughed at me before. She dug through my closet and found a navy pair. "Perfect," she said. So I changed into them and then we both looked in my mirror to admire the finished product. "Very good," she said. We hadn't noticed that Daddy was standing in the doorway, ready to leave.

"What are you girls doing?" he smiled.

"Amanda was helping me get ready," I said, smiling back.

"Well, you look wonderful. You did a good job, Manda."

Amanda smiled, feeling good about herself. She hugged both of us goodbye and went back to bed.

The day went by very quickly. Too quickly, in fact. I had never enjoyed school more. All of my teachers were wonderful and encouraging; and while I didn't quite find a friend, all the kids were friendly and inclusive. We were all new. We were all learning who each other was, so no one was better than anyone else. And we were all excited about the new school year. I was most excited knowing that I would no longer be in the shadow of my sisters. I was my own person now, and no one around me— neither teacher nor student—had ever heard of Amanda or Ashley Allen. And furthermore, no one in the world knew who Paige Allen was. It was absolute bliss.

***

My sisters started school that following Monday. Amanda was a junior and Ashley was going into eighth grade. Dinner was already on the table when my dad and I arrived home around six o'clock. We sat down as soon as we walked in. I didn't have time to change out of my uniform, and I feared Paige would laugh at me again, but she didn't. She seemed very subdued. My dad was asking my sisters about their first day and telling Ashley that, just one more year, and she would be in high school too.

"The three of you are growing up too fast," he said pensively.

I think that may have been when a sad feeling began to come over me. My dad and I had a great conversation on the train ride in that evening; but somehow sitting at the table that night, I began to feel very depressed and alone. It was hard to describe.

Dinner had been calm. Eerily calm. Paige never spoke. My

sisters talked some but were subdued as well. I wondered if they had the same feeling of sadness I had, but I never asked. The rest of the night was uneventful. As the night wore on, my feelings grew even more melancholy. It was a very dark, ominous feeling that I couldn't understand, and I couldn't shake it. My dad spent time with all three of us that night, one on one. When he came into my room, we talked about how much I loved my new school, which classes I liked best, and that I was getting along with the kids there. I could tell that was most important to him.

He seemed down. And just like me, he couldn't understand why. There were so many things I wanted to ask him about, but I just didn't. He had told me so much about when he and Paige dated and were first married, and he had been very honest about everything. I guess I just wanted to know one thing, but I didn't ask. I was hesitant because I wasn't sure I wanted to know the answer. I knew my dad well enough to know that he would tell me the truth no matter how painful it might be.

He spent about an hour in my room, and it was nice to have all that time just to talk instead of having to struggle through homework or studying. All that work had subsided through the years as I gradually got better in school. I never made straight A's, but I was getting A's, B's, and some C's. Not perfect but it was passable. Now with my new school, I was off to a great start. It was early, but I already loved my teachers and found them to be highly motivating and inspirational. I felt optimistic, and we talked about all of that. He seemed very pleased, knowing he and Mim had made the right move by getting me into the program. He seemed hesitant when he said goodnight, acting as if he had more to say; but he never said it. I fell asleep that night with an uneasy feeling I couldn't shake, and I tossed and turned all night.

The next morning, my dad woke me up before my alarm went off. He was sitting on the edge of my bed rubbing my hair, saying, "Wake up, sleepyhead," like he did when I was little. I opened my eyes and smiled up at him. He was in his pajama pants and t-shirt with his hair still messed up from sleep.

"Why are we getting up so early," I asked as I yawned.

"I forgot to tell you that I have an early meeting this morning, so I thought we needed to get an earlier start," he said gently.

"Oh, okay," I said, stretching.

"So hurry and get up, okay?"

"Okay, Daddy. I will."

I laid there for a minute after he left, realizing I still had that sad, ominous feeling. I could not figure out why. I tried to think of everything, but nothing made sense. I didn't have a test or an assignment that I was worried about. Paige had been subdued lately and nothing she had said or done bothered me. Amanda was being nice, and Ashley was rarely at home. I didn't have to deal with Allyson anymore. Nothing seemed wrong. The only thing I could think of was the question that had been nagging me. The question that I needed to ask my dad but had been avoiding.

My dad and I sat quietly on the train. He was studying his notes for the meeting, and I was sketching. I was glad I would be getting to school early. I was hoping to catch my algebra teacher for a quick tutoring session before class began. She had said she gets there early every morning, so that would be the best time to get with her if we ever needed any help.

"What are you drawing?" he asked after a while.

I looked up and smiled. "You."

He laughed. "Me? Why me?"

He had been sitting across from me, and I just thought he looked so handsome in his suit and tie with his glasses on. So I just felt like drawing him.

"Because you look so nice today," I said. "That's why."

He looked over at it and smiled when I turned it towards him. It was a good likeness, if I had to say so myself. He took my book from me and autographed the picture, trying to be funny as if he were some sort of a celebrity. I laughed at him, but I still couldn't shake the sadness.

With each step after we departed the train, my heart got heavier and heavier. By the time we were standing on the steps of my school saying goodbye, I started crying. It just burst out of me, and I had no control over it.

"What's wrong?" he asked, concerned.

"Nothing, Daddy. Nothing's wrong," I said, shaking my head.

"Now, Roda, something has to be wrong," he said soothingly. "Tell me what it is."

I shook my head. "I don't really know. I can't explain it."

He looked at me thoughtfully, not really knowing what to say. I knew he needed to get to his meeting, and I didn't want to keep him. "It's really nothing, Daddy. You need to go so you won't be late."

"Honey, I don't care if I'm late. Tell me what's wrong."

I stood there thinking, still trying to make sense of it. All I could think was that I needed to ask him "the question," so I did.

"Daddy . . ." I started, but then I hesitated.

"Yes?" he finally asked. "What is it?"

"Do you think . . ." He waited. "Do you think your life would be better . . . without me?"

His mouth dropped open. He was baffled. "Sweetheart, why would you *ever* think that?"

I shrugged and more tears came. "Just because," I paused. "Because you and Mother are always fighting because of me. And because she's never been happy with me. And I just think that if I had been different, your life would have been better."

He just looked at me with tears in his eyes, and he cupped my face in his hands. "Roda, don't *ever* think that way. Do you understand me? Don't ever think that you should have been different or that life could have been better. *You* are the best thing that has *ever* happened to me. Do you understand? Don't you ever, ever doubt that. What has happened with your mom has nothing to do with you. It has *everything* to do with her. Do you understand? She is the problem, not you."

He smiled down at me and then hugged me tightly. I was still crying, and so was he. He pulled back, looked at me, and said, "My sweet child, you are the most precious thing to me in this whole wide world, and I wouldn't trade you for anything. And one day, you'll know how wonderful you are, and you'll believe it. I *know* without a doubt that you're going to be something great, and I cannot wait to see what you become. Now listen to me, okay? From this day forward, I want you to work towards that. I want you to work towards achieving something great. Okay?"

I smiled, feeling better; and I nodded in agreement that I would do as he wished.

"You promise?" he asked, smiling.

I smiled. "Yes, Daddy. I promise."

We hugged and said our goodbyes as he kissed me on my forehead. He started to leave but then turned back. He dug in his pocket and pulled out a small slip of paper.

"I almost forgot," he said. "The message fairy left this under my pillow by mistake."

I tilted my head and smiled at him. He knew I didn't believe in the message fairy anymore, but he never failed to put the little notes under my pillow every morning. He handed it to me, and I unfolded it carefully. It read, *Everyone is worth knowing. Everyone.* A feeling came over me that I couldn't explain. It was a mix of happiness and sadness, of confidence and power, of compassion and forgiveness. I looked up at my dad and smiled.

"I like this one," I said.

He nodded. "So do I. It's true, you know? Everyone *is* worth knowing."

I stood there for a moment, thinking but not speaking. "Even Mother?" I finally asked.

He thought for a second and then nodded. "Yes, even her."

We said goodbye again, and then he turned to leave. I watched him walk away; and before he disappeared down the stairs to the subway, he turned and smiled and waved goodbye. For some reason—and I don't know why—but just as it was when I drew the picture of him on the train, I thought he looked more handsome than I had ever seen him look before.

Chapter 12

Sometimes in life there is a line of demarcation: a point where everything goes from being the same to never being the same again. It's the point where everything that happened before, during, and after is so deeply embedded in your mind that you can recall it as if it were yesterday—five, ten, even twenty years later. I had been feeling this eerie feeling since the night before and, for the life of me, could not shake it. Even as I sat in the hallway putting the finishing touches on the portrait of my dad that I had started that morning, I couldn't help but feel this sense of dread. I would pause, trying to figure out where it was coming from; but the answer eluded me. By getting to school early, I had hoped to meet with my teacher. I had forgotten, however, that her child was starting school that morning. So I just sat and sketched until my homeroom teacher arrived and opened the classroom.

Once inside, I immediately focused on the schoolwork at hand. Mrs. Wexler had vocabulary words on the board for us to copy and begin defining. My mind got lost in the task. It wasn't until about half an hour later that the sound of a distant thud jarred my focus. Everyone looked around at each other, wondering if they had heard it too. Our teacher went to the window to see if there had been a car accident outside. She turned from the window, perplexed that nothing was out there. Before she could cross the room to walk out into the hallway, sirens were racing down the street. She stood outside the door with other teachers who had begun to gather, insisting there must be an accident somewhere close by. All of the sudden, someone from the office down the hall had hurriedly motioned for them to come; so the teachers took off running, leaving their classrooms unattended. The kids around me talked in hushed tones, wondering what the commotion was about. For some reason, that eerie feeling I had been having overtook me, causing the hair on the back of my neck to stand up. That prickly feeling spread throughout my whole body, and I felt as if my blood were draining from me.

After a few minutes, the teachers began walking slowly back down the hall. Mrs. Wexler came in the classroom and closed the door very calmly. "Let's settle down now," she said in a subdued tone that masked her fear.

"What happened?" one of the boys asked. "Was it a bad wreck?"

"Let's just settle down," she repeated. It was obviously something bigger than a car accident. Something much bigger. And Mrs. Wexler was not at liberty to say at that moment. Whatever it was, the office administrator must have given instructions to keep the students calm and uninformed for the time being. But I noticed that when my teacher was looking around the room, gently telling some to sit down and others to turn around, her eyes landed on me for a brief moment. We locked eyes, and then she quickly looked away. My body went completely cold. I was completely numb, and all the noises around me were muffled and distant. Something was wrong, and I wanted to know what it was. I wanted to get up. I wanted to go talk to her, but I felt so weak that I probably wouldn't have made it to her desk without passing out. Tears started streaming down my face. Dread had begun to swallow me, and I felt as if I were drowning. She walked over to me and handed me a tissue and hugged me, wanting to tell me something but unable to do so.

Not too much longer, we heard another distant thud. This time, Mrs. Wexler bolted from her seat, flew open the door, and ran to the office. All the kids rushed to the door and filtered into the hallway. I sat there motionless, barely able to breathe. Within minutes, the teachers were marching down the hall with red eyes and tear-stained faces, directing students to return to their classes. All the kids were curious and asking what was wrong. Mrs. Wexler ushered all of her students back inside the classroom and closed the door.

"Boys and girls," she started in a serious tone, "please

141

begin packing up your things. School will be dismissed in thirty minutes. Your parents are being called as we speak to come pick you up."

She tried to sound authoritative and in control, but she was on the verge of tears.

"Mrs. Wexler, please tell us what's wrong," a girl asked.

"Class, there's been an emergency," her voice cracked. She looked down, trying to compose herself. When she looked back up, tears were falling down her face. She took a deep breath as the room grew dead silent. "There's been an emergency, and you will be dismissed for the remainder of the day."

"Did something happen to the school, Mrs. Wexler? Was there a bomb or something?"

"No, Michael. Now please pack up your things."

The intercom speaker crackled, and the principal made the same announcement, asking that everyone remain calm and orderly. Parents had been called, and students would be dismissed as their parent arrived. Mrs. Wexler stayed in the classroom momentarily and then appointed a girl named Lori to watch the class. She walked down the hall to the office and then came back to the room. She did so about three times. One by one, the students in my class filtered out as their mom or dad arrived. Soon, there were only five of us left. My dread continued to engulf me, and I began to shake. Moments later, I felt the earth tremble. Was it an earthquake? But it only lasted a minute or two. It didn't make sense. A new wave of panic came over the teachers, and again they headed for the office. Their faces were ashen when they returned down the hall. Surely by now the kids who had already been released knew what was going on outside, but the teachers were instructed to keep us calm and uninformed. All they would say was, "There's been an emergency." Sirens continued to blare down the street.

Before long, there were only three of us left. I decided it was time for me to go. No one was there for me yet, which was a grave concern. So as soon as Mrs. Wexler left the room and walked back to the office, I walked as quickly as I could out the door, ignoring Lori as she told me to stay in the room. I was still so weak, I wasn't sure I would make it down the hall. I broke into a sprint as I got closer to the main doors where parents and students

142

were still coming in and out, their faces contorted with sorrow. I rushed past a mother standing in the doorway; and as soon as I was outside on the steps, the sight of Mim stopped me dead in my tracks. She had just arrived and was about to walk up the steps. She stood there motionless with her cell phone up to her ear; and at the exact moment we were face to face outside, the North Tower of the World Trade Center fell in the distance. I saw it mere seconds before it collapsed and disappeared into a thick cloud of dust and smoke. Mim's phone went silent. She looked at it, and then she looked back up at me. I began to scream such a primal scream that it felt as if I was being turned inside out. I collapsed to the ground, and Mim rushed to hold me. "NOOO!!!" was all I could scream over and over. "NOOO!!! NO! NO! NO! NOT DADDY! NOT MY DADDY! NOT MY DADDY!" That's all I could say. And then I went into such a dark, sobbing state that I wasn't sure I was even conscious.

***

I collapsed at the exact spot on the steps where my dad and I had stood only a few hours earlier. I don't remember who picked me up off the ground. I don't remember leaving the school. I was never aware of moving from one place to another—whether by foot, by car, or by train. I had absolutely no memory of it. There was a vague recollection of being at my grandparents' house in Troy, but everything was dim lights and shadows, whispering and soft crying. I detected movement but didn't know who it was. I could feel covers being pulled up around me and someone trying to feed me soup or make me drink. I had no idea how much time had passed. There was no sense of time or space. At some point, I began to wonder where I was. I could fathom where I was physically; but mentally, I couldn't comprehend it. My thoughts were too muddled to know. I was somewhere in the recesses of my mind, trying to figure my way out. Everything was dark. The whole world was silent.

When I began to emerge from the darkness and became aware of my existence in life, the most excruciating pain overtook me. It was indescribable. My subconscious was waking up, and outside stimuli began to filter in. During my time in the darkness, I

143

was aware that my dad was gone, but I was in a protective dream state where consciousness didn't exist. When I began to emerge from it, I was overwhelmed with the reality of his death. The horrible, horrible reality of it. Mim would tell me later that it had seemed as if I were trapped in a bad dream, twisting and turning and screaming. They would try to gently coax me out of it by reassuring me everything would be all right. I could feel myself slowly waking up, but the pain didn't subside. It stayed with me. I would open my eyes and see the world clearly around me. I could hear people talking to me, but I couldn't respond. I do, however, remember the moment a conscious thought began to surface. It started as a soft whisper deep within the crevices of my mind and grew into a concern that would motivate me to return to reality. I thought of Amanda.

I began talking coherently early one morning two weeks after my dad died. Mim came in and opened the curtains, letting the morning light in. "What day is it?" I asked with such a parched mouth that the words croaked out of my throat. "Good morning, honey," she said softly as she sat on the bed and rubbed my hair. "It's Wednesday morning." That meant nothing to me. I wanted to know how long it had been since that terrible day. I asked; and when she told me, I began to cry. Two weeks, I thought. Two weeks without my dad. What made me begin to sob was the thought of having to live every single day for the rest of my life without him. She sat there and cried with me. I wondered how she and my grandparents had handled their grief while I was catatonic. She said by holding each other tightly and by tending to me. She said they cried most of the time, and then they would reminisce about my dad's life and laugh about things he had done, and then they would break down into tears again. "Healing," she said, "is a long process, and everybody does it differently."

I asked about my mother. I asked Mim if she had talked to her. She said she had. She called her that day and told her about me. She told her that she was taking me to my grandparents. She said my mother didn't object. Both she and my grandparents had called several times and talked to her in the past couple of weeks, offering for them to come to Troy and stay with us. She said my mother sounded kind but always said no to their offer. They never spoke to Amanda or Ashley. My mother always said they were sleeping. My grandfather had gone to check on them a few days after my dad died, and he said they were like zombies. He had asked if her parents were going to come and stay with them. My mother said no. Her parents were expecting out of town guests, and it had been planned months in advance; so they wouldn't come to her, and she and the girls couldn't go there.

I eventually got out of bed and took a long, hot shower. I had not bathed in two weeks. I had not eaten a real meal in that time span. Mim and my grandmother changed the sheets while I was up and had a hearty breakfast ready when I crawled back into bed. I was too weak to walk to the kitchen. It took time to build my strength back up. I pushed through the pain and willed myself to get better. My dad would not have wanted me to exist in such a state. He would want me to be strong. I made a promise to him that I would become something great, and my motivation was to make good on that promise.

Mim and I returned to her apartment on Thursday of the following week. It was a tough first step for both of us to take. Venturing back into the city after the devastation it had endured was far more difficult than I could imagine. The city seemed different. Quiet. Subdued. Paralyzed. For me, there was just emptiness. It was my dad's world, his favorite place to escape to; and now he was gone. Walking into the apartment for the first time was heart-wrenching. His absence was palpable. It was suffocating. I saw him everywhere, where he used to be. His shirts were there, his shaving cream, a crossword he did the week before he died. They were all reminders that he used to be but was no longer. I could feel myself sinking back down into that dark place. I could feel the depression returning. Mim saw it too, and she came over and hugged me tightly and rocked me back and forth. "Let's focus on the good times, okay?" she said, starting to cry. "Let's not be sad. He wouldn't want us to be sad." I nodded in agreement. "I know," I said. We sat on the couch and talked until late in the night, laughing and crying. I slept in Mim's room with her. Neither of us wanted to be alone.

I planned to return to school the following Monday. I had not talked to my mother or my sisters, and my mother hadn't called to summon me home. So for the time being, I stayed at Mim's. Going back to school wasn't easy. Remembering when I was last there and what had happened was overwhelming. I could feel a panic attack coming on, that darkness coming back. But I fought it. I took deep breaths, thought of my dad smiling, remembered the promise I made, and walked into Mrs. Wexler's first period class. Almost everyone was already in the room working on an early assignment. When I walked in, they all looked up. I froze, feeling the tears forming; but I smiled instead.

"Roda," Mrs. Wexler smiled and welcomed me as she got up from her desk, "we're so glad you're back. How have you—" she stopped herself. "I'm so glad you're back," she said, hugging me.

"Thank you," I said meekly. "I'm glad to be back."

"Roda, dear," she started, "I would like to talk to you for a moment, if I may." She looked over at a boy named Scott. "Scott," she called, "will you take Roda's things and put them away? Thank you," she said as he jumped up and took my backpack from me. She motioned for me to go out into the hallway and closed the door behind us.

"First of all, I want to tell you how very sorry I am for the loss of your dad. We all are," she said, looking at me gently.

"Thank you," I said. "I appreciate that."

She nodded. "I also wanted to tell you how sorry I am that I couldn't say anything . . . that morning. The administration made the decision to keep everyone calm by not telling what had happened. We've learned that other schools did inform their students as it was happening, but our principal . . . well, Mr. Garner . . . well, he just wanted to keep everyone calm." She paused for a moment. "I knew you had a feeling about something. I could tell from your tears and your demeanor. I wanted to say something, but I didn't know what to do . . . and I'm sorry I didn't. I knew your dad worked in one of the buildings, but I didn't know what might or might not have been happening to him. I just didn't want you to panic. I didn't want anyone to panic." She looked at me helplessly. "I'm sorry, Roda. I really am."

"Thank you, Mrs. Wexler," I said as I reached out to hug her. I felt as though I needed to comfort her because she seemed to have been carrying such a burden since that terrible day, and I wanted to release her from it. "It's okay. It wouldn't have made a difference one way or the other. It was better to keep everyone

146

calm."

She nodded in agreement. "I suppose," she paused, "but still."

We walked back into the classroom, both of us wiping away tears. I followed her to her desk where she handed me a small stack of makeup work to do. It was still the beginning of the school year, so I hadn't missed too much. Nevertheless, she told me to take my time. I sat at my desk and settled into the morning routine. It felt good to be engrossed in schoolwork. It was a good distraction, and there was solace in the normalcy of the day.

I learned throughout the day that four other students had lost a parent in the World Trade Center. One boy, Tyler Jackson, even lost both parents and had to go live with his grandparents in Minnesota. Mrs. Carson, a chemistry teacher, lost her brother-in-law. A couple of other students had an aunt or an uncle who had been in the Towers but had escaped unharmed. I could see where it was a wise decision to keep all of us uninformed the day it happened.

Everyone was very kind to those of us who lost someone that day. The teachers and the students went out of their way to help us. There was comfort in that. It made me wonder what it was like at my old school and how different it would have been for me that day and returning there as well. What would that have been like? I wondered how it had been that terrible morning for Amanda and Ashley, and I wondered if they had gone back to school yet. I decided I needed to go home. Not so much for my mother or even Ashley but for Amanda. I was worried about her.

Mim decided she would go with me that Friday because she was concerned about them as well, and she didn't want me going alone. We boarded the train that afternoon and headed to Greenwich. It had been a good week; but when I got on the train, a wave of sadness came over me again. Memories of riding home with my dad overtook me. Mim grabbed my hand and held it tightly the whole way home. We both had tears streaming down our faces, both knowing that this was going to be a very difficult experience.

When we were outside the train station in Greenwich, Mim dug in her purse for the keys to my dad's car. He had given her a spare set years ago. I knew where he always parked, so we walked over to the car. I was overcome with emotion when I saw it. I just stood there thinking that he was the last person to drive this car, he was the last to park this car, he was the last to lock this car; and all of it happened *that* morning, that terrible morning; and it hadn't been touched since. I could remember the last conversation we had in the car on that last morning and how we were laughing when we got out and shut the doors. I was standing there, remembering it almost as if I were watching a movie. Mim gently touched my arm, and it brought me back to reality. "Let's go, sweetie, okay?" she said. I nodded.

She hit the button and unlocked the door. When I got in, I could smell his cologne. Tears immediately fell down my face. His chewing gum, his favorite CD, a dry cleaning ticket, a Forbes magazine—they were all there. All of his stuff, and all last touched by him. I didn't want to move anything. I didn't want to disturb any of it. Mim wiped her own tears away and started the car. We drove in silence for the entire ten minutes it took to get home.

We pulled into the driveway, and Mim pushed the button to open the garage door. She parked the car in its usual spot. My mother's car was there. Amanda's car was there as well, parked in the driveway. We walked in the back door; everything was quiet. There was just silence. My mother's house was never messy, and it wasn't so much then, but it just didn't feel well kept. It was hard to explain. Mim called out, "Hello?" No one answered. I walked into the den; no one was there. I walked to my mother's room; she wasn't there either. My dad's room was down the hall, and I approached it carefully. I wasn't sure I was ready to face his room, filled with his personal belongings. That would be the hardest of all. But I walked that way as I looked for my mother, and I found her. She was asleep in his bed, curled up with some of his clothing surrounding her. It took Mim and me by surprise, and we stood there and looked at each other for a minute. I walked over and sat on the edge of the bed and touched her shoulder. I wasn't sure I had ever touched her before.

"Mother," I said quietly, "are you asleep?"

It roused her, and she turned over. She seemed somewhat dazed from sleeping. "What time is it?" she asked.

"It's five-thirty," I said.

She looked around, perplexed. She looked at me and then at

148

Mim. "What day is it?"

"It's Friday," I said.

She sat up, and I noticed she was wearing my dad's old Rutgers sweatshirt. She looked at me. "You're back?"

I looked at Mim and then looked back at my mother. "Yes, I decided it was time to come back."

She nodded. I had been imagining she hadn't called to tell me to come home because she and my sisters were doing perfectly well without me, but then I realized it was because she was stuck in the darkness. She was—and had been—where I was before, but she had no one to pull her out of it. She was dazed, and Mim supposed that she hadn't eaten anything in a while. She told me to go check to see where Amanda and Ashley were, and that we needed to look for some food to prepare. I left the room while Mim helped my mother get up and take a shower.

I walked upstairs sensing that, even though her car was in the driveway, Amanda would be out with friends. It was quiet upstairs, so I supposed both of them were gone. I looked in Ashley's room first, and I was right. She wasn't there. Next, I went to Amanda's room, expecting it to be empty as well; but I was wrong. It was almost six o'clock, and the room was growing dim. Amanda was lying on her bed facing towards the wall, still dressed in her school clothes. I suddenly remembered Amanda was a cheerleader. Shouldn't she be at the game? Yet she was here, sleeping.

I stood at her door. "Manda?" I said without realizing I had said her name the way my dad always did. She turned suddenly, startled. Disappointment suddenly crossed her face, and she burst into tears. She sat up and buried her face in her hands. I walked over and sat on her bed. I held her, and we cried together.

After a while, we started talking about that terrible day. That awful day. How we found out. The moment we realized our dad was gone. How the world changed that day. How it became small and empty and completely devoid of purpose. She told me how Mother fell apart and how Ashley exploded with anger and how she was stuck in between. She told me about friends visiting in the beginning and then tapering off. How people didn't know what to say. How Mother's parents never visited and still hadn't. She told me how supportive everyone had been at school, but how now they were acting as if everything was getting back normal; and she knew her life would never be normal again. So she floated through each day, trying to act as if she was okay, as if everything was okay. But it was just an act. She no longer felt like cheering and had quit going to practices and games. Her coach assured her that she was still on the squad and could come and cheer whenever she felt ready, but she didn't feel like she ever would again. Ashley was the opposite, though. She said Ashley threw herself into cheering and school—into everything—just to run away from the pain. She was never at home. She practically lived at Allyson's house, saying it was too depressing at home. Mother slept all the time; she was barely functioning. And in the middle was Amanda, and she was lost.

Mim came upstairs looking for us after a while. She walked over to Amanda and hugged her with one of those hugs only Mim could give. The kind of hug that envelops your soul and gives you strength and makes you fall apart at the same time. The three of us cried fresh tears, and we held on to each other. I was glad Mim and I came back. I was glad I didn't stay away, believing there was no use for me there. Amanda needed me, and she needed Mim. We talked for a few minutes before Mim told us that dinner was ready. She had found enough food in the kitchen to make vegetable soup and sandwiches.

When we got downstairs, my mother was already in the kitchen sitting at the table. Mim had fixed her a bowl of soup, and she was slowly eating. Her hair was still wet from the shower, and she had on fresh clothes but was still wearing my dad's sweatshirt. She looked up when the three of us sat down. She still seemed dazed.

"How are you doing, Paige? Would you like more soup?" Mim asked.

My mother thought for a moment. "No, I'm fine."

Mim disagreed and began to serve her more. "We need to build up your strength. Try to eat some more." My mother complied without objection.

Everyone had been eating quietly when I suddenly realized my dad's chair was empty. It hit me so hard, tears came to my eyes. How did I miss that? How did I walk into my house and not be as aware of his absence as I was when I got into his car? "You

150

okay?" Mim asked me. I nodded but felt as if I had somehow betrayed my dad's memory. Amanda looked at me and smiled a weak smile. She knew what I was thinking. She reached out across the table for my hand, and I reached for hers. She squeezed my hand to offer me strength.

"Sometimes," she said, "the living are distracted by other things. When you got here, you were worried about Mom and me. So for a moment, you forgot the sadness that you were feeling; and instead, you focused on us. And then you remember, and it comes rushing back. It happens in waves like that, you know? One moment, everything will seem okay; and then in the next moment, the world falls apart again."

I smiled sadly at her and nodded. "I know," I whispered.

The back door suddenly opened, and Ashley walked in. Allyson was behind her. They were just getting home from the game, still dressed in their uniforms. Allyson's parents were waiting in the driveway with the car still running. Ashley stopped and looked at us, and then she looked directly at me. "What are *you* doing here?" My mother looked up, still dazed, no response. I was speechless, but Amanda turned around and said, "Shut up, Ashley."

"Oh my God," was all Ashley said, and then she stormed upstairs. Allyson followed, but she no longer seemed haughty. She looked at me with a sad look and followed Ashley upstairs. A few minutes later, they came back downstairs. Ashley had an overnight bag packed.

"You're spending the night off?" Mim asked as she was putting dishes in the sink.

"Yes, I am," Ashley replied, sighing.

"You need to spend some time at home, Ashley. I want you to be back early tomorrow. Do you understand? By noon."

Ashley began to object, but Allyson interrupted. "We'll have her home by noon," she promised.

Ashley left without telling anyone goodbye. Amanda and I helped Mim clean up the dishes, and my mother retreated back to my dad's room and went back to sleep. The three of us contemplated watching a movie, but none of us really felt like it. Instead, we decided to pull out old photo albums and reminisce about Daddy. We talked quietly so we wouldn't disturb Mother.

There were times when Mim would have us laughing so hard, we had to cover our mouths to muffle the sound. Other times, we were crying. It was a healing exercise to remember his life instead of thinking about his death, and I think it helped Amanda more than anything.

Around midnight, we decided to go to bed. I told Mim that she could sleep in Ashley's room since she was gone for the night, but Amanda had a different idea. She asked if it was okay if she slept in my room with me, and Mim could sleep in her room. I was surprised but glad that Amanda needed me. My heart suddenly broke, knowing she had been alone for so many weeks, going through the pain on her own. I told her I would like that very much. Not long after, we collapsed in my bed, exhausted.

Chapter 13

Mim stayed with us for the next few weeks. Her primary goal was to get my mother up and eating and functioning. She would make her get out of bed every day, get her in the shower, fix her hair and makeup, and feed her three meals. She slowly weaned my mother off the antidepressants she was on; and before long, she had regained her strength. My mother was resurfacing, but she continued to live in silence. She expressed no appreciation, no opinion of what was happening around her. She was coming back to life; but she was still locked in a quiet, expressionless world.

Ashley continued to run away from the pain. Her anger made her meaner and nastier, so I just tried to stay out of her way. Mim would try to be the parent and instruct her when to be home or whether or not she could go in the first place, but Ashley continually ignored her. She was going through a rebellious period, and the only person who could possibly make her mind was my mother; but at that moment in time, she was completely useless. Amanda tried to talk to her—big sister to little sister, but Ashley didn't want to hear it. She tried to talk to her about our dad and that terrible day, but Ashley pushed her away. She spent so much time with Allyson and her family that we naturally wondered if they were offering her any guidance. We could only hope that they were. She continued to throw herself into schoolwork and cheering. She was trying her best to overcompensate and to be as normal as possible. Ashley, above all of us, refused to show any weakness.

Our dysfunctional family was trying to heal, but the dysfunction remained. I would like to say that we came out better on the other side of our grief, but that wasn't quite so. As things slowly started evolving into some sort of normalcy, we slowly started regressing into our former selves. My mother went from being a zombie to being distant and cold again. She was a shell of who she was before, but her superficial manner remained. I was astonished that even after Mim nursed her back to health, she could still be so ungrateful. We had really hoped that it could be a turning point and that some good would come out of such a horrific tragedy. We were wrong. Mim's presence was gradually not needed, and we went from her coming to our house every weekend to me going to her apartment again.

Amanda began to bend to my mother's will again. It was gradual and subtle, but I could see it happening. I could feel her pulling away from me. We had bonded through this tragedy and gotten closer than we had ever been before, but I could see her distancing herself as the weeks went by. She and I still had moments, but we were never as close as we had been. Ashley never improved. She was still bitter and continued to stay away, but that made it easier to avoid her.

My fifteenth birthday passed in November without recognition. Amanda did remember, and she wished me a happy birthday, but my mother and Ashley never acknowledged it. Mim took me out to eat the weekend following my birthday, and she took me shopping. She tried to make it a fun day for us, but I was just so profoundly sad not having my dad there with us. Something about turning a year older saddened me. Knowing each year that passed would push me further away from when he was there, and that each year would measure the time and distance from when I last saw him. I tried to look ahead, to guess how much longer I would live. That's a strange thing to do when you're fifteen, I suppose; but I was trying to estimate how many days I would have to spend without him. There were too many to count. I finally let go of calculating the infinite number of days, weeks, and months ahead of me by telling myself that my dad would not want me to live that way. He would want me to live my life to the fullest and to enjoy every minute of it. But above all, he would want me to work hard to fulfill the promise I made to him—to become something great. That became my motivation.

Christmas came and went. We didn't celebrate. We didn't put the stockings up or even a tree. My dad was the one who always got everyone into the Christmas spirit. That year, we just didn't have the energy. Mim and I spent Christmas Eve and Christmas Day with my grandparents. They had decorated for the season but not to the extent they normally did. There wasn't a big family dinner. It was much more subdued—just Mim, my grandparents, and me. We had asked my mother and sisters to come, but they declined. My mother's parents did visit briefly on their way to the airport. They flew out of LaGuardia on their way to London. That's where they spent the holidays.

I could sense that Amanda wanted to come with us but was too afraid, and my dad wasn't there to make the decision easier for her. Mim, my grandparents, and I tried to celebrate by remembering all the fun things about my dad during the holidays. He absolutely loved Christmas, and my grandmother had several new stories from his childhood that I had never heard. We had moments of laughter and smiles, but it was painful to celebrate without him. It felt empty and hollow, and I didn't think Christmas would ever feel special again.

***

I was surprised one day to come home and find my mother standing in my room. She didn't see me. She didn't know I was standing in the doorway. She was looking through my sketchbook that I had left on my bed; and when she got to the picture of my dad on the train the day he died, she stopped. It took her breath. I stood there watching as she stared at it and moved her hand across it. She took her finger and traced his signature and the date that he had playfully written. Her hand went up to her face as she wiped the tears away.

"I drew it on the train that morning," I said softly, hoping not to startle her.

She turned and looked at me, still holding the sketchbook. She nodded, and then looked back down at it. "It's really beautiful, Roda. Such a good likeness of him. You are as talented as he said you were."

I smiled, surprised at her candor. "You really think so?"

She looked at me. "Well, yes of course. But it's no surprise, really. You take after Miriam in every way possible, so it would

155

only seem logical that you were a good artist as well."

My mother was a master at the backhanded compliment. Yes, I did count it as an honor that I took after Mim in every possible way, but my mother meant it as a slap. That's all it was meant for. She closed my sketchbook and laid it back on the bed. She said it was time to start dinner, and she walked past me and out of the room. I thought for a moment that I should volunteer to help, but I was taken aback by what had just happened. For a brief moment, I thought we might actually have a bonding experience, but my mother made sure we didn't. How I would have loved to sit and have her look at the other pictures in my notebook, and ask her what she thought of each one, but it was not to be. I sat in the quiet solitude of my bedroom and began my homework.

A week later, I came home to a much different scene. It was report card day for Amanda and Ashley, and they were sitting in the den with Mother, who was most unhappy. I heard her lecturing when I came in the back door. She was berating Amanda about trying harder, making more of an effort, doing better than she had because what she had done was *not* acceptable. I walked up and peeked around the corner, not wanting anyone to see me. Amanda was sitting on the sofa as Mother paced back and forth in front of her, lecturing. "How could you do this, Amanda? How?" she asked over and over again, expecting an answer. Ashley was sitting nonchalantly in my dad's chair in the corner of the room, thumbing through a magazine. I walked in the room to find out what was going on. If my dad were there, he would want to know.

"What's wrong?" I asked, looking at Amanda. All three of them looked up at me: my mother and Ashley thinking I had just said something stupid, and Amanda with pleading eyes.

"Well, if you must know," my mother said smartly, "she got a B on her report card. Not all A's but a B!"

Well, this was a travesty, I thought. This was definitely, in the broad scope of everything, the end of the world. I looked at Amanda. "What did you get a B in?" I asked innocently.

Before she could answer, my mother interrupted. "*What* does it matter which subject it was? She got a B! She has never in her life gotten a B, and I will not stand for it now!"

I could imagine my dad mockingly saying, "Well, if you won't stand for it, how are you going to change it? It can't be changed." I smiled inwardly at the thought. I decided to be reasonable and try to help my mother rationalize the situation. I looked at Amanda and smiled gently, and then I looked at my mother.

"Mother, don't you think you're being a little harsh? Think about everything we just went through. It would not be unreasonable for our grades to fall. I think you should take that into consideration."

"Said the girl whose grades always fall," Ashley interjected flatly.

My mother eyed me viciously, daring me to try to make an excuse for Amanda's failure. "Is that so, Roda?" she asked with contempt. "Then will you please explain, if that is your premise, why Ashley was still able to make straight A's?"

"Yes, Roda," Ashley said sarcastically, "please explain why that is."

"I *can* explain it, thank you very much. It's because you, Ashley, handled your grief by throwing yourself into your schoolwork, trying to run away from reality. Trying to ignore the pain. Meanwhile, the rest of us suffered through the sheer agony of it all, not having the energy or even the gumption to do something as simple as brushing our teeth. Isn't that right, Mother?" I asked, looking at her and knowing she knew exactly what I was talking about.

She looked away, realizing I had a point. "Regardless," she said, looking at Amanda, "anything less than an A is unacceptable. You've always known that." Amanda looked down at her hands.

"Well, Roda," Ashley continued, "if what you're saying is true, then your grades must really suck. What did you get?"

I had my report card in my backpack and was waiting until the weekend to take it to Mim's, but I decided it was okay to show them and to have my mother sign it instead. I went to retrieve it from my bag, and then I went back into the den and handed it to my mother. Her eyebrows rose slightly. I had four A's, two B's, and a high C in Literature. Not perfect, but she was surprised my grades weren't lower. Instead of complimenting me, she turned it on Amanda. "Well now, it looks as if you aren't doing much better than Roda." She handed my report card to Amanda. Amanda looked at it and then looked at me. "Roda, you did really well."

She sounded surprised.

"Let me see," Ashley said, walking over. She grabbed the paper and surveyed it. "Not bad for you, I guess."

My mother grew impatient with the direction of the conversation. She was still furious with Amanda, so she told her to go to her room and stay there. She told her she couldn't stand to look at her anymore. She was grounded, she informed her; but that didn't matter to Amanda. She rarely went out since Daddy died.

A few days went by, and the consequences of the dreaded B began to set in. Mother gave her the silent treatment, and Amanda was all too aware why. Not cheering with the squad during football season was one thing—and could certainly be made up during basketball season, but a B on a report card was permanent. Mother bragged about Ashley every chance she got but ignored Amanda completely. The manipulation continued. I walked upstairs one day and heard Amanda crying softly in her room. I peeked in and saw that she was lying on her bed. I walked over and sat on the edge next to her.

"Hey," I whispered, "you okay?"

She turned over, wiping her eyes. "I can't stand how she ignores me. I just can't stand it. Like I'm not important. Like I don't even exist."

Ah, she was talking to the expert. "I know," I said.

"I've been trying my best. And the thing is, I don't want to try at all," she said, looking at me. "I don't want to do any of it. None of it matters to me anymore. I'm so sick of school and I'm so sick of my teachers and I'm so sick of the kids. They vote me class favorite like they worship me, and all I can think is that it's just so useless and *pointless*."

I nodded, agreeing with her. I thought of something, and I told her I would be right back. I went to my room and pulled out a box from under my bed. It contained hundreds of little pieces of paper that the message fairy had left me throughout the years. I had kept every one of them that my dad put under my pillow. I dug through them, hoping to find the one that I was looking for but knowing it might take forever. Luckily, I found it within minutes. It was a miracle, but I knew it was there. I took it to Amanda's room and handed it to her.

"This is what Daddy would say about it," I told her. She

looked at me curiously, almost as if I were delusional; and then she looked at the paper. It read, *A is for artificial because an A does not show how amazing or brilliant a person truly is.*

She looked at it for a moment, and tears began to form in her eyes. She rubbed her thumb over the lettering he had printed. I told her about the message fairy he had created, and I told her that he had left that particular note under my pillow the day after I got my very first report card and had nothing but C's and D's on it. She didn't speak for the longest time. Finally, she looked up at me.

"He did this every day?" she asked, holding up the message.

I nodded. "Every school day. But not during the summer or on weekends," I added, shaking my head.

She was very quiet and continued to look at the paper. "I never really felt like I had a dad. It always seemed like he was only your dad," she said sadly.

I was perplexed. "That's not true. He always tried to do things with you. He always tried to include you and talk to you." I didn't want to say what I was really thinking, that she always turned him down.

"Yeah, I guess. But he never did special stuff like this for me. He never left me messages."

"Well, I know. But he always felt like he had to build up my self-esteem. You know?"

She just looked at me.

"He was all I had," I said quietly.

"But you had all of him. I only had part of him," she said almost angrily. "It was never fair that he gave you so much attention."

"But I didn't have a mother. She has never been a mother to me. You know that. What she's doing to you now—ignoring you, that's what she has done to me my whole life. So he had to give me more attention because of her. Don't you understand? He had to be both a mother and a father to me. It's not that he loved me more than you. I promise it's not. I know how much he loved you and Ashley. He loved all of us very much. It's just that he couldn't always show it to you, or you couldn't always return it because you were too afraid of Mother."

"Do you know how jealous I've always been of you? Do

you?" she asked through tears.

I stammered. "You've been jealous of me? *You* have been jealous of *me*? Why?"

"Because you had his love and all of his attention. And because he always took you with him into the city, and then he got you into that school. It's just not fair! It was never fair!"

I didn't know what to say. I never even considered that she was harboring such jealousy. She always acted indifferent and aloof, but I began to understand why.

"I'm sorry, Amanda. I never knew you felt that way. And I'm sure Daddy never knew you felt that way either. He knew you were scared of upsetting Mother, but I'm sure he never thought he was neglecting you. He wanted us to do everything together. He really did."

She nodded. "Yeah, that's true. I know."

We talked for a while, and I reflected back on all the things he tried to get her to do. She was amazed at my memory. We talked about the trip to Mim's that weekend when we were little and how great it was. I told her that she should go with me one weekend to Mim's, but she said she couldn't. She knew Mother would be mad. She asked to see more of my messages, so we went into my room and looked through them. Before long, we heard Mother come home with Ashley. Amanda jumped up and ran to her room, and we pretended to ignore each other for the rest of the night.

Chapter 14

~*January 2002*~

On the surface, we were healing. It had only been four months since September 11th, but we were functioning. We were moving forward like we were supposed to, like everyone expected. We assumed our roles and acted accordingly. Nothing really changed except we added another level of dysfunction. We saw counselors, but that required getting in touch with our feelings, so it didn't last long. My mother didn't believe in such endeavors. So we just existed. Conversation, if there was any, was purely perfunctory. Mother never asked how we felt about losing our dad. She never expressed the emptiness she felt. She was a strong woman who showed no weakness, but we desperately needed her to break apart. We needed her compassion and her love, but all Amanda and Ashley got were her demands and her expectations, and all I got was her silence. Ashley was extroverted and ambitious to a fault, hoping to prove that the pain would not get the best of her. Amanda became quiet and reserved, withdrawing from her life. She was the antithesis of Ashley. Amanda had once considered her grades, her friends, and her extracurricular activities to be the most important things in life. Now she was well aware at just how inconsequential—how trivial—all of it was. Nothing much mattered to her because she had lost something precious, something special, something irreplaceable. And the real tragedy was that she didn't value its worth when she had it. Such is the definition of loss: not knowing how priceless a person is until they're gone.

So we existed inside our own grief bubbles, floating through life—life as we knew it at that point. I was still determined to succeed and to make my dad proud. But existing in the cautious state I was in kills a person's spirit. It's a slow, almost undetectable death, but it happens. Silently. Then one day, you look back upon your life and realize that you have made little to no progress. If you're not careful, you can become complacent in your grief and die right along with the dead. The land of the living is meant for the living, and the living must move on and let go of what once was. That is the way our loved ones would want it. That's the way my dad would have wanted it.

I had a dream one night. My dad came to me and said, "Let's take a drive." So we got in the car, and we were driving around twists and turns on a very hilly road, and I started crying. I was pleading with him to turn back because I was scared. I knew in my dream what was ahead. I knew his death was around the turn and down the road, and I pleaded with him to turn back. But he wouldn't. He just kept driving and laughing. And then the meaning came to me in his voice, saying, "Don't be afraid of what's ahead. Even if it's dreaded; even if it's scary; even if it means I'm not there. Your future is ahead, past the twists and turns and the bumps in the road. It is there. Go after it!" I woke up from my dream knowing it was time to make a change.

That morning, I watched the sun come up. I watched the darkness disappear and the fog on the horizon clear, and I smiled at the strength I felt. It was a strength that I felt from within. There was nothing external about it.

My mother had plans to take the girls shopping that day and then haircuts and manicures that afternoon. It was a typical Saturday for them, and it was typical for me to be left behind. I watched them leave. I watched them walk out the door, completely unaware that they would never see me again. It would be a relief for my mother. A breath of fresh air, an unwanted burden finally released. Ashley probably wouldn't even notice. I wasn't sure how Amanda would feel. It scared me not knowing that for sure, so I dismissed the thought.

I had begun to pack my things early that morning. My room was fairly sparse. It was never decorated the way my sisters' rooms were. It was plain, but that was fine with me. I had a few bags of clothes and a box full of childhood memories. I packed every book my dad had ever bought me and read to me. I would never part with those. One day, I hoped to try to mimic his voices and read them to my own children—if I ever had any.

I called a cab; and while I waited, I took care of two last things. I took my box full of messages and left it on Amanda's bed. I had thought to write a note to my mother but decided my absence wouldn't need explanation. I did, however, leave a note for Amanda, and I left it with the box. It read:

I'm sorry I have to go, but it's time. I can't live here any longer in a place where no love exists. When Daddy was here, I had his love; and that sustained me. But now, there is nothing. I feel close to you, and I'm glad we've shared the moments we have, but even that's not enough to keep me here. I want you to have this box of all of Daddy's messages. He gave them to me to build me up, knowing I needed encouragement. Now I want you to have them. Promise me that you will pull one out every day and read it. Just one a day. And hopefully, whatever is going on with you that day, whatever happiness or sadness you're feeling, hopefully his words will speak to you. I love you very much.

Love,
Roda

I looked around my house before I left—every room. I sat in my dad's chair in the den. I smelled the clothes still hanging in his closet. This would be the last time I was here. It felt sad but liberating at the same time. I walked from room to room remembering the good times. It was hard to believe there were any. My dad made this home for me, and I could see him everywhere. Should I stay and be content with just the memories? He would say no. So when the cabbie came, I had him load up all of my things. The last thing I did before walking out the door was to tear out a picture from my sketchbook and leave it on the kitchen table for my mother. It was the last portrait of my dad. It had touched her. It was something of mine she actually liked, so I wanted her to have it.

It took a couple of hours to venture into the city by car. The distance and the traffic were time consuming, but I reached Mim's apartment within a few hours. I had already planned to come that day, but she had no idea it would be a permanent visit. I rang the buzzer; and when she answered, I asked if she could come down for a minute. "Well, honey, why can't you come up?" she asked sweetly. "You'll see," was all I said. When she got downstairs and saw the cab and saw all of my things in the trunk, she immediately leapt with joy. She bounced up and down, clapping her hands and said, "You're staying! You're staying! You're staying! I'm so glad you're staying!" I told her to use some of that energy to help me carry all of my stuff upstairs. We had a lot to do.

I always made a point to know everybody's name, and the cabbie's name was Sylvio. He was Italian, and he hated his name but had learned to accept it. I told him my name was Roda. He winced. I said that I completely understood. He agreed. But Sylvio was a very nice cabbie—probably about thirty-five years old, and he helped us take all of my stuff up three flights of stairs. So in turn, Mim paid him a very large cab fare and a very large tip. It was well worth the money, and he appreciated it.

It didn't take us long to set up my room. We were done within an hour. Afterwards, we sat on stools near the terrace and painted. Mim was so excited that I would be there with her from then on. I was excited too, but I was nervous wondering what was happening at home. It was mid-afternoon, and my mother and sisters would be getting back around then. I wondered what their reactions would be. I wondered if my mother would call and demand that I come home. I wondered if she would even bother to call at all. One thing I didn't anticipate was how I would truly feel about leaving it all behind, knowing I would never go back. It was a very strange feeling now that I had ventured to the other side. Now that I had escaped.

The phone never rang that night. I had dreaded my mother calling, but it made me even sadder when she never did. I guess I would have to say that the greatest gift my mother gave me was letting me go, but how generous was it since she never wanted me in the first place?

***

My dad was a financial genius; and in his death, he provided quite well for my mother. She would never have to worry about money, not that she ever did. But one thing he knew without a shadow of a doubt was that she would never provide for me. So he had set aside a separate life insurance policy just for me, with Mim as the custodian. I had no idea until Mim told me, but it was a one million dollar policy with double indemnity for accidental death. I was glad to know he had thought of that because I did not want to be a financial burden to Mim. I knew she never saw it like that, but I didn't want it to be that way. I was glad to know that there would be money to go to college on because I had every intention of going. New York University was my first choice—and there was not a second choice.

My passion was art, and I wanted to follow in Mim's footsteps. I wanted a degree in art history. I wanted to have my work displayed in galleries all over the world. I wanted to be eclectic, and I wanted to sketch and paint the scenes of New York. I was a true artist at heart. I had a gift, and I intended to go as far as I could with it.

In February, an afterschool photography class started at McKinley. It started as an attempt to see how much interest there would be in making it a regular class elective. It was the brainchild of Dr. Henry Hawkins, a sociology professor at NYU. He sought to incorporate art with science—particularly as it dealt with the human psyche. Just out of curiosity, I went to the initial class on a Monday. I was immediately fascinated with it. Capturing time and space, human emotions and human frailty with a single picture. I wrote down the camera he recommended we have and was determined to get it that week. Mim's art did not venture into the world of snapshots, so her camera was pretty basic.

I returned the next Monday with my new camera, ready to capture the world. I realized very quickly that I lacked the knowledge needed to actually use the camera in the way Dr. Hawkins wanted us to. Aperture, backlighting, ISO speed, depth of field—it was all Greek to me. Perhaps a remedial course was needed. I just wanted to point and shoot. I bluffed my way through it and tried to appear as competent as possible. When I got home, I retrieved my owner's manual from the box in which it came and decided to at least study the basic functions of my very expensive 35mm professional zoom camera. I decided that I may have been a little too optimistic with this endeavor.

During the following week, I spent a lot of time outdoors

just trying to get the feel for my camera. Within a few weeks, I had become knowledgeable enough to actually take a decent picture in a variety of settings. Some of my earliest pictures were basic: a shot of the street below Mim's terrace, in black and white; a bird perched on a parking meter, in full color; children running in the park were snapped in full motion with a blurred background. We presented our first attempts at greatness to Dr. Hawkins, and he was quite unimpressed with all of them. The only thing remotely positive he had to say was about my picture of the view from the terrace. In it, there was a car parked at the curb and a man leaning against it with his head back and eyes shut. I hadn't really even noticed him. "What is going on here with this man?" Dr. Hawkins asked. "What is he thinking? What is he doing?" I looked around, perplexed. I had no idea. It was just a picture. He looked at me intensely. "Roda!" he said. "There is a story within every picture! Look for it!"

Afterwards, a girl came up to me outside, pointed to a man hailing a cab, and said, "Roda! Look at that! There's a story! Take a picture of it! Do it now!" She mimicked his gruff voice effortlessly.

"What's the story?" I shot back.

"I don't know!" she continued to mimic. "I was hoping you could figure it out and tell me!"

I laughed and said, "Well, I think he's just hailing a cab. End of story."

"No!" she said. "That cannot be it! There must be more! Some reason for the cab! Some place to go! Some reason he cannot walk! Human behavior is not that random! There is a reason!"

I could hardly catch my breath, I was laughing so hard. Her voice and her mannerisms were a dead-on imitation of him. She started walking away, so I called after her.

"What's your name?" I asked.

She looked back and waved. "My name is Charley Webber. I'll see you later!"

I waved back.

And with that, she was gone. How intriguing to initiate such a hilarious moment and then walk away so casually. That goes against all sense of common courtesy, but it leaves the person you walked away from that much more curious.

166

I grabbed my camera before she could get too far away, and I snapped a picture of her skipping down the sidewalk. She had jet back hair with a thick purple streak, and she was dressed all in black with white Converse sneakers. Very unusual. There was a story there, for sure. I decided I would title her photo "Uninhibited" because she was without fear or self-consciousness. She felt completely free to be herself, and I envied that.

***

I found out the next day that Charley was a new student who had just transferred from Ohio. Her dad was in the Army and had been assigned to Fort Hamilton in Brooklyn. Her family lived in Chelsea, however, which was within walking distance of the school. I didn't have her in any of my classes, but I overheard a boy mention the girl with the purple hair and knew exactly who he was talking about.

She spotted me at lunch and came over and sat down. "Hi, Roda. Mind if I sit with you?" she asked, as if I had known her forever. I nodded, admiring her confidence. I would have never been able to go up to a person in a group and start talking, even if I had talked to them briefly the day before. A few other students from my English class were sitting with me. They smiled and made room for her. She sat down and began eating her lunch, and she immediately inquired about everybody sitting around us. She asked their names, where they lived, and which classes they were taking. I was mesmerized at the friendly reactions she was getting and how quickly she bonded with everyone. I wished I could do that, to be so brave and so outgoing. She entertained us with the funniest stories of her life and the places she had lived. Since her dad was in the military, they had been stationed around the world. She was a fascinating person.

Charley and I met up after school, and we walked to her apartment a few blocks away on West 21st Street. Judging by her artsy appearance—which bordered on the alternative, I assumed she would have lived in an old building whose character surpassed its amenities. I was wrong. She lived in a very plush, upscale apartment complete with a dutifully dressed doorman named Sam.

"Hello, Sammy," she said brightly as he opened the door

167

for us.

"Good afternoon, Miss Webber," he announced regally as if he were greeting the Queen of England. "I trust your first day at school was satisfactory."

"Oh," she sighed, "it was lovely, Sammy. Really it was."

He nodded without a smile and dryly said, "Well, may you have many more just like it."

She playfully saluted him and then walked ahead. He half way saluted back. I looked at him and smiled. "My name is Roda." I reached out and shook his hand.

"And I am Sam," he said, returning my gesture.

"It's nice to meet you, Sam," I said.

"It is nice to meet you as well," he replied with half a smile.

I knew from her exchange with Sam that Charley and I were a lot alike. We both believed in acknowledging people who might otherwise be ignored. She told me in the elevator that she noticed when they moved in that Sam didn't talk much, and people didn't talk much to him either. So she had decided to make a point to talk to him; and in turn, he would have to talk back. I liked that about her.

Her apartment was amazing. It was on the 17th floor, had wall to wall hardwood, impeccable furniture, and nothing but windows. My God, the windows. The apartment faced northeast so there was the most extraordinary view of the city in all its splendor. The Empire State Building was center stage. I stood there transfixed for a moment before Charley's mom emerged from her bedroom. She was tall and thin like Charley, with shoulder length silver hair pulled back in a bun. She had a simple elegance about her, and she possessed the gentlest smile.

"Charley, darling! You're home. How was your day?" she asked, embracing her daughter. Then she smiled at me. "I see you have a friend."

"Yes, this is Roda Allen. I met her yesterday at the photography class I went to."

"Oh, yes, dear. You mentioned her last night. Roda, darling, it's so nice to meet you," she said warmly and embraced me with a hug as well. I smiled, surprised I had been discussed the night before. We talked with her for a few minutes, and then she excused herself to return to her work. They had only moved in the Friday before, but Mrs. Webber already had the apartment in such perfect order that it looked as though they had been there for months.

"Make yourselves at home, girls," she said as she was leaving the room. "There are snacks in the fridge."

Charley grabbed a small bowl of fruit, some cheese cubes, and bottled waters; and then led me to her room. It was spacious and a little messy compared to the rest of the apartment. And the décor was very different. It reflected Charley's alternative, quirky personality. Her bedding was black with different colored throw pillows: red, purple, electric blue, and lime green. The furniture was a more modern black laminate rather than the warm mahogany woods that were throughout the home. Her walls were covered with various movie posters—especially horror movies. There were a variety of photographs and paintings as well, all of them framed. In fact, even the movie posters were framed in the same sleek black frames as the others. I assumed the artwork was Charley's.

"My mom doesn't care what's hanging on my walls," she said, noticing I was looking around, "as long as she can frame it." She laughed as she opened a bottle and handed it to me.

I smiled. "Your mom seems really nice. Really . . . accepting," I said, searching for the right word. Her mother was poised and conservative, yet Charley was quite the opposite.

"She is," Charley nodded. "She's pretty cool."

I looked downward, pensive, thinking about my own mother.

She took a long sip of water and looked at me, tilting her head in curiosity. "What's wrong? Is your mom not?"

"No," I said, looking up, "she's not at all. In fact, I live with my aunt. I sort of ran away from home."

We settled on the bed, and I told her the whole story. She listened with rapt attention, a look of sad concern in her eyes. She cried when I described my dad's death. How he tried to call Mim at her apartment after the plane had hit, trapping him ten floors below it. How he finally was able to reach her on her cell phone. How she stayed on the line with him as she rushed to get to school so I could talk to him too, only to be lost when the Tower fell as soon as she got to me. The fear in his voice that Mim heard. How he had begged her over and over to tell me how much he loved me. How he had said there was no one more important in his life than me.

I told her about my sisters. I told her about Amanda and how she was the only reason I almost stayed. She nodded, understanding the sibling dynamic, especially when the sibling was brilliant. She told me about her older brother, Greg. How he was in his first year at West Point, following in their dad's footsteps. Smart, good looking, strong, athletic, conservative—the perfect son for Sergeant Major Carl Webber and Mrs. Elaine Webber. Then there was her: average intelligence, never serious, liberal leaning at a young age. There was a stark contrast between the two.

"I've always sort of been the idiot savant of my family," she said with a sad laugh.

"You're not an idiot savant," I told her. "What do you mean by that?"

She sighed. "It's just . . . I can be so fantastically smart one minute but so pitifully dumb the next. I can learn something quickly and then forget it the next day. My brother was extraordinary at birth. It took me forever to read—even longer to comprehend. It's actually a mistake to refer to myself as an idiot savant . . . their intelligence greatly exceeds mine."

She laughed at herself, but I saw the pain. Her parents didn't inflict it upon her either. She did it to herself, constantly comparing her ability to her brother's. It humbled her, and I admired that about her. I could relate to it. Our circumstances were very different, but we were very much the same. She was the happiest person I had ever been around, yet she was the saddest person I had ever met. I wondered if she felt the same about me.

"Your mother loves you anyway, doesn't she?" I asked.

She looked at me sadly and sincerely. "Yes, she does. Both my parents do."

"Then that's all that matters."

Chapter 15

Charley Webber was my first real friend. She was my best friend. I had met a lot of new kids at school and gotten along with all of them very well, but there wasn't anyone that I truly bonded with until Charley. There wasn't anyone with whom I had hung out with afterschool or spent the night with. She and I became inseparable. I absolutely adored her parents. I had been intimidated by her dad at first, thinking he would be a large, strict, overbearing man who barked orders at his family the way he would his cadets. But my fears were dispelled the moment I met him. He was a big teddy bear of a man who had tears in his eyes the moment he met me. Charley had told him about my dad, and he wrapped me within a warm hug and told me he loved me and was praying for my family. He immediately became like a second dad to me.

Charley loved Mim just as much. She immediately bonded with her and was fascinated by her career and her art. In that respect, she was really more like Mim than I was. Charley loved the coziness of Mim's apartment; and although it didn't have a punk flare, it really was more her style than her own prestigious apartment was. She spent just as many nights with Mim and me as I did with her and her family. I once showed her a picture of my mother, and she was shocked. She immediately said, "No, that cannot be. You are Mim's daughter. You really are. There was some mistake in the cosmos for you to be born from her. She gave birth to you so Mim could have you. I am certain of that!" I smiled at her certainty. Surely in some way she was right.

The school year was coming to an end, and Charley was spending the night with me one Friday night in mid-May. The three of us were having fun playing a game of Yahtzee and waiting for Chinese food to be delivered. Charley was doing her best impersonation of Dr. Hawkins as she played the game. She had Mim laughing so hard, she was rolling in the floor with tears streaming down her face.

"Roda! This cannot be! This is unacceptable!" Charley announced emphatically, mimicking his voice. "These dice are not complying! They are going against human emotion! Surely my extraordinary will and brain power can yield better results than this!" His strong belief in mind over matter was not lost on Charley. Mim, being a colleague of Dr. Hawkins, knew all too well that Charley was spot-on. She respected him above anyone at NYU, but she was amused as well by his idiosyncrasies. His wild gray hair that was a constant mess, his crazy bugged eyes that shifted in tandem as he talked, every statement that was said emphatically but without raising his voice, the way he held his hand up to emphasize his point. Charley had mastered them all. "Roda! I need new dice! Get them!" she demanded.

Mim was trying to catch her breath when the buzzer sounded from the street below. She rolled over, pulled herself up, and walked over to press the button to release the door for the delivery man. She cracked open the apartment door so Yang could let himself in when he reached the landing. She was wiping her eyes and digging in her purse, still laughing, when there was a soft knock on the door as it slowly opened. I had just rolled the dice when Charley and I looked up. It wasn't Yang standing in the doorway. It was Amanda. She was holding her pillow, a suitcase, and a few other things she had managed to carry up the stairs. There was a backpack slung over her shoulder, and she had a look of fear and uncertainty in her eyes. She looked at Mim and then at me.

Mim dropped her purse and hurried to her and hugged her. She took Amanda's things and put them just inside the doorway. I was stunned to see her. I never thought I would again. Charley looked at me, not exactly sure who she was. I slowly got up, never taking my eyes off of my sister. "Manda," I said and burst into tears as I walked towards her. She dropped her backpack, and we embraced as if we hadn't seen each other in years. We stood there hugging for several minutes; and Mim joined in, hugging us both.

The three of us were crying when we finally began separating ourselves. Charley had walked over and was standing by the kitchen table, smiling curiously. I turned and said, "Charley, this is my sister, Amanda."

Charley smiled at her and nodded. "I've heard a lot of good things about you," she said. Amanda smiled.

"Amanda," Mim said, trying to broach the subject tactfully. "What's going on? What are you doing here?"

Amanda looked around, realizing she hadn't been there since she was in third grade and was surprised she had actually found it. She looked at Mim. "I was hoping," she said quietly, "that I could live here too."

"You want to live here?" I asked, my excitement beginning to grow. "Not just spend the weekend but actually live here?"

She looked from me to Mim, searching for approval. "Well, I was hoping. I wasn't sure if I could, but I was hoping."

"Honey!" Mim exclaimed. "Of course you can!" She looked outside the door, wondering if Amanda had brought more stuff upstairs. "Do you have anything else with you?"

"Umm, yes," Amanda stammered. "I have more stuff downstairs in my car."

"Your car?" Mim was stunned. "You drove? You drove here tonight?!"

"Yes," she replied, not fully understanding Mim's surprise. "I left a few hours ago. It wasn't a bad drive," she assured us. "I had a map."

"A map?" Mim laughed. "Well, that's good, honey; but did that map help you fight Friday night traffic as you journeyed into this crazy city?"

Amanda smiled. "It really wasn't that bad."

Mim reached out and hugged her, proud of her bravery.

Yang arrived as we were focused on Amanda. Charley took the money out of Mim's purse and paid him, and then she began putting the food and plates on the table. "Well then," Mim said, seeing what Charley was doing, "let's eat. And afterwards, the four of us will go down and bring your stuff up."

Amanda nodded. "I tried not to bring too much," she explained. "I'm not sure there will be enough room for me *and* my things."

"Don't you worry," Mim reassured her as she came around her chair and hugged her from behind, "we will make room." I looked at Amanda and nodded in agreement. I was so excited to have her there.

The four of us worked diligently that night to put all of Amanda's belongings away. She had pared all of her possessions down to only her favorite things; but her favorite things filled the trunk, the backseat, and the passenger's side of the front seat. We used creative ways to store her things, and we were able to find a place for everything.

It was only when everything was put away and we were settled down on the sofa around midnight that we asked Amanda what had made her decide to leave. She sat there for a moment staring straight ahead but looking at nothing. She was deep in thought, trying to decide where to start. She took a deep breath and began telling us why.

"You know," she paused, "Mom told me once when I was younger that I was my mother's daughter. I was too young to know what she meant at first, but I learned later that it meant I was just like her." She paused again, thinking. "I wasn't proud of it at all. I didn't want to be like her. I *was* so much like her, but I didn't want to be. I could see how she acted. I could see how she treated people—and not just you and Daddy," she said, looking at me, "but everybody. How she would be so sweet and pleasant towards people and then rip them apart behind their backs. I didn't want to be that way. I could see it happening to Ashley. I could see her becoming more and more like Mom, but I knew with all my heart that I didn't want to be that way. And I could see how she was using Ashley against me to try to make me do better or try harder, and I was doing the best I could. Nothing was ever good enough for her. And how she treated Daddy," her voice cracked, and she began to cry. "And how she killed his love for her. And how she treated you," she said, looking at me again, "how she ignored you, and how she taught us to ignore you as if you didn't exist. You were right, Roda. Daddy did have to be both parents to you. For so long, I had been so angry that you got all of his attention and love, but you were exactly right. He had to give it all to you because you had nothing else. I don't want to be like that. I don't want to be like her. And my greatest fear is that I will be, no matter hard I try not to be." She paused again and thought for a moment. "And then when Daddy died . . . you were right, Roda. Every bit of love was gone from that house. Every single bit of it. And when you left . . . when you left, there was nothing. There was absolutely nothing. Mom sunk further into her silence, Ashley stayed gone, and I was just there. Existing. Alone. I don't want to be alone. So I left. Mom was gone on a field trip with Ashley today. Somehow she pulled herself together and put on a fake, happy smile and left. So I packed my stuff and left too. But for good."

We sat there listening until she was done. We nodded in agreement, knowing she was right in how she was feeling.

"Did you leave her a note?" I asked. "Did you tell her why?"

Amanda looked over at me and then looked down. "No," she said, "I didn't. I didn't know what to say."

Suddenly and strangely, I felt sorry for my mother. It was one thing for me to leave; I was the one she didn't want. But it was quite another thing for Amanda to leave. Mim got up to comfort Amanda and tell her everything would be all right. I sat there in a trance, wondering about my mother. Wondering how she reacted when she came home and realized Amanda was gone. Did she, I wondered, have a good day out on a fieldtrip among the living—among the happy—only to return and find that her daughter was gone? Simply gone and only because of her own actions. I wondered how my mother felt when she looked at Amanda's empty room. Was she stoic and sullen, or was she heartbroken? I could imagine her reacting in her normal way—unaffected and unafraid, but I couldn't imagine the opposite. Strangely though, my heart broke for her at the possibility that she had fallen apart.

"Aunt Mim?" Amanda said, jarring me out of my thoughts.

"Yes, honey?" Mim answered gently.

"I was wondering about something."

Mim waited for her to continue. "What are you wondering about?" she asked, prompting Amanda.

"Well, I was just wondering if you thought," she paused for a moment, unsure. "If you thought maybe I could go to McKinley too?"

A smile of disbelief crossed Mim's face. "Honey! You want to go to McKinley?"

Amanda nodded eagerly. "I do. I've wanted to go since last year. Ever since you and Daddy told Roda she was going."

Mim remembered Amanda was a promising artist when she was younger, and she remembered my dad had the feeling she would like to attend McKinley as well, but Mim never thought Amanda would actually give up everything to go there. She nodded in affirmation. "Yes, I don't see why not. It should not be a problem at all. I will make some calls Monday morning."

Amanda smiled. She seemed relieved knowing there was a chance. I smiled at her and reached out and hugged her. For the first time in my life, I was actually excited that she and I would attend the same school. Charley, being the funny girl she was, hugged us in such a dramatic way that it made Mim join in as well.

"Please promise us," Charley playfully begged. "Please, please promise us that when you're voted most popular, you'll let us be part of your clique!" All of us broke into laughter.

"Absolutely I will," promised Amanda.

She smiled through the tears that had dried on her face. She seemed genuinely happy at that moment. She had been set free. She had found the courage, taken the key, unlocked the door, and freed herself.

* * *

~September 2002~

When school started in September, there was a mix of excitement and sadness. Amanda had her coveted gray McKinley sweatshirt and a closet full of school uniforms that only she could make look stylish, and I couldn't wait to have Dr. Hawkins for Beginning Sociology. But the looming anniversary of our dad's death hung over us all summer. It felt as though it had been the longest year of our lives, yet it seemed like it had just happened yesterday. How is it that our minds can play such tricks on us? Mim was the voice of reason. The three of us were quiet and reflective the night before school began, but it was Mim who finally said, "Girls, your dad wouldn't want us to feel this way. He would not." She looked at both of us, and we nodded in agreement. "Amanda," she said, "he would be so excited about this step you've taken. He would be so proud of the choice you've made.

He knew last year that you wanted to go to McKinley, and now you are. He would love that." Amanda nodded and smiled. "And Roda, his dream for you came true this past year. He dreamed that you would finally be in a place where you could grow and learn and begin to love yourself. He would be so proud of you. And he would be so proud of the grades you've earned and the challenging classes you're taking. He knew better than anyone that you could accomplish anything." I smiled and nodded in agreement. "Let's be happy," she said. "Let's just be happy right now and not worry about that date until next week, okay? Let's just be happy now," she repeated. "He would want it that way." Amanda and I smiled and agreed without hesitation.

Mim was so excited on our first day that she went with us and took pictures. It felt as though we were little kids on our first day of school. The excitement on Amanda's face was priceless, so I grabbed the camera just before we went inside and captured a moment in time of the exuberant look she had on her face.

Charley was already inside the building entertaining a few new students when she spotted us coming in. She waved excitedly and broke through the small group she was talking to.

"You guys are *finally* here!" she gushed. In just a matter of a day since the last time we saw her, she had gone from jet black hair with green streaks to bright red all over. It was quite shocking. The looks on our faces most likely conveyed our thoughts.

"Do you like it?" she asked proudly, running her hand through her hair. "It's in honor of our school colors. My mom and I did it last night."

"Your mom had something to do with this?" Amanda asked without thinking. I elbowed her, warning her to watch it.

"Sure!" Charley said happily. "The red was her idea."

Amanda was still in shock. "Did she mean for you to do it . . . all over?"

At that point, I went from being mortified to amused. Amanda wasn't intentionally being snobby, but she was bordering on it. Yet, there was a friendliness about it. She was deeply concerned with Charley's choices, but she wasn't judgmental. She genuinely liked Charley and had grown close to her over the summer. My mother would have never liked my best friend. She would have labeled her as weird. But I could see that Amanda

177

didn't feel that way at all, and I was glad.

Charley sighed dreamily. "No, it was my idea to do it all over. I was getting tired of the black to tell you the truth."

"What is your natural hair color?" Amanda asked. "And how long has it been since it's been that color?" This was a question I had wanted to ask but didn't know how to bring it up exactly. Amanda was just direct that way.

"Umm," Charley thought. "Well, my natural color is sort of a dirty blonde or light brown. And," she thought, "I think it's been about three years. It's a boring color really."

Amanda nodded. "Aren't you afraid you're going to fry your hair with all the chemicals you put on it?"

Charley shook her head happily and smiled. "No, not really."

Amanda and I looked at each other and laughed. Charley, we agreed without saying it, was her own person. Her own funny, independent, creative person; and we loved her.

Before we could disband and go to class, we heard a voice coming down the hall, getting louder and louder. His baritone voice was singing something from an old movie that I couldn't place, but it was clear and strong and quite funny. He walked down the crowded hallway, people parting as he moved through them effortlessly. He looked at everyone as he sang, imploring them to smile. He was a new student and definitely an entertainer. He was thespian material for sure. He was about to walk past us when the beauty of Amanda caught his eye. He stopped abruptly: stopped singing, stopped walking, stopped everything. He immediately propped his arm up and leaned against the lockers, his eyes fixated on her.

"Well, hello there," he said in a deep, romantic voice. He obviously had not realized he was gay yet.

Amanda smiled, genuinely amused. "Hello," she said confidently.

"My name is Max Garrison. What's yours?"

"Amanda Allen," she replied.

"Well, Amanda Allen," he said, taking her arm and looping it through his, "it's nice to meet you. May I walk you to class?" He was such a flirt.

She continued to smile. "Of course you can, Max

178

Garrison."

They began walking together, and he started singing "The Sound of Music" at the top of his lungs. Amanda walked beside him proudly, not minding at all that everyone was looking at them. She enjoyed the attention and found him completely hilarious. I knew immediately that Amanda had just met her new best friend. Charley and I looped our arms together, mocking them; and since neither of us could sing, we just skipped down the hall and hummed the same song as Max. It was promising to be a good year.

Chapter 16

The day I had been dreading came too quickly. The first anniversary of my dad's death loomed heavily on my heart. The night before the anniversary, I replayed every moment of that same day the year before in my mind as if it were in real time: the train ride home with him that night, the quiet dinner we had, the feeling I couldn't shake, the sadness he seemed to feel. I woke up early the next morning remembering how he had woke me up on that last day. Remembering the train ride back into the city; the picture I sketched; how handsome he looked; the smell of his cologne. It all came rushing back as clear as if it had just happened.

We left the apartment early to make the short subway trip to ground zero for the memorial. My grandparents had spent the night with us so that the five of us could go together. Everyone was crying the night before except for me, and everyone was crying that morning except for me. As sad as I felt, I didn't know why I wasn't crying; but I was preoccupied with my thoughts. I was also thinking about my mother and Ashley. I was wondering what they were doing and how they were coping. Mim had called and left a message on the machine when there was no answer. She told my mother that we would be going to the memorial and suggested that she and Ashley go with us, but my mother never called back. We didn't expect to see her.

The closer we got, the harder they were crying; but I was still stoic. We walked down the long ramp into the footprint of the Towers. We were holding flowers and pictures of my dad. We gathered with other mourners. We weren't related by blood or by marriage, but we were related by tragedy. We were all family, all of us who gathered to mourn. I felt as if we were at a funeral. I guess it was an overwhelming sense in some way because we never had a funeral for my dad—not even a memorial. We waited patiently each day, wondering if his remains would be located in the rubble. They never were. He was never found. There was nothing left. I don't think I had ever cried harder about anything in my life than I did the day we realized that. I would often think of him on that last day, the last moment I saw him; and realize that in a matter of a few hours, that beautiful person wouldn't exist. Not one shred of him.

I stood there the morning of the anniversary thinking of the first time I had seen the coverage on television, when I had actually seen the first plane hit. It was my dad's building it hit, and he was not too far below it. I thought of seeing the Tower fall, knowing he was in it. The day it happened; a year to the day after it happened; five, ten, twenty years after it happened—the world watches and remembers how they felt that very day. Where they were and what they were doing is recalled with utter clarity. The world mourns but only from the outside. They cannot truly know how it feels to see it over and over again. They cannot truly know how it feels to relive it over and over again every single time it is shown before our very eyes. When the North Tower fell, that was the moment I lost my dad. The world watches and sees it as tragic history. When I watch it, I see the moment my dad disappeared from this earth. The moment he literally vanished. And every time, this deep wound is reopened over and over again. It never heals. Life moves forward, good things happen, happiness is found; but the loss of my dad—his absence every day from my life—never heals.

There were three moments I was holding my breath for. The first was when my dad's name was read aloud. Paul Michael Allen. His name echoed through the empty sky above; it echoed through my heart. I repeated it in my head as silence washed over me. I recited a mental obituary to myself: Paul Michael Allen, age forty-five. Forty-five years, two months, two weeks, and six days old. Brown hair, green eyes, a financial investment banker, husband, father, son, brother, nephew, cousin. Survived by his parents, Donald and Barbara Allen; wife, Paige Martin Allen; daughters, Amanda Lynn Allen, Roda Francis Allen, Ashley Marie Allen; sister, Miriam Annette Allen; various aunts, uncles, and cousins. My mind was lost in thought when I heard the first bell ring, marking the first plane hitting. Marking the moment my dad's life became a brief living hell.

'What had happened?' I let myself wonder. I imagined him in his early meeting. I remembered all the papers he was reviewing on the train that morning. Those would have been right in front of him. I imagined the plane hitting above him. Darkness, smoke, screaming, fear. They had tried to find a way out. I know they had tried. He told Mim they had, and there was no way out. He knew at some point that he wouldn't survive. The moment he knew, he got on the phone and tried to call Mim. When he reached her, he stayed on until the very end. He hadn't been able to comprehend what happened. He realized a plane had hit. He was able to discover that, but Mim told him the rest. The sheer terror of it all. He was scared, but his voice was strong. His voice would crack, and he would cry, but he was determined to be brave. "They'll get you out," Mim kept telling him. "Someone will get to you and bring you out."

The third moment I was waiting for was the ringing of the bell to mark the moment my dad's building fell, and that's when I lost it. That's when my tears flowed in uncontrollable waves. The moment I knew that a year to the day—to the exact moment—my dad was gone. Disappearing in the very spot where I was standing.

We filtered out with the others hours later, completely drained. We were quiet, lost in our own thoughts. At some point, Mim grabbed my hand and held it as we walked, squeezing it to give me strength. When we reached the apartment, Mim pulled out food and put on a pot of tea. We ate very little. Afterwards, we each found our own space and escaped into the solace of sleep. Hours later, we gathered on the sofa. Normally we would have reminisced. We would have talked about all the things we remembered about Daddy, but not this time. This time we were quiet.

The buzzer sounded, jarring us from our thoughts. Someone was below on the street. Mim's brow furrowed, not knowing who it could be. She pressed the button to the intercom, inquiring who it was. "It's me, Charley," was the response. "I hope it's okay. I was thinking you guys might want some company." Mim buzzed her in and stood in the hallway, waiting for her to come up. I got up and went out with her. Our sorrow turned to surprise when we saw not only Charley but her parents, her brother, and Max coming up behind her. They were carrying bags of takeout from Bellino's and greeted us with warm hugs.

Nothing could have lifted our spirits more than their company. The ten of us squeezed into the apartment and spent the next five hours together, eating and talking. They wanted to know all the details of the day. They had watched the news coverage but wanted to know how it felt to actually be there, especially since none of us had been back to the area since the attack. We showed them family pictures of my dad and told them all the stories we knew by heart. It was the catharsis we needed to end the day.

I sat there watching those wonderful people who had surprised us at our lowest point. New friends who had come into our lives in the past year. I realized how blessed I was. The past year had been the best and worst year of my life. I had lost and left the only family I knew, only to have it replaced by my new friends. My new family. I smiled, looking around at each one of them and thinking about how much I loved them. Then the thought of my mother came to mind. Why did it keep happening? Why couldn't I just forget about her? Surely she had forgotten about me. I tried to push the thought out of my mind, but it wouldn't leave. It stayed there, wondering how she was doing. Did she have friends who would come over and spend the evening with her in an attempt to lift her spirits? Was she as lucky as I was to have such caring people around? The thought haunted me, and a small part of me wished she were here with us.

Later that evening, after everyone had left and my grandparents retired to Mim's bedroom for the night, I sat in the den with her and Amanda. Mim was getting the pull-out sofa ready so she could go to sleep. We were all ready for this day to finally end. The question had been on the tip of my tongue, but I hesitated in asking it.

"What is it?" Mim finally asked me. "I know you want to say something, so just say it." She knew me all too well. I looked back and forth at both of them.

"Well," I finally started, "I was just wondering . . . do either of you ever think about Mother? Especially today. Have you been thinking about her being alone?"

Mim took a breath and was about to speak when Amanda answered quickly. "Not me. I don't."

We both looked at her, surprised at her brisk response.

"That's just how I am," she explained further. "Once I let go, I let go. I don't look back."

"What about forgiveness?" I asked.

Amanda thought for a moment. "It's not about forgiveness. It's not that I can't forgive," she paused. "I've just closed that door, you know? That part of my life is over, and I'm moving on."

"But she's our mother," I reasoned. "Doesn't that matter?"

Amanda looked down. "Maybe it will matter one day but not today. Not right now."

Mim was watching us, listening to our conversation. "You're worried about your mother, Roda?"

I looked at her and nodded. "Yes, I am; and I don't know why. I can't figure out why I am. I'm sure she's not worried about me."

Mim looked at me for a moment. "Honey, I can't speak for your mother, so I can't really say if she's worried or not. Truth be known, she's probably mad—mad at both of you," she said, looking from me to Amanda. "We all know how she feeds on her anger. It sustains her. Is it sustaining her now? I don't know. But what you're feeling is normal, I think. You are surrounded by people who love you. She probably isn't. She has isolated herself. Did she ever have any close friends? Really close, true friends?" Amanda and I shook our heads no. "Then she probably is alone," Mim said. "But Roda, honey, that isn't your fault. That's *her* fault. You feel sorry for her, sure. That's because you are a compassionate person. You have such a good heart, such a caring spirit. You want to take everyone's troubles and make them your own so that maybe it will be better for them, but you can't do that with this—with her. She is where she is because of what she has done. The choices she has made. You can't change that. And I did invite her, remember? I did reach out to her, but she chose not to come. So feeling sorry for her is normal; but remember, it's the choice she has made."

I looked down and nodded.

"I know what you're thinking, Roda," Amanda said. "You're thinking if you hop on a train and go to her that she will suddenly change and that suddenly she will come to her senses and love you the way you've always wanted her to love you. Right? That the compassion and love you show her will be returned."

"I would like to think so, but I know it wouldn't change things. I know she will never accept me," I said sadly.

"No, she won't," Amanda said emphatically. "She will not, so don't worry about it. That's how I feel about it anyway."

I knew they were right. I *knew* they were, but I still felt profoundly sad. I realized I couldn't make her change. I couldn't make her love me. Only she could do that. So I went to bed, resigned to the fact that there was nothing I could do for her. It had been a long day, and I was exhausted. I was ready to move past all of it. I looked forward to the next day because, starting the next day, I would get back to life at hand. I was determined to keep moving forward. The past was the past, and it was time for me to get on with my life.

Chapter 17

~October 2002~

My favorite class of my tenth grade year was Dr. Hawkins' sociology class. I had thoroughly enjoyed his photography class; but sociology was a far deeper, more intense study that fascinated me. He, with all his eccentricities, was a brilliant teacher who inspired his students to dig within themselves to truly understand the world around them. He wanted us to see society from a different perspective. He would tell us that it was far too easy to observe human behavior from a distance, to see it from an indifferent vantage point. The more difficult task would be to get close and involved with the situations we encounter. Not surprisingly, he asked us to employ the camera lens to do so. That had been the purpose of his photography class, to give us a brief introduction into capturing the world around us. I was hooked on this method of art, intrigued by the possibilities that were out there waiting to be found.

He assigned topics we were to look for in the world around us: moments of human kindness or human frailty. Everyone would be given a passing grade no matter the quality. It was purely on effort alone. It was actually his way of seeing through our own individual eyes the way we see the world. By this method, he would be able to gauge how his influences were affecting us. It was his own psychological experiment, I supposed. But it was brilliant. It caused me to observe my own environment around me, to notice people and things and moments that surrounded me. It gave me an appreciation for life that I had never known before, and I found myself searching for it at every turn.

We would be given a specific assignment on the first day of each month, and we would have a full month to find a proper subject and then present our picture on the last day. It was an intriguing assignment—a challenge I was up for. The topic for October was titled "Candid Compassion." It was up to each individual to interpret its meaning—how we perceived its definition—and then capture that meaning in a still shot. I was diligent in my search. Rather than riding the short distance by subway with Amanda, I started walking to school, staying above ground among the people passing by. On the subway, it was easy to ignore people. Just to sit and read, listen to music, or work on last minute homework. It was easy to drown everyone out, but I wanted to interact with the world around me. Because of Dr. Hawkins, I wanted to immerse myself in society.

On the first day the assignment was given, I began to look for situations that I would interpret as a compassionate act. Someone holding a door open for a stranger; someone giving up their cab for another. They were all so stereotypical. I wanted something different. Something unique. I didn't feel overwhelmed with my task. It was an exciting adventure, and I was sure I could find something that would suffice. But for me, the challenge was greater. I wanted to surpass my own expectations. So I remained diligent with my camera always around my neck, waiting for humanity to jump out in front of me.

It wasn't until almost two weeks later when I took a detour through Washington Square Park on my way to school that I found what I was looking for. That's when I found George. He was sitting on a bench on the edge of the park as people rushed by. They didn't pay attention to him, and he didn't pay attention to them. What I saw was so surreal to me, and I was so entranced by it that I almost forgot to snap a picture. I gathered myself quickly, took the lens cap off my camera and began shooting. What I captured was as magical as it was tragic. Within the photograph was a homeless man sitting on a park bench, disheveled and forgotten and ignored by the busy people walking by. He was the center of the photograph, framed by the blurred people passing by, too busy to notice.

The symbolism was evident, but that was not the subject of the picture because that is not compassion. The subject was

187

George, the homeless man, feeding a small group of pigeons gathered in front of him. A hungry homeless man who no one offered food to was, himself, feeding birds that stopped and offered him a bit of company. Such is compassion—and candidly so.

I stood there for a moment after I had taken a few pictures, just watching. I was at a distance, so he never looked up at me. He never sensed me watching him. I was mesmerized but didn't really know why. I had seen plenty of homeless people before; but for some reason, I couldn't walk away. It would have been hypocritical to do so. How different would I be from everyone else who passed him by? It would actually be worse: to notice him so clearly, to take a picture of the beauty and sadness of it, and then to walk away. That would be shameful. I replaced the lens cap on my camera and timidly walked towards him.

He was so focused on the pigeons that he didn't look up until I was standing at the end of the bench. When he looked up at me, a slight expression of happiness and confusion crossed his face. I smiled at him and said hello. He said hello back, his voice parched. He probably thought I was crazy. Chubby me in my school uniform with a backpack and a camera around my neck. I extended my hand and told him my name. He shook my hand and said his name was George Mickler. I sensed people passing by, looking at me talking to him; and I wondered if those same people forget that someone like him actually had a name.

"May I sit down with you?" I asked him.

He was perplexed but nodded. He moved over to make room for me. The first thing I noticed was that he didn't smell like alcohol. It's common for homeless people, but it could also be a stereotype. He was dirty but as well kept as he could be. He was scruffy, but his hair and beard were not too overgrown. I immediately noticed how blue his eyes were. A very light, clear blue that was so intense, I felt he could see straight through me; yet I wasn't intimidated. My heart was suddenly full of love for him. I had such an overwhelming desire to show him he was important, even if he was only important to me. He wasn't menacing or belligerent. He wasn't angry at the world or resentful of people who passed him by. He was calm and polite and somehow generous even though he lacked any possessions. He held out the small paper bag of bird seed, offering for me to take some. I dug a handful out and scattered it sparingly as the pigeons pecked at the ground. How surreal it was to step into this picture with him. I shut out the world that was walking by, and I smiled at the solitude of it.

After a few minutes, I looked up at him. "Are you hungry?" I asked. Such a dumb question, I immediately thought.

He nodded. "I am."

I reached in my backpack and pulled out my lunch. It was a paper sack that contained a turkey and cheese on rye, chips, an apple, cookies, and bottled water. I handed it to him. He touched it timidly, not wanting to appear too eager. He thanked me quietly, politely.

"Are you here every day?" I asked.

"Most days," he said.

"Will you be here later this afternoon?" I asked.

He thought for a moment. "I probably will be."

"Okay," I said, already planning to bring him something to eat for dinner. "Will you be here every morning?"

"Yes," he said without hesitating. "My little friends here would be disappointed if I didn't show up. Who's going to feed the little birds if I'm not here?"

It was such a simple thought that it made me smile. "Are these the only friends you have?" I asked delicately.

He nodded, and I nodded in agreement. I knew exactly how that felt.

I wanted to know everything about him. I wanted to know who he was, where he came from, and why he was homeless. I wanted to know where he slept and how he ate. I wanted to know what he did during the day. I wanted to know why he seemed to have given up on life. Or had life given up on him? I knew I needed to get to school, and I knew I would see him again, so I excused myself and told him I would be back to visit him and the pigeons if that was all right with him. He said that it would be quite all right.

I walked to school thinking of George and thinking of my dad and remembering his last message to me. That everyone was worth knowing. Everyone was important. Everyone. It was very true, and it made me smile.

***

I couldn't explain it, but I had been in some sort of trance all morning after my encounter with George. I concluded that it was a realization of how good it felt to make someone feel important. Growing up, I had often wondered how people like my mother and Allyson and even Ashley got any pleasure out of treating people the way they did. How could doing such a thing make anyone feel good about themselves? Treating someone with kindness and decency always made me feel better. I couldn't imagine being any other way. But there was something different about George. Something special, something very tender. He was docile and quiet, but something within me told me that he could be full of life if given the chance. I floated though the morning anticipating the next time I would see him.

Charley and I stood in line together at lunch talking about a history test we had taken second period. It had been multiple choice, and we were comparing our answers. None of them matched, so we knew one of us had bombed. Amanda and Max were sitting at our usual table, so we walked over and sat with them. They had already finished eating, and Amanda was reading a fashion magazine as Max painted her fingernails. The two of them were more inseparable than Charley and I were. They were the epitome of best friends. They could practically finish each other's sentences.

I sat my lunch tray on the table and began to unwrap my cheeseburger.

"Roda, I thought you brought your lunch today," Amanda inquired, looking puzzled. Max's attention diverted from her nails to my food, and he instantly crinkled his nose. He had finished his chicken Caesar salad with light dressing and bottled water. He watched as I opened a packet of ketchup and spread it on my cheeseburger. He believed red meat was the devil and wasn't entirely sure if cafeteria meat was even real food. Regardless, he found it disgusting. I smiled at him as I took my first big bite.

"It's going straight to your thighs," he said wispily.

"It's already there," I shot back with a mouth full of food, causing him to cringe more. Honestly, he was the closest thing I had to a brother, and we treated each other as such.

"Roda," Amanda repeated, "I thought you brought your lunch."

"I did," I said, swallowing my food with a sip of soda, "but I gave it to a homeless man." I said it nonchalantly as if there wasn't anything strange about it.

"A *homeless man*?" she asked, alarmed. "You talked to a homeless man? Are you crazy? You could have been mugged or something!"

"Okay, listen up, prom queen," Max interrupted, rolling his eyes at Amanda. "There is nothing wrong with talking to a homeless man. They are people too. They just haven't showered in a while, that's all."

Amanda just stared at him. "Okay, listen up, drama queen," she mocked. "Nobody needs your input."

"Whatever," Max sighed and continued to paint her fingernails.

I was always amused by them. Their playful banter and sarcastic wit were entertaining. But the truth was they loved each other. They adored each other. They accepted each other without judgment. Max knew he was gay. He knew it at a very early age. His parents knew it before he did. They tried to ignore it, tried to deny it; but at a certain point, he couldn't hide it. He had been rejected by his classmates for years at the prestigious prep school he attended, and he begged to go elsewhere. Finally, they decided to let him choose. That was the only mercy they showed him. They were wealthy, and he didn't want for anything except their love. That was the one thing they wouldn't give him. By the time he was old enough to truly realize his sexuality, they kept him at arm's length.

Amanda knew that about him, and it endeared him to her. She knew rejection. She understood it. She knew what it meant for a parent to show love from a distance, to not truly accept the person you were. It was conditional, and a parent's love is not supposed to be conditional. Her greatest fear in life was being like Mother. She knew how similar she was to her, but she was determined to be different. In that regard, Max was perfect for her. He balanced her. If Amanda ever showed the slightest hint of Paige Allen—a snobbish reaction, a judgmental comment, even a certain look that would cross her face every now and then. If any of those things happened, Max would call her on it without fail. And she loved him for that. Theirs was a love that was deeper than friendship. They were soul mates, but only in the platonic sense.

"Roda!" Amanda whispered sharply, rousing me from my thoughts. "Who is this man? Where was he at?"

"Washington Square Park," I shrugged, taking another bite of my cheeseburger.

"Roda!" she said again, trying to convey the urgency she felt. "You do not need to be talking to strange men in the park, especially homeless men. Why in the world did you approach him anyway?"

"I was taking his picture," I said casually.

"His picture?" she asked. "Why?"

"For my sociology assignment," I replied.

Amanda looked at me and then at Max and then at Charley and then back at me. "And?"

"And what?" I asked innocently.

Max sighed and looked at me, feeling sorry that I wasn't quite getting it. "Roda, darling, Mommy Dearest wants to know what in the world prompted you to actually go up and talk to the poor derelict on the park bench."

"Ohhh!" I said in my most air-headed voice. "I get it. Well," I said, "I felt sorry for him."

"Roda! Enough with the short answers!" Amanda demanded. "Tell me what happened!"

So I told her the whole story from beginning to end. Her fear and skepticism gave way to understanding, even compassion. I told her how excited I was about the picture and that I couldn't wait to develop it and get it ready for the presentation at the end of the month. I would tell the story behind it, and I was sure Dr. Hawkins would be impressed. I told her I was going back by the park after school and take him more food.

"Oh!" Charley spoke up excitedly. "I want to go see the homeless man!"

The three of us just stared at her. "Charley," Amanda said kindly, "he's not a circus attraction."

"Well, I know. I just want to see him. He sounds nice."

I smiled at Charley. "You can go too," I told her. Then I looked at Amanda. "Promise me that you won't say anything to

192

Mim. Do you promise?"

She hesitated but promised she wouldn't.

***

After school, Charley and I went by a Mexican restaurant and picked up sacks full of tacos, burritos, and rice. Then we went by a little store and bought crackers, cookies, and bottles of water. We were determined to feed George well. We spotted him before he saw us approaching. He was sitting on the same bench, feeding his birds an afternoon snack. I stopped Charley before we walked any further. "Be nice, okay?" I told her. I knew that she would be. I completely trusted her, but I wanted her to be respectful. I felt very protective of him. He was my friend, and I wanted him to know that I was his friend as well. Charley nodded, and we continued walking.

He saw us approaching before we got there; and when he looked up, he smiled. Charley and I smiled back.

"Hi, George," I said happily. "This is my friend, Charley. Charley," I said introducing them, "this is my friend, George Mickler."

Charley reached out and shook his hand. "Hi, George. It's nice to meet you."

"It's nice to meet you too," he said, looking somewhat amazed. "You remembered my name?" he asked, looking at me.

"Well, of course," I said, smiling. "Why wouldn't I? Do you remember mine?"

"Yes," he said. "Roda Allen. I remember."

I smiled at him and nodded. "Hey," I said, holding up the bag from El Doros, "we brought Mexican. Shall we have a picnic?"

"I haven't had Mexican in a long time," he smiled. "That would be nice. Are you two sure you want to eat with me?"

"Of course we do," Charley said, and I nodded.

The three of us found a spot under a nearby tree. We sat on the grass and ignored the world around us. We ate and talked about all kinds of things. Charley entertained us with stories about her experiences on the subway. I desperately wanted to ask him about his circumstances—how he got there, where he came from; but he seemed to be enjoying our company and the brief escape from the reality of his world, so I didn't detract from the happiness he was feeling.

We left a little over an hour later. When I got home, Mim and Amanda were already eating dinner. Mim asked if I was ready to eat, but I lied and told her I had already eaten at Charley's house. I had never lied to her before. Amanda just looked at me, knowing the truth. I excused myself and went to the bedroom to change clothes and start on my homework.

Later that night, I printed off my favorite of the ten pictures I had taken of George. It was actually the first picture I had snapped. I printed an 8 x 10 copy and decided on black and white. I carefully glued it to a black matte board and then began to type the story about my picture. That was when I realized I didn't have the full story, only my side of it. Only the part about meeting him. I would need to know his story for the assignment to be complete.

"I can't believe you lied to Mim," Amanda hissed when I came in the bedroom that night.

I looked down at the floor. "I know," I said, ashamed, "but I couldn't exactly tell her the truth. She would freak out more than you did."

"You do *not* need to keep seeing him. He's a vagrant. He could be dangerous."

"He is *not* a vagrant. He is a very nice man, and I am going to find out his story," I argued. "Here, look at this," I said, handing her the picture.

She took it and held it, looking at it for a few minutes. It was a powerful picture. It was very moving; and until I had enlarged the actual print, I hadn't realized how profoundly sad he looked. Amanda thought he was just a lazy bum who could work if he really wanted to. But what I saw—and what the picture showed—was how sad and helpless and alone he was.

"His name is George," I told her. "I'm going back tomorrow, and I wish you would come with me so you can see how completely harmless he really is."

She slowly handed the picture back to me and nodded her head. "I'll go with you," she said. "If you're going to befriend him, I need to know him too."

Her protective nature made me smile, especially since she

was being protective of me. We went to sleep that night talking about him, and I wondered aloud where he slept at night. I told her every detail about that morning and that afternoon with George and Charley. I wanted Amanda to truly know him before she ever met him.

The next morning, she and I found him sitting on the same bench. He was holding a small bag of bird seed and feeding the pigeons. It was his morning ritual. He was no longer looking down, lost in thought. He was alert and looking around, watching for me. He spotted me just seconds after I spotted him. He not only smiled, but he smiled a big smile and waved.

"Hello, Roda!" he greeted as I approached. "It's a beautiful day, isn't it?" The change in his demeanor was amazing.

"Hi, George! Yes, it is a beautiful day. I brought someone else for you to meet," I said, motioning towards my sister. "This is Amanda. She's my older sister. Amanda, this is George."

George extended his dirty hand on which he wore a fraying knit glove with the fingers cut out. Surprisingly, Amanda shook his hand without hesitation.

"It's nice to meet you," she said.

"It's nice to meet you too," he replied.

We brought him breakfast from a nearby diner and had packed another lunch for him. He was grateful but still timid. He was always careful not to seem eager. He was polite and well spoken, and that intrigued Amanda. It piqued her curiosity, just as it had mine, as to who he really was. I decided it still wasn't the right time to ask such questions, so we spent a few minutes with him, just talking. He was in a very cheerful mood, much different from the day before.

I said goodbye to George, promising to see him after school. We turned and waved as we walked away. I saw him break up a crust of bread into small pieces and throw them to the birds still waiting there. He was a generous, good-hearted man.

Amanda was quiet for the majority of the time as we walked to school. She was deep in thought. Before we rounded the corner a block away from the building, she stopped and gently touched my arm.

"Roda," she said, looking at me, "I want you to know," she paused, "that I think you're amazing."

195

I was slightly stunned. The whole time walking to school, I thought she was mad; but I was wrong. "Y-y-you do?" I stuttered. "Why?"

She thought for a moment. "Because you're nice to everyone, and those people . . . people like George . . . everyone ignores them. They ignore him, but you don't. You talk to him, and you don't care who sees. You don't care what anybody thinks. I'm proud of you. I'm proud that you're my sister, and I wish I could be more like you."

I thought I was going to faint. I really did. I literally thought I was going to fall over. Amanda wanted to be like me? There was no way. But the gentle look on her face and the tears in her eyes made me realize she was telling the truth.

I smiled at her. "It's not hard to be like me, Manda. It's really not."

She nodded. "I know. It's easy to follow your lead. What's hard is having the compassion that you do, to know to reach out like that in the first place. But I'm learning," she smiled. "You taught me an important lesson today."

I nodded smugly. "Well, it's good to know that you have the ability to learn."

She laughed and looped her arm in mine, and we walked the rest of the way to school. Amanda did a lot for my self-esteem that day. The sister who was taught to despise me and who was horribly mean to me growing up, had grown to like me and now even looked up to me and admired me for something I taught her. It was an amazing moment for me. One that I will never forget.

***

That afternoon, I went to see George by myself. I took him a couple of hotdogs from a vendor in the park. We sat on the bench and talked. He was in a subdued mood. Subdued but not sad. I asked him how his day had been, and he said it had been a good day. It was a good time to ask about his past, and the conversation naturally led to it.

He said he had been homeless for about three years, and the transition from normal life to life on the streets had happened within the time span of a few months. The catalyst for the change was the death of his son, Landon.

Landon was only four years old when he was diagnosed with leukemia. It was a shock to George and his wife. Their son had been healthy and active one day, and it seemed the very next day he was tired and listless. They took him to the doctor a few days later, and that was when the leukemia was discovered. They were suddenly thrust into the world of doctors and oncologists. They were discussing treatment options and bone marrow transplants. And within weeks, among the flurry of it all, Landon died suddenly and without warning. It was pneumonia, a case so severe that it took his life. A normal child could have survived it; but in his weakened condition, it was deadly.

George and his wife fell apart. Their world fell apart. Landon was gone and nothing else mattered—not even each other. Their grief separated them. Within weeks, she moved out of their beautiful Manhattan apartment and back home with her parents in Maryland. George couldn't function: he couldn't eat, he couldn't sleep, he could barely even breathe. He had a high level position in a corporate firm and was close to making partner when his life fell apart. His bosses understood to begin with but quickly cut him loose when he continually failed to show up for work. Within a few months, he lost everything, including the apartment. His first night on the street, he had slept on the park bench that he sat on every day. He had no safety net. His family was gone. His parents were dead. His extended family, what little there was, was scattered across the country. He had no one to lean on. So he shut out the world and retreated into his own.

I sat there grieving for the loss of the life he had. I grieved for his little boy who would have been turning eight soon. I sat there and thought of my own mother, knowing her life could have easily ended up the same way. How diverse people are when tragedy strikes. How some can grieve and move forward while others are engulfed by it. I sat there and cried with George, and we talked for hours. I truly believed it was the first and only time he had ever opened up to anyone about it. It was a moving experience for me and a very cathartic moment for him.

When the time came to leave, I hated to go; but he insisted I should. It was beginning to get dark, and he was worried about me getting home by myself. I asked where he stayed at night. He said a shelter a few blocks away. I was glad to know he had a bed somewhere.

It was dark when I got home, and Mim had been very worried. I told her I had been out shooting pictures and lost track of time. She threatened me within an inch of my life that I better not do it again. She was so upset, she bought cell phones for Amanda and me the next day; and she dared us not to answer them.

That night, as Amanda and I were going to bed, I told her about George. She was so moved by it, she cried herself to sleep. From the next day forward, she wanted to go with me every day to see him. "We need to help him, Roda," she kept saying. "We need to help him."

***

A few weeks later, it was time to present our photographs in sociology class. Mine was ready well ahead of time, and I was quite proud of it. I showed it to Mim but was careful to omit the story about its subject. She was fascinated by it and was certain it would impress Dr. Hawkins. I needed someone else's approval though. I needed George's. I was uncertain as I approached him that morning. I began to doubt myself, thinking I had overstepped a boundary that I had not even bothered to seek permission for. If he had just remained a stranger, I wouldn't feel such conviction; but he had become a friend, and I felt as though I were taking advantage of him without his knowledge.

I approached him as I usually did every morning and brought him three of Mim's homemade cinnamon rolls and a cup of black coffee. I had nestled them together perfectly in a small paper sack so the coffee would keep the buns warm. We smiled and said hello. The weather had turned much colder, and he was bundled up in a heavy coat. I wondered where he got it from but didn't ask.

We talked for a few minutes before I told him I had something to show him. "It's for a school project," I said. He was anxious to see it. Before I slipped it out of the paper sleeve I was carrying it in, I paused and sighed. "I have to tell you, George, it's a picture of you." I suddenly felt horrible. I felt as if I were

198

betraying his trust somehow. Taking a picture of him without his knowledge and without ever telling him, and then using it to impress my teacher and my peers—it was shameful.

"A picture of me?" he asked, intrigued. "When did you take a picture of me?"

I pulled it out and showed him. "The day I first met you, before I came up and talked to you."

I fully expected him to be offended. I held my breath as he sat there staring at the picture. "This is me?" he asked in almost a whisper. "This is what I look like now?" It was as if he had not looked in a mirror in three years. Perhaps he had not. But he was shocked by what he saw, subdued into silence. He looked up with tears in his eyes. "I can't believe I've become this man," he said sadly. He shook his head in disbelief. "I can't believe it."

"You know what I learned a long time ago?" I asked as he handed the picture back to me. "I learned that the person we truly are is who we are on the *inside*. The outside doesn't matter, really. The outside, good or bad, is just a shell. The heart of who we are is on the inside. That's what truly defines us."

He nodded somberly. "You're exactly right, Roda. But still, it's quite a shock."

"Well," I assured him, "I think you're a beautiful person."

"You do?" he asked humbly.

"Yes, I do," I said, smiling at him.

He smiled a warm smile in return. "And I, dear Roda, think you are too."

"So," I hesitated before I had to leave, "is it alright with you that I show this today? I really wish I had asked you ahead of time. I feel just awful about it."

"Nonsense," he said. "Don't feel awful. You saw something unique and made it your own. I think it's wonderful. Really I do."

I thanked him and reached out for the first time and hugged him.

"I love you, George. I really do."

"I love you too, Roda. Now go on and get to school."

Having George's permission, I couldn't wait to present my project to the class. I waited patiently as others before me showed their pictures and told brief stories. A unique one was of a young

199

business woman standing on a street corner waiting to cross, and beside her was a very old woman. The two were undoubtedly strangers. Apparently, a sudden shower had come up; and the older woman only had the protection of a newspaper. The well prepared business woman was armed with an umbrella and was reaching out to offer the elderly woman protection from the downpour. It was captured from behind and developed in black and white. It was a powerful image of the proverbial generation gap being bridged in kindness and compassion. I noticed that Dr. Hawkins, who was sitting in a student's desk on the front row, was nodding his head in delight. He loved the image.

Suddenly, I was nervous when I got up to present mine. I stood fumbling for a moment before I began. The typewritten story was glued on the back of the thin foam board that displayed the picture, but I didn't need to hold it out in front of me to read it. I knew the story by heart. I rested the matted picture against my torso just beneath my chin and began to tell the story. Immediately, Dr. Hawkins sat straight up in his seat and leaned forward to examine the picture as closely as he could. I heard the word "unbelievable" escape softly from his lips. I hesitated when I heard it but kept going with the story.

I talked in a concise but heartfelt manner, telling George's story. I finally conclude eight minutes later. I had the longest presentation by far. Dr. Hawkins was completely engrossed in my photograph and the story that followed.

"Absolutely brilliant," he said breathlessly after I had finished. I was still standing in front of the class when he got up from the desk and stood before me, placing his hands on my shoulders. "Roda! This is the most magnificent picture I have ever seen! It is pure magic!" He stood back with his hand covering his mouth, looking again at the photograph and shaking his head in disbelief. "Simply amazing! Simply amazing!" he kept repeating. "Roda," he said sincerely, "you are brilliant. You have a unique eye for things. You truly do. You see things that others don't see. And better yet, you engage the things you see. You not only found a subject and captured the uniqueness and the vulnerability of him, but you put yourself within the picture—figuratively speaking, of course. You engaged your subject and became part of his world. You have accomplished what I had hoped for you . . . for all of you," he said, looking around and gesturing with a sweeping wave of his hand. "You have made yourself a part of your art. You have embraced the magic of it."

I was stunned. I had no doubt that he would like it and appreciate the story behind it, but I had no idea I would elicit such a reaction. I had impressed a professor who no one could impress. I had rendered him almost speechless. It was *the* most epic moment of my entire life. Certainly a moment that I would never, ever forget for as long as I lived.

Chapter 18

I had been so excited about my sociology project that I hadn't even entertained the very thought of the minutest possibility that Dr. Hawkins might say something to Mim. Obviously I should have anticipated the fact that it was bound to happen—and happen it did. Apparently, he called her as soon as he could to gush about my project and even more so about the humanitarian work I was doing in caring for and feeding this poor homeless man. He went on and on, sure that she was aware of every aspect of the story I had told. She was not, but she didn't let on to him in the least.

Unaware of the development, Amanda and I had stopped to visit George after school and take him soup and a sandwich from a local deli. I told him about my presentation and how much my teacher loved it. So much so, he kept the picture, hoping to enter it in a local contest at the beginning of the year. George was happy that I was happy. We didn't get to stay long because it was Friday, and Mim had planned a girls' night for the three of us. However, the moment we walked in, Mim's wrath was unleashed.

"RODA FRANCIS ALLEN!!!" I was greeted as the door opened. "I DEMAND TO KNOW THIS INSTANT WHAT IS GOING ON!!! I MEAN *THIS INSTANT*!!!"

Amanda quickly ducked out of the way, hoping not to be implicated in the supposed scandal.

"Well . . ." I started to say, not sure where to start.

Mim was impatient. "WHAT HAS BEEN GOING ON WITH THIS HOMELESS MAN?! WHAT EXACTLY HAVE YOU BEEN DOING?! TAKING HIM FOOD?! DO YOU *KNOW* HOW DANGEROUS THAT CAN BE?! YOU DO NOT

INTERACT WITH STRANGERS!!! YOU DO *NOT* DO IT!!!"

"I—" I tried to begin.

"WHAT ON *EARTH* POSSESSED YOU TO DO THIS?! WHAT ON EARTH?! THERE ARE HOMELESS SHELTERS AND SOUP KITCHENS FOR THOSE PEOPLE!!! CERTAINLY A GIRL YOUR AGE SHOULD NOT TAKE IT UPON HERSELF TO CARE FOR SUCH A PERSON!!! DO YOU REALIZE HOW DANGEROUS THAT CAN BE?!" she repeated. "DO YOU REALIZE YOU COULD DISAPPEAR AND I WOULD NEVER KNOW WHAT HAPPENED TO YOU UNTIL YOU FLOATED FACE UP IN THE HUDSON?! DO YOU REALIZE THIS?!"

"But I—" I attempted to interject.

"BUT NOTHING!!!" she continued to yell, unable to control herself. "YOU WILL NOT CONTINUE THIS!!! DO YOU HEAR ME?! YOU WILL *NOT*!!! YOU WILL ALLOW HIM TO FIND HIS OWN FOOD IN PLACES THAT SERVE FOR SUCH REASONS!!!"

I understood her fear, but I was suddenly shocked at her words. Mim was one of the most generous and charitable people I knew, but she sounded heartless and judgmental.

"Mim," I asked quietly, surprised she had paused from her rant to listen, "have you ever helped a homeless person?"

"No," she admitted, taking a breath, embarrassment suddenly creeping up on her. "No, I haven't."

"Why not?" I asked innocently.

Her eyes darted from me to Amanda. She swallowed hard, suddenly realizing the gravity of it all. "Well," she started. "Well, I guess because if you give them money, they'll just buy booze with it . . . and if you give them food . . ."

"They'll what?" I asked. When she didn't answer, I completed her thought. "They'll eat it?"

She looked away. "Roda, it's more complicated than that."

I just looked at her.

"Roda," she said defensively, "you cannot feed someone three meals a day. It's . . ." her voice trailed off. "It's not that I don't admire what you've done. You've been very generous. But, honey, I'm just afraid . . ."

"Afraid of what?" I implored.

"I don't know," she said, shaking her head. Her anger

subsiding and giving way to reason. "I just think you should stay away from this poor man. He will come to expect your charity and perhaps take it for granted."

"He's not like that. Not at all!" I argued. "He's a person who needs someone to help him, to believe in him. He needs friends and a family."

"Roda, it is not your place to give that to him. You cannot work miracles."

"I can be part of it, Mim. I can be his friend."

"Roda," Mim finally said sternly, "I am telling you to stay away from him. It's for your own good." She looked at Amanda. "From now on, you will go with her every day. Do you hear me? And you will make sure she doesn't go near him."

Amanda looked at me, and I looked at her. A knowing look passed between us that Mim didn't detect. "Yes, ma'am," was all she said in response.

Amanda and I both felt horrible about disobeying Mim, but there was no way we would stop seeing George. We continued to visit him regularly, and eventually Max came too. We took George extra gloves and scarves and knit caps to keep him warm. The weather was getting colder, and snow would set in soon.

***

~February 2003~

As fate would have it, Mim needed a wrench one day. For what, I did not know; but she sent me down to maintenance to ask Joe for one. Joe was our building superintendent and was a small, frail-looking man who was about sixty years old and missing a few teeth. He had worked there for as long as I could remember and maybe decades before. I always loved talking to him because he was a wisecracking old man who never failed to make me laugh.

"What does Big Mama need now?" he asked as soon as he saw me appear in the doorway. Mim had never been offended by his pet name for her because she was the one who first referred to him as "Shorty."

"A wrench," I said, rolling my eyes in mock exasperation.

"Which kind?" he croaked as he searched for batteries for his small radio.

"There's different kinds?" I asked naïvely.

"Well, yes, the hell there is," he said, looking up at me like I was an idiot. Oh, he loved me so. "There's a monkey wrench, an allen wrench, a socket wrench, an adjustable wrench, a hammer wrench, a flare nut wrench, an open wrench, a combination wrench. Dammit!" he said. "The possibilities are endless."

"Well, Big Mama just said a wrench," I told him, adding to his pseudo-irritation, "so your guess is as good as mine."

"Well, hell," he said, not minding throwing around the occasional cuss word, "I'm gonna have to go up there and take my whole damn tool box so she can figure it out!"

"Such is the life of a super," I sighed. It was our usual banter. Mim was notorious for needing his help but never knew exactly how to describe anything beyond calling it a thinga-ma-jig or a whatsit-called. Joe would never admit it, but he loved the interaction. Not too many tenants were like us. They usually kept to themselves and rarely expressed appreciation to him for doing the job he was hired to do.

"Yeah, yeah, yeah," he complained as he started searching through his tools, instinctively locating the wrench he knew Mim would need. "But guess what, missy? You ain't gonna have ol' Joe here to kick around much longer."

I stopped, suddenly serious. "What do you mean? Where are you going?"

He looked up and cocked his head. "Now, don't go gettin' all weepy on me. My daughter lives down in Florida, ya know. She's movin' me in. Thinks I'm gettin' old and all that shit. She's makin' me move out of the luxurious conditions I have here to sit on a beach somewhere with my grand-youngins and drink lemonade out of a straw. It'll be hell, I'm sure; but I ain't got no choice."

I wanted to laugh and cry at the same time. I loved Joe, and I didn't want to lose him, but I knew he would have a much better life with his daughter and her family.

"No, I'm happy for you, Joe. I really am. When will you be leaving?"

"Well, hell fire and damnation! You ready to get rid of me that quick?! Damn child, I thought you actually liked me!"

I laughed. "No, Shorty, that's not what I meant."

205

"I know," he winked. "I gotta keep up my reputation of being a hard-ass, ya know."

I nodded. Boy, did I know it.

"Well," he said, "I'm stuck here 'til they find me a replacement. It's in my contract that I signed a hundrer'-fifty years ago when I was young and wet behind the ears. Damn if I knew when I was twenty-seven that I'd be denied retirement 'til those owners found somebody suitable. I may never get to that beach," he grumbled.

A thought suddenly hit me. "Have you already told them that you want to leave?" I asked quickly.

"Well, yeah I have! Haven't you been listenin'?"

"When? Have they started looking yet?"

"See! You are anxious to get rid of me. Well, ain't that a load of horse shit! You sure find out who your friends are, that's for damn sure."

"No, that's not it," I said quickly. "I was just wondering if they've started looking yet."

"Well, hell no they haven't. I told them three weeks ago, and they said they'd discuss it when the Board met. Damn slave drivers. That's a whole two weeks away! I'll be dead by the time they get around to findin' anybody."

"What if you found your own replacement? Would they go for that?" I asked, almost out of breath I was so excited.

He thought for a moment. "Well, I guess." The question had actually stumped him. "I never thought of that." He shrugged. "But hell, I wouldn't even know anybody to ask."

"What if I do? What if I know someone who could use the job? And you have your own little apartment, don't you?"

"Well, yeah, I do. So?"

"So the apartment comes with the job, right? Do you pay rent, or is it part of the job?"

"No," he said, "it comes with the job. Not a bad set up, to tell ya the truth."

It was one forty-five on a Saturday afternoon, but I couldn't contain myself. I had to go look for George. I wasn't sure if I would find him, but I had to try.

"Go upstairs," I directed Joe, "take the wrench and tell Mim I had to run to Charley's. Something I just remembered for school. I'll be back as soon as I can, and I'll bring your replacement with me." I didn't wait for the response that he was obviously formulating. I ran to the park as quickly as I could. Miracle of all miracles, George was there. He was reading a newspaper.

"George!" I said, out of breath from running. "Come with me! You have to come with me now!"

He looked up in surprise, almost alarmed. "What's wrong?" he asked. "Is someone chasing you?"

"No!" I said. "Nothing like that. I want you to come meet somebody. I may have just found you a job!"

"I can't go looking like this!" he said.

"It doesn't matter," I said, shaking my head. "It won't matter, I promise. Now please come with me," I insisted.

He got up and followed me, walking away from a park bench that I hoped he would never have to sit on again. I had no doubt that everyone we passed looked at us like we were crazy: a homeless guy following a teenage girl. But the look of determination on my face let everyone know that I was on a mission, and I was not to be stopped.

When we arrived at Joe's tiny office down a small hallway off the foyer inside the building, he was banging on a metal box, trying to get it open. He apparently had forgotten the combination to the lock. Cuss words were flying out of his mouth, the kind I had never heard him say before. I cleared my throat to get his attention; and when he turned around—surprised, a look of utter shock froze on his face.

"WHAT IN THE HELL HAVE YOU GOT HERE, RODA?! WHERE IN THE HELL DID YOU FIND THIS DAMN HOBO?! YOU THINK THE DAMN BOARD IS GONNA ALLOW ME TO LET A DAMN HOMELESS MAN WORK HERE?! HAVE YOU LOST YOUR DAMN MIND?!"

I had warned George that Joe's reaction would not be good. I told him not to be offended. And Joe did not disappoint. I let him scream and holler and cuss until it was out of his system. When he finally stopped to draw a breath, I asked if I could please speak.

"Well, go ahead! But it ain't gonna change a thing! Those horses' asses won't hire a damn homeless man!"

"Well," I insisted, "they will if they don't know he's

207

homeless. We can fix him up."

"Fix—" he started. "Fix? Fix *him* up?" Joe shook his head. "This ain't no makeover show. This ain't no before and after fixem' up show."

"Joe—" I started to say, but George interrupted me.

"Sir," he said politely, "I'm sorry we've taken up your time. Roda here is just trying to help me. I've had a run of bad luck, and she's just trying to help."

Joe was taken aback by George when he spoke. Apparently, he assumed he was a drunken vagabond. Joe realized very quickly that he was mistaken.

"Joe," I begged, "please give him a chance. We can get him all cleaned up, and he can stay here with you for the next couple of weeks until the Board meets. I'm sure they'll be thrilled you found someone, and they won't have to deal with the hassle of it. George would be great at this, I swear."

Actually, I wasn't sure if George knew the difference between a socket wrench and a hammer wrench, but it was worth the bluff. Joe thought for a moment and finally agreed.

"Don't matter no way," he complained. "Damn women always get their way anyhow."

***

I had a few hundred dollars saved in a box in my room, so I ran upstairs to retrieve it. When I walked in, Mim was baking cookies.

"Hi, honey! Where've you been? Shorty said you ran to Charley's?"

"Uh, yeah, I did; but she wasn't at home," I lied. "I'm working on a project with Shorty now, so I'll be back later. Where's Amanda?"

"Max stopped by earlier, and the two of them decided to go shopping. Apparently Max has his mother's Amex card, and they're going to take full advantage of it," she reported. "It's sad how his parents brush him off by throwing money at him."

"Yeah," I said absentmindedly, "one of the perks of rejection. Listen, I gotta go. Shorty's waiting on me."

"For the life of me, I don't see why you like hanging

208

around that old coot. There's only so much of him I can take."

I was out the door before she finished her sentence. I flew downstairs and was at Joe's apartment within minutes. He and George were sitting at the small kitchen table, eating a sandwich. It was a warm little three room apartment. The living area and kitchen were all one room and spacious enough for one person. There was a bedroom just large enough for a double bed, a nightstand, and a dresser. The bathroom was off the bedroom, and Joe kept it impeccably clean. Surprisingly, everything about his apartment was neat and warm.

I rushed in, holding up the money. "Okay, let's go!" I said.

Joe told us where his barber was, just a block down the street. That was the first stop for a shave and a haircut. Next, we went to a thrift store three blocks down. That's where Joe got all of his fine clothes. I bought three pairs of jeans for George, four button-up shirts, two t-shirts, a sweater, underwear, socks, shoes, and a coat. It was a good start to his wardrobe, and it cost a little over a hundred dollars. A bargain indeed. I had thought we would need Amanda's expert advice, but we did fine on our own.

George shed his tattered clothes and walked out of the thrift shop wearing one of his new outfits. I was amazed at how handsome he looked. Almost GQ material. He seemed like a new man and had suddenly begun to regain a sense of pride that he had lost several years before. He kept thanking me; but at the same time, he kept saying I shouldn't do it. He promised to pay me back, but I refused the offer. I was glad to do it.

Our last stop was at the corner drugstore to pick up a toothbrush, toothpaste, shampoo, shaving cream, and soap—all the essentials. We picked up a few small groceries to help stock Joe's apartment since he was taking on a guest. When we returned, Joe was shocked. "What the hell?!" was his reaction when George walked in. Knowing Joe as long as I had, I knew that was a compliment.

George was, in all reality, unrecognizable. I knew Amanda and Max were still out but would be back soon. I called her cell phone and asked where they were. They were in Max's town car, and the driver would be dropping them off within ten minutes.

"Come to Shorty's apartment as soon as you get here," I instructed. "There's something I want you and Max to see."

They were there a few minutes later, knocking on the door. Joe was sitting at the table when I opened the door; and George was standing in the middle of the room, waiting for them to recognize him. They didn't. Amanda looked around, noticed there was someone there she didn't know and asked, "Well? What is it?"

"You don't know? You're not curious about anything in this room?" I asked, smiling.

She sighed. "Roda, what is it that you want me to see? I see Shorty, and I see a new guy."

"Roda, dear," Max interjected. "Blondie here doesn't know what the fuss is about. Could you please enlighten her? I, myself, think it has something to do with this gorgeous man standing here. Could that be it?"

I smiled a broad smile. "Maybe."

Amanda sighed again. "Roda, quit playing games. What is it?"

George finally spoke. "Hello, Amanda. Hello, Max."

They froze. They recognized his voice, but their eyes deceived them. As he stood there smiling at them, the truth finally began to sink in. They were both speechless.

"Is this—" Amanda tried to speak.

"Is this who I think it is?" Max asked, completely dumbfounded.

I nodded. "Yes, it is. It's George."

They shook her heads in disbelief.

"How . . . why . . ." Amanda said, trying to form her thoughts.

They sat down, and I told them the whole story that had happened only hours before. It was a quick transformation but well worth the effort. And now George was safe and had the promise of a stable life. Relief washed over us in that little room, and we couldn't stop smiling.

Two weeks later, Joe had George fully trained. It turned out that George was quite the handyman. He was also a quick study. He learned the ropes very quickly and had already begun to learn many of the tenants by name. They seemed very pleased with him since he wasn't as gruff as Joe. Not everyone understood Joe the way I did, and that was a shame.

The Board approved the hiring of George and the

retirement of Joe, so everything was set. George had a place to call home, and Joe would be relaxing on the beach in a matter of days. Mim had not had the pleasure of meeting the new building superintendant yet, so it was my idea to have him and Joe over for dinner one night. Sort of a going away party for ol' Joe. Mim eagerly agreed and began planning the menu.

She didn't mind that Amanda and I invited Charley and Max as well. "The more the merrier," she had said. The four of us helped her cook all afternoon; and when George and Joe arrived promptly at six o'clock, they were greeted with the smell of Cornish game hens roasting in the over, sautéed vegetables, and freshly baked bread. Mim's kitchen always smelled like heaven.

Mim was quickly enamored with George. "Well, hello," she greeted him. "You must be Joe's replacement." Joe and I looked peculiarly at each other, wondering why she used his real name instead of the nickname she had given him years ago.

"This here's the one you gotta look out for, Georgie," Joe said, pointing to Mim. "She never knows what the heck she needs, but she'll bug the stew out of ya 'til ya figure it out."

Joe felt comfortable enough around Mim and me to use his crude language, but he always tempered his words when he was around Amanda. Mim rolled her eyes at his playful insult, and George just smiled at them. "Well, come in," she told them. "Make yourselves at home. Dinner will be ready in a few minutes."

Everyone settled in the living area while Mim and I set the table and prepared to serve the food. "My goodness, he's cute," Mim whispered to me. "Where did Shorty find him?"

I shrugged. "Beats me," I lied. Then panic began to slowly set in.

I had thought to cover all my bases this time. Amanda and I had sworn Joe, Max, and Charley to absolute secrecy as to who George really was. The one flaw in my grand plan was that I had forgotten to tell George. My worse fear was realized halfway through dinner when Mim asked where he was from and how he knew Joe.

'No, no, no, no,' I thought to myself, knowing George would tell the whole story. Joe, Max, Charley, and Amanda all froze suddenly, bracing themselves for Mim's reaction. 'How did I miss this?' I thought. 'How did I forget to tell George?'

211

I actually did know how I forgot it. I had avoided it. I didn't want to tell George what my aunt had said about my charitable work. I didn't want to hurt his feelings or give him a false impression of how she truly was. I knew Mim was not that hard-hearted. She was just worried about me. But still, I had not told George.

George looked around, unaware of why Mim didn't know the truth about how he got the job. He had assumed she knew everything just like everyone else did.

"Well, I was homeless," George said, "and Roda came up to me one day and insisted I come with her. That's when I met Joe. That's when I got the job."

You could have heard a pin drop, the silence was so deadly. The look of shock that fell on Mim's face was indescribable. George was instantly perplexed as to what the problem was. The other five of us had our heads bowed, looking down at our food with a little too much interest. Mim cleared her throat and folded her hands, resting them in front of her mouth. The truth was sinking in. She was trying to process it and trying to contain her anger, realizing that I had defied her. Her eyes landed on Amanda, my supposed guardian.

"I didn't have anything to do with this," Amanda quickly insisted, throwing her hands up in defense.

"You didn't?" Mim accused.

"No, ma'am. I didn't have anything to do with all of this," she continued to defend.

"I didn't either," Max interjected. "Nope, not me at all. I was just shopping that day. That's all. No guilt here whatsoever."

She continued to stare at Amanda. "Did you ever go with Roda to the park to see him?"

She was trapped, and she knew it. There was no way around it. She couldn't lie. "Yes, ma'am," she admitted, "I did."

Mim's eyes landed on me, her glare burning into the top of my head as I continued to look down at my plate. Her hands were still folded in front of her mouth. It was her way of keeping herself from shouting.

"Well, damn," Joe said, trying to break the tension, "I knew he was homeless. What the hell is wrong with that? He's a good man! There ain't nothin' wrong with that." Joe had grown quite close to George in the weeks he had been with him. George became the son that Joe never had.

"Mim," George said, beginning to understand the problem, "don't be angry at Roda because of me. Amanda either. They were only trying to help me. I understand that they must have lied," he said, looking at me and then Amanda, "but they were just worried about me. I don't want them to get in trouble for that."

Mim softened as she looked at George. She sat back in her chair, putting her hands down and resting them in her lap, her anger slowly subsiding.

George looked around and then looked at me. "Roda is an amazing person. She's a godsend, really." He smiled at me, and I looked up at him. "I was lost and she found me. I was alone in a world full of people, and she was the only one who spoke to me. She made me feel important." He nodded and began to get choked up. "She didn't wait for me to tell my story. She asked me. She wanted to know about me because she cared about me. She's the first person—the only person—I have ever told my story to. The only person I have opened up to. And now, because of Roda, I have a new chance at life. If it weren't for her, I would still be sitting on that park bench. People always think, 'Why can't they help themselves? Why can't they find a job?' But sometimes it's not that easy. Sometimes it's not that simple. Sometimes people aren't strong enough to climb out of their grief. Sometimes it takes someone stronger to pull them up out of it. That person for me is Roda, and I will always be grateful to her for that."

By the time he finished, we all had tears streaming down our faces. Even Joe, who quickly wiped his away.

Mim sniffed loudly. "I know Roda is strong," she said, smiling at me. "I've always known that."

Everyone at the table nodded. Everyone agreed, and that made me smile—even if I didn't believe it about myself.

"Well, hell," Joe said, breaking the mood and forgetting about tempering his words, "can we just eat now, dammit? Enough of this sappy shit." Joe was not a touchy-feely kind of guy, that was obvious; but he looked at me and reached out and held my hand for a brief moment and squeezed it.

We spent the rest of the night talking and laughing. George had a wicked sense of humor that I never knew about, and he and

Joe together were a riot. It really was a shame that Joe was leaving. I was enjoying the two new additions to our family. But leave he did. He flew out of JFK bright and early the next morning. He promised to keep in touch and possibly even visit if his damn daughter would let him.

That night, Mim apologized to me. She said how sorry she was for not trusting my judgment and that she knew I had done a wonderful thing. She felt great conviction in how she had reacted to all of it. I assured her that the reaction she had was quite normal. Any parent would have done the same thing. We laughed when I told her that Amanda had even said some of the very same things she had said. I think that made Mim feel better.

When Amanda and I went to bed, she laid there for a moment before she said anything.

"Roda, you are so brave."

"What do you mean?" I asked.

"You see what needs to be done and you do it, no matter what. Despite the consequences. Despite everything, you do it. Don't you see how brave that is?"

"Yes, I suppose," I agreed.

"No," she argued, "there's no supposing. It's true. It's absolutely true. I wish I could be like that. I wish I could be as brave as you are."

It was at that point that I turned on my side to face her, resting my elbow on my pillow and propping my head up with my hand. "But you are brave."

"What? No, I'm not. I'm a coward. That's all I am."

"Are you kidding me? Do you not remember what you did to get here? You loaded your car and *drove* here . . . by yourself! That's a scary thought. I would never have been so brave."

She thought for a moment but dismissed it. "So what? That doesn't really matter. You did the same thing basically."

"No," I disagreed, "what you did was different. I left a home life where I was rejected. I left a mother who never loved me. What you left was your whole life. You walked out on that wonderful life you had, as wonderful as it looked anyway. I walked away from an empty life. You walked away from everything you knew. To me, that is far braver than anything I've ever done."

214

She laid there quietly. "I guess," she finally said. "Roda?" she asked after a moment.

"Yes?" I answered.

She paused before she spoke. "After you left, did it bother you that Mom never called?"

I couldn't deny it. "Yes," I said truthfully, "it broke my heart like I never thought it would."

She began to cry softly and nodded. "I know. It broke mine too. I really thought," she paused, choking back more tears. "I really thought she would come after me. I really thought she loved me enough."

"I know," I said. "I had hoped the same thing too, but I wasn't surprised. I was heartbroken but not surprised."

"Do you think she'll ever forgive us?" she asked, looking at me.

I thought for a moment. "I don't know. Maybe not. But maybe she wonders if we'll ever forgive her."

Amanda nodded sadly. "Yeah, I guess I never thought about that."

"But regardless," I told her, "we have to live our lives the best way we know how. And we have to try to fulfill our dreams. We have to work to achieve them. And I know that we can."

"You're certain of that?" she asked. "I know *you* will. You can do anything. I'm not so sure about me."

"Well, I'm sure about you; and I know *you* can too."

Somehow she believed me and gained strength from my words. We promised each other that night to follow our dreams and to not let anything stand in our way. We would be brave. Together.

Chapter 19

~September 2005~

It's easy to see how big events can change the course of one's life. My dad's death put me on a completely different path. But, amazingly, it's also the little things that can change the direction of our lives as well. Something that touches us in a way that nothing else has and gives us a new perspective on life. It can be a class that we take, it can be a speech that we hear, or sometimes it can be one particular person. Yes, there are people who come along, even if for a brief moment, and can change your life in an instant. For me, that person was Sarah Sewell-Cothran.

I was in my freshman year of college at New York University. New York University! My dream had been realized. I had long ago decided that no matter what class Dr. Henry Hawkins taught, I would take it, even if it didn't pertain to the curriculum path for my chosen major. He was my mentor, my inspiration. My goal in life was to impress him, and I was determined enough to do so every chance I got. He sensed this about me, so it was no surprise to him when I walked into his Psychology 101 class first semester.

"Well, if it isn't Roda Allen," he announced as I walked through the door. The students who were already seated looked up at me, but I wasn't embarrassed. It was an honor that the professor who everyone feared the most knew my name and announced me as if I were someone important. I smiled and went over to his desk to talk to him before taking my seat when class began.

I learned long ago that Dr. Hawkins' passion was the study and understanding of the human mind. While he was fascinated by the sociological aspects of the world, his desire was to understand them through the human psyche. That was the reason why he always employed the method of photography for his students. No surprise, that method would be used in Psych 101 as well. I was ready for it. The only difference this time was that our grades *did* depend on it. It would not be optional, and it would not be based on effort. It would be a requirement. He gruffly said to the class, "If you do not own a camera of the caliber I require, if you do not wish to own a camera for this endeavor, if you are not up for this challenge, then leave this classroom immediately. I am the only professor at this university who requires this. I am the only professor at this university who has integrated this into his curriculum. If you have no interest in it, then you may take this same class under Gilbert or Christensen."

No one left. I think they were too afraid to. But I noticed at the very next class session that the number of students had dwindled by half. I realized what an advantage I had over the others who were brave enough to stay. No one else in the class had ever heard of Dr. Hawkins before arriving at NYU, so no one else truly knew what they were getting into. But I did. I had been introduced to it my freshman year of high school and mastered it by the time I graduated. I was ready for it on the college level. No one else was. So I knew, once again, I would be his star pupil; and I was very proud of that.

The semester was only four months long, running from September through December. Within our class syllabus, each photography assignment was listed on the outline. September's assignment was "Commitment," October's was "Fear," November's was "Courage," and December's was "Peace." In my mind, I began to formulate ideas for each picture. Being the overachiever that I had become, I wanted to get all of them done ahead of time, not just month by month.

"Commitment" would be easy. I already anticipated that everyone else in the class would find a wedding to go to somewhere and snap a picture of the bride and groom. My first thought was to go to the park and find an elderly couple walking hand in hand and find out their story and how many years they had been married. That is true commitment: when it's near the end and you have proven yourself faithful. Not when it's at the beginning and it's only a promise. Or better yet, I thought, an elderly man sitting at his wife's bedside holding her hand while she lay dying. That was true commitment.

That's when I had the idea to look for my subjects at a medical center. As my mind formulated a plan, I realized that every assignment could be fulfilled within a hospital. The underlying theme for all four assignments was death. Aside from commitment, they somehow encompassed the different stages of death itself: the fear of dying, the courage that must be found, the peace that comes, and the person who is committed to being by your side. I looked at Dr. Hawkins when I realized this. I had that *Aha!* look on my face—that look of realization. He knew that I knew, and he nodded and smiled.

I talked to Mim about my idea, knowing I would need to get permission from the hospital. She said she could make a few calls and see what the protocol was to obtain a visitor's pass at NYU's medical center. Within days, my request was approved by hospital administration. A meeting was scheduled with Dr. Herman Warner, Chief of Staff, so that I could explain my mission and would be given a tour of the facilities by an executive assistant. Hopefully, at some point, I would be able to search out my subjects alone.

Thanks to Mim's extensive contacts, the red tape was kept to a minimum; and within a week, I was wandering the halls on my own, camera in hand. Two things that had been stressed by Dr. Warner were discretion and permission. "Be discrete in *how* you take pictures and *where* you take pictures. And above all, permission must be given by the people whose picture is being taken." That was not unlike how it was in everyday life. I had learned that being a photographer in a delicate situation required patience, understanding, and a certain measure of invisibility. To capture a candid moment, the subject should be oblivious to your presence, but you must later gain their permission. That could be a difficult bridge to cross. And even if you had the perfect picture, if they withheld their permission, you could not use it. That could be heartbreaking. I understood my task at hand, and I was willing to take it.

I started my search in geriatrics. That's where the idea was born, so that's where I was determined to start. The nurses on the floor were instrumental in directing me. They knew the patients, the rooms they were in, and the people who visited. There were rooms and rooms of elderly patients who always slept, and whose spouses, if they were alive, slept in the chair the whole time as well. And there were those whose children or grandchildren visited, only to pay attention to what was on television while they impatiently waited for their visit to end. But there was one patient—just one—who they thought would be perfect for me. Her name was Margaret Tanner. Maggie. Her faithful husband was Johnny. They were both eighty-nine years old and had been married since they were eighteen. Seventy-one years. They never were able to have children, so at the end of life, it was just the two of them. She was at the end of her battle with Alzheimer's, and he was unable to care for her properly. She had been in long term care for weeks, and he never left her side. When I walked in the room, I saw what I had pictured in my mind in Dr. Hawkins' classroom: a frail man sitting at his wife's bedside, holding her hand. He was humming softly to her. It was the most beautiful scene I had ever witnessed.

The nurse introduced me to him, and he was glad for my company. I sat with him for over an hour as he told me their life story. His eyes lit up when he talked about her. It made me smile. I told him about my project and asked if it would be all right to photograph him and his wife. He didn't hesitate to say yes. He even offered an idea. My thought had been to have him sitting as I found him, beside her bed holding her hand; but his idea was so much better. He took her hand and pulled it gently up to her chest and held it in his. Then he leaned forward, bending down to kiss her on her forehead. I zoomed in just enough for the two of them to be the dominate objects in the picture but still being able to capture the hospital equipment in the frame. Even though it wasn't a candid moment, it didn't look posed. It looked very natural, and he and I were both pleased with it. I wrote down his address and promised to send a copy to him. I spent a few more minutes with him before leaving. When it was time to go, I left the room wondering who would care for him when it was his time to die.

My next stop was in pediatrics. As much as I enjoyed talking to Mr. Tanner, it had depressed me. I wanted something happy. I wanted something young and vibrant and new. Of course, my next topic was "Fear," so that might be difficult. But then I thought, 'What do children fear the most?' I knew the answer to that. Shots. So I found the cutest little six year old boy named Jared, who was about to receive a vaccination; and I asked his mother if I could capture the moment on film. She agreed, and the picture I took was priceless. Jared was afraid but tried to be brave. Yet, the moment the needle was about to enter his arm, he looked at it. Wide eyed and his mouth about to let out a scream, the fear on his face was genuine. It was absolutely perfect. I felt sorry for him; but he was immediately given a grape lollipop, so he was happy.

My idea for "Peace" was a mother holding a sleeping newborn. When I arrived in postpartum, I told a nurse about my idea. She directed me instead to the neonatal unit. She knew of a premature baby who was finally strong enough to be removed from her incubator briefly enough to be held by her mother for the first time. My timing was perfect. It was a tender moment as the nurse gently removed the preemie from her bed and placed her in her mother's arms. She was a tiny little girl, not much bigger than a doll; and she had been born six weeks before. Her name was Emily, and she was the most beautiful baby I had ever seen.

Finally, there was "Courage." I wondered how I would depict courage as it pertained to death. I thought for a moment. Not surgery, I reasoned. Surgery saves us from death, for the most part; and while some may die in surgery, it's never certain. Courage meant bravery in the face of possible or even certain death. This meant a battle—a fight. That was when it hit me. Cancer. I found my way to the oncology ward. That's where I found Sarah.

Sitting among the other patients receiving chemo was Sarah Sewell-Cothran. She stood out among the others. Everyone else was reclined back, covered with a blanket and sleeping. Sarah was sitting upright, her legs elevated in the recliner and covered with a blanket; and she was wide awake. Her daughter, Julie, sat beside her. They were talking and laughing in hushed tones, sipping coffee and soda. Sarah was finishing a crossword, and Julie was starting her third Sudoku puzzle. Both were confident enough to do them in pen. "Only wimps use pencils," they agreed.

It was hard to believe that Sarah was a cancer patient. She was on her third round of chemotherapy and had completed one round of radiation. She had been battling lung cancer for almost a year, yet she looked healthy and vibrant. She had never been sick a day during treatment.

I sat with them as Sarah told me her story. She had been scared to death when she received her diagnosis. Her family doctor had been heartless when telling her she would be dead within months. He offered no hope. Regardless, she was referred to an oncologist and began her first treatment on her sixty-fourth birthday. Except for the initial diagnosis, her daughter had been with her for every appointment; yet Sarah felt completely alone. Julie was with her through every step, but Sarah was the only one facing an uncertain future. Sarah was facing death, and only she alone could fight it.

She knew her prognosis was not promising. There were only five types of chemo to combat small-cell carcinoma, and she was on number three. The small clusters of tumors were inoperable, and chemo and radiation had done little to shrink them. But she chose to fight every day, and that was the definition of courage: never giving up, even when consumed with fear.

I asked what her greatest regret in life was; and she told me, "Not doing something that I loved. I spent my whole life doing what I was supposed to; but out of fear or obligation or lack of time, I never did what I truly wanted to do." What she had wanted to do was write. She had so many stories in her head but had never been focused enough to put them on paper. She never took the time, and now she had very little time left. "Find something you love and do it," she told me. "Not something you're good at, not something others expect you to do, but something that you love. Something that makes you feel alive." When she said that, a spark ignited within me. I had been entertaining an idea gradually throughout the day; but when she said that, it became a burning flame within me.

I asked to take her picture because, to me, she was the epitome of courage. She agreed without hesitation. Before I could snap the picture, she ripped off her wig, revealing her bald head with fuzzy white hair that was trying its best to grow back. She put up her fists as if she were a boxer and smiled, her eyes dancing. Of the four photographs I took that day, hers was the only one I printed in color just so I could show how truly marvelous her green eyes looked.

***

It was late afternoon when I left the hospital. I was excited about the photographs I had taken and the people I had met, but I was most excited about my new mission in life. Yet, I was also afraid. I understood what Sarah meant by not doing something out of obligation. There were things I was good at, things I liked to do; but it wasn't necessarily what I loved. I was good at art, good at sketching; but even that was giving way to photography. Thanks to Dr. Hawkins' influence, photography had become a passion; but I realized it wasn't what made me feel complete. I had thought I might become a photojournalist. I could travel the world taking pictures and telling stories, just as Dr. Hawkins had been conditioning me to do. I was good at it. What motivated me to excel was simply to impress my mentor; but other than that, it wasn't what I loved. What I loved was people. I had a heart for people, and I wasn't sure I would be content to merely observe them through a camera lens. I wanted to interact with them. I wanted to help them. My only concern was how Mim and Dr. Hawkins would react. They both expected me to follow the path of the art world. I didn't want to disappoint them. But like Sarah said, I shouldn't do anything out of obligation. I should follow my heart and do what I love. And what I decided I wanted to do more than anything was to become a doctor.

I needed an objective opinion. I decided the only person I could talk to was Charley's mom. I went directly from the hospital to their apartment. Charley had an afternoon class, so she wasn't there. It was actually better that way. I asked Mrs. Webber if she had some time to talk, and she gladly welcomed me in. I told her about the project and the day I had. I even cued up the digital pictures on my camera to let her see them. She was very impressed with my work and with the life stories I had learned. I told her how I had always loved taking pictures and telling stories, but now I decided I actually wanted to help people by becoming a doctor. This came as an unexpected surprise to her.

"A doctor? Really? When did you decide this?" she asked.

"I think today, really. Does that sound crazy?" I asked, unsure.

"No, darling, there's nothing crazy about it. But have you ever thought about it before?"

"No, not until today. The older I've gotten, the more I've realized how much I love people and how much I love helping them. And today, spending all day at the hospital, I realized I was somehow in my element. You know? I felt completely comfortable there. And whenever I would hear the doctors or nurses talking in medical terms, I somehow understood what they were saying. Does that sound crazy?"

She shook her head. "No, it doesn't. If that's the case, you may have a very high aptitude for medicine. If you already have some basic knowledge or understanding, then you should be able to excel at it with your education."

I nodded, believing she was right.

"Roda, darling, I think you should go for it. Just like what this dear lady, Sarah, said, you should go for it and do something you love. I think you would make a wonderful doctor. Really, I do."

I nodded again but was more pensive. "It's just that . . ."

"It's just that what?" she asked lovingly.

I looked at her. "It's just that my aunt and my professor are sure I'm going to be an artist. It's what I've always dreamed of doing. Really, it is. But now, suddenly, I want something else. And I'm just wondering if I'm jumping into it too quickly. Does that make sense?"

"You need to choose your own path, Roda. No one else can or should choose it for you. You need to weigh all of this in your heart and then decide. Give it some time. Don't decide right now. But with time, you will know."

"I'm just afraid they'll be mad at me or disappointed in me."

She smiled. "No one is going to be mad at you for deciding what you want to do with your own life. Anyone who loves you will encourage you to follow your dreams. I don't believe either of them will be mad or disappointed."

I nodded, agreeing with her. She made sense. "I'm just afraid to tell them, I guess."

She smiled. "You know, we adults . . . we parents . . . are used to our children making their own decisions as they get older. It's part of being a parent. Parents have to learn to let go when their children grow up. We can't decide for them what they should do or should be. That's their decision to make." She smiled and tilted her head, a thought suddenly coming to her. "Do you know Charley's real name?" she asked.

I looked at her curiously, not understanding the question. "I thought it was Charley," I finally said.

She smiled. "No, it's not; and I'm not surprised that she never told you. She hates her name. But if I tell you, you have to promise to keep it a secret."

I smiled, somewhat amused. "I definitely will," I promised.

"Her real name is Charlotte. A little too traditional for her, don't you think?" She paused, smiling; and I nodded. "I love the name Charlotte," she said. "I always have. And when she was born, that was the only name I would give her. She never said anything about it as she grew up. She would ask how she got her name, and I would simply say that it was my very favorite name in the whole wide world. Little did I know that she loathed it. Then when she was twelve and we had just been stationed in Ohio, she came home with her schoolwork and had the name Charley written on everything. Well, I was quite surprised, to say the least. I knew it was her work; I could tell it was her writing. Instead of making an issue out of it, I just simply asked her when she decided to start going by Charley. She said when she started school that first day. She had told her teachers and the students it was her name. She wrote it on everything. So from that day forward, we quit calling her Charlotte and started calling her Charley, as if that were her name all along."

I smiled as I listened to her story. "Did she expect you to get upset?"

"Well, I'm sure she did; but what would be the point? It broke my heart, I won't lie to you. I still love the name Charlotte, but I love my daughter more. That's all that matters."

I nodded. "That is all that matters."

"You know, Roda. Your mother . . . well, you know that I know about your mother; but do you know what I believe about her? I believe that maybe it's not that she doesn't love you, because somehow I believe that she does; but what I think, from what you've said about her own mother, your grandmother . . . I just think that maybe your mother doesn't know *how* to love you or even Amanda. How to really show love. Do you understand?" She paused and thought for a moment. "You see, our parents teach us how to love. It's true. That is a very important part of being a parent, showing your children love. And in turn, children learn to love and to show love. Perhaps your grandmother never taught her that. Perhaps the only things she really taught her were competition and perfection. I truly believe that, Roda. So please don't go through life thinking your mother doesn't love you, because I believe with all my heart that she does."

Tears were welling up in my eyes as she spoke. I really wanted to believe it was true, and maybe it was.

"Parents are supposed to love unconditionally," I said.

"Yes, that is true. But we, ourselves, need to be loved unconditionally as well," she added. "Perhaps she wasn't."

I nodded. "You know, Ms. Elaine, I really admire you. I always have. Charley is so very different from you, but you love her so much. I really do admire that."

She laughed a little. "Well, Charley *is* different, but that is what makes her so unique. So special. So priceless."

"I think Charley is the coolest person I've ever met. I've always thought that. I've always wished I could be as outgoing and as funny as she is."

"Oh, darling," Mrs. Webber replied, shaking her head a bit, "Charley is not as outgoing as you may think. She is actually one of the shyest people you will ever meet."

I shook my head and laughed. "That is not true at all. You should see how she is, especially when she first started McKinley. I was so jealous!"

She smiled knowingly. "Roda, you have to remember that Charley is an Army brat. She has grown up going from school to school. She was never in the same place for more than a year or two. She had to learn to be that way just to survive. When she was younger, she was painfully shy. Her brother has always been the outgoing one. He was too many years older than her to be able to take her under his wing though. So Charley struggled through school, and she struggled with making friends. But then that day when she started calling herself Charley, the world suddenly changed for her. She learned to play the part and act her way through it. But she was still that scared, shy girl with low self-esteem. She really was."

I was amazed. I had no idea that such a thing could even be possible. I thanked Mrs. Webber for taking the time to talk to me, and I left there that day feeling better about myself. I was beginning to feel confident with my decision, but I would give it some time before I told Mim and Dr. Hawkins. I wanted to be absolutely sure about my choice.

***

~December 2005~

I waited until the end of the semester before I decided which career path to follow. I knew I needed to decide before pre-registration, however, so that I could get on the right track with my undergraduate work. The medical field required a lot more math and science courses than art did. And I had decided that I definitely wanted to become a doctor. I wanted it with all my heart and soul.

At the end of the semester, I presented my last picture. It was of baby Emily and her mother. I told their story, and Dr. Hawkins was enthralled as usual. He had thoroughly enjoyed my whole series of photographs. "Insightful!" he exclaimed to the class. "Very insightful! Brilliant!" Everyone knew I was the teacher's pet. It was obvious.

I had decided to wait until after our last class to tell Dr. Hawkins my news. I was extremely nervous; and it didn't help that he started the conversation with, "Roda, you are going to make an excellent photojournalist! Excellent!"

I swallowed hard and said, "Yeah, about that."

He looked up at me with a hint of surprise. He raised his eyebrows. "Yes?"

"Umm," I started but hesitated. "Yeah, I was thinking . . ."

"Let's not beat around the bush," he said. "Out with it."

I cleared my throat. "Well, you know, a funny thing happened when I went to the hospital that day to take all of my pictures for class," I explained, thinking that was the best way to approach it.

His eyebrows rose further, and he just stared at me. "Out with it," he said.

"I think I've decided to become a doctor," I announced. He preferred the straightforward approach. He didn't care for all the details.

His expression softened, and he began to rub his chin thoughtfully. "You think you've decided? You're not sure?"

"No," I corrected, "I am sure. I don't think, I know. I know I want to be a doctor."

"Have you decided which field?" he asked.

"Field?" I asked.

"Yes, field. Field of study. What type of doctor do you want to become?"

"Oh," I said, suddenly feeling stupid, "sorry. Well, I'm not exactly sure yet, but I was thinking oncology . . . or maybe pediatrics."

"Or maybe geriatrics or neonatal?" he asked, smiling. "I can see where this project did have a great deal of influence on you. Are you sure that's not what this is?"

"No," I said matter-of-factly. "The project was the catalyst, I will say that. But no, it was the feeling I had inside the hospital. I felt a sense of empowerment. A sense of self-worth. I know I can do this. I know I can help people, and I want to help people more than anything."

He smiled at me. "I know that about you, you know? I've always known that about you. The way you see people through your camera lens, it's amazing. It's genuine. You have a heart for people, dear Roda. I have always known that. You see the downtrodden, and you want to reach out and take care of them. I think that's a wonderful quality to have. It's a rare quality to have. In fact, so rare that it's actually a gift. Yes, you, dear Roda, have a gift; and I think taking that unique gift into the medical field is the most brilliant idea I have ever heard."

"You do?" I asked, taken aback. "Really? You don't think I should use it to capture the world and tell its story?"

"No, absolutely not. You have already studied the world in this way. Now it's time to live it. And I have every confidence that you will excel beyond your wildest imagination."

I was so overcome with joy that I actually lunged towards

him and hugged him. He laughed in surprise and hugged me back. "Oh, dear Roda, I am so very proud of you. So very proud indeed." He broke our embrace and held me at arm's length. "You do realize, don't you, that you have always been my favorite student? You have been my prized pupil. While others sighed and moaned about my assignments, you took them head on as an intriguing challenge. And you, dear Roda, have never disappointed me. I am truly proud of you. I truly am."

His words were like manna from Heaven. Something inside of me craved affirmation. It was what could build me up, could feed me, and give me strength. I was ignored for so much of my life, but he was always the one teacher I had who truly believed in me. I was blessed beyond measure to know him, to study under him, and to have him as my mentor.

When it was time to go, he followed me out of the classroom. Turning off the light and locking his door, he said, "You do know, don't you, that you will have many, many classes with me if you take pre-med?"

"Oh really?" I asked, smiling. "Will you require photography assignments in those classes as well?"

He winked. "Perhaps."

When we reached the end of the hallway and we were about to go our separate ways, I stopped him and said, "Please don't say anything to Mim just yet." I knew he could be such a blabbermouth where she was concerned. "I haven't told her, and I need to be the one who does it."

He nodded. "Yes indeed. I will leave that up to you, but do not worry. I have a feeling she will be quite pleased."

***

After having such a good conversation with Dr. Hawkins, I decided to tell Mim that night. It was just the two of us now. Amanda was in her third year at NYU, studying fashion merchandising and design. Max was in his second year at NYU and was happily immersed in theater arts. He hoped to be on Broadway one day. Max's parents were eager to finally get him out of their Upper West Side penthouse, so they gave him an allowance to have his own apartment in Greenwich Village. He and Amanda lived together in a purely platonic manner and had been doing so since Max graduated high school. They were like an old married couple. Their bickering was quite hilarious. They were a good match because they balanced each other well.

When I arrived home that night, George was at the table and Mim was serving him her homemade Italian wedding soup, which was absolutely to die for. I had noticed throughout the past few years that George spent a lot of time fixing things in our apartment, and Mim always fed him well. Very ironic, I told her once, since she didn't want me to feed him to begin with.

I sat down as Mim offered me a bowl as well. "What's up, sugarbug?" she asked.

"Well, honey pie" I began, still loving that she called me pet names even though I was in college, "I just had a long conversation with Dr. Hawkins." I thought that might be the best way to break the ice.

"Oh really?" she said as she sat down with her bowl of soup. "What about?"

"My idea to be a photojournalist," I said. "Or rather, to *not* be a photojournalist."

Mim looked up at me. "*Not* be a photojournalist? But you've wanted to do that for years now. What's changed your mind?"

"I just have something else in mind," I said casually.

"Are you going back to sketching? Please tell me you're going back to sketching," she pleaded.

"No," I said sadly. "I still like to sketch. I won't give it up completely, but that's not what I want to do."

"Well, what do you want to do?" George asked.

I looked back and forth at both of them, waiting to gauge their reactions when I said it. Waiting to see if there would be disappointment or surprise or anything negative that would indicate they didn't think I could actually do it.

"I want to be a doctor. A medical doctor," I finally announced.

Mim's hands flew up to her mouth, covering a large smile. Her eyes became wide with surprise and joy. "Oh, Roda, honey! I think that would be amazing! Really I do!"

"You do?" I asked, shocked. "You really do?"

"Yes! I think that would be the most wonderful thing in the world! Just wonderful!" She grabbed my hand. "You are brilliant, Roda. You are. You have a brilliant mind, and I have no doubt that you can accomplish it!"

I smiled bigger than I ever had before. "You really think so?" I still didn't quite believe it about myself. I wasn't completely sure I could accomplish it.

She nodded emphatically. "I *know* so!"

I looked at George. He had a sense of pride beaming on his face. He looked like a proud dad, as if my own dad were sitting right there looking at me. "Roda, I think it's wonderful. I know you can do it. I have no doubt that you can. You have a heart for people. I can attest to that. I think you will make the best doctor anyone has ever known."

I was so excited I could hardly stand it. I knew I had made the right decision. Before we were even finished with dinner, I went and grabbed the NYU course catalog and began charting my path towards med school.

Chapter 20

I met the love of my life on October twentieth during my second year of medical school. He was the most handsome guy I had ever met, with short brown hair, the bluest eyes, and the cutest crooked smile. He approached me on our third day of chemistry lab. He had chosen me to be his partner. I was, to be quite honest, shocked. His opening line was peculiar, however. I was already sitting at the lab table when he came up to me and said, "You have a very unusual name." Well, tell me something I don't know, I thought. But I smiled and said, "Yes, I know I do." He placed his books on the black table top and sat down.

"Do you have a story behind your name?" he asked, smiling.

"Oh, do I ever," I replied, fumbling in my purse for a pen so he couldn't tell how nervous I was.

"Well, spill it then," he laughed.

So I told him the short version of how my name came to be, transcription mistake and all. I ended by telling him that my dad had refused to change it, saying that there was a reason. Boy, was there; and I discovered it that day. It's what attracted him to me.

"My mother's name was Rhoda," he said. "Rhoda with an *h.*"

I smiled, for the first time in my life absolutely *loving* my name. "Really?" I asked. "Is there a story behind her name?"

He smiled and shook his head. "Nah," he said, "I think it was just that her mother's favorite flower was a rhododendron, or something like that."

We both laughed. He was very charming and witty. We had instant rapport.

"My name is Ben," he said, shaking my hand. "Ben Emerson."

"Hi, Ben," I said stupidly. "My name is Roda Allen." What an idiot.

"Yeah, I kinda know that," he said, laughing. "I knew that on the first day of class. I don't guess you picked up on mine, did you?"

"Umm," I started to say but not wanting to say it.

He laughed again. "It's okay if you didn't. It's a pretty big class. There's got to be about a hundred . . . well . . . maybe only fifteen people in here. But who's counting?"

His laugh was infectious, and his self-deprecating humor was endearing. I had butterflies in my stomach; but I tried to remain cool, hoping he wouldn't notice.

"You said *was*," I said, suddenly catching it. "Your mom's name *was* Rhoda?"

He nodded. "Yeah, my mom died of breast cancer when I was seventeen."

"Oh," I said sadly, "I'm so sorry."

"Thanks," he said. "Yeah, it's pretty young to lose your mom, you know?"

I swallowed hard and nodded. "Yeah, I know. I lost my dad when I was fourteen."

"Fourteen? Really?" he asked with concern. "That's really too young. What happened?"

Before I could answer, the professor started the class. I was surprised that I felt relief about the interruption. I supposed it was because I felt defined by the event of my dad's death and had just truly realized it. Everyone knew that about me, that my dad was a victim of September 11th; therefore, I was a victim of September 11th. Ben was new, and he didn't know. He didn't know to look at me with that sincere look of sadness that comes with the realization of who I truly am and what I went through. It is much like a person who has cancer. Before that person reveals the knowledge of their disease, they are seen as a person. After they reveal the knowledge, they are seen as a person with cancer. Not just a person anymore, but a person walking around carrying this huge thing inside of them, even if it's only microscopic cells. It's still cancer, and they are no longer just a person.

The same is true for victims and the families of the victims. The event becomes part of the story of our lives, and we can either embrace it or run from it. But when the rare chance occurs when you meet someone new, and they have absolutely no knowledge of it, and they just see you as a person—a *person*—and not a victim, it's refreshing. I knew I would tell him. I wasn't going to keep it from him since he asked. But for one hour, I sat there, barely paying attention to what was being taught, savoring the time I had with him before he knew.

When class was over, Ben and I walked out of the building and stood outside on the sidewalk. He had sensed my demeanor during class. He had noticed I was preoccupied with my thoughts.

"What's wrong, Roda?" he asked with deep sincerity. "Is it about your dad? I'm sorry if I've made you feel uncomfortable."

"No, you haven't," I said, shaking my head. "You haven't at all." I took a deep breath. I was going to tell him. Why was it suddenly so hard? I dreaded it. I dreaded seeing that look of sympathy on his face. Dreaded him acting like he didn't know what to say. I just wanted to be normal. I just wanted to feel normal again. But have I ever known what normal is, really? No, I haven't. So I just said it. "My dad died on September 11th. He was in the North Tower when it collapsed," I said, choking back tears, "and I saw it fall."

It wasn't a look of sympathy that he had. His reaction actually mirrored my emotions when I told him. Tears welled up in his eyes, and he became so choked up that he could barely speak. It was as if someone had just told him *he* had lost a family member on that fateful day. He instinctively hugged me and told me he was sorry. The ninth anniversary of my dad's death had just passed the month before; but suddenly, it felt as if it had just happened, and I was being consoled all over again.

His embrace was warm and caring, and I could have stood there in his arms forever. I lost my sense of time and space. I was unaware of anything around me and unaware of how long we had been standing there. When he pulled away slightly, he looked me in the eyes. "Why don't we go get something to eat," he said, "and we can share our sad stories?"

233

I nodded, and he put his arm around me. We walked two blocks to a Chinese restaurant. We sat there talking for three hours. It wasn't a sad conversation but an uplifting one because we didn't dwell on the tragedy of either of us losing a parent so young. We focused, rather, on the people we had become *because* of the events. Ben said the way we—as survivors—needed to see it was, that if the tragic events made us become better people, then their deaths were not in vain. I completely understood that and believed it. I knew I had become a better person because of what I had endured. Ben knew he had too. Up until he was seventeen, he had wanted to follow in his father's footsteps and become an engineer. After his mother's illness, he knew he wanted to go into medicine. He wanted to help others the same way I did. We had very different stories, but we had ended up at the same point in life. And from that day on, we were inseparable.

***

The next two years of med school were a whirlwind of classes that seemed endless. Ben and I charted our course together, taking many of the same classes and pulling all nighters studying for every exam. We became quite the team. Friday night date nights consisted of pouring over piles of medical books in the library. Weekends were spent quizzing each other about the skeletal system, the muscular system, general pathways of the brain, and renal and digestive functions. It was all very romantic. But we enjoyed each other's company and quickly became each other's right arm.

~*May 2016*~

We took our relationship slowly, knowing the direction we were headed but not being in a hurry to get there. We both agreed med school was a huge commitment that we needed to get past before any other long term plans could be considered. It was upon graduation from med school, however, when Ben proposed to me. I knew the next step would be coming, but he completely surprised me by proposing that very night.

The graduation ceremony was at two o'clock in the

afternoon, lasting well over two hours. Mim and George, who had married during my junior year of college, planned a catered celebration dinner at the new art gallery they had opened together two years prior. She had retired from teaching at the university, and she finally realized her dream of owning her own gallery. It was a beautiful space she had found in Chelsea. It was open and airy with exposed brick walls and hardwood floors. Mim Allen-Mickler was finally a successful art dealer, and her gallery had become all the rage.

I was astounded when Ben and I arrived that night at six o'clock. There was a long table set up in the center of the gallery, decorated with my grandmother's china, a large center piece, and place cards for seating. Our closest friends and family were in attendance, including Ben's dad and younger sister; Charley and her parents and brother; Max and Amanda; and Dr. Hawkins. But what surprised me was that Mim had removed all of the gallery art from the walls and, in its place, had matted and framed much of my artwork from throughout the years: sketches I had drawn when I was in elementary school, paintings I had done in middle school, and pictures I had taken in high school and college. The picture of George when he was homeless was on prominent display, as was the series I had taken at the hospital my freshman year of college. I looked at the four pictures, wondering where those people were now. When had Mr. Tanner's wife, Maggie, passed away; and where was he now? Was he even alive? How old was Jared now? How big had little Emily grown? And what ever happened to Sarah?

Those four pictures had been a turning point in my life, and each of the people depicted in them had changed my life for the better. They never knew they had, but they did. I had written their addresses down and mailed their pictures, but I never kept in touch with them the way I had intended—especially Sarah. It had been eleven years ago. I doubted if there was any chance of finding out where they were now.

Ben saw me transfixed by the four pictures, and he came up behind me and slid his arms around me.

"Whatcha looking at?" he asked sweetly. "You seem to be in deep thought."

"These are the pictures I took that day at the hospital my

freshman year. They're the reason I'm a doctor."

He nodded. "They're wonderful. You really captured their spirit in each one."

"I just wonder where they are now," I said, reaching out to touch Sarah's picture.

He nodded. "I know."

I took a deep breath as Mim approached, and I turned and smiled at her. "Mim, this is just amazing. Thank you so much for doing this for me. All of these pictures bring back such memories."

She smiled. "Ah, honey, you've always had such talent. I wanted to show it off, and I thought this would be the perfect way to do it. And," she said, looking around, "it shows how you've progressed throughout your life. The experiences you've had and the people you've met."

"But there's one missing," I said sadly. "One that I regret giving away."

Mim nodded. "I know, honey."

"Which one is that?" Ben asked curiously.

"The portrait of my dad that I drew on the train the morning he died. It was a beautiful picture, and I left it for my mother to have. Now I would give anything to have it back."

"Yeah," Mim said, "this collection isn't complete without it." She looked around. "Listen, let's stop dwelling on things we can't change. Let's just focus on the joy of today. You two have graduated medical school!" she said excitedly. "It's time to celebrate!"

Ben and I both smiled and agreed.

We had a wonderful dinner. Everyone talked and laughed. Tears were shed because it was a bittersweet celebration without my dad and Ben's mom there. The greatest heartbreak of losing a parent so young is not having them around during the most important moments in life. My dad wasn't there for my high school graduation or my college graduation, and now he wasn't there to see me graduate from medical school. It was an accomplishment I'm sure he never dreamed of. All of those nights sitting in my room doing math problems over and over and over again. Back then, I doubt he would have ever imagined I would become a doctor.

I was lost in thought when Ben took his fork and tapped his

wine glass, garnering everyone's attention. He slid out his chair and stood up. He took me by the hand and guided me to stand beside him. Putting his arm around me, he began to speak.

"Roda and I want to thank everyone here tonight. Thank you for coming, and thank you for supporting us as we made our way through med school. Thank you for believing that we could actually accomplish it. Thanks to all of you for loving us and being there for us throughout our whole lives, not just the past few years."

I smiled in agreement, looking lovingly at everyone around the table. Then Ben looked at me. "I must tell all of you the story of when I first saw Roda." He smiled at me. "She walked into chem lab, and Dr. Gregory greeted her by saying, 'Well, Roda Allen! My favorite student is finally here!' I was intrigued, to say the least. 'Who was this girl?' I wondered. The professor obviously knew her well, and she had the same name as my mother—which was rare. So she got my attention. She sat at a lab table in the front and took copious notes. 'She seems very smart,' I thought. I decided she would make an excellent lab partner." He paused while everyone laughed. "I couldn't take my eyes off of her. She was the most beautiful woman I had ever seen. Now when I told her this later, she disagreed. But it was true. There was something I saw in her when she reacted to Dr. Gregory's greeting that convinced me she was not only beautiful on the outside but on the inside as well. There wasn't any haughtiness about her. Most students would have puffed up with certain arrogance, but Roda just smiled a shy smile and said, 'Hello, Dr. Greg.' She was the only one allowed to call him Dr. Greg, by the way. I found that out the hard way. Apparently, it didn't even matter if you were dating Roda. Dr. Gregory would *only* allow Roda to call him by that name." He paused again for more laughter. "I realized then that not only was she beautiful, not only was she smart, not only did she have my mother's name, but she had something even more valuable. She had a way with people. I don't even know if it has a name. But it's just a presence that puts people at ease, that draws them to her, that causes them to trust her. Causes them to love her. She just has a beauty all her own, and I count myself lucky to have had her fall in love with me. And now, I have one more question to ask her. One very important question."

He pulled a little black box out of his pocket, got on one knee and opened it. "Roda Francis Allen, will you marry me?"

You could have literally heard a pin drop. No one expected it. No one. Not even me. My hands were shaking as I drew them to my face in disbelief. Tears began streaming down my face. I nodded and could barely speak, but I managed to say yes. It was probably only a whisper, but I managed to say it nonetheless.

Mim squealed in delight and jumped up to be the first to hug me. Everyone applauded and began getting up to come over to personally congratulate us. They all wanted to look at the ring, which was a two carat princess cut diamond, set in platinum, with half carat diamond baguettes on each side. It was breathtaking.

The night could not have been more perfect. My head was spinning, and I don't think I had ever been happier than I was that night. I had finally graduated medical school and was about to start my internship. I was in love with the most wonderful man on earth, and he had just asked me to marry him. I was absolutely floating the rest of the night; and the next day, I would begin planning our wedding.

***

Well, planning a wedding while interning at the NYU medical center turned out to be quite the challenge. I ended up relying on Mim for the vast majority of it. I trusted her judgment. Amanda helped as well. She had graduated from the university with a business degree and a focus on fashion design and merchandising, so she was definitely in her element. I basically left it all up to them and joked that they could just tell Ben and me when and where to show up.

I experienced an earth-shattering moment when Ben and I had our engagement pictures taken. We decided to have them made in Central Park, and the day couldn't have been more beautiful. It was inherent in me that I loathed pictures. Growing up overweight and not so pretty, I avoided the camera at all costs. I was more comfortable behind the lens. So other than the obligatory ID badge photo needed for school or for the hospital, I had not seen a real picture of myself in quite some time. Ben and I had been too busy in our dating years to socialize much, so there weren't many pictures taken during that time period.

When we were given the proofs, I was astounded at what I saw. It was me, but it didn't look like me. I somehow looked tall and thin. That wasn't me. It couldn't have been me. I had cheekbones. Actual cheekbones! My face had always been chubby and round, but now it appeared in the pictures to be slim and defined. How was it that I didn't notice such a change when I looked in the mirror? Somehow our minds play tricks on us, causing us to believe that who we have always been is who we will always be. In my mind, I was still that pudgy thirteen-year-old girl. I still felt like her. I still believed I looked like her. But those pictures proved differently. I had grown and matured. I had changed.

Ben noticed my stunned demeanor. "What's wrong?" he asked. "You don't like the pictures?"

"No," I said, staring, "that's not it. I just," I stammered. "I just don't think this is me. How is this me?"

He was confused. "What do you mean? Of course it's you."

I shook my head. "I know it's supposed to be me, but it doesn't look like me."

At this point, he probably thought I had lost my mind. "Sweetie, you've always looked like this."

"No, I haven't," I argued.

"Yes, you have," he countered.

"*No*, I haven't. I've always been fat."

He shook his head. "No, you've always been pretty small, and I think you've lost more weight since we first met. Probably the rigors of med school took care of that. I think you're just fooled because you wear clothes that are too big for you. And now we basically live in scrubs, so that can kind of fool you too. But no, you've always been thin."

"That's impossible," I said, stunned. How had I not noticed? How had Mim, George, Amanda—anybody—not noticed or said something? I thought back to my college days and med school. Yes, it had been rigorous. I was always sleep deprived and consumed large amounts of coffee. Always taking a full course load. I barely had time to breath yet alone eat. I remembered eating lots of salads and usually anything portable, like fruit or a granola bar. During those years, I learned to live on very little sleep and very little food; and now it had transformed me into someone completely different.

I called Amanda immediately. When she answered, I completely ignored her greeting and hurriedly asked, "What size is my wedding dress?" Amanda had been in charge of the dress, and she was doing an impeccable job. She had never mentioned what size it was; and I, always avoiding knowing what size I needed, had never asked.

"Well," she hesitated, stunned at the abrupt question, "because of fittings, dress sizes can vary; but technically, you're a size six."

"A size SIX?!" I asked, raising my voice in excitement. "I'm a size SIX, and you never told me?! Why haven't you told me this, Manda?! Why?!"

"Well," she hesitated further, no doubt thinking I had lost my mind, "I thought you knew."

"No, I didn't know this! You should have told me! I've always been fat! I thought I was still fat!"

"No, Roda," she replied, "not at all. You are very slim. I thought you knew."

I hung up without responding and immediately called Mim. "Why didn't you tell me?" I asked as soon as she answered the phone.

"Tell you what, honeybee?" Mim asked, confused.

"That I was skinny. Why didn't you tell me?" I felt crazy and happy all at the same time. Euphoria was overtaking me.

"Well, sweetie, I thought you knew. With your crazy schedule, you started losing weight a long time ago. In fact, now I think you're losing too much weight. That hospital needs to give you time to eat."

"But I," I stammered, "I didn't know."

"It's probably those baggy clothes you wear. You need a new wardrobe. Manda has wanted to take you shopping, but she knows you never have a minute. You should take some time and go with her."

I nodded absentmindedly, but she couldn't see me. "Yeah," I finally said.

"By the way," she continued, "have you noticed that I've been losing weight also?"

"No," I said, surprised. "You have?"

"Yes, I have. I've lost about thirty pounds in the past year. It's a drop in the bucket, but I'm making progress."

"No," I said, dumbfounded, "that's great. Great progress."

My life, I concluded, was too hectic if I hadn't noticed mine or Mim's weight loss. I decided to start paying better attention to the world around me. How could I allow such significant events to escape my notice? I immediately texted Amanda and said, "Let's go shopping soon!" Then I smiled at Ben, feeling like I was suddenly a new person. We picked out our favorite pictures and decided on one in particular to use for our engagement announcement. I sat there for the first time looking forward to taking our wedding photographs. I was literally in awe at the thought.

~June 2017~

Our wedding turned out to be one of the most beautiful weddings ever held at the Plaza. Mim and Amanda did a fabulous job planning it. Everything was perfect. The men were dressed in traditional black tuxes, and the bridesmaids were dressed in a soft shade of periwinkle. The flowers were cream colored roses. George looked handsome as he proudly walked me down the aisle. We were married on June twenty-first, on what would have been my dad's sixty-first birthday. Ben and I both wanted to acknowledge our lost parents in some way, so we chose that date in honor of my dad and laid a bouquet of cream roses mixed with pink rhododendrons on the chair where the mother of the groom would have been seated in honor of his mother. Our tears were tears of joy that day but also bittersweet tears because we missed them so much. We both longed to have them there with us on such a wonderful, beautiful day in our lives. Such is the sadness of losing a parent too soon.

We honeymooned in Bora Bora. It was a relaxing getaway from the madness of life. Ben and I promised each other that we would not let the craziness of life interfere with our marriage. Somehow we would make time for each other and not evolve into strangers in the years to come. That was of utmost importance to us.

A week later, we returned to our two-story brownstone in Gramercy Park. We were refreshed from the thrill of our marriage and our amazing vacation. The following week, we were both scheduled to start our residency at Mt. Sinai Hospital. We had interned at NYU Langone Medical Center, but we were both miraculously accepted into Mt. Sinai's surgical residency. Ben and I both decided to become cardiothoracic surgeons; and by getting accepted at Mt. Sinai, we were both able to go straight into surgical training involving our field rather than general surgery with a cardiac fellowship. We were ecstatic.

Many people we had known throughout med school had always joked that Ben and I seemed to share the same brain. What Ben didn't quite know, I knew; and what I didn't quite know, he knew. That made us perfect study partners, compensating for each other's weaknesses. He knew medical terminology like the back of his hand, and I was an expert at coming up with anagrams to study and remember facts. That was something my dad had taught me.

The only area we differed in was the sub-specialties we fellowshipped in. We were both cardiothoracic surgeons, but Ben specialized in cardiac transplantation while I specialized in pediatric cardiac surgery. When we were in our third year of residency, we both assisted the chief of surgery during a heart transplant on a nine year old girl named Sydney. It was after that one surgery, when we knew it had been a success and we were basking in the exhilaration of it all, that I knew I had achieved a milestone in my life. I knew I had achieved something great. And I smiled as tears fell down my face because somehow I knew my dad was looking down upon me, full of pride and knowing I had kept my promise to him. I had become someone he knew all along I could be, and I had achieved something he believed I could achieve. Something great. And for the first time, I believed it too.

Chapter 21

It has been twenty-five years since my dad died. Twenty-five years. That seems like an eternity, yet it still feels like yesterday. I miss my dad every day. Every single day. Ben and I have a son now. We named him Paul Allen Emerson, after my dad. He's three years old and is the spitting image of my dad. It's amazing. The same green eyes, the same brown hair, the same crooked smile. Mim constantly pulls out baby pictures of my dad to verify that this phenomenon is true. He's a virtual clone. How intriguing genetics can be. How amazing that someone so dear to me who I lost so long ago can somehow be brought back through my own child, if only in image alone. Sometimes I hold him and feel like I'm hugging my dad again. I am careful, however, not to worship my own child. I could easily fall into that trap, so I resist it.

Ben and I just found out that I'm pregnant with a little girl. She's due to be born in April. We've decided to name her Amelia. I resisted at first, associating any and every *A* name with my mother. But I love the name Amelia. Amelia Michelle—part of the name I would have had if my dad hadn't changed it. But Michelle was a variation of Michael—his middle name, so I wanted to use it. And I am proud of my own name now. It was the name my dad gave me, it was the name he believed in, and it was the name that attracted my husband; so I'm happy with it.

I have spent the better part of a year recounting my life. I hid so much of it away in my heart and conveniently forgot about it. But when I put pen to paper, it all came rushing back. How extraordinary it is that our brains can recall events and conversations from so long ago. I have journeyed through the madness of my childhood that I experienced with my mother. I have cried tears of joy and sorrow as I remembered the shelter I found in my dad. I have finally put the pieces of the puzzle together, and now I can see my life in the big picture. I can finally see so clearly how my mother influenced my life. As sad and as horrible as it was to endure, it made me the person I am today. I was deprived of my mother's love; therefore, I learned how to love others. I was denied compassion; therefore, I understand the need for compassion. I was inadvertently shown that only certain people matter; therefore, I believe that everyone matters. I was made to feel stupid and ugly; therefore, I treat everyone as if they are beautiful and smart. No one deserves to be treated otherwise.

There is purpose in everything. Nothing is by chance, or so I believe. I was my mother's daughter for a reason; and that reason, I believe, was to make me a better person. I often think about my mother. I haven't had any contact with her for the past twenty-five years. I have no idea what has transpired with her or Ashley. Sometimes if I dwell on it, it saddens me. But I've always fully believed that it was my mother's place to reach out to me. It's not that I can't forgive. I've just always stood firm on the belief that if she truly loved me, she would reach out to me.

Mim always invited her to the ground zero ceremony every year. My mother never responded. When Amanda and I both graduated from McKinley, Mim sent invitations to her. She never came. By the time we graduated college, Mim declined to invite her. Our mother's silence, even from an hour away, could always hurt us. Her silence could take a perfectly wonderful day of celebration and ruin it with just the simple thought that she didn't even have the decency to at least say no. Mim decided at some point to take that power away from her and just not invite her at all. That way, she could no longer hurt us.

My life as it is now, with all its craziness, is exactly how I always wanted it to be. It was the life my dad had wanted. A close family with a husband and wife who loved each other desperately, a beautiful child, and the excitement of another baby on the way. A happy, loving, laughing family that would be lost without each other. That's what I have, and that's what my dad always dreamed of.

Ben and I have continued to keep our promise to not lose sight of each other and to balance our personal lives with our professional lives. We are still fully immersed in our careers and leaders in our field, but we are both careful to set our family as the priority.

I love my job. I love saving lives and putting people at ease. I love diagnosing and correcting problems. I love the challenge of my work. I wouldn't trade it for anything. But there are days, I will admit, when I allow my mind to wonder what might have been. Charley, who I am still best friends with after all these years, became what I had wanted to be. She went on to become a photojournalist and is currently in Uganda on assignment for National Geographic Magazine. Sometimes I'm almost jealous. But then a patient comes in, a case is presented to me, I solve the riddle of what is wrong, and I dive in and correct the problem and save their life. Then it's all worthwhile, and my jealousy evaporates.

***

Ben came home exhausted from his shift at the hospital. He had hoped to be home before Paul was asleep, but a last minute consultation delayed him. I wasn't due to be at the hospital again until the day after next, so we made plans to spend a quiet family day together. Early in our marriage, we always tried to schedule our shifts together; but after Paul was born, we staggered them so that one of us would always be at home with the baby. It shortened our time together, but we usually had a day or two in between to spend with each other.

The next day was Thursday. We decided to keep Paul out of preschool, and the three of us packed a lunch and headed for the park. It was a beautiful fall day in early November, and it was a welcome relief to spend a relaxing day together.

We had just finished lunch. Paul was asleep on the blanket, and Ben was reading a book. I was sketching when the hospital messaged me. Technically, I wasn't on call; but I had instructed them to contact me if there was a dire emergency. A nurse, who was a close friend of mine, alerted me, saying, *ASAP! 17 y/o female. Need you!* I sighed, not wanting to go. I had been enjoying the day with my guys. But Ben kissed me and said to go. He would stay at the park until Paul woke up, and then they would go home. He knew that, whatever the emergency was, I could take care of it and be home by late afternoon. He felt sure about that. He promised to have dinner ready when I was done. I kissed my guys goodbye and caught the first cab I could.

I arrived within fifteen minutes, quickly heading to the doctor's lounge to change into my scrubs. Gabby Foster, the nurse who paged me, came in behind me, wanting to fill me in on the situation.

"Girl, you got here fast. Where'd you come from?" she asked as she assisted me with my clothes.

"We were at the park. I got here as quickly as I could."

"I'm sorry to interrupt your day, but I just felt you needed to be here for this one," she said, folding my clothes and putting them away. "They already got her up in surgery, prepping her. You need to get scrubbed."

"I'm going as fast as I can, Gab," I said, motioning for her to follow me out of the lounge. We sprinted to the elevator to head upstairs to the surgical floor. She filled in the details as we rushed to get there.

"Seventeen-year-old girl. Mother says she's been short of breath and congested lately. Figured she was battling an upper respiratory infection. Had a doctor's appointment scheduled for tomorrow. Then today at school, she started feeling dizzy and her heart was racing. Later, she felt pressure on her chest and could hardly breathe. So they immediately took her to the pediatrician. Why in the world they didn't take her to the ER beats me. Pediatrician examined her and immediately sent her here. Why in the world they didn't send her to the ER in Greenwich beats me. All I know is that the pediatrician sent her to you, so I felt the need to text you." She took a breath while I began scrubbing. The patient was prepped and ready, and everyone was waiting on me. "Keller diagnosed it. Said she was in atrial fibrillation. Looks like a congenital defect of the aortic valve, just now showing up. They ran some tests and saw that the valve was leaking. Decided to knock it out instead of waiting for it to get worse."

"Thanks, Gabby," I said, backing into the OR with my hands up, ready for gloves. "You did well. Excellent run down. I'll see you in a bit." And with that, I immediately took charge of the room and began cracking her chest open to repair the valve.

I worked meticulously to the sound of piano music. Surgeons have their own preferences as they work. Some like Bach, some like Beethoven. I just prefer soft contemporary piano. Most surgeons like to talk. I know Ben does. But I prefer silence because I'm a thinker. Unless instructions need to be given, I ask that everyone remain quiet. No chatter. It makes me nervous. I like the calmness of silence so that I can allow my thoughts to wander. Today, I was thinking about Gabby.

Gabby is sixteen years older than I am; and she has had a much rougher life, to say the least. She's a petite African-American woman who is so skinny she looks like she would just blow over with the slightest breeze. But I know that she is as strong as any man.

Her name was originally Wanda Higgins. She was born in a small, impoverished town in southern Georgia to a teenage mother who was too young to truly care for her and to an older man who began sexually abusing her by the time she was five. Gabby resisted him with all her might but soon learned that it was less painful to give in and avoid the inevitable beating that would occur if she didn't. She quietly took his abuse and her mother's neglect until she was seventeen. That's when she met a boy named Reggie Foster.

Reggie was two years older than Gabby and, at first, treated her well. He worked construction and made a good living for an eighteen year old kid. She quickly saw him as her way out of the hell she endured every day. He got hired on a construction job that would take him to North Carolina. It was then that they married and ran away, making their new home in Asheville. For the first time in her life, Gabby was happy and content. Reggie earned the money, and she kept the home comfortable and calm, full of good food and affection for her hard working husband. Wanda Foster had rid herself of her father's name and had finally found normalcy.

That normalcy lasted for two years. Reggie was a good man, but he was impressionable. He began to take up the habits of the co-workers around him. Mainly drinking, which began with Friday nights at a local bar to blow off steam and led to nightly visits that gradually turned into all-nighters. The first time Reggie struck her was when she waited up for him on a Friday night. It had been their anniversary, and he didn't come home until two o'clock in the morning. She was upset and hurt, yelling hysterically at him. Without a word, he punched her in the face and went to bed.

The abuse grew from there. Gradually at first but became increasingly frequent even when unprompted. Not only was he physically abusive but he became sexually aggressive as well. Given the abuse Gabby endured from her father, she regressed towards her husband to the point where he was literally raping her. And just as her father had done, Reggie would beat her if she resisted. She was caught in the same trap as before. She felt as though she were in her father's house all over again.

It took Gabby seven months to save enough money to quietly file for divorce and buy a bus ticket. Leaving with only what she could carry, she escaped in the middle of the night when Reggie was at a bar. What few possessions they had, she left behind. Fearing that he might come after her, she decided to head north instead of south. Reggie would never have expected her to go north. Not only that, but knowing she was more of a small town girl at heart, he would never expect her to go to New York City. So that's where she went.

Having very little money, she mainly stayed in women's shelters to begin with. Within two weeks, she found a job in the custodial department at Mt. Sinai hospital. Within three months, she found a roommate at the hospital: a co-worker who was widowed and lived in a small apartment in Harlem. Ten months later, she was working in the cafeteria. She saved her money and began taking night classes within a year. She decided to become a nurse, and she put all her energy and ambition into that endeavor.

Wanda Foster quickly received her nickname in nursing school, and it followed her. She was outspoken and easily knew all the answers. She was always talking, and it was one of her instructors who began telling her that she gabbed too much. Soon, he was referring to her as his gabbing student. Finally, he just started calling her Gabby. She walked into class one day, and her teacher said, "Well, there's Gabby Foster. She will enlighten us with her knowledge today." Other students laughed and from then on called her Gabby as well. She assumed it was meant as an insult, but she rather liked the name. It suited her, and it allowed her to shed her past identity. She was no longer Wanda Higgins Foster. She was no longer her husband's wife or her father's daughter. She was her own person, achieving her own goals. She had always wondered if maybe her teacher called her that name to intimidate her, but it didn't work. It only made her that much more determined to speak. By the time she graduated nursing school, she had legally changed her name, proud of the badge of honor he had bestowed upon her. She felt like a new person with everything bad behind her and everything good ahead of her.

Working from the bottom up, she had learned every square inch of the hospital. She knew it inside and out. She was smart, and she paid attention; and by the time she had earned her degree, she could easily direct more seasoned nurses above her. She was confident and spoke her mind easily. Sometimes this was well regarded and sometimes it wasn't.

As years passed and Gabby gained more experience, she grew to despise the interns who came in already thinking they were smarter than the nurses just because they had a medical degree. She was quick to put them in their place, and all of them grew to respect her. I was a resident when I started at Mt. Sinai, but I was still intimidated by her. I saw how demanding she was of the other nurses and how she kept the doctors on their toes. I tried my best to stay below her radar and not make a mistake. She didn't engage me at first. I was pleasant and respectful towards her from the beginning, and she was to me as well. I didn't quite understand it to begin with, but I realized later that we saw something in each other that was familiar. There was a vulnerability about us both that stemmed from a childhood of victimization and neglect, and only we could see it in each other. Only we could recognize it. It was a secret, unspoken language. But the beauty of our past circumstances was that we both overcame them and became better people because of them.

I hadn't been there very long when I realized she was looking out for me. Exhausted after an eleven hour stretch, I inadvertently grabbed the wrong size intubation tube for a patient in cardiac arrest. Gabby was right beside me, taking the tube from me and handing me the correct one. But what surprised me the most was that she took the blame, saying, "I handed you the wrong one." No, she hadn't. I knew it was my fault; and above all, I knew Gabby Foster never took the blame for something that wasn't her fault. She was more likely to point out everyone else's mistakes. After the patient was stable, I went to the nurse's desk to chart my notes. I looked at her and asked why she covered for me. "I know you tired," was all she said. Then while she walked away, she turned and said, "I don't really consider it covering, by the way. I know you smart. I know you know what you're doing. I was just helping you out." And with that, she walked down the hall to check on a patient.

From that day forward, we protected each other. She was always a step ahead of everyone on patient care, even with the patients she wasn't in charge of. She immediately comprehended their history and diagnosis. She would enlighten me before I would even get to them, and the other nurses always wondered how I knew everything beforehand. They never knew Gabby was my secret weapon. In turn, I defended her. What I realized very quickly was that the others misunderstood the tough exterior she had. Sure she was tough. She was demanding. But she was fair, and she was loyal. She had a good heart, a loving spirit. They were just too blind to notice. But in their defense, it was no surprise they were blind to it because Gabby never let herself get close to anyone—except me. She trusted me and I trusted her. We were bonded together through memories of an unhappy childhood and our drive to succeed and make something out of ourselves. When others would complain or gossip about her, I would quickly correct them and tell them that they had better listen to her and do what she said because I knew they would learn more from her than from anyone else at the hospital.

What makes Gabby an excellent nurse is that she is ferociously protective of the patients. Not just her patients but everyone's patients. If the patient needs something, she's there. If she can't get there, someone else better—and fast. If she sees a nurse sitting when a patient has buzzed, she lights a fire under them. And everyone *knows* not to let it get to that point. Gabby is one of the most respected nurses today, and many have encouraged her to go into the administrative side of nursing, but she refuses. The patients are her life. They are the children she never had; the mother she left behind; the fellow downtrodden who haven't found their way up yet. She will never give them up. And from the beginning, I have made sure to have her by my side whenever possible.

***

I emerged from the operating room almost four hours later. The surgery went well, and I wanted to chart the procedure before talking to the family members anxiously waiting down the hall. Gabby was ready for me at the nurse's desk with orange juice and a turkey sandwich from the cafeteria.

"You been on your feet too long, girl," she said, directing me to sit down. "You got to rest. Don't want that little baby girl to get too stressed."

I smiled up at her. "The baby isn't going to be stressed, but thank you. My back is killing me."

"Here," she said, pushing the sandwich towards me, "you got to feed baby girl." She was like a nervous grandmother waiting for her first grandchild to be born. I complied and took a couple of big bites before looking at the chart.

"So everything go well with Anna?" she asked.

"Who's Anna?" I asked, my mouth full of food.

"Who Anna?" she said indignantly. "Anna's the girl you just operated on."

"Ah," I said, swallowing and then taking a sip of my juice. Baby girl needs her vitamin C. "Well, you didn't tell me that, Gab. I guess your pre-op rundown was a little deficient," I said, smiling. I knew that would get her.

"Deficient? I know you didn't say that," she said, crossing her arms.

"Well, did you expect the patient to sit up and tell me her name?" I asked smartly.

"What they say when you went in there already knowing what to do?" she asked, changing the subject.

"Completely shocked when I asked for the mechanical valve. Simmons was thinking biological, if not something altogether less invasive. He disagreed because she's a teenager, but I told him the symptoms were too far gone. We could do ring

251

annuloplasty; but judging from the ultrasound, she would be right back in the OR within a few years. Better to nip it in the bud."

"You did the MAZE procedure?" Gabby inquired.

"Sure did," I answered, nodding.

"Simmons hates anything invasive," Gabby said knowingly.

"Yep," I agreed, "but you can't put a band-aid on a gunshot wound. Anyway," I shrugged, "it's for the best. I did one of these on a thirty-four year old last year. Just something that has to be done. I've just never had to do one on somebody so young."

She nodded. "Reckon they'll ever figure it out? How you already know what's up?"

I shook my head. "I doubt it. They should, but I doubt they ever will," I laughed. Our sharing of inside information was our little joke.

I sat there finishing the sandwich, knowing I needed to hurry and get to the waiting room to put the family at ease. I suddenly felt pensive, thinking about the girl's name. Anna. That was supposed to be my name. I had not encountered very many girls named Anna in my life, but it was always just a little bit surreal when I did. It wasn't so much about them personally as it was just me wondering what my life would have been like if that had been my name. Would it have been any different if I still looked the same? And what if I had looked different? What if I had looked like my sisters? How differently would I have turned out? But I would dismiss such thoughts. It wasn't that such a life was a road not taken. It was more that it was a road never offered. My life was my life, for better or for worse; and I was quite pleased with how it had turned out. Yet sometimes, I would still wonder.

Gabby saw me sink into quiet reflection, and she knew why. "We are who God makes us," she said, her deep faith leading her. "The Lord in Heaven knows our name before we do. Your name was never meant to be Anna. You know that? God knew your name would be Roda before your daddy even knew it."

Tears came to my eyes, and I nodded. "I know it, Gabby." I paused, trying to let go of my thoughts. "Or should I say Wanda?" I joked, trying to break the somber mood.

"Well," Gabby said, looking at me sideways, "God always knew my name should be Gabby. He told me through Professor

252

Hillman. It was those fools in my family who were too stupid to know."

I laughed as I opened the chart for the first time.

Chapter 22

I charted my notes, procedures, and times first. From begin time to end time, it took exactly three hours and twenty-seven minutes from incision to closure. About average. Patient roused from anesthesia but was kept sedated in recovery. I checked to make sure everything was noted. Blood pressure, oxygen level, and all other pertinent information during the procedure. Everything was there.

I flipped to the front page with family information, preparing to talk to her parents. Her name was Anna Michelle. Goosebumps formed quickly. How odd. My exact name. Supposed to be my name. Anna Michelle Ingram. Ingram. I looked at the parents' names. Brad and Ashley Ingram. Ashley. I felt myself suddenly begin to hyperventilate. Brad Ingram. Allyson's brother. Allyson Ingram's brother. No, this could not be. I saw the city. Greenwich. Hadn't Gabby said something about Greenwich ER? Why hadn't they taken her to the Greenwich ER?

My whole body went cold. I felt as if all the blood were draining from me. I was pale as a ghost. I couldn't move. I couldn't breathe. Gabby saw me and rushed over. "You okay? What's wrong?" I looked at her, but I couldn't focus. Her words echoed. I could hardly hear. I laid my head on the cool desk trying to calm my breathing before I passed out. I was close to passing out. I could hear Gabby calling for help, but I raised my hand and managed to tell her no. She hesitantly complied and got a cold wash cloth instead. She pulled my hair up and placed it on the back of my neck. She made me drink more orange juice. The world slowly began coming into focus again.

I kept my head down on the desk for a few minutes. Gabby

sat in the chair beside me, concern written all over her face. "What is it Ro? What's wrong? You okay? Is baby girl okay?"

I nodded. I pointed to the chart. "Where are they?" was the first thing I managed to say.

She looked curiously at me. "They down the hall in family waiting? Why?"

I kept pointing at the chart, beginning to feel foolish that I was falling apart. But at least it was Gabby. It was only Gabby, and she would understand. "Have you seen them?" I asked.

"Yes, talked to them too. What's going on?" she asked, patting my back.

I pointed to my sister's name. "It's Ashley. It's my sister, Ashley. Who all is down there?"

Gabby suddenly turned the chart towards her to look at the name. Then she sat back in her chair, astounded. "Three women, one man," was all she admitted to.

"An older woman?" I asked.

"Two younger women. Youngish. Not real young," she dodged.

"Was there an older woman?" I asked, barely whispering.

She hesitated. That meant yes. She finally nodded, confirming my worst fear. My mother. Was it my mother? Maybe it was Allyson's mother. Reading my mind, she confirmed it was my mother. Ashley had introduced her. The chills came back. I was freezing, yet I was sweating profusely.

"Calm down," Gabby soothed. "I'll go tell them Anna's out of surgery and that the doctor will be there soon. I'll buy you some time. Just breathe, okay?"

I nodded.

I could hear her walking down the hallway. She didn't have to go very far. They were just mere yards away. I could hear her voice. I could hear hushed tones. My mother was here. She was here. I tried to get that straight in my mind. I tried to reconcile that fact. They named her Anna. Anna Michelle. How did that happen? Why did that happen? I hadn't gotten a good look at her. She was intubated, so I couldn't see her face. She had a surgical cap on, so I couldn't see her hair. What did she look like? She was listed as 145 pounds. A seventeen-year-old at 145. She wasn't thin. How tall? Five three. No, not thin at all.

Suddenly, I had a burst of strength. I sprinted to recovery. She was lying there, sedated as ordered. Round face. Dark, curly hair. She looked like me but prettier. Tears fell down my face as I looked down at her. I heard the nurses asking me something, but I ignored them. I just stared at her. She was me. Not just like me but close. Were they mean to her? That was my first thought. Were they mean to her they way they had been to me? Anger welled inside of me with either answer. Either they were, and that infuriated me; or they weren't, and that infuriated me as well. Why would they be nice to her if they hadn't been nice to me? Why would she be any better?

Gabby found me standing there. "Roda," she said, but I didn't hear her. "Roda," she repeated sharply, causing the other nurses to gasp. How dare a nurse talk to a doctor in such a way. But they didn't know. They didn't know us, and they didn't know my circumstances. I turned, crying like a stupid little girl and shaking my head no. She held her arms out. I went to her, and she held me as I cried. I felt so dumb. So very dumb. Why was I falling apart like this? Why?

Gabby saw the other nurses gawking, and she reprimanded them. "Mind your own business!" she snapped, and then she walked me out of recovery. Later, she would explain it away on pregnancy hormones; but for now, she wanted to get me to the doctor's lounge so I could lie down.

"Roda, girl," she said softly, "you got to get yourself together. You got to go talk to the family." She paused. "Your family."

I nodded. "I know," I said. "I can't figure out what's wrong. Why am I panicking like this, Gab? Why?"

"You just in shock, that's all. All these years, you never had to see them. Never had to think about them if you didn't want to. But now they right here, right down the hall, waiting."

I nodded. "Thank you for the reality check. But why?"

"Baby girl, I think you built up such a defensive wall for yourself when you was younger. You guarded yourself so they couldn't hurt you." She nodded, tears forming. She was talking from experience. She had done the same thing with her family. "You don't have that wall up no more because your life is so different, and you don't need it. But now suddenly they're here, and you don't have that wall, and you don't know how to protect yourself."

Yes, that was true. It was all making sense.

"Lord, I don't know what I'd do if my daddy showed up. I'd like to think I'd cuss his sorry ass out, but I think it would be more likely that I'd fall apart too." She looked pointedly at me. "But you know what? Ain't nothing they can do to hurt you now. Nothing. Look at you. You a successful heart surgeon. What are they? Not that! I can guarantee you that." She was trying to build me up, and it was beginning to make me feel better. But still, I was scared to death.

"Listen," she said, "you ain't got to do it. I'll get someone else. I'll tell them you ain't feeling well. They'll understand. They'll do it for you. I'll get Dr. Penn. Yeah, he'll do it."

I shook my head. "No, Gabby. I have to do it. I'm going to do it. Just give me a minute."

She agreed and sat there for a moment. She started humming, knowing it would make me feel better. "You know," she said after a few minutes, "I'd like to think that if my daddy did show up, if he showed up by accident or however, I'd be so proud of myself; and I'd be so glad for him to see what I had made out of myself. I'd want him to know that he didn't break me, you know? That I overcame the hell he put me through, and that I survived even though he told me every day of my life that I'd never amount to anything. I'd like to show him that." She stared off in the distance as she said it. Then she shrugged. "But he probably wouldn't even know me. He probably wouldn't even recognize me if I was standing right there in front of him."

I blinked.

"That's it!" I said, sitting straight up. "That's it, Gabby! They won't recognize me! There's no way they'll recognize me! They haven't seen me in twenty-five years! I look so different now! I am different! I'm not fat anymore! Well, not really."

She grabbed my hand. "You ain't fat. You hear me?" Then she nodded. "But you probably right. They won't recognize you."

A sudden burst of energy and I was up again, digging in my locker for makeup and a hairbrush. I looked in the mirror. God, I looked awful.

"You look beautiful," she said, reading my mind again.

"You really do, Roda. You have such a glow about you, it's amazing."

It's not that I didn't believe her, but I applied a little makeup anyway. I began brushing my hair. It was showing the slightest sign of frizz, and I began to get impatient. Why must my hair look so bad? Suddenly, I stopped. "Do you see what they do to me, Gabby? I never worry about how I look. Never! Now look at me. It's like I'm obsessed. It's ridiculous."

She walked over and took the brush from me. "You look beautiful, Roda. I promise you. I wouldn't lie to you," she assured me.

"You know what it is?" I asked, turning towards her. "They still have this power over me. I'm still trying to prove something to them. I still feel like an awkward, ugly thirteen-year-old girl to them. That's how they make me feel. That's how they always made me feel."

She grabbed my shoulders. "But you are *not* an awkward, ugly thirteen-year-old girl. You a beautiful forty-year-old woman who is astonishingly successful in her field and has a gorgeous husband and a gorgeous son, and you *are* better than they could've ever imagined. But you know what? It don't even matter. It don't matter what they used to believe or what they believe now. All that matters is what *you* believe about yourself. That's all that matters."

I nodded and put down the brush. "You're exactly right," I said.

She nodded, believing her job was done. "Okay then. I'm gonna go back to my desk, and you gonna go in and talk to them." She nodded. "Right?"

I nodded. "Right."

She left me alone in the lounge. I stood there psyching myself up for something I never thought I would have to face again. But deep down, I still felt thirteen; and I couldn't shake it. Then suddenly, I heard a voice inside my heart. It was clear and distinct—and probably crazy, but I heard a voice say, "Can you hear my voice? It's deep inside your heart. It's deep inside your soul. It's saying, 'Only believe.'" It was my dad's voice. How could that be? How? But I heard it clearly, as if he were standing right in front of me saying it. *Only believe what?* I wanted to ask. Only believe that I can do this? Only believe that they won't recognize me? Only believe what? Only believe, it suddenly occurred to me, that I'm not what they think I am. Only believe that I am so much better than what they see. That was my answer, and it gave me the strength to open the door and walk down the hall and face my greatest fear.

***

I paused before I walked through the door, flipping my ID badge around so they couldn't see my name. I didn't want them to know who I was. I was just hoping to get through it and for them to be oblivious to who I truly was. When I walked in, only Ashley and Allyson were sitting there. I didn't see my mother anywhere. I had to remind myself to act completely normal. Any fear on my face would immediately be perceived as a problem with the surgery—that something was wrong. They both stood up when I entered the room, worry etched on their faces. So I smiled and introduced myself as Dr. Emerson, pediatric cardiac surgeon who had performed the procedure on Anna. I apologized for the delay, citing administrative problems and reassuring them that Anna was fine and in recovery. I asked where the patient's father was, and Ashley said he had walked with her mother down the hall to the bathroom. I was told they should be back momentarily. My stomach sank knowing I would be face to face with my mother within mere moments.

I took a deep breath and began giving Ashley preliminary information on what had been done. But at the same time, my mind was racing. She had grown into such a beautiful woman, still looking a lot like Amanda. She was petite and thin and had a soft look about her, but her eyes were very sad. I could see past the worry on her face, and I clearly recognized the stress and sadness within. Allyson was beautiful as well. That was no surprise. She still seemed very confident, yet I didn't detect arrogance. I had been afraid that I would choke, that I would still feel so intimidated by them; but surprisingly, I wasn't. They didn't seem to recognize me at all.

Ashley had a million questions about Anna. "What caused this? How did it happen?" Specific questions about the surgery. I didn't want to say too much without her husband present. I wanted to tell them together. I began telling her that with someone Anna's age, the condition was most likely a heart defect, with her heart developing only two aortic leaflets as opposed to three. I was in midsentence when, out of the corner of my eye, I saw her walk in through the doorway on the other side of the room. Ashley's husband followed behind her and was surprised when my mother stopped. It caused me to look over at her, and our eyes met. She had aged, and my mind couldn't quite comprehend if she had aged well or not, but she had aged. She looked small and frail. Her hair was much shorter and white, and her blue eyes had faded.

We held each other's gaze a moment too long, and suddenly her eyes filled with tears. Her hand covered her mouth in disbelief. "Roda," she whispered.

I didn't want to give myself away. I wanted to deny who I was to her, but she said my name in such a way that my heart broke for her. I could almost count on one hand how many times I had heard my mother actually speak my name; but of those few times, it was said with such disdain that it crushed my spirit. But this time was different. This time she said it as if she had just found a lost treasure.

I didn't respond at first but kept looking at her. "Roda," she repeated, tears streaming down her face. My emotions failed me, giving way to tears that I was trying desperately to hold back. She dropped her purse, spilling it everywhere; and she rushed towards me and grabbed me in a tight embrace.

"Mother! Have you gone mad?!" Ashley asked, a look of horror on her face. "What has gotten into you? Why do you think this woman is Roda?"

My mother pulled back from me and cupped my face in her hands. "Because it is Roda," she said. "She's my Roda." She wiped the tears from my face.

Seeing my reaction, Ashley was suddenly speechless. She looked at me in awe. "Roda? You're Roda? *My* sister, Roda?"

I didn't answer. I kept looking at my mother, and she smiled as she began to cry harder. "Yes, Ashley. It's Roda."

Allyson was stunned. Absolutely stunned. She reached for my ID badge and turned it around, revealing what had become apparent. Dr. Roda Allen-Emerson, pediatric cardiologist. Her hands flew up to her mouth as she sank back down into the chair in

260

disbelief. Ashley suddenly burst into tears, grabbing me and hugging me.

"You're a doctor?!" Ashley said. "My God! You're a doctor?! How did that happen?! *When* did that happen?!"

The questions started coming like rapid fire. Ashley was always inquisitive, and I could see that it hadn't changed. My mother just kept looking at me, smiling. It was strange to me. Something so foreign that my mind couldn't quite comprehend it. Allyson remained sitting. Silent. Stunned. The look on her face was priceless. I could almost read her mind. How did *that* girl become *this* woman, was what she was thinking. I was sure of it. I intentionally ignored her. It was against my nature, but it felt good to finally have some semblance of revenge.

Ashley's husband, Brad, politely interrupted. "I don't mean to spoil all the excitement, but can I please ask what's going on with Anna?"

We were brought back to reality, and I began explaining what had occurred and what was done to correct it. I expected Anna to have a full recovery, although she would need to take it easy from now on. Because of the mechanical valve, she would need to be on a blood thinner for the rest of her life. She would gradually regain her strength but would need to take it easy.

I told them they could see her in recovery but that she would remain sedated for the next few days while her body healed. We were walking out of the waiting room when my mother grabbed my hand. "You saved Anna's life, didn't you? You saved her life." I smiled down at her, my heart completely letting go of all the hurt and all the pain I had endured. I nodded, trying to hold back the tears. She smiled back at me and squeezed my hand because she was unable to speak.

I walked down the hall to recovery with them. I answered all of their questions and continued to assure them that she would make a full recovery. I had never felt so happy and so light before. It was an odd sensation, as if a weight I hadn't even know was still there was suddenly gone. I had been reunited with two people I never thought I would see again. And what's more, my mother recognized me. She actually recognized me. I didn't know how or why, but she had. And even more than that, I had finally achieved something I never thought I would. I had gained my mother's approval. I stood there thinking of the last conversation I had with my dad when he told me to do something great, and I think this was why he wanted that for me. So my mother would be proud of me.

Chapter 23

I arrived at the hospital the next morning dressed in my favorite red blouse, black slacks, and heels. I spent thirty minutes straightening my hair, and it looked absolutely perfect. My makeup was flawless. I felt beautiful. I went to the doctor's lounge first thing to put on my crisply pressed white coat. Stethoscope or no stethoscope? It covered up my name on my coat, so no stethoscope.

I approached the nurse's desk casually, looking at a patient's chart. When I reached the desk, Gabby was just staring at me.

"Girl, what is up with this?" she asked pointedly.

"What's up with what?" I asked innocently.

She cocked her head and pushed out her lips. "Girl, you know what I'm talking about. Now what is up with *this*?" she repeated, circling her hand in front of my face and pointing to my clothes.

"Oh," I said casually, shrugging, "I have a meeting later today."

"A meeting with who?" she asked, glaring at me. "Miss America judges? What you doing dressing up like all that?"

"I'm not dressed up," I denied.

She gave me that look. That girl-now-I-know-you-lying-to-me look. That's what always kept me straight, especially when I wasn't being honest with myself.

"Okay, so maybe I'm dressed up," I agreed.

"Maybe?" she asked, still giving me that look.

"I just felt like dressing up today. No big deal. I don't have any surgeries scheduled."

She was still giving me the look.

"I have scrubs in my locker if an emergency comes in," I continued.

The look plus raised eyebrows. Not good.

I exhaled. "Okay, fine. Yes, I'm dressed up. Yes, I'm trying to impress them since I looked so horrible yesterday." I shrugged. "I just wanted to look nice."

"Ro, you do look nice. You look very nice. Stunning. But you don't have to try so hard. You don't have to impress them."

"I'm not trying to impress them," I said, thinking. "I'm just…" my voice trailed off.

"You just trying to show off what you got. I get it. But you ain't got to try so hard. You the most beautiful person I know. Don't matter what you look like, makeup or no makeup. Don't matter what you wearing, bloody scrubs or a ball gown. You the most beautiful person I know because you are beautiful on the inside, and it just comes out on the outside." She looked into my eyes. "You know?"

I swallowed hard and nodded, suddenly feeling foolish. "Yeah, Gab. I know. And you're the most beautiful person I know too. And for the same reasons."

"Now why you got to go copying my eloquent speech like that?" she said, lightening the mood. "Every time I go saying something meaningful and sweet, you just basically say 'ditto.' Ain't you ever got anything heartfelt of your own to say?" She smiled and winked. "Now go in there and show off what ya got. Go on now."

I rolled my eyes, turned on my heel, and headed towards Anna's room.

***

I walked into the room and found Ashley sitting alone beside Anna's bed. She was sitting in a chair with her head down on the bed, looking at her daughter and holding her hand. She sat up quickly when she heard me enter. She blinked, wiping her tears away. "Wow, Roda. You look beautiful."

I suddenly felt foolish, knowing I was over dressed. I shrugged, attempting to downplay it. "I have a meeting later."

264

I smiled, walking over to begin a quick assessment of how Anna was doing. "How are you this morning?" I asked Ashley.

She took a deep breath. "Good, I guess. I'm just ready for Anna to wake up. How much longer?"

"Another day or two," I said, charting information into the computer. "We just want to keep her under while her body heals. She'll be able to wake up. Don't worry, okay?"

She nodded. "Okay."

"Roda," she began hesitantly, "why is her heart ticking?" She stifled a sob. "I wanted to hear her heart beating, just to know it was; and when I put my ear up to her chest, I could hear ticking."

I sat on the edge of the bed, facing my sister. "It's the mechanical valve. The ticking you hear is the leaflets in the valve pushing her blood through."

"She'll always have that ticking sound?" she asked sadly.

"Yeah. That's the downside, I know. But she'll get used to it. Others won't necessarily be able to hear it unless she's in a very quiet room."

"Like when she's at school taking a test?" she interjected.

"Well, yes. That's true," I answered.

She took a deep breath, still trying to hold back a sob; but it didn't work. "Other kids will make fun of her because of that, won't they?" she cried.

I tilted my head sympathetically. "Maybe," I said. "Do they already?"

She nodded. "Some do. Not all of them. She has a few friends but not many. It's not as bad as it was . . ." her voice trailed off, and her eyes were downcast, "as it was for you."

I nodded slightly. "Well, that's good at least." I looked at her, but she avoided looking back at me. She was ashamed.

"Listen," I said, "with something like this, it's better to confront it head on. If she goes back and this condition is not explained to kids at school, they will be more likely to make fun of her. But confrontation is power. Confront the issue, get it out there, and take that power away from those who would tease her. You know?"

Ashley looked up at me. "Yeah, I guess. Maybe."

"I'll be glad to go to her school and do that. I actually do it more than you would think. Oncology even asked me to go to a little girl's school to talk to the other kids about the fact that she would lose her hair and not be able to play. It's a common thing for me to do."

Ashley nodded, looking worried. "Yeah, okay. I guess that would be okay."

"How is she at school? Grade wise, how is she?"

She shrugged. "She does alright. Her grades are pretty good. She actually likes math. She does pretty well in that."

"Is she good at art," I asked out of curiosity.

She shook her head. "No, not really."

"She has friends?" I asked, touching on what she had already said.

"Yeah, she has one close friend. Megan. They've been friends since second grade. She and Meg are best friends, and they're friends with two other girls who are best friends. So they're like a little group." She sounded sad.

"Well," I assured her, "at least she has that. I didn't have anybody when I was in school. That's a tough thing, you know?"

She bowed her head. "Yes, I know. I get that now."

I let it go. I didn't torture her with it. "Is she athletic at all?" I asked, changing the direction of the conversation.

She looked over at Anna. "No, she isn't."

"Well, that's actually a good thing. Like I told you yesterday, this was a heart defect from birth. If she had been more active, it could have triggered this incident sooner."

"Yeah," she agreed, "that's true. Sounds logical."

We sat in silence for a moment. Finally, I asked what I had been wondering. "How is Mother with her?"

She looked at me and actually smiled. "She's great with her. She really is." She paused, looking over at her daughter. "Anna being born is what brought Mom out of her depression."

For some reason, there was a spark of jealousy within me. I looked over at Anna, and somehow I was suddenly jealous.

"Really? How?" I asked.

"Well, it's a long story," she began.

"I've got time," I said, switching my gaze from Anna to Ashley.

"Well," she said, searching for the words. "Well, first of all, Brad and I . . ." she hesitated. "Brad and I had to get married. I was pregnant." She looked down, embarrassed. I waited for her to speak. "I ran away just like you did, you know? I practically lived at Ally's. And Brad and I . . . well, you know . . ."

I nodded, understanding her. "Allyson was like a sister, but he wasn't necessarily like a brother?"

She nodded. "We liked each other, and one thing eventually led to another. I was nineteen when I got pregnant. Brad was twenty one. His parents didn't even know about us, to tell you the truth. To them, we seemed like brother and sister. Anyway, they were furious. Absolutely furious. Felt like they had been deceived and all that. Welcomed me into their house and now look. The whole nine yards." She paused, sighing. "So anyway, Brad and I were in love and wanted to do the right thing. Problem was, we were young. No money. No jobs." She shrugged. "His parents wouldn't let us live with them, so going back to Mom was the only option. I think I hadn't been home in two weeks when I went back to talk to her. I was scared to death," she said as she looked directly at me. "You know how crazy she would get when things didn't go as planned. So when I got there, she was in her usual zombie state. She was really pitiful. But I sat down and just told her. Just got it over with. And for the first time in years, she actually looked at me and actually focused on me. She had this odd look of concern and happiness. It was very strange. I expected disappointment and anger; but she actually smiled, believe it or not. I told her the problem and asked if we could live with her for a while. She started crying and hugged me. It felt like I was in the twilight zone or something. Very weird. But that's what we did." She paused again, looking at Anna. "I think it just gave Mom something to live for, you know?"

I nodded, my mind racing. "How did she react when Anna was born? How did she react when it was obvious she would look like me?"

Ashley looked at me blankly.

"You don't know how Mother reacted when I was born, do you? You don't know," I said, shaking my head. "Daddy never told you, but he told me. She wouldn't hold me. She wouldn't even look at me. Said I wasn't worthy of the name Anna. So I want to know exactly how she reacted when she saw Anna. I want to know *why* she rejected me. I want to know *why* she didn't reject Anna."

My anger was rising, anger that had been suppressed for years; and I suddenly felt foolish and childish. On the one hand, I was immensely glad that she loved Anna; but at the same time, I was furious that she loved her when she didn't love me.

"Roda," Ashley said, barely able to speak, "it's because of you that she loves Anna." Her eyes filled with tears. "You want to know what she said the moment she saw her with her shock of black hair and chubby cheeks? I will tell you because I remember it perfectly. She cried and said that she had a second chance. I didn't understand what she meant at first. I thought she just meant a second chance in general. But then she cried every time she held Anna. I mean, she practically bathed her in tears. So I asked her why she was so emotional, and that's when she clarified and said she had a second chance with you. In some small strange way, she felt she had a do-over. She felt she had a chance to correct the mistakes she made. Roda, she poured her heart into Anna. She has given her every ounce of love she has. It's amazing."

I sniffed loudly, tears pouring down my face.

"Roda," she said, reaching out and taking my hand, "it was Mom's idea to name her Anna Michelle. She asked if Brad and I would do her that favor because she was so haunted by her regrets, and she felt it was a way to honor you."

I was still torn by my feelings. The anger was subsiding, but my emotions were torn. "Mother felt she was worthy of the name? Did she feel Anna was the daughter I never was?"

"No, Roda," she said sincerely, "it's nothing like that. It's more like she was replacing the daughter she threw away. But to tell you the truth, she's never been able to let go of her guilt. You should have seen her last night. She was so happy. Worried about Anna but so very happy. She kept saying, 'I can't believe I found Roda.' It was like, if she didn't say it, it wasn't true. Do you know what I mean? As if it were a dream. But she kept saying it over and over."

I sat there trying to understand it all. After a few minutes, I got up to leave, saying I needed to do my rounds. I had just turned to walk out when Ashley called my name.

"Roda," she asked timidly, "where's Amanda?"

I smiled. "She's in Paris right now, but she'll be home soon."

"Paris?" she asked, surprised. "What's she doing there?"

"She went for fall fashion week but decided to take an extended vacation. She'll be back next week."

She shook her head, trying to comprehend what I was saying. "Fashion?" she asked.

I nodded. "Yes, she's a designer. She's quite good."

"So you're a doctor and Amanda's some sort of jetsetter, and I'm just a stupid girl who got pregnant too young. Both of you went on to do something incredible, and I'm just nothing."

"No, Ash, that's not true. You're the one who saved Mother. That's something incredible right there. It really is. You did something neither Amanda nor I could have done. You and Brad and Anna were the miracle Mother needed. That *is* incredible." She nodded in hesitant agreement, and I smiled at her sincerely and walked out the door.

***

Gabby was sitting at the nurse's station when I came out of the room. She smiled at me. "Your mother asked about you," she said.

"She did? When?" I asked.

"About ten minutes ago. I told her you were in with your sister, talking about Anna. She said she would wait for you. She didn't want to disturb the two of you."

"Where's she at?"

"I put her in the private waiting room down the hall," she said, tilting her head in that direction. The private waiting room was where families who would be receiving bad news were directed. But in this case, Gabby knew that my mother wanted to talk to me; and Gabby also knew that no one would disturb us in there. She would make sure of it if anyone dared to try.

I approached the room slowly. Why was I being so timid? I stood outside the door, looking through the small window. She was sitting on a bench in front of a large window, staring out at the city. I watched her for a minute, trying to remember how she used to be. How beautiful she was back then, how cold she always was, and how she used to stare at me. That version of her was gone now, replaced by a frail, aging woman. After all I had endured, I had compassion for her. My whole life, I had never imagined I would be able to forgive her for how she treated me; but now I knew it was possible. I opened the door slowly and stood in the door way. Her thoughts were a million miles away, and she didn't notice I was standing there.

"Mom," I said, surprised that the word came out of my mouth.

She turned and looked at me and smiled. "Hi, Roda. Come over here and sit by me." She patted the bench. I walked over, wondering why I felt as if I were five years old. "You look beautiful today," she said.

I smiled as I sat down. "Thank you. So do you."

She sat there, twisting a tissue in her hands. "It's a beautiful day," she said, staring out the window.

"Yes, it is," I agreed, looking out the window also. She grew quiet, and I began to feel uncomfortable with the silence.

After a moment, she spoke. "I've only been to the city once," she said, looking at me. "When Daddy and I were dating." She looked back out the window again. "That was the best day of my life. Honestly it was. I've never had so much fun. It was New Year's Eve."

"I know," I said quietly. "He told me."

She looked at me, wondering how much he had told me.

"Did he ever tell you that I had a gymnastics scholarship to Yale?"

I was stunned. "Yale?" I searched my memory and shook my head. "No, he never told me that. Yale University?"

She smiled. "Yes, Yale University. A full scholarship. I was recruited my junior year. I was an Olympic hopeful. Did he tell you that?"

I shook my head again, sad that I never knew that. I wondered why he hadn't told me. She looked down at the tissue she was still twisting. "I was quite good," she said.

I instinctively took her hand. "I bet you were amazing."

She looked up at me and smiled. "I suppose I was."

"So what happened? Why didn't you go?"

She looked wistfully out the window, wondering where to begin. How to begin.

"I had lived under my mother's oppressive hand for

270

eighteen years. I was tired of it. She had been at every single practice and every single meet since I began gymnastics at the age of five. She eyed me so intensely and critiqued my every move to such a degree that, when I actually competed, the judges didn't scare me. My mother scared me but the judges didn't. And God forbid if I did make a mistake because I would get an hour-long speech from her about the importance of being perfect."

She looked at me. "I didn't want to live like that anymore." She wiped away a tear and looked out the window. "I hated gymnastics. As good as I was, I hated it. She caused me to hate it. Then one day, during my senior year, one of my best friends told me she was going to Rutgers to try out for their cheerleading squad." She laughed. "I went with her on a whim. I didn't expect to make it. I had never cheered before, but I was a natural. And I made it." She smiled to herself, remembering the thrill of it. And then she sank into quiet reflection.

"How did you tell your mother?" I finally asked.

"I didn't. I was too afraid of her. I told my father, and I let him tell her. And I knew the day he did because she stopped speaking to me. My mother was a proud woman. She loved to brag about what she had. She especially loved to brag that her only daughter—her only child—was an Olympic hopeful. She loved to brag that her only daughter was going to Yale. She loved to brag about her daughter, but she didn't love her daughter. There's a difference." She paused. "So what was she going to tell people when her daughter didn't go to Yale? What was she going to tell them? That her daughter was going to Rutgers? Rutgers?! In New Jersey? New Jersey, for God's sake. My mother couldn't even utter the words New Jersey. She would rather tell everybody that I was dead. I had embarrassed her," she concluded, "and to her, that was the ultimate sin. An unforgivable sin." She took a deep breath. "Do you remember when Amanda made cheerleader? Do you remember how my mother acted?"

I nodded. I remembered it well.

"That's why. It was because of me. Because of what I had done. She never forgave me. Except for one brief visit, they never came to see me after your dad died. Do you want to know why? It was because of my rebellion when I was eighteen. Everything was due to that. In her mind, she rationalized that if I hadn't gone to

Rutgers, I wouldn't have met your dad; and therefore, I wouldn't have lost him that day. Do you understand? It was like her twisted form of punishment not to come see me. It was her essentially saying, 'I told you so.' That's how she was. That's how she had always been. She sat there, waiting for me to come to her and say I was wrong; but I never did. I never did."

"Is that why you didn't like Mim?" I asked. "Because of your mother's disapproval?"

She looked at me and blinked quickly. "Yes," she finally admitted. She looked ashamed. "Paul was perfect," she said, smiling to herself, remembering how she felt about him in the beginning. "Everything about him was perfect, and I allowed myself to think that my mother would approve." She paused, looking down. "When I saw Mim . . . I can't explain what came over me." She shook her head, trying to think of the words. "Even to this day, I can't explain it. Just . . . I just knew what my mother's reaction would be. '*That* is his sister?' she would've said. I knew that's what she would say. Incidentally, she didn't say anything. She just gave me that look of hers, and I knew she was thinking it. That made it even worse. I saw Mim as a flaw, another disappointment for my mother. My mother began lecturing me at a very young age about the importance of choosing the perfect mate with the perfect pedigree—the perfect bloodline. Genetics. My mother understood genetics very well. So when I saw Mim, I saw a genetic flaw." She looked at me apologetically. "According to my mother," she added quickly.

I nodded. "And then there was me. I was the result of that genetic flaw, wasn't I? Your worst fear come true."

The look in her eyes said yes, but she didn't speak the words.

"I fought so hard not to be like my mother," she said. "It was easy when I was in college, when I had that distance from her. That trip we took to Europe my sophomore year, right before I met Mim, my father planned it as a surprise for my mother and me. He was hoping we would reconcile. In a way, we did. But then I met Mim, and I knew it would start all over again. And then your dad and I got engaged, and I knew I would have to deal with that— with Mother meeting Mim." She put her hands up to her face and began to rub her temples. "The more I tried to not be like her, the

272

more I became like her. I knew she would despise Mim; so therefore, I despised Mim. I didn't include Mim in the wedding because I was hoping my mother wouldn't notice her or ask about her. I wasn't so lucky. She noticed her right away. My mother demanded perfection. Any imperfection was a glaring flaw. So I tried to compensate by making everything else perfect. The house, the yard, everything. And of course my children had to be perfect. I had a two-fold problem with her on that. First of all, she expected perfection regardless. But then there was the genetic factor. My mother was *waiting* for me to have a baby who resembled Mim just so she could say, 'I told you so.' And, as I said, that was because of her anger with me choosing to go to Rutgers. So when you were born . . ." her voice trailed off. She stared out the window, sinking into quiet reflection, not seeing beyond her own memories. "When you were born, I was so angry. Angry at myself, angry at you, angry at Mim, angry at the world. My mother would gloat. That's all I could think about. She would gloat. She would be so full of her own self righteousness, it made me sick. And everything just grew from there. The next fifteen years. Your dad would tell me what I was doing. He would tell me I was being just like her, and I would vehemently deny it. I denied ever being like her. Yet, I knew what I was doing. I could see it, but I couldn't control it. I could see how I treated you; but I would justify it in some sick, twisted way. I was furious that I had to try so hard to please my mother, but I worked so hard to do so. It was crazy. And you were the constant flaw that prevented her approval." She looked at me sadly. "I'm sorry. I don't mean that now. It's just how I felt back then. Do you understand?"

I nodded that I understood.

"My perfect life fell apart when your dad died. I thought I could control everything. I tried to. But I couldn't control that. And then when you left . . ." She looked down and took my hand. "When you left, my world fell apart."

"How?" I asked. "You didn't even love me."

"No," she said, shaking her head and bursting into tears, "that's when I realized how much I *did* love you. It ripped my heart out. There's no other way to describe it."

"Then why didn't you come after me?" I asked.

"I didn't think you loved me," she said, smiling sadly. "I

thought you would be better off with Mim. She was always a better mother to you than I ever was. I guess I just thought you deserved better."

"And Amanda? What about when she left?" I asked, always wondering how that had made her feel.

"When Amanda left . . . that's when I knew I had become my mother." She nodded to herself, having no doubt about it. "Just as I ran away from my mother, so did she. It was déjà vu, except I was on the other side of it. I was my mother. *That*, Roda, was my worst fear. You think you being born looking like Mim was my worst fear—but no. Being like my mother was. It was my worst nightmare. And when Amanda left, that nightmare came true. And from there, I just sank deeper into my depression. I had lost everything. Everything that I loved. Everything that I should have loved. It was all gone. And why? To please my mother. I wasted my life trying to gain her approval, and I sacrificed everything I loved."

Out of compassion, I put my other hand on top of hers. "But now you have a second chance. You know that, don't you?"

She took a deep breath. "Do I?" she asked. "Do I have a second chance?"

I smiled. "Of course you do. We both do. I would love that."

"You would?" she asked meekly, through her tears.

I nodded. "And you know what? Daddy would have loved that too."

She smiled. "Yes," she agreed, "he would have."

"Can I ask you something?" I began. "How is it . . . how did you know it was me? How did you recognize me?"

"Ashley asked me the same thing. I told her the truth. When I saw you, I saw your dad, and I saw Mim, and I could see Anna."

I smiled. "You could see Daddy in me? Really?"

She nodded. "Yes, I could see him. But that wasn't the only reason I knew it was you." She paused, and I waited for her to speak. "At first, that's what I saw. I saw how you resembled all of them. But what really convinced me, what really clenched it, was how you looked at me."

My brow furrowed. How did I look at her, I wondered.

She pressed her lips together and sniffed. "You always had this look," she said, her voice shaking. "When you looked at me, you always had this fearful look on your face. It was subtle because you always tried to suppress your fear when you were younger, but I could see it. A glimpse of it. And when I walked into the waiting room and you looked at me, I saw it. I recognized it because it has haunted me all these years. So that's how I knew."

I wiped tears away and nodded. She squeezed my hand. "I never want to see that look again, Roda. I don't ever want to see it again."

I shook my head. "You won't. I promise."

She grabbed me and hugged me tightly. "I love you more than anything, Roda. More than you will ever know. And I am so sorry for what I did to you. I will go to my grave apologizing everyday for how I treated you."

"No," I said, shaking my head, "you won't have to because I forgive you. I don't want you to feel that you'll never be forgiven. That's something your mother did to you. I don't want to be that way."

She pulled back, wiping her face. "I don't feel worthy; but thank you, Roda. That means a lot to me." She paused and looked at me seriously. "Do you think Amanda will ever be able to forgive me? Where is Amanda?"

"Yes," I said slowly, "I think she will. She's in Paris right now. I was just telling Ashley about it. She's a fashion designer, and she's been over there for the shows."

Her jaw dropped. She was almost speechless. "A fashion designer?! Does she have her own line?"

"Yes, she does. She and her friend from school have been in business together for years now. They're a great team."

"What's the name of her line?"

"Manda and Max," I answered.

A look of awe came over her face. She quickly took off her cardigan and looked at the tag. *Manda & Max*. She sat there staring at it. "Ashley gave me this sweater for my birthday," she said, rubbing her finger over Amanda's name. "I always thought it was an intriguing coincidence." She smiled sadly, looking at the label. "Manda," she whispered.

"Do you think," she said suddenly. "Do you think that the

two of you would come to my house for Thanksgiving this year? Your families too, of course. Is Amanda married? I know you are," she said, pointing to the name embroidered on my coat.

"Yes, I would love to come for Thanksgiving. We would all love to."

"Mim too," she insisted. "I want her to come too."

I nodded. "She would love to, I'm sure."

"Is Amanda married?" she asked again.

"No," I said, shaking my head, "she never got married. She was too afraid to."

"She was too afraid of being like me, wasn't she?"

I was honest and said yes.

We sat for a few minutes longer before she said I should get back to work. But before I left, she said she had something for me. She pulled a tote bag out from underneath the bench. She retrieved a hard, flat object that was wrapped in tissue paper and handed it to me. Curiously, I took it and folded back the paper. It took my breath when I saw it, and I immediately choked up. It was the picture I had sketched of my dad on September 11th. I looked at it for a moment, running my hand over it and tracing his signature with my finger. I hugged the frame to my chest and rocked back and forth, crying.

Mom was rubbing my back gently. "I've had it all these years, and now it's time for you to have it back. Brad went back home last night and got it for me. I wanted you to have it."

I smiled at her. "Thank you, Mom. Thank you."

"I was surprised you left it for me when you moved out. I couldn't understand why you did, but I was glad. I held it so much that Amanda put it in a frame so I wouldn't ruin it," she said, smiling. "Why did you leave it behind?"

"Because," I said, "I knew you liked it. It was the only thing I had ever done that you actually seemed to like, and I just wanted you to have it so that in some small way you would remember me."

"Roda," she said, cupping my face with her frail hands, "a mother never forgets her daughter. Even a horrible mother like me."

I smiled and nodded, and she kissed my forehead. My mom and I were finally at peace.

276

***

A couple of weeks later, we were traveling by van to Greenwich. It was a trip I never thought I would make again, but I was glad to be going. Mim and George were with us, as was Gabby. I insisted Gabby go. We were the only family she had, and she always spent the holidays with us. It took some coaxing to get Amanda to agree to go, but she finally did. Max had a long talk with her about it, telling her that if she had a parent who actually wanted to see her, then she ought to be thankful. He had not seen his parents since sometime during college. They had basically disowned him. He was with us, though. He was part of our family, and that was all that mattered.

It was surreal when we pulled up in front of the house. Amanda and I hadn't been there in over two decades, but it looked exactly the same. Nothing had changed. My mom saw us drive up, and she was outside before we even got to the door. Her eyes landed immediately on Amanda, and her face contorted into tears. Amanda had been very resistant, so I was surprised when her heart melted, and she sprinted to Mom and hugged her. Mim looked at me and smiled.

I walked up with Paul in my arms. It was the first time my mom saw him, and she was astounded. "My goodness," she whispered, "he does look just like your dad." She touched his face gently. "What a beautiful boy." She looked at me. "How are you feeling? How's the baby?"

"I feel really good, Mom. The baby's doing great."

She smiled and rubbed my stomach that was beginning to show. "Hello in there, Amelia," she said.

She looked around. "Come in, come in," she told all of us. She was excited to have her family home for the holiday. Brad and Ashley were at the front door, so we all walked ahead. Mom stopped Mim as the rest of us went in.

"Mim," she started to say, "I'm so sorry for how I've always been."

Mim reached out and hugged her, forgiving her because I forgave her and because Amanda forgave her. "All is forgotten, Paige." She smiled at my mom. "We've lost a lot of time, haven't

277

we? Now let's go in there and start being a family."

Mom smiled and nodded, and they walked into the house together.

I walked through the house, amazed at how very little it had changed. It felt smaller for some reason. Probably because everything seems larger when we're younger. I found Anna reclining on the couch, still recuperating from her surgery. She was doing much better and looked very healthy. I sat with her for a little bit, asking how she was feeling. For a moment, when no one else was around, she leaned over and whispered to me, "Am I going to be as pretty as you when I'm older?" I smiled and told her, "You'll be even prettier." She smiled back at me, hoping it was true.

Everyone had a wonderful time cooking together, and the meal was magnificent. We were entertained by Mim's hilarious stories and Max's dramatic flair. The house was full of love and laughter, just as my dad had always wanted. I sat in his chair for the longest time, smiling and laughing with my family. I thought of my dad, wishing he was there and believing in some small way that maybe he was. I thought of how he influenced my life as I grew up, and the wonderful parent he was. I looked at each one of my family members who was there with me, and I was thankful that we were finally all together. All that we had been through, all that we had survived—all of it led us to this point of forgiveness and acceptance. I thought about the words my dad left me with, the words that I still cling to: that everyone is worth knowing. The hateful mother whose heart breaks, finally allowing her to feel love. The perfect daughters who ran away, only to come home again. The abused daughter and wife who, rather than believing she was only a victim, had the determination to make something of herself. The homeless man who found a new life after the one he had was lost. The man who was rejected by his own parents for being different. All of them were my family, and all of them were worth knowing. Everyone, I truly believe, is worth knowing. Everyone in this world. Even me.

The End

Made in the USA
Charleston, SC
21 October 2013